A Nameless Oath

Book Two of the

Realms Curse Duology

GW Prouse

Written by G.W. Prouse

Edited by Megan Amato

Rose and dagger chapter header by Dominique Callegari

Storygraph art by Jesse Robling

Map by Angeline Trevena

Chapter Header fox by Ashley Wilson

Blurb by Jessie Cunniffe

ISBN: 9798987648629

ASIN: B0D8WTPKGC

https://prousebooks.com

For everyone without a clear definition of the
titles they are bound to and the roles society expects them to play.

Other books by G.W. Prouse

A Realms Curse Duology:
A Nameless Curse
A Nameless Oath

Content Warnings:
Contains death, death of family members, gore,
and consensual sexual scenes.

**An important note for family and friends or those who
prefer a closed door experience...**

When things start to heat up in the chapters found below,
start to skim or go to the end of the chapter:

Chapter 33
Chapter 47
Chapter 51

Final note to family and friends: If you chose to read the above
chapters fully then do **NOT** speak to me about what you have read.
I'm shy. I turn bright red. You know this. Be nice.
Thank you.

TALAMH
TINE
FIOS
DOMHAIN
VAEN
TOWER
SAOL
N

ÉARDROM
KOSELIG
CNOC
AER
SCÁTH
VISCE
THE
OILEÁN
ISLANDS
DORCHA
DUN BRIG

Prologue

The Night of Lughnasadh

F eet touched ground. Shadows slid from Marquette's body, slithering to hiding places among rock, trees and grass, existent from the moon and stars above. Her knees buckled from the strain of using too much magic to save herself and Fiadh.

But not exhausted enough to quiet the scream as she crumbled to the ground, tore the grass at its roots, sending it flying in all directions. It wasn't enough to stop the agonizing desperation that rose in her throat and chest at the broken bond. Roald's absence tore open her heart and tears slid down her cheeks. She screamed again.

And again.

Beating the ground until only dirt was left beneath, her nails chipped from stone, she clawed for something to grasp onto but only found the cold earth. The place where her husband, her heart, lie if their enemies were kind enough to bury him.

She gasped on a breath of fresh air as her sobs softened. Arms gripped her shoulders and forced her to look up. Eyes unfeeling as a chasm and yet held a touch of understanding met hers. Eyes she recognized.

"They will pay. We know this. Roald knows this." Fiadh's grip tightened as she pulled Marquette to her knees.

"She—" Marquette bit into her cheek, the sharp taste of blood coating her tongue. The sound of the earring meant to spell the spy's world to silence hitting the ground rung in her ears. Felicity had heard every word about the ward's connection to her. A prince and princess. Siblings. Enough to break the curse that had barred the entirety of the world of his existence. Of his entire family's name.

And when that wretched female uttered the ward's true name, one Marquette hadn't heard in years, she had called on the shadows. Not quick enough though. The image of that sword of starlight sliding through her own heart as it cleaved through Roald. The way his body was torn in half.

"There had been something about her... In a way, she assisted in our plans. You don't need a crown for what's to come. We have allies." Fiadh spoke the words as a promise.

Marquette spat to the side, clearing her mouth and her thoughts. "I had her right in my grasp the entire time and hadn't remembered who she was. A spy within my own court and to think I saw myself in her. Thought she was more of a kindred spirit than the wrath of the forgotten."

"She will pay. As will her brother. They are weak now. We should go for their father. Find him and—"

"No." Marquette jerked free of her friend's hold and stood. Fists tightened at her side as she glanced around the field at the edge of Tine and Éardrom—the farthest she could whisk the two of them safely away without being completely spent from their escape. They needed to keep moving. "We'll let them search for Bastien. It will keep them distracted—give us the time we need."

She took steps, checking that her muscles and mind were in line with one another again, then brushed cheeks now certainly smudged with dirt to remove any remnants of tears. The ones she had let fall would be enough. Let the rest of them turn to fire and prepare to burn those who scorned her.

"And your son?"

Marquette stopped. Disappointment coated her tongue at the mention of the male who shared her blood, and she grimaced. Turned. "He doesn't know enough. Never had. Even so, Alarian will be on a wild chase attempting to catch up with the little he has to go on. Besides, that would mean they would have to trust him, and my son has made that difficult all on his own. They will learn how deep his indiscretions go."

He had never understood what the pain and agony of her parents' and own sister's death had cost her. His time in Scáth had meant to show him the truth. That Scáth and Visce—no, the continent deserved to be punished. Instead, those who had forgotten her had turned him against his own mother.

Fiadh moved in alongside her as she continued their trek. Away from what once had been the closest thing to a home she'd ever known.

"We need food and rest for the night. Tomorrow, we reach our allies and then the next day, we prepare to destroy the continent."

Fiadh's smile was twisted, teeth brightened by the light from above. "Yes, My Queen."

Marquette returned the grin. "I will never tire of that. Even if it was short lived."

Fiadh cackled. "We'll all have our revenge for what Talamh has done to us."

That they would. "Are they still well hidden?"

Fiadh nodded.

"Good. We have much to do. I hope you're ready."

"I'm always ready." She paused, her eyes closed, lids fluttering. "There are two coming. Near, but I don't know who. We must move."

Marquette drew her shoulders back. For now, they would run. But soon they wouldn't be the ones running. Felicity had only forced her to move sooner than expected, but the spy princess would bow to her once again.

Chapter 1

Alarian didn't tap his foot, bounce his knee, or thrum his fingers against the armrest of the chair he sat upon. It took active thought to ensure he didn't do any of these things. He was supposed to be concentrating on the court proceedings—particularly because they would decide his fate.

"Hundreds were imprisoned. Many died," Lord Chartow growled. "And he stood by and watched."

A sigh to his right caught Alarian's attention, but he didn't dare look that way. That was where Prince Kellan, overseer of these proceedings, sat next to her. Auburn hair. Warm, brown eyes that could easily change to sharp daggers when she was pissed. Lips he desperately...his foot tapped.

Nope. Concentrate.

He wouldn't—couldn't—look at Felicity right now. Then he would think about the hand he held out to her the day before. A choice. Words spoken. And every emotion she felt that he could now, for some unknown reason, sense. The part of herself she tried so hard to suppress and keep hidden he could now feel wafting off her. He was trying to get better at blocking it but failed when she felt as strongly as she did now. Annoyance. Anger. All hidden by a mask of indifference.

He swallowed, remaining outwardly composed.

Prince Kellan ran a hand through his dark brown hair. "With the facts brought to you today, do you honestly believe he should be sentenced for crimes he didn't commit? It was his parents. Not him."

Lord Chartow looked at his fellow advisors one at a time. None of them were thrilled with the prospect of Alarian being exonerated, but there was also nothing they could say. Alarian had been a scapegoat. Someone to be used to show the rest of Talamh that they had everything under control when chaos was on their doorstep. Alarian understood all of this, but more importantly, he wanted to stop his mother and protect the continent from utter ruin. And the clock was ticking...

When Felicity stood, Alarian could no longer resist looking towards her. Protectiveness tattooed against his skull. She had played varying roles during her employment under his father. A spy. A courtier. A damsel in distress.

As she smoothed her skirts for the umpteenth time, not that he'd been watching from the corner of his eye, he followed the movement. Noted the sleeves of her dress that went to her wrists, the neckline at her throat, and her hair was in a tight bun at the nape of her neck showing off the clasp and chain at her ear. The clasp he had thought she'd thrown away with the curse. Her hard gaze, a contrast to the light blue dress that softened her curves, was the only indication of her frustration. Buttoned up and proper. What part did she mean to play now?

Her tone was even and to the point. "Let's go over the facts. We have proof and accounts that Alarian was not only a rebel but their leader. One such account is a letter written by Lady Chartow. One that you have confirmed was by her hand." She held that letter she had received from Sloan up. Lady Chartow hadn't known for certain, but she had been curious of Alarian's true allegiance. Alarian would reprimand Sloan for keeping damning evidence on his person, but for once, it hadn't bitten him in the ass.

Felicity continued, "More proof from Sloan, who a few of you have claimed was your contact." His friend waved from his seat amongst the advisors, a grin etched on his face as he leaned against his chair looking for all the world as if they were in a pub. "I have brought forth information regarding the ship Alarian had ready in the harbor under an alias. You all were aware of a Master Harlin working with the rebellion but hadn't met him. Alarian was aware of the plans to free the abducted townsfolk—something he wouldn't have known since he'd been imprisoned for the past ten days."

Alarian forced his gaze away from her as she spoke of his alias as a merchant. The supply ship he had ready in the harbor the night of Lughnasadh when the rebels infiltrated not only the palace, but the ravine to free those abducted from their homes. Alarian had offered a place for families and orphans to come together to eat and celebrate near the docks. Unbeknownst to them, his plan was to reunite them with their loved ones and, if necessary, offer a quick escape if all hell broke loose and his parents remained on the throne.

He hadn't expected the curse to break. Hadn't known there was a way for Prince Kellan's name to be remembered when Felicity didn't seem to know who she was. Even Alarian had questioned his assumptions of who she was at times. The curse wasn't supposed to have affected her memories.

And he couldn't ask. It would have been too dangerous to speak aloud. Secrets spoken to the wind had been uncovered on more than one occasion. He wouldn't dare have put her in danger. When she admitted to him the previous day that she hadn't had her memories, it took all his willpower not to shadow straight to the Tower to demand answers.

This time it was Lord Denizen of Saol who spoke. "It doesn't matter. He was a bystander for years. A silent and willing participant as his parents made every-one suffer." The portly man grumbled a few words under his breath that had Lady Grandeur of Visce chuckling. The two must have been the only options as stand-ins on behalf of their realms since neither were politically inclined. But they had been a part of the rebellion, so they were loyal to the rightful rulers.

Lady Avyanna Solfire stood up at Felicity's side. The princess stepped back to her chair. Impassivity, a sensation like a dying flame, curled off her and that bothered him more than her silence.

Avyanna shifted her long, curly orange hair behind her shoulder as she looked at those who opposed his innocence. Alarian knew quite well that they weren't wrong for questioning his loyalty. None of what was being said was wrong—he deserved punishment. For years he'd been complacent, had never risen against his parents on behalf of the people. He had even disappeared and submerged into the world of drinks, parties, and brothels. There was nothing to show for that time of frivolity, except for the blind eye towards his parents' sins.

Later, that world had built up the persona he would use to raise a rebellion. To discover what he could about his parents' plans and what they hoped to achieve with the heartstones.

But it was a little too late. His father might be dead, but his mother had escaped with the witch, Fiadh.

Avyanna's shoulders drew back. "He made mistakes. The best of us have. May I ask, if you're almighty and get to choose which faults he is held accountable for, where were all of you during those years? Where were you before the rebellion strengthened and their numbers rose? Were you leading at the helm or silently watching from the back of the room? I don't remember any of you standing up to Roald. I didn't see you question Marquette. If you're to blame Alarian for what all of us, including myself, have done for years, then tell me—how many trials should we hold?"

Silence expanded through the room.

Avyanna took a seat and Prince Kellan stood. "Are there any other objections, or have we unanimously decided that Alarian shouldn't be tried as an enemy of Talamh?"

No one spoke up. Lord Denizen looked as though he wanted to say more but remained still with his mouth pursed and brow furrowed.

"Good." Prince Kellan fixed the lapel of his jacket and turned to face Alarian. "As Prince Regent of Talamh, I hereby announce you as not guilty. With your freedom, what do you choose to do first?"

That had been a discussion they already had the night before. A small meeting to explain himself and put a plan in place. Alarian was going to do exactly what he did best. "With your permission, I'll leave tomorrow morning and search for my mother and Fiadh's location."

He didn't mention the heartstones. Not everyone in the room was privy to that tidbit, and it had taken longer than he'd hoped to get Prince Kellan to believe that the stones were real and not a bedtime story. Well, mostly believe. He knew the prince still had doubts.

Besides, such information was dangerous. It was kept between himself, Felicity, Avyanna, Sloan, and Prince Kellan.

Chartow snorted, but the others ignored him.

Prince Kellan glared at the advisor from the corner of his eye. "Safe travels. When should we expect your return?"

"As soon as I have something to share—or within twelve days' time." That should be enough to check in with his allies for any insight on Marquette and Fiadh's whereabouts and see if he could collect information regarding the location of the other heartstones. Hopefully when he returned it would be enough to begin his penance.

"How do we know he will keep his word?" Lady Grandeur rose a brow. "Maybe this is his plan all along and he's running to his mother's side."

"You can't spew accusations when we've just agreed he's free," Sloan all but growled, his fists tightened.

Alarian was growing tired of their attitude. It had been easier when he had operated within the shadows. Ignored, except for speculation on his relationship with whoever they connived for him to court. Lady Grandeur had wanted him to consider both of her children at one point.

He stood, hoping he wasn't overstepping, but he needed this to end. "If you truly think I'm guilty, then come find me and tear me apart where I stand." His tone was a dangerous whisper and the shadows spread along the floor. "I never got along with my parents. Everyone knew it."

"You didn't stop them when my wife was chained at your father's feet."

Chartow had been chewing on those words for a while now. Alarian had been waiting. "I know you're upset that my family killed your wife. She was one of the best of us. But I didn't betray her. She knew the danger of being a spy amongst wolves and did what she could for Talamh."

"She didn't know you existed," Chartow snapped. "She thought the leader was him." He pointed at Sloan.

Sloan chuckled, but it was one of malice not humor. "That was the point. Because of moments like these and the doubt that his name brings. Alarian was the mastermind and the one who brought together countless civilians, courtiers, and associates. He trusted a select few to be the face of our cause. I'm not the only one who knows his identity. Would you like to take the time for them to be brought here to give the same testimony? Or would it even matter when all you want is someone to blame?"

"Or," Felicity began in a sharp tone. The spy and assassin present—that darkness in her gaze as she leaned forward from her high-backed chair. "Will you allow him a chance to prove himself to you and find his mother?"

Air caught momentarily in his throat. He expelled a breath. He wasn't good enough for her.

Chartow swallowed and leaned back. "Of course, Your Highness."

She didn't look Alarian's way. Not once. He diverted his attention back to the others. That's what this all came down to—proving himself. Not to them, though. They could all go to Ankus, the realm of the dead, as far as he was concerned. If they didn't want to trust him, then fine. But her...he would prove himself to her. That he was worthy of her trust, at the very least.

"Twelve days." Prince Kellan diverted the conversation back to where they were before the interruption. "We hope to hear from you sooner with news."

Alarian had to bite back a smile. Prince Kellan wasn't enthusiastic about his return. He hadn't exactly warmed to Alarian and only trusted him because Felicity and Sloan had evidence of Alarian's true identity. But...

Alarian turned to face the Prince and Princess of Talamh but kept his attention on Kellan. "Before I go, I need to apologize to you both, but mostly to you, Prince Kellan."

Avyanna breathed in a sharp gasp.

Prince Kellan swallowed, his eyes widening. "For?"

Alarian drew back his shoulders and then crossed his arms over his heart. A sign of fealty. This was meant to be more than an apology, but a show of his loyalty. "I abandoned you at your greatest time of need. I didn't stand up to my parents when I should have, but what is worse is that I left you behind. I could have been an ally. A friend. I should have shown you that you weren't alone. Instead, I left. For that, I will always have regrets."

Alarian held the prince's gaze. Waited.

Prince Kellan's grip tightened on the armrests of his chair. "I appreciate the apology." He looked at the other members of the council. "Time will tell if you deserve forgiveness."

Spoken like a true king. Well—someday. Prince Kellan needed to show his strength and stability to those who watched him for mistakes. Who questioned if he could maintain control in the absence of his father. Sloan would be leaving soon to search the last of the Oileán Islands for King Bastien, but in the interim, Prince Kellan had to remain steady. Felicity was young and unknown as far as the continent was concerned, but to have her by his side showed a united front.

Alarian turned to her. Allowed himself to take her in. Stoic. Once again hiding any sign of emotion. How the world had shifted and changed so much since Lughnasadh. "I'm going to do everything in my power to prove that I deserve your trust."

He turned and walked towards the double doors at the end of the hall without looking back. It was time to pack and prepare. If his assumptions were correct, Marquette and Fiadh would make their move soon. His mother didn't like to be backed in a corner and although Alarian didn't have all the facts, he knew she was collecting the stones. Knew she planned to use them. It was common knowledge that the veil was at its thinnest on Samhain. If she planned to use the heartstones, she would use them then. He just needed confirmation that he was correct.

Which meant their time was dwindling. They had less than eighty days.

Let the countdown begin...

Chapter 2
Felicity

Felicity bolted upright, dagger in her grip as she searched her room. A cold sweat dampened her skin, her sheets sticking to her clammy body. She brightened the dim light beside her bed and placed her dagger back under her pillow before checking her fingernails for the blood she couldn't wash clean. The corpse's empty eyes, the smell of burnt skin from unchecked magic was etched into her mind even in her waking hours. A dream pivoted to a nightmare.

The nightmares had become more frequent. She had been a spy, but more than once someone had died by her hand. She didn't know which ones she should feel guilty about. There had never been a time she had remembered asking the Tower why. Or if they deserved to die. Now their faces haunted her.

Emotions. Guilt. She was still working through them. She wanted to ignore the feelings welling up, but that wasn't an option anymore. Not with the knowledge she'd gained.

Then there were the memories she still didn't have. The dreams of a family without faces. Hauntings of running through a field with her mother. If her father was found and returned, she wouldn't know him.

But there were more important things to pursue, like understanding heart-stones and stopping Marquette.

She ran a hand through her hair and breathed a long sigh, her head pounding from thoughts that buzzed like flies. Felicity couldn't bring herself to do more than research in the library or attend the many meetings. She was a princess now. Sequestered to a palace for her protection. Followed by guards who vowed to give their lives for her.

With a heavy sigh, she stood and slipped on her robe. Usually that was enough of a signal for Meira to appear as if summoned. It was an ability that Felicity still hadn't been able to pinpoint but tonight was different. Silence was the only response to her movement and Felicity welcomed the opportunity to head towards the kitchen alone. Tea would do. Anything to change her train of thought.

Felicity walked into the kitchen and the sweet scent of chocolate filled her nostrils. But the sound of laughter caught her off guard. She stilled in the entryway, spotting Meira in a cream apron that brightened her green skin and rosy cheeks—and Alarian across from her with a measuring cup in hand wearing a pair of loose-fitting pants and a thin, white tunic that clung to his body. Felicity swallowed and looked around the kitchen to ignore the heat building within.

Ignore the memory of his touch from that night at the *Rose & Wisteria*.

"Oh." Meira straightened at the sight of her. "Princess, I apologize. Is there something you need?"

She bit her lip, crossing her arms over her nightdress at being caught loitering. No matter how many times Felicity had requested the handmaiden to resist using the title, Meira ignored her. Felicity relaxed, forcing warmth into her expression. "Of course not. I'm sorry for interrupting. I was going to grab some tea then I'll be out of your way."

"Let me." Meira rushed across the room and began fiddling with the bronze kettle that sat on the large wood burning stove.

Alarian stepped in her way. "Nana, why don't we finish the cake icing?" He nodded towards the bowl that had been left on the counter.

"Cake?" Felicity's eyes widened. "You're baking?"

Alarian reached for a wooden spoon. "Meira and I used to bake all the time. We hadn't had a chance to in years, so we decided to take the opportunity." He winked at Felicity who ignored the fluttering in her stomach.

"You did?" She couldn't keep the surprise from her voice.

Meira's blush deepened. "Rian dear, the princess doesn't need to hear about all of that. She came for tea and I—"

"Will there be enough cake to share?" Felicity glanced between the two of them, making her way across the room. She added water to the kettle and stroked the fire back to life. "I can handle the tea if you finish the icing. Would anyone else like tea?"

Alarian grinned as Meira fidgeted. It was clear she wasn't certain how to move forward. Even after all their warm conversations, the handmaiden was still hesitant around her.

Alarian reached for the tin. "I'll take some." He held out the wooden spoon towards Meira and pushed the tin towards Felicity. She picked up the canister and her fingers grazed over the orange blossom imprinted onto the side. Saol. *The Tower.* She bit her lip and popped the lid to the citrus scent and was pulled into a memory. *Cool soil. Grass stained with blood.*

Meira took the spoon from Alarian with a sigh, forcing Felicity from the past. "Thank you, Your Highness. I would love some tea."

They worked in silence, a sense of comfort taking over as the seconds ticked by. While Meira mixed ingredients in a bowl, Alarian collected what was needed. Felicity grabbed milk from the ice box and searched for teacups that materialized in front of her with a wisp of shadow. Alarian smirked and she turned away, unable to look at him. He made her weak. Feel too much. While she had loved Harrison, the pull towards Alarian was taut. She needed to break it before it broke her and hold onto whatever glimpse of control she still had because it faded every day.

The sweet smell of the cake grew stronger, and Meira took two round pans from the oven and placed them on a shelf to cool. When the tea finished brewing a moment later, Felicity poured three steaming cups, the citrus and floral scent wafting up as she handed them off.

Alarian sipped and grinned at her over his mug. "Perfect."

Felicity stared at the floor, her thumbs fidgeting with the rim of the cup before she asked, "Did you two bake often in Scáth?"

The handmaiden glanced at Alarian who was leaning against the counter in that careless way of his. He took another sip and nodded. "Meira thought it was important to learn how to keep myself alive. Basic needs beyond fighting stances and sneaking up on unsuspecting targets." He chuckled to himself. "It's where she cultivated my need for chocolate."

"I didn't give you your sweet tooth," she grumbled with a roll of her eyes.

His grin widened. "I feel it's best I blame you."

"I didn't know you liked desserts." The words were out of Felicity's mouth before she could hold them back. *See me.* There was so much she had ignored.

He shrugged, unaware of her inner turmoil. "My parents removed everything I loved from my life when I returned. Not like I could sneak to the kitchens and bake with Nana on a whim."

Meira glanced up at the clock settled against the wall, then drained the last of her tea. "I should check on my charges. Some of the new handmaidens have a habit of sneaking to their friend's rooms when it's past their bedtime."

Felicity cleared her throat. "You don't have to leave—"

"Duty calls. Feel free to ice the cake when it's ready and I'll be back a bit later for a piece. Thank you for the tea." She bustled from the room.

Alarian chuckled.

Felicity's cheeks flushed. "That was an excuse, wasn't it?"

"I'm sure she will do just as she says. Meira is honest to a fault." He took another sip of his tea, watching her over the rim.

She had the strangest thought that he was waiting to see if she ran. From him. Schooling her expression, she wrapped both hands around the still warm cup and asked, "How do you feel after today's proceedings?"

"I was certain they would find some fault with me, but not enough to hold me." He shrugged noncommittally. "For the most part, I think they're glad to be rid of me. Even if it's only for a short time."

She bit her bottom lip, not wanting to venture to far on thoughts of him leaving—or being rid of him. "I don't know...I think you caught my brother off guard with your apology. Imagine how he would have reacted if you got on your knees and begged for forgiveness?"

A coolness licked Felicity's bare feet, and she looked down to find the tendrils of shadows. Hesitantly, she met Alarian's darkened gaze. "I won't get on my knees for just anyone, Starlight."

Need slid through her and settled in her core. She broke their stare and averted her gaze to the cup in her hand. He couldn't be flirting. Her body was betraying her. The last kiss they had shared—their only kiss—he'd cut short. Then there were the words they've said to each other since. Just the day before, his hand held out offering a choice. Again...

Her thoughts turned towards her previous opinion of him—when she had thought him on his parents' leash. She wished she'd known more then, but regret wouldn't change anything. There were much more important matters she needed to concentrate on now.

She made her way to the chocolate sponge cake—an easy distraction. She picked up the wooden spoon covered in chocolate icing before placing it back in the mixing bowl. "I've never iced a cake before."

Alarian made his way across the kitchen, hovering his hand over one of the cakes. "They are ready to come out of the pans to finish cooling. Would you like to help?"

Alarian responded to Felicity's nod with a smile and pointed towards a drawer near the sink. "We need a knife. I'll grab the rack."

While she retrieved the knife, he removed both pans from the shelf and placed them on the counter next to the metal rack he'd found. "You need to cut around the edges of the pan. I'll show you." He took the knife and sliced the blade between the cake and pan, moving slowly around the edge. Then he held out the knife towards her. She did the same, then watched as he turned the cake over, and with some shaking, the cake plopped onto the rack. After she mimicked his movements, he took the pans to the sink and turned on the water.

Her brow furrowed as Alarian began to wash the dishes. "You clean up after yourself too?"

He laughed. "I was brought up by a handmaiden—of course I clean up after myself."

"Your room said otherwise," she mumbled under her breath.

Alarian snorted. "It isn't always that chaotic. Lots of research, plenty of time to do it. I meant it when I said you ruined my system."

She rolled her eyes and he chuckled. "Fine. I usually live within controlled chaos. But in spaces that are shared, I'm a perfect gentleman."

Felicity grinned, and he stilled before turning back to his task. When she held the knife out to him, he shook his head. "We're going to need that for the icing."

Once the dishes were cleaned, Felicity dried them, and with a little trial and error, they found where everything needed to be put away. There was normalcy to their movements, almost synchronized like a dance as they moved about the kitchen.

Felicity watched as he poured the frosting in the center before spreading it in a thin, even layer. He carefully placed the second layer on top, then handed her the knife. She iced the second layer, and he advised her the best way to cover a bare spot without tearing the cake.

"It's done." Felicity smiled at their creation. The icing was thicker in some spots, but her mouth watered in anticipation. "Should I grab plates?"

"Sure." Alarian reached for the forks and at the same moment Felicity dabbed a dollop of icing on his nose.

He froze. She froze. Her hand was still outstretched and icing plopped to the floor. Had she just done that?

His expression lit up as he faced her, his emerald eyes shining, the corner of his mouth lifting. "Really?"

She shrugged, popping her finger in her mouth to lick off the excess. His gaze slid to her lips, and she paused, suddenly aware of how close they were to each other. How his throat bobbed. How she wanted to close the distance between them. His smile expanded, but before she could decide, he smeared icing onto her cheek.

At Felicity's mock gasp, he chuckled and winked. "Two can play at that game. You won't win."

"Oh?"

Then chaos ensued, both fighting for control over the bowl amidst laughter and jabbing elbows.

A tittering sounded at the door followed by a small groan, and with the wooden spoon raised in Alarian's hand and Felicity coveting the bowl she'd just won, they both turned to face Meira.

"What is happening in here?"

Felicity blinked once then turned to survey the room. Chocolate icing was splattered on the counter, shelves, and all over their clothing, arms, and faces. Felicity began to apologize but instead of looking upset at the mess, the handmaiden's eyes misted with unshed tears.

Alarian straightened, lowering the spoon. "We'll clean it up."

"I know you will." Meira waved her hand without looking either of them in the eye. "But first things first—let's have cake."

As the handmaiden collected the ignored utensils and plates, Felicity and Alarian went to the sink to wash their hands. When their gazes met momentarily, they grinned at each other. Felicity's smile faded as her arm brushed his and heat rushed to her cheeks. She quickly turned away.

They kept to easy-going topics while Felicity attempted to ignore the male who stood beside her as they ate. Meira was sharing a story about Alarian's youth, but Felicity's attention wandered and got lost on the day before. When she had taken a chance—and his hand—and been rewarded by him choosing to confide in her about his part in the rebellion. How he had led them in secret. Then a decision had been made.

"And then snap." Meira clapped and Felicity nearly jumped. "The branch broke and Alarian was in a heap on the ground. That's when we learned he could heal himself. Didn't stop him from having to deal with the pain of a broken limb though..."

"Have to learn some things the hard way." Alarian took his last bite of cake before scraping his plate with his fork.

"It's late." Meira took his plate from his grasp. "Time to clean up before you start licking the plates."

Felicity smiled, taking her own things to the sink before Meira could.

As they cleaned, Meira continued to tell stories as if they were children preparing for bed. On more than one occasion, she caught Alarian chuckling to himself. She didn't ask. Didn't speak at all. When the kitchen was orderly again and the icing cleared off all surfaces, Meira bid them goodnight and bustled from the room.

They were alone. Again.

The large kitchen suddenly felt small. The walls edging closer. The lanterns and hanging pots lowered. "Goodnight," she murmured and headed towards the door, uncertain what else to say.

"May I escort you back to your room, Princess?"

Felicity shuttered and rolled her shoulders to loosen the weight suddenly pulling them down. "I could—" She cut her rejection short at his tender grin and hopeful emerald eyes. "Use the company." Why did she say that?

He nodded towards the door, and she led him out.

They walked together towards the stairs, and each step felt like agony with the arm's length between them. She repeated their agreement over and over in her head. The definition of their relationship. She examined their surroundings while she tried to think of ways to fill the silence. The faded tapestries hanging on the wall really should be replaced. And there must be better art than the depictions of war the traitors had used to decorate.

He cleared his throat and clasped his hands behind his back. "I hope you're able to sleep well tonight."

"Uh..." That damn heat spiked through her cheeks, and she hoped the dim lights guiding them weren't bright enough to draw attention to her blush.

He ran a hand through his hair. "I mean, I hope that the cake and tea helped," he rushed, and she was relieved to see his own cheeks reddening.

"Oh...I'm sure it did." Why was she a bumbling mess around him now? To calm her racing heart, she took a deep breath and lifted her chin, her shoulders drawing back. Her mask, persona, in place. "Where will you head to first?"

He was silent for a step. Then two. "Aer, then probably into Domhain."

"Do you think your mother or Fiadh are in either location?"

Alarian shrugged. "There is a chance. They have connections in both."

"Will you miss me?"

Her carefully crafted façade cracked, and she turned to him.

"While I'm gone?" That grin of his played at the corner of his mouth.

"It's only twelve days. You'll be back before we know it." She nearly asked him if she could go with him. To step away from the suffocating title placed on her. But her duty and responsibilities to an entire continent had to come first.

Alarian sighed. "I see. And what about you?" He stopped and faced her.

Felicity halted, realizing they were outside her room. "What do you mean?"

His jaw flexed. Felicity's attention pinned on that movement—he was going to say something she wasn't going to like.

He folded his hands behind his back. "Are you going to figure out what's bothering you or continue to ignore it?"

Instincts had her fingers twitching for her dagger. To feel the handle in her grip. Ground her. But she'd left the blade in her room. "What the hell do you mean?" she repeated in a hiss.

"You're trying to make yourself disappear. Just now, in the kitchen, was the first time I saw a sign of the female I was getting to know."

Her eyes widened. "Excuse me?" How was it that he could go from charming to a thorn in her side within one breath?

"I noted it when you came to my room yesterday. But today's proceedings solidified it. I never thought I'd see you let anyone speak for you. Not after you'd been forced to silence."

After all this is over, don't ever let anyone use you again. A request after a kiss. After he returned her to her room from the brothel. Then he'd disappeared.

Fists formed at her side, and she stepped into his space. "What the fuck, Alarian? You think you can throw these accusations? You have no idea what I'm thinking, and I have good reason to hide my emotions." Not that he needed to hear what they were. She was only a little shorter than he was, but in that moment, she hated that she had to look up to meet his eyes.

He didn't back down from her anger. "I don't care if you have reasons or not—stop it now. At least for those you care about. For yourself. Remove the clasp from your ear. Let that light that's always been a part of you out."

Unconsciously, she grazed the dampener clasp she wore, and her mouth grew taut, her eyes sharp. "I can't believe you," she snapped. "It's been less than a day, and I already want to throw you back into a cell and toss the key." Felicity pushed past him to her bedroom door.

He grabbed her arm, pulling her close to him. "If I didn't tell you the truth every now and then, you would hide behind that mask you work so hard to maintain. That's how we have always worked. I tell you a truth you don't like, you hate me for it. You'll get pissed for a few days and then we figure it out. Works both ways, because you do the same for me. But I couldn't leave without saying something. Besides, we're friends and we promised to be honest with each other."

Friends. The word stung. She didn't know why she cared. It wasn't like she could have more with him. Or wanted more. But she had taken his hand, took a chance, and when he'd asked her if they could be friends, something solidified within her—that was all he saw with her. "Is this why you offered to walk with me? To throw this crap in my face?" She realized he still held her. How close they were to each other. But as angry as she was, she didn't pull away.

Alarian's grip loosened, his eyes scanning her face. "No. In fact, I wasn't going to say anything at all, but I can't stand seeing you this way. Half alive. You're not the dutiful spy used by the Tower anymore. And you *are* a princess." When she drew herself up, he shook his head and continued, "I see how you react every time someone says that title. *Your* people deserve the smart, loyal, and powerful female you are. Don't just show me the real you, Felicity. Show the world."

He turned to leave, then paused with a glance over his shoulder. "I know you didn't ask, but I will."

She lifted her chin, her mouth a thin line. "Will what?"

"Miss you." He stuffed his hands into his pockets and walked away.

She watched him until he disappeared around the corner and considered running after him to either punch—or kiss him. Neither were a good alternative, so she entered her room and leaned back against the closed door.

Felicity caught her reflection in the mirror across the room and stared at herself. Chocolate stained her nightdress. Her hair hung loose at her shoulders. She had lost weight. Her muscles ached, but not from training. She hadn't trained since she uttered her brother's name, and her entire world turned on its head. Instead, she woke up sore from tossing and turning throughout the night.

She clutched her chest to combat the sudden heaviness. The rush of her heart. Breathing became difficult as her lungs constricted.

The sharpness in her gaze was gone. She looked as tired as she felt. She turned away, willing herself to breathe. To think. Darkness edged into her vision as her legs buckled. *Count*, she demanded herself.

But she couldn't. Her reflection was branded in her mind. Changes she noted, Alarian had noted. But she didn't know what to do. Not anymore.

She lowered to the ground and placed her palms to the floor to feel the wooden grooves against her skin. She pinched her eyes closed, forcing her attention onto tapping the rate of her heart. Willing it to slow.

Breathe. One. She tried to count like Kellan had shown her, but it was impossible.

Weapon.

Princess.

Spy.

Royalty.

Alarian saw her when she tried so hard to ignore him. He had told her today that he'd prove himself, but she knew she was the one who needed to prove herself. To him. To the entire continent. And gain some control in her own life again.

The door flung open, banging against Felicity's foot as Meira appeared by her side. "Princess Felicity, are you all right?"

Her foot ached from the impact, a hiss that forced air into her lungs. A gasp. The darkness slipped from the edges of her vision as warm hands gripped her arms. She couldn't speak as the handmaiden pulled her to a seated position and searched her face. Worry edged Meira's eyes. "Let's get you up."

Felicity nodded as Meira assisted her to the bathing room and settled her on the stool. "We need to clean you up first you." She tutted, mumbling words Felicity couldn't discern as she retrieved a clean nightdress and a towel.

She sat in silence, only moving when the handmaiden told her to. Once she was in clean clothes and the chocolate was removed from her hair, Meira led her to her bed and tucked her in. "There, that's better."

Meira sat down in the overstuffed chair. One that she'd occupied in the past. It seemed the handmaiden wasn't planning to leave tonight. Felicity almost asked her to go, but Meira took a throw blanket from a nearby basket and gave her a look that dared her to try. "Do you need anything else?"

Felicity shook her head, then curled into the blankets.

She didn't know how to answer that question.

Chapter 3
Kellan

*H*is father was chained to the floor beside him. Both of them on their knees with iron manacles at their wrists. Blood dripped from a harsh slash across Bastien's cheek where Roald's talons had sliced.

Kellan wished his body would stop trembling. That he didn't look terrified when it was anger that pulsed through him.

"Are they gone?" Marquette stalked into the throne room and glanced at where Roald sat. The exquisitely carved chair that used to be his father's throne. Until a coup...

Kellan spat as she passed, saliva hitting the toe of her pointed black stiletto. She paused, looked down at him, then kicked him square in the jaw. The heel of her boot cut into his mouth, which filled with blood and he coughed.

Roald stood at the action, his talons tearing away the wood of the throne. He took a step towards them, but Marquette raised her hand and the male immediately stopped. "Don't worry, my heart. He will feel the pain of his choices soon enough."

"Where are my wife and daughter?" Bastien thrashed against the restraints. He had an extra manacle around his neck, and Kellan had watched his father's skin pale further as his body drained from his attempts to reach the magic the iron suppressed.

Roald chuckled and sneered as Marquette curled her arm through the crook of her husband's. "Dead—or they will be soon enough. Maybe we will be lucky enough to show you their heads as proof. No one can run from his reach."

"*What have you done?*" *Kellan fought back the tears.* "*How could you kill innocents?*" *His sister—his stepmother. One held little magic, and the other was too young.* "*Call them off.*"

"*They are unnecessary.*" *Marquette tilted her head, considering them.* "*You will do as we say.*"

Bastien twisted against the restraints. "*We never—*"

Roald roared, "*You will. If you want your son to survive. You will give us everything we want.*"

Kellan pulled at the restraints, knowing it was futile. "*You might as well ki—*"

"*No,*" *Bastien bellowed.* "*Don't touch my son.*"

Marquette's smile was feline. "*That's what I thought.*"

"*Father…*"

Marquette nodded at her husband and the male stalked down the steps, stopping in front of Kellan. He grabbed Kellan by the throat, his claws grazing the sensitive skin. He tried to yell but sputtered as air was cut off from his lungs. Roald pulled him from the ground, his feet dangling as the male transformed further into the beast.

"*Stop.*" *Bastien's voice still held the authority of a king.*

Kellan wouldn't beg. Not even as darkness edged his vision.

Bastien shuffled forward on his knees. "*Let him go. I'm listening.*"

Kellan was slammed to the ground. Air engulfed his lungs, but he wished it wouldn't because then his father wouldn't have to succumb to their hatred. His eyes settled on the few advisors who stood on the outskirts of the room. The ones who had been allies, friends even. Who had betrayed them. He would remember each and every one of them. If he survived this, he'd tear their worlds apart.

Revenge would taste sweet.

Marquette stood in front of them, shadows wrapped around her shoulders and cascaded behind her like a train. "*We would love to kill you, but you have information we want in time. And your blood*" *—she leaned forward and Bastien shuddered as she ran a finger down his clawed cheek—* "*is necessary.*"

"Leave him alone," Kellan snapped. Blood slid down his chin, as he fought to sit upright, his head spinning. "He'll never help you."

Roald chuckled. "He will if he wants you to live." He pushed Kellan's shoulder and although the tap wasn't rough, exhaustion more than the force had him crumbling to the floor. Roald walked around his fallen form to face Bastien. "He will remain here while you'll be sent far away. You will give us what we want and, when the time is right, you will prove your use."

A gasp scratched his throat. Warm hands held his arm. He tore free from their hold.

"Kellan."

Her voice. *Avyanna.* He shuddered as her hands cooled, touching his forehead. "Kellan. Your name is Kellan."

Tears pricked his eyes as he concentrated on her voice. He buried his face in his hands, and she moved to wrap her arms around him.

"Your name is Kellan," she whispered the reminder over and over like a mantra in his ear. Those words, his name on her lips, grounded him to the present. *It was the past—not the present.* The residual effects of the dream slowly dissipated.

"Thank you," he whispered into the crook of her neck.

Her hands stroked circles on his back and they warmed again, on instinct, he was sure. Her desire to fix wounds that couldn't be touched by her magic. Scars that always would remain, even if not with a physical reminder. "I wish I could do more."

"You're here." He looked up and met her gaze. "That is more than enough."

The moonlight shimmered on her cool, dark skin, another reminder that he was free. Under Roald's rule, they would not have stayed in each other's rooms. Certainly not with the windows open. There had been some close calls. A few too many times that both had taken chances.

"Which nightmare?"

There were too many of them lately. "My father's banishment. I saw Marquette's face in this one. Not just her voice."

"Did the witch appear?"

He shook his head. "No." After so many years, all he could remember of the witch who had enacted the curse were her blue eyes. Not Fiadh's but another, unknown but somehow familiar.

Avyanna's touch cooled again, relieving the stress a little further. "I need to talk to the witches. See if one of them can give me clarity."

"Have you talked to Felicity about this?"

"No, I don't want to bother her. She has enough going on." He'd noticed her withdrawal into herself but couldn't figure out how to broach the subject. She was drifting like a wraith through the castle, barely aware. Her mission to find proof of Alarian's innocence had brought her to life since she had been titled, but now that was over. She was present—but not.

Avyanna's shoulders slumped. "She worries about you too. You cannot ignore this forever. Sometimes I wonder if you both need to go to the Tower."

"Why?" His brow furrowed. It may have been the place that had housed his sister, but the Tower had also put her in danger. He had mixed feelings about the Countess and her tactics. Especially since they had stolen Felicity's memories.

She brushed a strand of hair from his face. "I don't know why, but I think they can answer the questions you both have."

He shook his head. "I'm needed here."

"Their information could be vital in helping us understand Marquette, the curse, and why Felicity still has holes in her memories." She took a deep breath. "But I agree now isn't the time for you to leave. Even with the curse broken, the realms are on edge. Send Felicity."

Kellan froze, his mouth drawn tight and a pulse pounded in his temple. "What?"

Avyanna folded her hands in her lap. "She needs this. We need her, but she doesn't realize it. I care for her almost as much as you do. She already feels like a sister to me."

Kellan leaned forward and rested his forehead against hers. He closed his eyes, breathed her in. "You're wise. Beyond us all." He meant every word. Even if he tried not to speak them aloud too often. Couldn't let the truth go to her head or she might realize she was too good for him.

"You've seen her behavior these past few days."

He sighed and leaned back. He'd hoped that Felicity would snap out of whatever was pulling her under, but once Alarian had left three days prior, Felicity had fallen deeper into herself. "You think I should send her to the Tower? For answers?"

"And maybe with Alarian. She needs a mission."

"What the hell, Avyanna? He's—" Kellan was still trying to accept who Alarian truly was. The drunken, rakish prince he'd known had led an entire rebellion. He hated to admit that his pride hurt to be wrong about the male who had been hidden in plain sight for years.

And then there was that apology he had been unprepared for.

"Stop."

Kellan froze. He learned within the first year of their relationship what *that* tone meant. He snapped his mouth shut.

Avyanna settled back against the headrest. "There is something I have never told you."

His brow furrowed and a heaviness settled in his chest at the seriousness in her tone.

"He knew about our relationship."

Silence. No words came to mind. Only that sudden rush of needless fear because Roald and Marquette weren't in charge anymore. His mouth a thin line, Kellan stared at her without interrupting.

"He found out early on and kept it a secret for us. Never said a word except for one time to me." She swallowed.

"To blackmail you?"

She shook her head sadly. "He's not his parents, Kellan. In fact, he told me that he would keep speaking of his interest and curiosity in me to ensure my presence in the palace. That's also why he brought me along to Koselig that night. To allow us a chance to spend time together under the guise of keeping his options open."

It went against everything he thought he knew about the male—a regular recurrence in the past few days. Alarian had more surprises up his sleeve than a court jester. He considered Avyanna's words. "Then why did he offer to go to Koselig with Felicity if not to..." Kellan trailed off as he recalled all the times he had warned his sister away from the male. Told her of Alarian's rakish ways and said he wasn't trustworthy. How far had Alarian gone to make everyone believe that side of him? "He was helping her?"

"I think so."

"Why? As far as he knew she was working for Roald."

The corners of Avyanna's mouth twitched. "I think he had his reasons."

He shook his head. "What are you implying?" He noticed Alarian's interest from the very beginning. That's why he had warned Felicity away from him. But he thought his curiosity a passing fancy since Alarian only ever had short-term infatuations that usually ended badly. "He can't care about her like that."

She rolled her eyes. "If you prefer to think that way, then fine. Stay in your fantasy world." Avyanna sighed. "Besides, you have time to accept him. She's resisting every other emotion so I doubt she will show any interest in him. It's near impossible to read her."

He couldn't help but smile at that. "True. And he's gone right now. Gives me time to discreetly plan his death."

She pushed his arm with more strength than she realized and he winced, feigning a pain-filled groan. Avyanna rolled her eyes. "Kellan, that's enough."

Kellan groaned, closing his eyes as he considered the evidence. If Avyanna was right, Felicity was still hesitant. But maybe he was the only one who had walls up to the traitors' son.

Did Alarian deserve it? Everything he'd endured as the ward, his stolen identity, couldn't be blamed on Alarian. But he'd abandoned him while Marquette and Roald tormented Kellan's people. Even with the mock trial and Alarian's apology, it was hard to separate the two.

"What proof do you have?" He didn't open his eyes, unwilling to see the truth on her face. He needed to hear her say it aloud.

"I'll keep it simple," Avyanna said in her matter-of-fact tone. "When he invited me to Koselig he wouldn't stop bringing up Felicity, saying that she shouldn't have to deal with you two brutes alone. Then he'd try to cover his tracks by mentioning that you would be there before steering the conversation back to Felicity. While we were there, his attention was completely on her. He wanted her to have a good time. To experience Koselig to its fullest."

Kellan tapped his head against the wooden headboard. "She can do better."

She sighed. "When he returns, watch him. I'm curious what you will see when your mind is clear."

He snorted. "Is my mind ever clear?"

"All I'm trying to say is that he's an ally and one we need right now. He deserves a second chance. For her sake." She kissed his temple, then snuggled down into the blankets.

"You think she needs to go?" An easier topic.

Avyanna pulled his arm around her waist until he was flush against her back. "Yes. And you already knew that. Maybe even considered it yourself."

He hadn't. Not once. He didn't want his sister out of sight again. Even if she'd grown into a capable female, he'd lost her once and was terrified of losing her again. But he also couldn't deny that whenever their father was brought up in conversation, it felt like she curled in on herself. He wouldn't let her suffer anymore, even for his own sake.

Kellan nuzzled Avyanna's neck and kissed her cheek. "How is it that you always try to act as if I'm as wise as you are when we both know you're just telling me exactly what you want me to do."

"Because" —she closed her eyes, a deep sigh of contentment— "that's why we work so well together. You might be a prince..."

"But you will always be my queen," he replied without any hesitancy. "I love you."

His hand slid to her thigh, her skin smooth against his palm. "Now did you want to help lull me back to sleep?"

"I thought you'd never ask." She turned to graze her lips against his throat.

He growled. "I don't deserve you."

She turned slowly in his arms and rested a hand against his cheek until his gaze met hers. "Yes, you do."

They kissed again, deeper this time, both their hands exploring. Lost in each other. Where he always wanted to be—

The walls shook. A roar sounded.

He shifted above her to cage her in his arms, eyes wide. She blinked up at him as the world stilled. Without a word, they jumped from the bed. Kellan grabbed his robe and tossed Avyanna's to her when a pounding sounded at the door. Felicity didn't wait but stormed inside.

"What was that?"

He rushed past her and down the hall with the two quickly following behind. The halls were quiet except for a few doors that had opened, courtiers and staff peering out from rooms. Kellan didn't pause until two guards nearly ran into him. "What happened?"

The guards glanced at each other, then back to their regent. One strapped on his breastplate, the gold-plated armor with the emblem of the sun and dragon. The insignia had been tainted by the traitors, but there wasn't time to consider a new design. "We don't—"

The other nudged the first to silence as Felicity and Avyanna caught up. "I can't be sure, but it came from the battlements."

"Your Highness," the first added in haste.

Felicity moved, not wasting another second and Kellan and Avyanna followed, the guards on their heels.

When they reached the battlements, the wind whipped at their clothing, a chill in the air. A captain called down to them, "Your Highness, up here."

Kellan's eyes widened at the sight that awaited them. The dust had barely settled. Stone and rock were scattered everywhere. He stumbled to a stop in front of the captain. "What the hell happened?"

"The guard's tower—it's gone."

Avyanna gasped. Felicity cursed.

Kellan's jaw tensed, and he glared at the vacant space above the captain. "I can see that. But how?"

"We—" He glanced at the two other guards then the one behind him. "We didn't see. We were completing our rounds when all of a sudden it became really dark and we heard a roar. One of my men was posted here." He grimaced. "We heard his screams and bones crunch. The darkness disappeared and the sky came into view and all we saw was this…"

Felicity moved amidst the rubble, her hand pressed against the remaining stone. "There are claw marks."

"What?" Kellan pushed past the captain as Felicity picked up the pendant at her neck and illuminated it with her magic. Starlight bounced off the white stone. That's when he noticed. The curve of her ears. The face he'd come to know wasn't the same shape. He inhaled, stared. She looked human, a glamour in place.

Felicity wasn't paying attention to him, her other hand curving through the grooves in the wall. "Dragons don't usually come this far north but these look similar to marks I've seen in the Balla Mountain pass between Saol and Domhain."

"Felicity?" he whispered.

She turned to face him, her bottom lip caught between her teeth and a divot at her brow. A sign of emotion. But the glamour told him more than any expression could. "Why?" He couldn't keep the worry from his voice.

Her features sharpened—her mask fell into place and emotion wiped from her face. "Concentrate."

He blinked, shook his head, and turned his attention to the wall. He would listen for now, but they would be discussing this soon. "Are you certain this was a dragon?"

She shrugged. "It's my best guess. They usually remain within the mountains. There isn't much reason for one to come this far north unless…" She turned to the captain. "This tower, was it different from any of the others?"

The captain took a moment to consider her question before nodding. "Minor difference. There was a brick left out of this one near the top, and a stone was within the gap that sometimes caught the sun's light. We figured it was the symbol of the Light Realm."

Avyanna gasped.

Felicity ran a hand over her face. "Well, that's unfortunate."

Kellan glanced between the two of them. What were they thinking? His brow furrowed…

Shit. Alarian was right—something he never wanted to say aloud. All this time they had it right within sight and he'd never known the heartstone existed. Only thought them to be a myth like so many others.

"What did this stone look like?" Kellan blinked himself to the present.

Felicity started to dig through any debris she could move. Avyanna bent over to assist and Kellan, needing something to do with his hands, joined in.

The guard was silent for a moment, watching them. "Should I help, Your Highness?"

Kellan shook his head and tossed aside pieces of the broken white brick. "No, just describe the stone and how it was mounted into the tower."

The guard's face scrunched up. "White. But unlike the wall stones, it didn't repel the sunlight but seemed to soak it in. It was smooth and had an iridescent look to it. It was bracketed to the open space by metal prongs."

Avyanna straightened. "Don't speak of this to anyone. We need to assess."

The guard nodded. Trials had already been held to ensure the guards who remained were loyal. If he wanted to keep his position, he'd stay silent. "If that's what you're looking for, I'm certain it's gone." He waved a hand to their surroundings. "We have guards searching the grounds for any remains or a trail, but it's like the tower vanished."

The three of them straightened. "Let me know if you find anything."

Only moments ago, he'd been wrapped in Avyanna's arms. Now there was a dragon somehow involved and a good chance that Éardrom's heartstone had been taken. It all seemed futile, but he couldn't give up. They had to find Marquette and put an end to all her plans.

He drew back his shoulders and donned the expression of surety—the one a prince regent, interim king, needed. "See if there is any sign of life at the very least. Does this lower our defenses?"

"If another flight attack happens, yes," the captain said as he gauged the destruction. "We'll be on higher alert. It's—"

"Not your fault," Avyanna interrupted before he could apologize. "I've searched for any sign of life." She swallowed. "Besides those of us standing here, there are no others."

The captain ran a hand over his haggard face. "I'll prepare the archers. We'll double the guard and ensure we have a Light Fae up here for extra sight."

"I'll have workers up here tomorrow to clean up." Kellan glanced around and saw Felicity heading towards the stairs. "Ensure the families are aware of loss and one of us will reach out to them tomorrow with our condolences." He glanced at Avyanna who gave him a small nod. Without a second thought, he jogged after his sister.

By the time he reached the top of the stairs, she was already out of sight. He rounded the corner to enter the hallway, his lungs burning from running and the dissipating of adrenaline, but she was gone.

He considered going to her room but knew she wouldn't be there. She didn't want to talk or be found. He ran a hand through his hair and leaned against the wall. A glamour...

Avyanna had been right. He could no longer ignore what was happening.

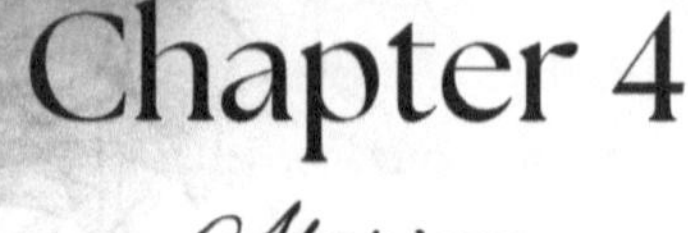

Chapter 4

Alarian

A larian didn't have enough light for the battle he found himself in. Shadows flew around him in sharp tendrils, slipping through the cracks of his attacker's stone exterior. He'd thought he had stayed far enough on the outskirts of the canyon. He'd been warned at a nearby outpost that the Fomorians had settled within the last known location of the Earth Realm's heartstone. The crevices and maze of caverns allowed the protection from the sunlight that blinded them. The stone troll faeries usually settled within the caves of the mountains that banked Domhain on the south and north, only outcasts traveled outside the protection of the shade. But by the numbers here—these weren't outcasts.

Alarian had been using what he thought was a boulder for cover before it shifted and stood. He had froze, dumbstruck. It was only when the Fomorian guard had alerted his comrades before almost pounding his skull into dust that he had moved. Why had he thought he could observe and remain unseen at night? He should have come during the day.

Alarian stepped into one shadow he drew from a nearby petrified tree, his position shifting farther away from the closest stone faerie with its fist twice the size of Alarian's bicep to reappear in a shadow cast by a fallen log.

Another Fomorian barreled down from his left. Alarian barely managed to dodge and slid into the shadow of the faerie to appear an arm's length away from another attack. Why had he used his magic in excess earlier? He hadn't been prepared and should have known better. His pull on the shadows was weakening, his muscles ached, movements slowing. He couldn't get far enough away from their attacks.

Shit. Shit. Shit.

This is what his reconnaissance got him. Not a step closer to the Domhain canyon, but trouble times two.

A roar sounded to his left, and Alarian sent the shadows directly at his assailant. Smoky tendrils slipped within the creature's gaping mouth, cutting off its airway. The Fomorian choked, sputtered, and fell to his knees as it clawed at its throat. Alarian's reached for nearby shadows but they only inched towards him before dissipating. His brow furrowed, sweat sliding down his temples. He needed to reserve whatever strength he had left.

Alarian only had one choice left. He ran towards his mount and jumped onto the gelding's back. With a squealing whinny, the horse raced away as fast as he could. The two Fomorians were on his heels, their grunts and roars urging the gelding faster, but Alarian didn't dare look back.

The sounds of the heavy footfalls, the shaking of the earth slowed then stopped as the terrain changed from stone to dirt and weeds. Alarian glanced behind him to see the faerie's silhouette shrinking in the distance. While he caught his breath and attempted to slow his racing heart, Alarian turned his mount east towards the nearest outpost. He had a contact he planned to visit anyway and who would hopefully be able to shed light on why the Fomorians had left the shadows of the mountains.

It couldn't be coincidental that the faeries had chosen now to venture into the canyon that had once housed the realm's heartstone. He had hoped to find clues he could use in his upcoming search for the other realms' stones. And give Prince Kellan more proof that he was trustworthy. That he was worthy.

It was past midnight when Alarian reached the outpost. Few candles were lit and the haggard buildings he could count on one hand were silent. The communal fire in the center of the ramshackle town burned embers, no longer overseen. More than once he had considered going to his aunt but dismissed the idea. He had two reasons for coming to Domhain. One was the stone. The second, information. His aunt might be able to answer his questions about Domhain, but she didn't know the inner workings of the other realms like Braum did.

He tied his horse with a gray gelding at the shed near the closed store where hay and water were kept for the rare traveler. He added a flake into the feed bin and ensured the water was filled before tossing in one of the apples he had brought along. One for each day he planned to be gone. One for each day he reassessed what to do about *her*. Or, to put it simply, what not to do about her. He'd sensed her fear when he'd left her at her door that night. She was trying to control so much. He had almost turned around, but knew he was the last person she'd want to see. So he'd sent Meira...

He shook his head, trying to clear his mind.

Alarian passed the incomplete homes and structures. Walls half built. Thatched roofs with holes, some of which only covered the corners. A realm slowly torn apart by stolen magic, and the people suffering because of it. He'd seen the paintings and heard stories of what the realm had once been—fertile landscape, grassy knolls, beautiful forests, and animals in abundance. He couldn't let that happen to the rest of Talamh or allow his mother to succeed in stealing the heartstones and open the veil to the human world.

He stopped at of a piece of thick red cloth that hung over a board acting as a door. "Braum?"

Decorum required an invite within another's home before one could step inside. Even if you could technically step over the one-stone high perimeter that outlined the structures.

"Rian?" The drape was pulled aside to a grinning face. Mussed dirty blond hair, blue eyes hooded by sleep. His large frame took up the entire opening from side to top. "About time. You've been gone for too long."

He moved aside, allowing Alarian entrance. "Well, between my parents and then the imprisonment—"

"I heard about that. That piece of gossip spread like wildfire. Or is it wind? Either way, it was what everyone was talking about."

Alarian quirked a brow. "And you didn't consider coming to the palace on my behalf?"

Braum guffawed, grabbing a mug from the lone table, and pouring contents from a pitcher before he took a swig. "You know me." He wiped his arm across his mouth. "I only do what I'm told. Figured Sloan had things under control or he'd come calling."

"Sloan wasn't here. Took him ten days to return."

"Then how did you get out?"

*Starlight...*a subject he didn't want to bring up.

"Sooner or later it all got figured out." Alarian shrugged and took a seat. "Have any water?"

Braum shook his head, nodding to a second pitcher at the edge of the table. "Not until morning. Ale?"

Alarian's nose scrunched. He had long been tired of the partying rake role. The taste and smell of ale had become unpleasant. It had done its part when he needed to fool the continent, but now he didn't touch the stuff on a regular basis if he could help it. There were better options out there anyway. "Naw. Thanks."

"So, what brings you to these parts? Figured you'd be sending Sloan to check in with all of us when the time was right." Braum took another swig.

"What's going on with the Fomorians?"

Braum snorted. "Damn them. Were you in the center of the realm? That's where I've heard they've been congregating. You know there is nothing there. Hasn't been for years."

Alarian nodded. All the towns had been abandoned when resources became sparse. Without the heartstone, Domhain had slowly transformed into rock—the once fertile land now dust and fossils, forcing its people to either leave completely or move to the edges of the realm where they could still access goods needed for survival. There were only a few outposts left within the realm itself and they were mostly used for protection—the last line of defense—and a safe haven for those who made the mistake of traveling too far. The supplies at these outposts were thin at best, relying on weekly rations being delivered. Rangers, like Braum, traveled between them from time to time to check on their status.

"Don't think I didn't notice that you ignored my question." Braum's gaze pinned on Alarian's arm where blood had dried on the slashed fabric of his tunic, the injury already healed. "Why you and not Sloan?"

"Sloan's busy." Maybe he did want a drink. It was easier to fall into habits with an old friend than take his incessant questioning. "So I came instead. The advisors weren't exactly thrilled to let me go, but the prince agreed to let me collect information and check in with my contacts."

"Looking for your mother? Or running from something?"

Alarian reached across the table and grabbed a tankard, poured some ale from the pitcher, then took a long gulp.

Braum laughed. "Both it is."

"Screw you."

"Sounds like that's exactly what you need."

The ale soured in his stomach. "You're a pig."

"That's offensive to pigs everywhere. They're majestic and smart animals—I'm neither. Now, besides searching for Marquette—who hasn't been seen by the way—what brings you to Domhain?"

Even if he trusted Braum, the fewer who knew about the heartstones the better. "There's been whispers of disruptions within the Balla Mountains, and with the Fomorians' movement it felt like a good place to start." It wasn't a lie. The Balla Mountains separated Saol, the Life Realm from Domhain. On his stop in Aer, Lian and Dimitri had informed him about dragons being seen outside of their mountain dwellings.

"The dragons have been throwing tantrums. They haven't attacked any of the towns yet, but they must be pissed off enough to kick out the Fomorians. It's a chain reaction, but we haven't figured out where it started."

Alarian leaned back, thumbing the handle of the tankard. "How many do you have looking into what's going on?"

"Two. But I can double it." Braum was more than a contact—he had various ways of uncovering information that others could not. As a ranger of Domhain, he met many diverse people on his travels who he either befriended or made enemies of. Either way, if there was someone you wanted to find or an object to uncover, he was a good ally to have.

"Triple it. Have them contact you if they hear anything about my mother or the witch. We'll set up a regular correspondence." Fiadh had been forgotten by many. She was sneaky and easily undetected, often hiding within plain sight.

"Got it, boss."

Alarian took another gulp, and immediately regretted it. He smacked his lips. Braum leaned forward. "Now, why are you running?"

Alarian sneered at the mug, not meeting his friend's gaze. "I'm not."

"When you drink, it's usually because of something personal."

He considered his options. Sloan's keen eye was exhausting and even if he gave solid advice, it wouldn't work with Felicity. She wasn't a female to woo, and while Sloan tried not to show it, he was a romantic at heart.

Braum on the other hand...

"You know I've made a lot of mistakes in the past."

Braum nodded, leaning forward.

"Well, they've come back to bite me in the ass."

"They freed you, so obviously not that hard of a bite." His brow rose. "Unless there is more?"

Alarian winced. "They don't trust me now. I have to prove that I'm loyal to Prince Kellan and the princess." A half-truth—an omission of facts.

Braum chuckled. "Princess, huh? I see." Alarian had a feeling he saw more than he wanted Braum to. "Well, running won't fix it."

"I plan to return. I just needed to get my head straight. Gather as much intel as I can." Something he'd failed to do as he would be returning empty handed.

"There are a few ways to do get your head straight. Odette is in town tonight. Her sister came with—"

"No," Alarian growled.

Braum smirked. "Had a feeling." He stood and took Alarian's tankard from his grasp. "They will see the truth of your actions, Rian. Go back and face this shit. You're not a waste of space."

A shudder rolled down his spine. He pinched his eyes closed and blocked out his mother's voice. Her proclamation of exactly the opposite on multiple occasions.

On a drunk night many years before, he'd cried to his friend about the pain his parents had caused. The emotional and physical abuse. Once, he and his parents had been happy together. A family. Especially he and his father. But they had sent him to Scáth, and it had all changed almost overnight. Now, all he had were the memories of harsh words and violent jabs.

Braum rested a hand on his shoulder and gave it a squeeze. "The bed is yours. I'll go to Odette's for the night. See you in the morning before you head back."

"Maybe I should stay a day or two?"

"You know you won't. You don't run anymore." His friend pulled aside the drape and peered over his shoulder. "You're not going to prove to whoever has your all riled up—or yourself—that you're worth the time if you're here." The drape closed with a swoosh behind him.

He was right. Mostly. But he also had one more stop to make.

Chapter 5

Felicity

Alarian had been gone for seven days, and all Felicity could think about was that she hadn't apologized. For doubting him. For questioning him. For not *seeing* him. Which was ridiculous. It wasn't as though she wouldn't have an opportunity to talk to him again. After he returned, they could begin their friendship properly. Besides she was mad at him. Or she should be anyway. He had called her out, then left.

The phantom sensation of soft, demanding lips against hers. The trail of his hands along her skin. She pinched her eyes closed to clear her thoughts.

All of this came down to one very annoying, tiny obstacle—she was *feeling* again. Everything. Her emotions had been a bother since she took that first drink from a vial, but this level of doubt and conscious thought was new to her. Even the idea of apologizing was foreign after years of not even considering the need for forgiveness.

And it hurt. The guilt. The dreams—

"Felicity?"

She blinked, turning towards her brother. A divot between his furrowed brow showed his trademark concern. A look she was becoming all too familiar with in the past few days. He had attempted to speak to her privately since the night of the attack, but she'd been good at evading him. However, his current worry was warranted since she was supposed to be paying attention to the proceedings.

"Do you have your final verdict?"

Shit. She had barely listened during the trial. Another guard. Another attempt to find out who to trust and who to punish. Or, in some cases, removed from the court and transferred to another position elsewhere. Most defendants had claimed that they had only followed orders of who they believed to be their sovereign. Understandable, but that didn't exactly abstain them from any guilt.

Felicity turned to face the young man in front of her. His hands were shaking at his sides. With his head downcast, he took a small glance towards her, a timidness in his expression that spoke volumes. She'd seen him before. He hadn't been in *that* room. Hadn't bound the hands of Lady Chartow. Held her while the traitor king brutalized and killed her. Unlike the last guard's trial... This guard had been at the stables. Held her horse as she dismounted upon her and Kellan's return from the canyon. That day she learned the truth of Roald and Marquette's villainy.

"Not guilty."

Kellan nodded. "Then by order of this court you're sentenced to a one-year probation within your current position. If any evidence is brought forward that contradicts the statements you shared or were covered in this court, then you will be punished accordingly. In one year, barring any such issues, you will be permanently reinstated."

The guard's shoulders sagged, a large breath released as he bowed and turned on his heel to head down the aisle of chairs and out the double doors.

Felicity watched him leave, her bottom lip slipping in between her teeth.

"We'll close out for the next two hours. How many more do we have scheduled for today?"

Fergus pulled out his notebook. As one of the rebel gardeners, he had been a member of the previous court and a document keeper for years under their father. He picked up the position easily and with vigor. "Three, Your Highness."

Kellan turned to look at the other members of their committee. It consisted of all the remaining advisors they trusted and kept close—only five. Avyanna sat in as no other representative had arrived from Tine. Sloan also sat in on behalf of Dorcha as his ship was preparing to leave in two days for the Oileán islands.

At first Sloan had hoped to make a portal with his dark magic, but the distance was too great and he wouldn't have been able to return with King Bastien. It made more sense to send a small fleet to check the last remaining outlying islands for Marquette and Fiadh. But that took more time. Time that they weren't guaranteed.

Avyanna crossed the room as the others left, stopping in front of Felicity with a hand held out. "Walk with me?"

Felicity's leg bounced. Nervous energy bubbled up inside of her. "I—yes, of course." She stood, taking her friend's arm.

Kellan trailed behind them. Felicity could feel his presence but tried to ignore it, hoping he'd take the hint and give them privacy.

Neither of them spoke until they exited the room, sauntering down the hall as Avyanna led her to the once-barren gardens now overgrown with rose bushes, wisteria, peonies, dahlias, and daffodils. The colors and scents melded together and momentarily shocked Felicity. It was different from the trailing scent of her mother's roses that always seemed to linger in her room after a particular nightmare. The one that faded to black with the scream of horses and thunder of hooves. She often wondered if that would be the only memory she would have of that night. And if she even wanted to know the truth of what followed.

"You need to talk." There wasn't a question in Avyanna's words but a command.

"What?" Felicity balked at her bluntness. "You asked me to walk with you."

"You're distant," Kellan interjected, moving in beside her.

Avyanna rolled her eyes. "I didn't invite you along."

"I'm just worried as you are," he grumbled.

Felicity pinned her brother with a glare, but he met it with his own piercing look. She turned away with a shake of her head. He was a mother hen if she ever saw one, and she'd tried to hide from him these last few days. He always saw more than she wanted. Felicity peered at Avyanna's grip on her arm. She should have known neither of them were going to let her be.

Avyanna took them to the gate and stopped. The field between the cliffs shifted in the breeze. Stalks of grass rolled, the color changing from light green to a shiny white as they bent to the wind. The willow sat stoically—alone.

Something tugged in Felicity's chest.

"Is it him?" Avyanna whispered the question, but Kellan leaned in anyway.

Her attention didn't move from the willow. "Who?"

"Don't play coy with me. From your own account, you searched for every way you could to prove Alarian's innocence. Trips to a brothel. Chats at the docks. Now you just walk the halls as though you're barely here." Avyanna squeezed her arm. "Have you been training? Using your magic?"

How much had Kellan told her?

"We notice," Kellan added. "You're wearing a glamour at night. Why?"

Obviously, he'd told her enough. Felicity pulled her arm free, ready to bolt, but Avyanna's gaze pinned her in place. "It's not like a princess is needed as a spy or assassin or did you forget that was how I was raised? Now I have this title and no purpose for nailing front rolls or how to throw the proper punch."

Her brother and Avyanna shared a look concealing a thousand unspoken words. Concern, knowing, understanding...pity.

Kellan rubbed his forehead. "Fine. You're right."

Avyanna beamed. "Remember those two words. They will be a part of your repertoire for the remainder of your days."

"Oh, I will, my love." He winked at her.

Felicity rolled her eyes. "What are you two yammering about? I didn't come along to see you give doe eyes to each other."

Kellan folded his hands behind his back. "You need to leave."

"What?" Felicity balked. Not again. This was finally becoming her home. Or so she thought. Now, he was telling her to leave...

"You're lost. I hope I'm not at fault, but I think what you need is exactly what you want—answers. You've searched for them for Alarian. It's time to find them for yourself." Kellan reached out and squeezed her shoulder.

She shook her head. "I can't leave. Father is meant to return. We have a war on the horizon."

"We aren't promised tomorrow, Felicity." Avyanna wrapped her arm through Kellan's. A united front. "And it's more important to us that you find yourself now."

"You shouldn't be hiding behind a glamour. As much as it pains me to admit it, Alarian is right about Marquette's hunt for the heartstones, which means we will need you when the time comes." Kellan reached for her hand with his free one and squeezed it. "Not just as the princess, but as the spy and assassin. You have experience that could benefit the realms."

But how could she claim all those titles? Spies and assassins were not princesses. A princess was to be loved, a symbol of hope and prosperity. She had been raised as a weapon to be wielded. Sharpened. Her memories brought back more than her past. It also unearthed her sins. The lives she ended without question—and the guilt that went with it. For too long she had buried every feeling she had. Now they bubbled, making it impossible to think clearly. Hard to concentrate.

"All of those pieces don't fit under one pivotal title." How could they not see? *Princess*. The word had a clear connotation. A meaning. She didn't have options anymore.

"They can if you want them to. Only you can make that decision." Avyanna patted her hand.

She pulled her hand free from them and flung her arms in the air to wave at the castle in the distance. "This is ridiculous. I can't just leave. There is too much to do."

Kellan scoffed. "You mean the trials? The planning for a war? Finding Marquette? All of which we can do while you get your own answers. Hell, maybe you can assist us in finding the stones and make connections in the other realms and we won't need Alarian after all."

Avyanna groaned. "That's enough of your negativity."

Felicity glanced between the two of them, defeated. "I'll think about it."

"Good." Avyanna smiled brightly. "Now may I hug you? I know that's not exactly your thing…"

Felicity's shoulders relaxed and couldn't help but chuckle. "Fine. This once."

Before Felicity could prepare, Avyanna had her in a tight embrace, the scent of a apple cider clinging to her skin.

Kellan laughed. "Just so you know, Avy will get more than one hug out of you before you leave."

Felicity sighed. "I haven't agreed yet. Not like you can kick me out if I'm my own person as you so claim." She wiggled out of Avyanna's grip. "It might be best I stay for now." Even as she said it, she knew it was a lie. If her life with her family, as a daughter, was in her past, she had questions and needed answers. At the very least, she wanted to honor her mother's memory and know the father who was hopefully about to return.

"So you can stare off in the distance and act like a ghost?" Kellan growled. "Not anymore."

Alarian's words came to her. *Your people deserve the smart, loyal, and powerful female you are. Don't just show me the real you, Felicity. Show the world.*

To admit such thoughts aloud… "I said I'll think about it. Besides, I won't be leaving prior to your big announcement." A missive had arrived at her door the previous day declaring a ball. In two days they would celebrate a much-deserved union. "I would have liked to have received the invitation in person." She glared at her brother.

"Then stop avoiding me," he said point blank.

Felicity winced. True, that was on her.

"That's right, you won't." Avyanna's eyes narrowed. "You must be there to celebrate with us."

"That doesn't mean I'm dancing."

"Good luck. I think Lord Walsh might have something to say to that." Kellan actually smirked. Felicity hated it.

"Doesn't mean I have to say yes."

"No, it doesn't. It also doesn't mean that he might make his intentions known."

Felicity balked. "Intentions?"

"Kellan—"

"He asked me personally if he could court you. As if I have a right or say in your life." Kellan rolled his eyes. "He seems to think that was the proper protocol."

Before her brother could finish the sentence, her stomach squeezed tight and she rubbed her temples where a pulsing had begun. Lord Walsh put his foot in his mouth all too often and then seemed surprised by others' negative reactions. He was too forward to the point of discomfort and disregarded when others requested space. And his favorite topic of conversation—himself—was a bore since his daily life involved numbers. A topic she didn't want to discuss at great lengths, yet he never seemed to get enough.

There was someone out there for him. It was not Felicity.

"Not the time." Avyanna shook her head. "Not the time at all."

Felicity's lips pursed tightly. "I suppose I'll just have to politely set him straight."

"Good luck." Kellan turned on his heel and headed towards the palace. "Think on that trip."

Avyanna caught up to him and took the hand he held out for her. Felicity was certain she heard the two of them whispering about her as she followed at a distance. Not exactly secretive. When she heard Alarian's name come up once, Felicity stopped and took a seat on a bench to stare at the flowers and will memories of her mother to the forefront of her mind. This place held them, she knew it.

It wasn't until she grazed the grooved wood under her palm that she was reminded that this was the bench where Marquette had confided in her about her murdered family and alluded to her revenge. Felicity stood and walked away. They should burn that bench.

***

Two nights later, the ballroom was decorated in shades of reds and white with accents of silver. The staff had outdone themselves ensuring that the event was unlike those that the previous tyrants held. For one, the local people had been invited—the main hall, gardens, and ballroom opened for the event. Not just the upper class but everyone. Of course, this required a higher number of guards since they were still uncertain who to trust. But tonight, the extra protection seemed unnecessary. The people were relaxed, enjoying the food and music. There wasn't a heightened degree of inebriation, and Felicity believed that was because Avyanna had planned for the drinks to be served in short intervals. But with the abundance of delicious delicacies that ranged from stuffed dates from Oileán and caviar canapés from Visce making the rounds, no one was complaining.

Felicity stood as an outlier, observing as Kellan and Avyanna walked around the room. They had made the announcement of their impending nuptials just moments before and everyone had cheered. After keeping their relationship a secret for so long, she was happy they could finally be themselves out in the open.

As Felicity moved along the perimeter, a habit she'd adopted long ago, she heard giggling behind a pillar and gossamer drapes. In slow, careful steps, she moved until she found two young fae females wrapped in each other's arms. Felicity cleared her throat.

The two flung apart, and Felicity bit her lip to stop the smile as Miss Isleen's eyes widened. "Oh, Princess, I'm—"

"Having a wonderful evening? Just a hint that it's a little early to be finding corners to hide in together. Usually, one waits until the majority of the guests are deep in their drink or caught up in the dances. Unless you don't mind being caught by your mother...?"

The other fae's, a Visce delegate's daughter, azure cheeks darkened. She hadn't meant to embarrass them but only let them know that they weren't as inconspicuous as they thought. "Well, off you two go. Have fun."

The delegate's daughter rushed away, but Isleen stopped mid-step and grabbed Felicity's hand. "Please don't tell my mother."

"You don't think she'd accept your choices?" Grit entered Felicity's voice.

"No. Worse." Miss Isleen swallowed and quickly glanced over her shoulder. "The options would double, if not triple in her eyes of whom to force me upon. And I know she'd want me to try to seduce you—I respect you too much for that."

It took Felicity's training to keep a straight face. "Understood. I wouldn't have said a word either way."

"I always did like you."

Felicity's façade cracked with a grin when the female ran off after the other. Had she ever been so young and naive?

When a string quartet started playing a waltz, and someone cleared their throat behind her. She turned and had to stifle a groan. The male straightened, his shoulders drawing back. His ashy blond hair hung past his shoulders, and he shook his head to make the casual waves flutter. He was taller than Felicity. Broader too. Attributes he had made certain to mention his muscles were larger than hers during their second conversation where he went into vivid details on how he'd come to this conclusion.

"Lord Walsh." She nodded as he stepped in beside her to observe the crowd.

"It's lovely tonight. Delightful news about your brother and Lady Solfire."

"It is." She folded her hands behind her back.

He moved in front of her, giving an exaggerated bow. "The only way this evening could get better is if we dance. We can make the rest of the room jealous of our good looks and agile moves."

Felicity approved of confidence. This...he was something else entirely.

She looked down to his hand was held out towards her. "Was that an invitation to dance?"

"Of course. What else could it be?" He looked at her as if she was the naive one in this scenario. For the past week, since his arrival, Lord Walsh had found her whenever possible to brag about who knew what—because she either hadn't listened or, by this point, had forgotten.

Felicity opened her mouth to decline when she caught Kellan grinning at her from across the room.

Since their conversation she had tried to be more involved. She considered his offer to leave. Was this a test to see if she could handle anything? She'd dealt with worse that oblivious braggarts. With a deep swallow and resolve she pulled from thin air, Felicity took his hand. "Yes, let's."

Chapter 6

Alarian

Alarian had returned to the palace an hour after dusk to find it full of people. He was back early, so it was no surprise that he had interrupted an event he wasn't meant to attend. He'd attempted to find distractions to fill his time but shortly after leaving Braum, he found himself heading back and tempting fate to run into her.

Because no matter how he'd tried to ignore it, he was drawn here. The lack of her emotions troubled him more with the increasing distance between them. If he hadn't felt the snap of the bond in place—at least that was how it was described to him—he would have thought it had happened without his knowledge. And he didn't even know whether the emotions he felt from her were due to a bond or not.

The bond was a magic rarely discussed, and his research hadn't uncovered anything helpful. He had asked Meira once as a child and that had resulted in a fairytale of love and loss about a friend of hers. It was a question he'd never asked his parents. However, Lian and Dimitri might be forthcoming with information. He'd considered asking while he had visited them but hadn't wanted to deal with their questions. Besides, he wasn't supposed to be thinking about her.

After a quick bath and a change of clothes, Alarian made his way to the ballroom and entered through a side door so as not to draw unwanted attention.

He glanced around the crowded room, looking for someone he recognized. The mood was so different from what he had grown accustomed to within these walls. There wasn't the heaviness of threat that lingered. A need to impress. Even if some of the same stuffy courtiers were present, glancing with snide expressions at some of the townsfolk, it was relaxed. A good start for Prince Kellan and Felicity's first official event.

He shouldn't have come. He hadn't been invited—although it looked like all of Koselig were in attendance. Even Meira, who wore a simple indigo gown that complimented her green skin, talked with members of the staff and guests.

"You're back early." Sloan appeared beside him.

Alarian shrugged. "Not much needed to be done."

"Didn't think there would be now that most of the rebels have returned home or settled." Sloan cleared his throat. "You missed the announcement just moments ago. Prince Kellan and Lady Solfire are to be wed."

"About damn time." Alarian chuckled. He remembered the first time he'd seen Avyanna slip into Prince Kellan's room behind him. The lingering glances between the two that thankfully others had ignored. "It seems they invited everyone to celebrate."

Sloan nodded. "They did. Even hired extra staff to let the regulars enjoy the evening and to allow everyone to attend the event in shifts. They thought of everything."

Alarian glanced about the room and Sloan nudged his shoulder with his. "She's over there." He pointed and Alarian's magic bristled at the sight of Felicity taking another male's hand. As he led her towards the dance floor, Alarian took an involuntary step forward.

Sloan grabbed his arm. "Easy, friend. It's just a dance."

"I—" Alarian shook his head, stepping back. He leaned against a pillar, crossing his arms. "I just meant to say hello."

"Sure you did," Sloan scoffed. "Have you not realized it's obvious?"

Alarian schooled his features. "I don't know what you're talking about."

"You know you can't lie to me. I know your tells."

"You only think you do." Alarian crossed one foot over the other. Curses, she was straight in his line of sight. Right over Sloan's shoulder, dancing with *him*.

He frowned as he examined the *him* in question. Alarian didn't recognize the male as a member of the previous court. Maybe he wasn't one at all. He was dressed well enough, with an air of superiority by the way he looked down his nose at her. Curses he wanted too—

Were they bickering?

Felicity gave one of her saccharine smiles to the male as they moved around the dance floor. He knew that look. Words rushed from her lips, but he couldn't tell what she was saying from a distance. He sparred back. They *were* bickering.

That was *their* thing. His and hers.

Alarian started forward again, about to move around Sloan when another body intercepted his path. "Alarian, you're back."

"Who is he?" He didn't mean to growl at Avyanna, but—he shook his head, blinking and turning away to stare at a pillar.

"Lord Walsh. The least of your concerns, I assure you."

"They are—" He was about to admit it. To say it out loud. That he was jealous of Felicity having a confrontation with someone else. Curses, he was sick.

Sloan chuckled beside him. "Maybe you should return to your room for the night."

"You're taking too much joy from this."

"Only because you won't admit it."

Avyanna shook her head. "He shouldn't have to. Now, you—behave." She poked Alarian in the chest. "Felicity can handle herself. She's probably denying Lord Walsh's request for courtship right now."

"Courtship?" The music hit its crescendo and drowned his protest from most nearby, but a few glanced in their direction. He felt their gaze, but his eyes remained on the pair as Lord Walsh dipped Felicity in a long arc. Alarian was certain the male's gaze rested far too long on Felicity's chest. Oh, hell no—

"It seems she needs another partner."

He didn't wait for the song to end, nor did the others attempt to stop him. Alarian was within the throng of dancers before he realized what he was doing. Felicity was attempting to smile through gritted teeth but her usually well-crafted façade was beginning to crack.

"Your Highness." Alarian bowed, holding out his hand. He knew she'd hate the title. Would probably give him an earful for it later. Or so he hoped as her wide-eyed surprise turned to annoyance. "May I have this dance?"

Lord Walsh opened his mouth but before the male could say a word or Alarian could counter, Felicity took his palm and pulled him away. "Of course."

It wasn't until they were in the center of the room, surrounded by the other revelers, that she stopped. "I don't know whether to thank or hit you."

"How about just a dance and we call it even?"

She considered him as the musicians started up the next song. A slow melody. "Depends—does this count as one of the dances I owe you?" As her hand met his palm and the music began, he could feel the raised skin of the scar brush his own. The blood oath in effect based solely on that one little promise remaining between them—one more dance.

"No." *He was selfish.* "This doesn't count. I saved you from Lord Walsh."

"Saved?"

He chuckled, drawing her in closer, and whispered in her ear, "That's right, Starlight. I just saved you."

She rolled her eyes, and he instinctively inhaled her wildflower scent as the music built up and offered a perfect opportunity to relish the way she felt in his arms. But only for a moment as a glance at the throne reminded him of what his family had done...

"I'm sorry."

He jerked and focused his attention on the present. "I should be the one—are you apologizing to me?"

"Because I was cruel and passed judgement before I got to know you. So many times I thought the worst of you and that wasn't fair." She didn't look up. "I should have said it earlier."

"You've nothing to apologize for." He twirled her away from him, needing a moment to collect himself before pulling her back.

Close to him again, she met his gaze. "Yes, I do. Maybe things would have been different. If we could have found a way to work together, and then your mother wouldn't be free doing hell knows what."

At the mention of his mother, he took a step away from her, his fingers barely grazing her waist and holding her hand. "I was angry and frustrated because I wanted you to know the truth but I never blamed you. Especially not at the beginning and certainly not after what you witnessed and overheard. The truth...wasn't much better. I was desperate for—" He snapped his mouth closed. Too close...

"For what?" She met his gaze, her hand tightening around his.

This. This was what he had been desperate for. For her to give him a chance. "A friend."

The safe answer. Not the one he wanted to declare. He knew the truth now more than he had before—he didn't deserve a chance.

She bit her bottom lip. His eyes dropped to her mouth, and he nearly stumbled. Felicity adjusted to the small misstep easily.

With a smile, she gave his arm a squeeze. "Well, you have a friend now. I guess that means I shouldn't be annoyed with you anymore."

He smiled back and a blush crept up her neck. She glanced away. Alarian stepped a touch closer. "I never really annoyed you. You enjoy my witty personality."

"Witty? Is what how you think others describe you?"

"I don't care about what others think. Only you." The words were out of his mouth before he could stop them.

This time it was her turn to falter, his hand tightening on her waist to keep her upright, their gaze holding each other hostage. It took them a few moments to realize the music ended. The guests clapped for the musicians but the two of them stood there, staring at each other.

Felicity stepped out of his arms first. "Thank you for rescuing me from Walsh's clutches."

He nodded. "Anytime."

She turned on her heel and paused. "Welcome back," she said before disappearing into the crowd.

Damn it. He needed to reconsider his presence here. Maybe it would be best to leave sooner rather than later. He couldn't do this anymore. She wanted to find herself and get her father back. He was interfering. He needed to concentrate on stopping his mother's plan. Maybe then he'd be worthy of her. Maybe.

Sloan cleared his throat as Alarian left the dance floor. "Tell her?"

He groaned. "There is nothing to tell." He straightened the lapels of his jacket and allowed one final glance in her direction before he turned to Sloan. "I'm calling it a night."

"The old Alarian would have gone to the nearest brothel and spent his worries on the first consenting being to cross his path and all the booze he could handle."

Alarian stilled, his jaw quirked. "So? How do you know I don't plan to do just that?"

"We know you won't." Sloan rested a hand on his shoulder. "You've grown. It's about time." Then with a final pat on his shoulder, he walked away.

Alarian closed his eyes for a breath and inhaled deeply before he slowly let it out. When he opened them again, he turned in the opposite direction he last saw Felicity and ran into a body.

"Oomph. Sorry." He unconsciously gripped their shoulders, straightening them.

"It's quite all right." Lady Isleen grinned a coy smile that Alarian had witnessed on many and had succumbed to before.

Alarian dropped his arms to his side and stepped back. "Lady Isleen, how are you?"

"Doing well, Milord." She tilted her head, her body sashaying side to side to make her skirts move. "Haven't seen you around. You've been missed."

What a flighty female she was. Alarian had always known that she craved a mystery. She had never been interested in him in the past, but Alarian knew it was because her mother had desperately wanted to place her within his sights.

Whenever they had been left to talk, she'd always turn the conversation to Prince Kellan. The once-cursed ward without a name had been intriguing to her young fancies. "It's nice to be out and about. If you'll excu—"

She curtsied, cutting him off. "This is forward, I know, but I was hoping we could dance."

It would be rude to decline, but it would be even worse to acquiesce. "I appreciate the offer, but I was just leaving."

"You could make her jealous." Her brows rose. "I'm willing to help." She glanced over her shoulder towards whom she spoke. Felicity was talking to Prince Kellan and Avyanna, or at least that was where he had last seen her. With Isleen's careful eye on him, he couldn't look now. But he did consider her offer and immediately hated himself for it. "Have a good evening, Lady Isleen." He bowed, then made his way towards the exit without looking back.

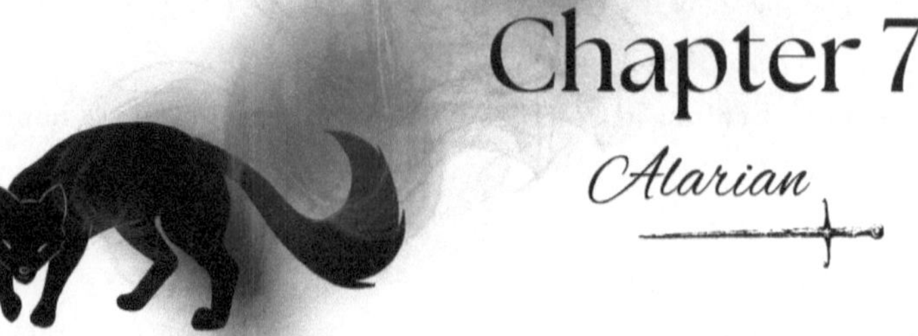

Chapter 7
Alarian

Alarian hadn't slept well. When he had drifted off, he dreamed of that male's hands on *her* hips. The way he maneuvered Felicity closer. Then his imagination took it from there...usually with him pulverizing the male into the ground before suffocating him with his magic. He woke surrounded in wisps of shadows and his sheets plastered to his skin from a cold sweat. He shivered and ground his teeth as the first rays of morning light snuck in through a slit in the curtains.

He didn't know if this dream was worse or better than ones he'd had while he'd been away. In those instances, he had woken up in need of a cold shower or a dip in the closest river.

Even worse was the ache in his chest. She didn't owe him anything. And he didn't expect her to return or act on his feelings. It made the sensation of her emotions and his draw towards her more difficult. When he'd ended their kiss...

He couldn't think about that now.

He had to concentrate on not allowing the other nightmare to come to fruition. All the blood. The scent of it. His mother's cruel laughter as she tore through Felicity's throat with a shadow hand of magic...it had felt too real.

Alarian dressed slowly, ran a comb through his bedraggled mess of red hair. He would need a haircut soon—it was beginning to curl at the nape of his neck. With a splash of water over his face, he wiped away the sleep still stuck to the corner of his eyes. The only evidence that he had any semblance of rest.

He arrived early to the meeting he had requested from Prince Kellan the previous night by missive. He had expected no one else to be there, but Prince

Kellan sat in his chair, waiting with a stack of books and parchment in front of him.

"Morning." Prince Kellan looked up from the pages he was perusing. "I was hoping we could talk."

Alarian took a seat a respectable distance away. They hadn't spoken since before he had been pardoned. No other words on the apology he'd given the regent. No expectation of forgiveness. At least he'd said the thoughts that had sat heavy in his mind for too long despite knowing words accounted for little after what Prince Kellan had been through.

Actions. He would prove himself with actions.

"I hear congratulations are in order." He smirked, forcing the expression even if the emotion was genuine. "Glad to hear Your Highness and Avyanna are finally to be wed."

"Thank you." Prince Kellan's jaw twitched and he sighed, placing the pages down on the stack. "On that note, I heard you kept my relationship with Avyanna from your parents. And Felicity informed me that you kept the secret about her magic and guided her in training as well."

Were all his secrets out now? *No*—he knew that wasn't true. There was some that couldn't be spoken. "Seemed the right thing to do."

Prince Kellan ran a hand through his pristine hair. "There was an attack to one of the towers while you were away."

Alarian stilled. "What? Was anyone hurt?"

Prince Kellan pinched his eyes closed and released a long breath. "These are moments when I'm confused by you. To realize you have empathy, humanity—" He shook his head. "It goes against everything I've believed."

Alarian wished he hadn't been worried about being a disappointment to his parents and instead had aligned with Prince Kellan. They could have been friends. Allies from the start. "I don't expect you to understand me. All you need to know is that the best interest of this continent is my priority."

"And Felicity?" Prince Kellan met his gaze. Held it.

He had to ask about her. The one subject Alarian would have bet against. Prince Kellan had never trusted Felicity and Alarian's tentative understanding prior to the break of the curse. He kept his expression impassive. Did Sloan or Avyanna hint at something or was this the prince's own concern?

Prince Kellan considered Alarian then when he realized he wasn't going to comment, he sighed. "One guard was killed during the attack. Felicity believed it was a dragon. Either way, it looks like Éardrom's heartstone was taken with a huge chunk of the tower. We haven't noted any change to the realm yet, but if what you've said was true, then your mother must have been behind it all."

A string of expletives rushed to the tip of his tongue. If this was true, then his mother had at least one heartstone. She was collecting them, and their time was short. Did she have any others? And how was a dragon involved? The news he uncovered on their unrest in the mountains must be related. "You believe me now?"

Prince Kellan stood, slowly. "There are claw marks that even I cannot explain. The attack happened in the dead of night and witnesses recounted that they couldn't see through a haze of darkness—probably shadow. As much as I'd like to consider you a culprit, Avyanna says that doesn't make any sense."

"Glad to hear that I've received a touch of trust from one of you." Alarian waved his hand. "I know it would be easier to blame me—the womanizing drunk. Lazy through and through."

"Except, as Avy pointed out and according to the records that Felicity collected, that's not true. Particularly the ones that spoke of your trips to the brothel and the information she retrieved were quite telling." Prince Kellan steepled his hands in front of his chin. "The madam stated that you stopped visiting the females around the time Felicity arrived. Your drinking habits changed too. That I noted on my own."

The prince regarded him under his penetrating stare, but Alarian had been up against tougher opponents—his parents. And Felicity. He wouldn't fall apart under the male's gaze. Even one he desperately wanted to impress. Not only because of his parents' sins or Felicity, but because despite Prince Kellan's prickliness, he had more good in him than the continent deserved. Someday, he would make a great king.

The prince sighed. "Your mother and Fiadh need to be stopped from opening that veil and if finding the stones is going to end it, then I agree you need to go." Prince Kellan considered him for a moment. "Have you been to the Fios in Aer?"

Alarian clenched his jaw. The great library of Aer had been one of his stops years ago. "Of course—but they weren't exactly warm or helpful during my visit." His charms hadn't worked on the elder, and the female intern didn't have enough clout to get him what he needed or wanted. Since it was nearly impenetrable, he hadn't attempted to steal what he needed. The wards would have been difficult to overcome on their own, but to peruse the collection of over ten thousand tomes without assistance would be impossible.

Prince Kellan chuckled. "My aunt is the head librarian. I haven't spoken to her since prior to the curse, but I'll write a letter for her to expect you and give another one for you to deliver upon your arrival. She'll be more forthcoming with information."

Alarian's gaze narrowed. The irony wasn't lost on him that the prince happened to have a connection with the last place where he would have any chance of finding information unaided.

"What do you plan to do while I'm gone?"

"Besides search for your mother and Fiadh, make a connection with Scáth in an attempt to gain an alliance, and prepare for my father's return?" Prince Kellan chuckled to himself. "Avyanna is going to visit the hospital tomorrow and check with those your parents had imprisoned and enslaved. See if they had a reason for their presence in the canyon."

Your parents. The mention still hurt even though Alarian knew he deserved it. He wished he could erase them from his history but that wasn't how life worked. You didn't get to pick whose blood you came from. "I can tell you what they mined for in the canyon."

Prince Kellan paused. Stared. "You can?"

Alarian nodded. "Control. Something to keep their imprisoned busy and the dungeons clear. It was also to find gems to pay off their allies. They had made promises, and some were harder to keep than others."

Prince Kellan's eyebrow twitched. His mouth a thin line as he rubbed his neck. "Sloan also leaves tomorrow on the second ship to search for my father and to ensure your mother and Fiadh haven't taken refuge in the island territories."

The door creaked opened and both males straightened as everyone filed in. Prince Kellan stood to kiss Avyanna on the cheek and pull out the chair beside him. When Felicity entered, Alarian averted his gaze while Prince Kellan pulled the other chair beside him for her too. Sloan sat next to him, and when everyone was settled, Prince Kellan nodded towards Alarian. "You requested this meeting. The floor is yours."

All eyes shifted towards him, but he kept his own pinned on the prince. "I believe my mother and Fiadh will open Saol's veil on Samhain."

"Saol?" Avyanna tilted her head at the same time Prince Kellan asked, "Where did you get this information?"

Alarian cleared his throat. "A seer. She was part of the resistance, and her magic can find certain...things when given a map. I had her pinpoint the weakest point of the veil."

"The lore among Saol always spoke of it as the place where humans first came through the veil. It's why so many humans are said to have remained in the realm."

The sudden sound of Felicity's voice felt like a shock to his system, and he steeled himself against it.

"Yes, that's correct." Alarian shifted in his chair. "The seer was able to discover that the thinnest point would be the ocean side of the realm, on the west near the mountains that divide Saol from Domhain. I have no doubt my mother will already have this information. We need to get to her first."

Prince Kellan's expression was grim. "What do you propose we do? Currently, we have spies scouring the realms for Marquette and Fiadh. And now a dragon. Until then, our hands are tied, and we don't want to pass on the information of the stones to others."

"I'm going to ensure the other heartstones are either safe or accounted for. I would recommend checking on the advisors my parents kept. They might not be here anymore, but that doesn't mean they are not in contact." He felt Felicity's gaze thinning on him. "As for the dragon...I have some information to share." He filled them in on his findings in Domhain. The Fomorians, his attempt to uncover the location of some of the heartstones, and the dragon's activities.

The prince nodded. "I see. This may go deeper than we know. What else would you have us do? It seems you have contacts on the disruption in Domhain."

Alarian ran a hand through his hair. "I would advise uncovering as much information on what is happening in Tine. There is a good chance they are still allied with my mother. If that's the case, it will be dangerous to waltz into the realm in search of the heartstone and alert her of our plan. And make connections with Scáth, but as for their stone, I'm sure it's well protected."

"Will you go to either realm?" Avyanna asked.

"Not until you have insight on Tine. I'm going to head south first." He could sense Felicity's curiosity heighten. Could she read him? Did she note he avoided mention of Scáth? He didn't want to return home for many reasons but sharing why...it would be inconsequential right now.

"Dorcha's stone is safe," Sloan scoffed and crossed his arms over his chest. "I'm sure of it."

Prince Kellan's head snapped towards him. "You know the whereabouts of your realm's heartstone?"

Sloan shrugged. "Of course. Why else do you think I believed Alarian so many years ago? We've guarded it for centuries. Not every realm has forgotten where their magic comes from."

Prince Kellan's magic swirled around the room. The prince really needed to work on his control. The lack of connection to his magic must have made him rusty after so many years.

Alarian intervened. "Either way, I figured I would visit your family and advise them to double the guard. It's not often I find myself that far south."

The room was quiet as the prince tapped his fingers in succession on the arm of his chair, his magic now stilled. "What do you plan to do with the stones once they are uncovered? It's not like you can remove them from the realm."

Alarian considered how best to phrase his answer so more questions wouldn't arise. There were some promises he was meant to keep. "I've requested assistance from a witch to come up with a way to hide objects in plain sight."

"Do they know what you want to hide?" Avyanna asked.

Alarian shook his head. "No."

"I assume, by your lack of information, that the identity of this witch is a secret?" Prince Kellan asked. At Alarian's nod, he breathed a sigh. "What do you need from us?"

"Provisions. Maybe a horse."

Sloan tilted his head. "You should take a guard or two at the very least. Just in case—"

"I'll go." Felicity straightened at her declaration.

Alarian's mask faded, his expression morphing to shock before he quickly diverted his attention towards Prince Kellan. "I appreciate the offer, but it's best I travel alone." Space, he wanted space. All right...maybe he didn't *want* it but that wasn't the point. If she came along, it would be difficult to get over her.

"It wasn't an offer." Felicity pinned her brother with her glare. "Or a request."

Alarian beseeched the prince in silence, hoping his instincts were right that Prince Kellan wouldn't agree. The prince worked his jaw and stared at his sister. Was he considering? Alarian tried again. "You have enough to do here. Your brother needs you."

She stood and slowly leaned, resting her palms against the tabletop. "I can—"

"No." Prince Kellan cleared his throat and stood. He was just a touch taller than her, but it was enough to look down upon her. "You can't go with him. That wasn't what we discussed."

Alarian's brow furrowed, and he leaned back. This wasn't how he meant for the prince to react. He'd hoped Prince Kellan would resist, but with tact and compassion. Maybe he shouldn't be surprised.

The two siblings glared at each other.

"You wanted me to go to the Tower." She turned her sharp gaze towards him. "Tell me, Alarian, are you going to Saol?"

He straightened at her attention, thrilled to see the life within her however, he didn't want to be pulled into the conversation. But how could he resist pestering the prince and fueling her flame? "Yes."

The glare he received from Prince Kellan would have torn down a lesser man. Alarian only shrugged, trying and failing at indifference.

Prince Kellan shook his head. "He doesn't want you to go, and I don't trust him enough for you to travel with him."

Ouch.

"Oh?" Felicity pursed her lips. "So, you trust him enough to put the fate of Talamh in his hands as he searches for heartstones? Yet, you don't trust *me* to be able to handle myself."

"You know how I feel about him. And you," Prince Kellan snapped back. "You're my sister and he's—" He waved in Alarian's direction with his piercing gaze kept on his sister. Alarian felt like a pile of forgotten laundry settled in the corner.

"This is a dangerous mission and Alarian should have backup. And if you want to get petty, I could also say that giving him a pile of coins and not expecting him to lose it on brothels or drink seems irresponsible on our part." A corner of Felicity's mouth rose. "And I can get real petty if you want to fight me on this."

"Can you get petty at someone else's expense?" Alarian mumbled under his breath.

Avyanna chuckled. Sloan outright laughed when Felicity shot a glare in his attention. Obviously, he hadn't been quiet enough. Alarian cleared his throat. "I'd like to think I'm not that bad and have proven that I can handle this alone."

Avyanna reached for Prince Kellan's hand. "You know she needs to go."

"Not. With. Him," Prince Kellan said through gritted teeth.

"I don't need to ask your permission." Felicity drew herself up. "You said you wanted me to find out the truth. Well then, I'll be ready to travel by dawn." Without a glance in anyone's direction, she left with her shoulders back and head held high.

"I guess the meeting is over?" Sloan stood next. "Unless there is something else?" He still was grinning as he made his way towards the door.

Alarian ignored him and turned to Prince Kellan. "This wasn't my idea."

Avyanna answered, "I think it's perfect. The two of you will be more successful together. Besides you're traveling in the same direction."

Prince Kellan spun around on his fiancée. "This is the worst idea I've ever heard."

"Stop coddling her." The words were out of Alarian's mouth without thought.

"It's my fucking job," Prince Kellan snarled at them both. "I lost her once."

Alarian swallowed. Hell, he knew how the male felt. "I'll try to talk her out of it."

"Don't you dare," Avyanna warned. "If I hear that either of you tried to stop her, I'll make your lives living hell. Do you understand?"

Alarian glanced between the two of them. "I—"

"She's right." Prince Kellan didn't look happy but nodded at his fiancée. "You heard her. I don't think either of us have a say in the matter. Besides, there isn't enough time to debate this. If you're correct, we need to find those stones or we need to be in Saol before Samhain. I don't think you can travel by shadow through the entire continent." He stood, pushing in his chair. "We'll ensure you have what you'll need for your trip. We should discuss communication measures for while you're gone."

Avyanna rested a hand on Alarian's shoulder as she passed to follow the prince. "We all know you're not really disappointed." Then she walked out, leaving the room empty except for Alarian's own thoughts.

He reached across and grabbed a map of the continent off Prince Kellan's pile of papers. And stared, unseeing. She was coming. What could he say to make her understand why she shouldn't? None made sense and his heart wasn't in it anyway.

"Of course you're still here. Ankus help me."

Alarian glanced up, Prince Kellan in the doorway. "I'd appreciate you not calling hell down upon me. Especially right before I'm meant to travel." He turned his attention back to the map. A breeze ruffled the hair at the nape of his neck.

"If anything happens—"

He closed his eyes and took a deep breath. "I know I'm not worthy of your sister, Prince Kellan."

"If you force or manipulate—"

Alarian growled as he slammed the map onto the table. "I would never. Do you really think I'm that horrible? Besides, I like my balls—and my heart—exactly where they are, thank you."

Prince Kellan winced. "That was low of me. I just...I worry about her. I've lost her once. And you're—"

"The last individual you'd ever want near your sister. I'm aware. Made that perfectly clear many times."

The prince didn't deny it. "I was coming back for my things, but I guess we should discuss correspondence." He reached for the pile. "To the library?"

Alarian stood, rolling up the map. "Not going to give me a speech about bringing her back alive?"

Prince Kellan glared. "You have your own life to worry about. I know she can take care of herself—just don't get her killed with your stupidity."

At least they had that in agreement. Maybe someday Prince Kellan wouldn't despise him so much.

Today would not be that day.

Chapter 8

Felicity

Felicity had packed the day before but a final go-through before she left wasn't a bad idea. She snapped the wardrobe closed and stomped across the room to the leather pack on her bed. After another count of the daggers, she put them back in place and confirmed the whetstone was added to her pack. The contraption Lord Lian and Dimitri had sent—a trick glove of blades—was strapped to her wrist. An extra pendant, this one clear instead of the deep red crystal she always wore, was stuffed in her pocket.

That should be everything she would need. Her clothes and extra layers were already packed. She ground her teeth when she noted that the wardrobe hadn't closed, a piece of cloth barring the way. With a deep sigh, she went back, ready to push it in when her fingers grazed the fabric. She stilled. The familiarity of the coarse cloak was not enough to bring back the past. Felicity opened the door and pulled out the clothing.

"May I come in?"

Felicity was about to stuff the cloak away again when Avyanna paused at the entrance, her gaze pinned on the fabric in Felicity's hands.

Her eyes widened. "Is that blood?" She trotted across the room, reaching for the cloak. "Are you bleeding?"

"No." Felicity stood still as the female glanced over the fabric. "It's old. Stained." She cleared her throat. "This was the cloak I was found in on the doorstep of the Tower."

A part of her didn't know why she said it. That was information only the Countess and Harrison had ever known. Likely Bishop too, but she and the

Tower liaison had never gotten along, so if he was aware he hadn't said a word about it.

She and Harrison had spent countless hours making up stories about the individual who it had belonged to. Back when she had most of her memories. Even if those from her childhood were still missing at that point too.

The thought had come unbidden, but Felicity breathed a sigh at the memory of Harrison always making the owner of the cloak a protector. Felicity would say that they were the villain, and she had stolen it from whomever it had belonged too as a trophy. It sounded like more of an adventure. Now, looking back, she was more likely to believe Harrison's hypothesis.

"Oh?" Avyanna looked over the fabric, a finger grazing the cloak's hood. "It's a generic traveling cloak. Hard to determine whom it might have belonged to."

The same information she already had learned from a shop clerk years before. "This might be a question I'll never have answered."

"Unless you find out what is holding back those last memories."

"Or if the Countess still has them," Felicity grumbled under her breath. In her time at the Tower, Felicity had looked up to the Countess. Now—now she didn't know how to feel. There had been too many secrets between them. Plans that involved her and she had been unaware. So many questions she deserved answers to. It was time to get them. "Have you seen Alarian? He didn't leave without me, did he?"

"So that you could track him down and beat his hide? I doubt it." Kellan entered with Alarian on his heels.

Felicity blinked in surprise at the two of them entering together.

Alarian glanced at the cloak in her hand with a raised brow. "Where did you get that?"

She sighed, unwilling to explain and turned to stuff it back into the wardrobe. "It's old. I'm not bringing it along." Felicity and Kellan hadn't spoken since that tense meeting the previous morning. She'd purposely steered clear of him, not wanting to give her brother another chance to talk her out of going.

She turned around to find Alarian staring at the wardrobe with a puzzled expression and when he noticed she was watching him, he cleared his throat. "Are you ready?"

"It's dawn. Of course I'm ready." Alarian had also disappeared, unable to be located no matter how hard she had searched after a certain missive had arrived.

Meira walked into the crowded room, carrying two pouches. "I packed some breakfast for your ride." Another fae walked in behind her, carrying one pack over his shoulder and reached for the pack Felicity had on the bed.

Felicity went to stop him. "I can handle—"

"Let him take it, Felicity." Kellan stepped in her path. "You have to say a proper goodbye first anyway."

Her brother nodded towards the attendant, who exited the room with their things. Felicity sighed, turning towards Kellan. "I could have taken that."

"Oh, I know. You can handle everything." His arms widened and a grin etched his features. "Right now, though, I need a hug from my sister. Please?"

Felicity felt the gazes of the others on her. Considered telling him to stuff it. "I didn't know I was in a family of huggers."

Avyanna chuckled. "We just want to show you we love you."

With a sigh, she let him wrap an arm around her.

Kellan whispered in her ear, "And we know it bothers you." She nearly stepped on his toes in response, but he pulled back, holding her at arm's length. "Be careful. Come back safely and in one piece. Understood?"

"I know how to take care of myself."

He snorted. "Yet you grimace at a hug."

She rolled her eyes while the others laughed. Avyanna didn't wait, inserting herself between the siblings to grip her tightly. "You must be back in time for the wedding. And your father's return."

Felicity's internal clock ticked down the seventy days that remained until Samhain. "And to stop Marquette," Felicity added as they parted. "Trust me, I'm aware that we don't have much time."

They all walked the quiet halls and left the castle through a side door that led straight to the stable. The sun couldn't be seen by the wall surrounding the yard, but a glimpse of dawn light illuminated the sky. No one except for the stable hands were out and about doing their chores. The birds were only beginning their song. Dew gathered on the edges of the rooftops, dripping to the ground.

Alarian walked over to a waiting chestnut gelding and mounted with ease. The stable hand let go and headed back to the barn.

Felicity did the same atop a gray mare, checking her daggers were still in the right place so she wouldn't be stabbed by her own knives.

"Be careful. Keep in contact." Kellan glanced between the two of them. "I expect an update every three days. I'll make sure to have one for you with a letter in the place we discussed."

Of course they discussed. Without her. With a shift in the saddle, she urged the mare forward. "Goodbye." She waved at the group over her shoulder without a backwards glance. She had never good at goodbyes, so why start now?

A moment later, trotting hooves sounded behind her. The mare tossed her head, dancing in anticipation as the gelding caught up. "What was that all about?"

Felicity snapped her gaze to Alarian and slowed her mount, his gelding settling into a walk. "Oh? Are you talking to me now?"

Alarian hadn't spoken directly to her since their dance. Except for the arrival of a letter in the same place the last shadow missive had landed—the one asking if she was all right after a particularly vivid memory had nearly knocked her unconscious. This time he asked for her to reconsider coming along. She'd spent until midnight searching for the male with no luck. "A letter. Really?"

"Maybe you had changed your mind. I wanted to offer an out."

Her jaw clenched, the tattoo on her thigh itched as a reminder of all the past missions she had completed using the anger that currently seethed inside her. "I didn't reconsider. In fact, it only made me want to come more." She turned a saccharine grin in his direction. "If only to drive you as mad as you drive me."

That grin appeared. Hell, she hated it sometimes. Other times she tried desperately to ignore the warmth that spread at the sight of it. He slowed his mount, raising the hood of his cloak. "I drive you mad?"

She bit her tongue and turned her attention back to the road to see Koselig's squat buildings. The outline of *The Rose & Wisteria's* signpost sticking over the roadway. She turned away as a door opened to their left and a man began to adjust the shutters to his apothecary. Felicity raised her own hood and lowered her head to remain discreet and not draw attention to the princess and once-prisoner now leaving together.

They trotted in silence through the town, passing shop owners making their way to their stores to open for business. Carts were being dragged in from the surrounding farms with freshly picked fruit and vegetables. Chickens squawked as a young child dug their hand into their roost boxes.

No one paid them any mind, too engrossed in their own morning habits to pay attention to two passersby.

When they were deep into farmlands, where houses were well off the main road and farmers were in the midst of their morning chores, Felicity slowed her mount to a walk. She lowered her hood and Alarian did the same.

Felicity reached into her pocket and removed the map she had drawn last night. "Have you also decided where we are headed or is that still up for discussion?"

"We aren't done with our previous conversation."

"I'm not in the mood for your innuendos and pathetic attempts at humor." She shifted the reins to one hand and flattened the map on her thigh. "Where are we headed first?"

He was silent and she looked up to find him staring, a small smile on his face. She rolled her eyes, but he pointed at the map before she could speak. "What do you have there?"

"What does it look like?"

"Tell me why you're angry, Felicity?"

She pulled the mare to a halt and glared. "Fine. Let's get this all out then. Why didn't you want me to come? You challenged me before you left. Called me out. Then I make a move and do what I think is right and of all people, *you* try to stop me."

He turned his gelding to face her and leaned back in the saddle, taking her in. "I've missed this."

She hated that she noted he'd trimmed his hair but hadn't shaved, stubble ghosting his jaw and lips. "I told you—"

He cut her off with a wave of his hand. "I shouldn't have written that letter." Alarian sighed. "You're right. I tried to stop you from being yourself. That was wrong of me and I apologize. It was for selfish reasons."

Selfish reasons? She wanted to ask but her mouth remained a tight line.

"You don't have to forgive me right away."

Curses, what had she been thinking going with him? She nudged the mare forward and urged her past Alarian's horse. "Good. I'm not ready to yet."

He chuckled as she passed and turned his gelding to follow. "Now what's that map about?"

"Well, while you and my brother were becoming life-long friends, I planned out a route."

"I don't think we'll ever be life-long friends. We were in the library discussing some plans and trying to find information on what could happen to the realm without its heartstone."

"The library?" She blinked. "Seriously? That's the last place I expected you to be." She'd searched the kitchen, his rooms, and even went to the willow. In all the time she'd known him, she'd never seen him in the library no matter how many times she'd collected books there.

"Aw, Starlight. At this point, you should know that, when it comes to me, the last place should be the first place to look."

How this male could drive her to the point of wanting to reach for her dagger yet remained unscathed...

"Before you get stabby, can you tell me your route?"

Felicity brushed a finger against the blade at her hip as a reminder of its presence. Alarian chuckled as she turned her attention back to the map on her thigh. "Aer to start. Then head into Domhain to search the old catacombs for clues about the previous stone followed by a stop in Saol. After a visit to the Tower, we make our way to Dorcha. Figured you could reach out to Sloan's family."

He winced.

Felicity caught it. "You already did, didn't you?"

Alarian had the audacity to look apologetic. "When I first decided to leave. So far, you're on the right track, but we'll need to make Dorcha a priority. Their cold front comes in sooner than ours seeing as they lack the light of the upper realms. I had us starting at the Fios in Aer."

"The Fios?"

He nodded. "It's a prestigious library protected by Guardians. There are multiple levels and only those with special privileges can receive certain information. I've tried multiple times to get what I need from there but have never been granted access. It seems your brother's aunt is the head librarian, so he's sent a letter ahead to ask permission."

"Of course—books."

"The keepers of knowledge and the weapons of the wise."

She inhaled. "I'm honestly surprised you and my brother are not best friends."

"Put in a good word for me?"

She rolled her neck. "I have. Now, after the Fios, where next?"

He shrugged. "Domhain, Dorcha, then Saol and Visce."

"And last stop is Scáth?" She had noted his hesitation yesterday in their meeting.

"No." His shoulders drew back, chin lifting. "They will see it as a lack of faith. We can't go there. Besides, you can trust they're protecting the shadow heartstone."

"We can't ignore them either and it's best we show them that we are on the same side. They haven't come to court. They might see it as—"

"No." The word was final—harsh and sharp. A small breath. "Please."

"Is there a reason you don't want to go there?" Many explanations crossed her mind. Had he hurt his relationship with the realm after returning to his parents' side?

"Just trust me on this."

See me.

She pinched her eyes closed and took two breaths, a slow inhale and exhalation. *Don't let the anger use you.* The mare shook her head, bringing Felicity back to the present. She leaned over, patting her neck to calm her and then took in their surroundings. The farmhouses were no longer in view. Instead, they had reached the rolling grasslands that would soon lead to the flat plain lands of Aer.

"Her name is Laochra." Alarian's soft voice broke the silence and brought her out of her own reverie.

She blinked in surprise, then the quiet way he said the name echoed in her mind. Her face burned crimson. Was this why he had been ignoring her? Why he wanted only to be friends? It would make sense with the distance he put between them. They had kissed. Once. And he had a lover. "What?"

"Your horse. She's spunky—figured she would be a good fit for you. So far you don't seem to be having any difficulty." He gave her one of his half smiles.

And she despised that a little bit of that anger was snuffed away. Jealousy was new. She turned to hide her blush, folding the map and put it back in her pocket. "Where are we staying tonight then?"

Alarian chuckled. "A small town that you might remember well. Cnoc."

"Are we going back to the same inn?" The one he had gotten stabbed in. His cocky grin was confirmation enough. "You better resist any card games tonight."

"Aw, but where is the fun in that? You going to babysit me and make sure I behave?"

"No."

"Then maybe you should join me for dinner?"

"Again no." Laochra snorted. "Even she knows that's a bad idea. I'm about to spend weeks with you. Tonight, I'm going to enjoy a quiet night and a good long soak in a bath."

"Was that an invitation?"

She glared at him. "You might not make it through this mission."

Alarian laughed, the boisterous sound sending a flock of quail running from a bush. His gelding jumped at the sudden sound, Felicity's mare whirling around with a start. She soothed Laochra, turning her towards Alarian just in time to see the gelding kick out. Alarian fell off the side, landing hard and getting a mouth full of dirt.

As he stumbled to his feet, he wiped his face and spit. The gelding trotted in a circle around them and stopped to stare at the male as if surprised to see him on the ground.

Felicity was the one laughing now.

Chapter 9

Felicity

The Fios was like looking at a mirror of the Tower. But instead of an iron gate that circled the building, it had an inviting white picket fence. And while the Tower had always had an 'enter at your own risk' exterior, the Fios was bright and welcoming even though it was made from similar stone. Felicity stared upwards while Alarian paid the stablehand to care for the horses.

The previous night they had stayed in Cnoc. Alarian had been in the room next to hers and it appeared he had followed her lead and stayed in for dinner—an empty tray had sat outside his door when she had placed hers there too. That morning, he had been whistling when he'd met Felicity for breakfast in the tavern downstairs. After riding for half of the day, they entered the town of Aimsir to a hubbub of activity.

Alarian moved in beside her. "He told me there's an Inventors Fair in town. We might want to find lodgings before all the rooms are taken—if they aren't already."

"What happens if someone recognizes us?" She mostly worried about him with his red hair and his previous title of prince. She doubted that anyone would recognize her yet.

"The princess is on a tour of the realms. Wanted to see the festival and check out the Fios. Very simple to play it off as a trip to get to know the realms of Talamh."

"Thought of everything, have you?" She sighed.

"That was off the top of my head. I think you would have figured it out if necessary." Alarian winked at her. "Give yourself credit, Felicity. Remember—you killed an advisor in a room full of people."

Felicity tore her gaze away from the building. "Did the stablehand have any recommendations close by?"

"Yes, he pointed out two options. Follow me." The roads were narrow and most people traveled by foot. All castes of faeries and humans brushed past each other, in their own worlds of curiosity or annoyance. Once they had entered the town, there were flat paths for carriages and horses that led to a central location where three large stables, two storefronts, and the Fios curved around a central grass knoll. From that point, cobbled walkways veered off in every direction. A few humans and fae sat on contraptions with three wheels—one in the front and two in the back—that they used to carry their wares and hawk their goods to passers-by.

Others had the same contraption but with two wheels instead of three and they zoomed around corners distributing pamphlets or information before disappearing around another curve.

The town was a mecca and Felicity was in awe. "This is unlike anything I've ever seen."

"This is the second largest town in all of the continent. It's also where most inventions are on display. If someone has come up with it, it can probably be found here." He pointed to the ridable contraptions. "Those, for instance, are called bicycles. I had always thought it would be fun to learn to ride. But outside of the town, they don't last long on the dirt roads. They are best used on smooth roadways."

"Then why have them if they are only useful here?"

Alarian shrugged. "Someday more towns will adjust. I've heard they can be found on Oileán too since many roads have been paved to allow for easier access to travel."

Felicity listened intently as he spoke. "Should we go to Oileán to search for the stone?" She didn't want to sound like Miss Isleen, but like the young fae,

Felicity had become interested in the island territories during her research on the realms. The long beaches, candied treats, and unique landscapes boasted about in the books had intrigued her.

"We shall see what we discover in Visce."

Felicity didn't broach the subject further. A visit to the islands would be a goal to fight for. A touch of hope when everything else seemed bleak. Felicity followed him to the first inn, halting at the packed tavern with a line at the entrance.

"We might want to go to the next one. It might be best if it's farther down the street."

They left the first, the second, and the third inn without any better results. It was a short trek to the fourth, which was rundown with a cracked window, its door barely on its hinges. Alarian carefully held it open for her. She stepped in to the smell of cigar smoke mixed with sweat and stew. The three patrons didn't look their way, but their grizzled appearance matched the room's ambience. Or lack thereof. The dusty floor and unkempt tabletops showed their lack of care. A family of three entered behind them, took one look around and left as quickly as they arrived. Felicity didn't blame them, but they had exhausted all other options.

Felicity made her way to the innkeeper's bar. "We need a room."

"Desperate if your kind is here." The barman didn't glance up at her as he poured a tankard and slid it down to a patron's waiting hand. "I only gots one, so if you want it, it's going to cost ya."

Alarian growled, but Felicity took a small step in front of him and leaned onto the bar. A mistake. Sticky residue coated her hands, but she swallowed her disgust. "You'll charge us the same as any other."

The man peered up then, his gray eyes barely visible between the strands of greasy hair that hung over his brow. "Pretty sure you can pay a little more and its hard times right now. You're not going to find another room—and you gotta pay for scarcity."

The dagger at her thigh itched. Called for her to grab hold in a way that it hadn't in a long time. "Last chance, *sir*."

Alarian sidestepped and tossed a bag of coins on the bar. "That's all we got."

The man picked it up, weighed it in his palm. "This'll do."

Felicity glowered at Alarian as the innkeeper turned to grab their key from a hall that likely led to the kitchen judging by the scent of steamed cabbage and burnt toast that leaked out. "You shouldn't have done it."

"Don't worry." Alarian shrugged. "It's a place for two nights. That's all we need."

She crossed her arms. "Fine."

The innkeeper returned with their money strapped to his belt.

Arrogant ass. The grin on his face told Felicity that he knew he'd gotten the better deal out of this.

He led them up a narrow staircase to the third floor, put the key in the lock and twisted. "Biggest room we got."

If that was true, then the other rooms must have been as small as coffins. There was one uncovered window over the bed, a side table, and a desk sans chair settled against the opposite wall where one couldn't stand due to the vaulted ceiling. "Shared bathroom is down the hall."

She took in the tattered patched quilt and rumpled pillows—

There was only one bed. "Are there no other rooms? Really?"

The man guffawed. "You could always room with me, sweetie." He slammed the door behind him, his laughter following him down the hall.

"I think I should slit his throat. Or push him down the stairs."

Alarian's gaze darkened. "It might be frowned upon for one of your subjects to wind up dead."

"I doubt he'd be missed."

Alarian snorted. "There is the future Dearmadta I know so well."

She snapped her mouth shut and reluctantly glanced back at the bed with crossed arms. It was easier than thinking about the title she no longer had in her grasp. The Dearmadta—an elite group of spies—wouldn't want to invite a princess into their ranks.

"Well? How is this going to work?"

Alarian dropped his pack on the lone table against the drafty wooden wall. "You on one side, me on the other." He spoke so matter-of-factly that Felicity wanted to smack him.

Could she share a bed with him? After last time—

"We did it before. Wasn't a problem then. Don't expect it be so now."

I remember a problem. She didn't turn to look at him but sensed him behind her. With a heavy sigh, she crossed the remainder of the room in two steps and put down her own pack on the desk. She opened it and rummaged for a heavier cloak. "I'm going to check out the Inventors Fair. Want to come?" She kept her voice light and inviting.

There was a moment of silence and she wondered if he had heard her. When she turned, the shadows had expanded lightly through the room. But instead of an encompassing darkness, they reminded her of that moment in the training hall. As their magic moved in sensual curves, calm sways, and an inviting embrace. A touch soft and warm. "Alarian?" she whispered.

His gaze snapped up, the shadows dissipating. "Yes, I'll come."

For the next hour they made their way by booths and saw inventions she'd never considered possible in her limited imagination. Magic was intriguing enough, but when used to create contraptions that sent flares of bright light into the air as a signal or spelled with magic to dry clothes—it was impossible to take it all in at once. As afternoon shifted to night, more people were out mingling and the crowd thickened. Alarian was nearly cut off from Felicity, so he grabbed her arm and pulled her close. She nearly fell into him, but he caught her. "All right there?"

She nodded, unable to speak—snared by his emerald eyes as they glanced over her. They always unsettled her in the worst—best—way. He winked, his hand grazing her arm as he reached down and tangled his fingers with hers. He led her down the cobbled road, cutting through groups and darting around travelers.

They arrived at the Fios at nightfall and found the door locked with a posting announcing it would open an hour after dawn the following day. "Disappointing. I had hoped to see if they could find some of the books prior to their closing tonight." Alarian huffed as he turned. "Let's grab something to eat. Don't know how much I trust the food at the inn."

"Or the prices," Felicity grumbled under her breath.

They purchased bite-sized sandwiches with pork and delectable sauces and her favorite—a sticky bun drizzled with white icing—as they walked back towards the inn. The room that awaited them was heavy on her mind. It shouldn't be. He was right. They'd shared a space before and it wasn't like then. They had an understanding and a title for their relationship. Friends. Simple.

When they reached their room, Felicity made her way to her bag and searched for her whetstone. She needed to do something with her hands.

Alarian watched from the edge of the bed where he was removing his boots as she selected her first dagger and took a seat on the desk. "Are you planning to stab me during the night?"

She didn't glance up as she slid the stone against metal. "I'd considered it before."

"And tonight?" There was a vulnerability in his tone that had her pausing to meet his gaze.

"Not unless you give me reason too."

That grin returned. She told herself she hated it. Over and over. Even as her eyes skimmed over his lips—

At a sudden jolt of pain, she glanced down to find her thumb cut open, blood beading at the slice. "Dammit."

Alarian was by her side in a breath. "Are you all right?" He reached for her hand and before she could say a word, her hand was in his palm as he inspected the wound. "You're lucky this isn't deeper."

"It's fine." She tried to pull away, but he only gripped her tighter.

"It still needs to be cleaned and bandaged. Where's your kit?"

She blinked, surprised. "I can handle it." Felicity had dealt with multiple stab wounds, a dislocated shoulder, and there was that run in with the gang in Domhain who had nearly killed her. She never did figure out how she had had woken the following morning from that particular exchange with most of her wounds nearly healed. At least, enough for her to make it to her contact in a nearby outpost to rest.

"I know you can. But I can help."

This time, when she moved away. he let her. His mouth a thin line as she stood and stuck her injured finger into her mouth as she got her kit from her bag.

"I was just trying to help."

"But I don't need you too."

"I never said you *needed* me too. There is no doubt in my mind that you're a strong and independent female. That, if I wasn't here, you would have that finger bandaged in no time at all. But you don't have to do it alone. Instead of doing it one handed, I could offer two."

She paused, kit in hand, then peered over her shoulder at him. "Why is it so important to you?"

He swallowed. Sighed. "Because everything doesn't have to be all on your shoulders. That's what friends are for—to share the burden."

They held eye contact for a few bated breaths, then with a sigh, she took the position she'd recently vacated and held out the kit. "Here."

A warmth radiated from his skin as he took the pouch from her, their fingers grazing. "Thank you," he whispered.

She nodded, uncertain if she should speak.

With deft and practiced hands, he cleaned the wound. "You know you shouldn't be distracted when sharpening a blade." There was a lilt to his voice, a smile on his lips.

She glanced at her dagger that sat on the desk beside her, considering its many uses.

"Nope." He applied the ointment. "Don't like where that look went." He leaned closer blowing gently to dry it on her skin. With each pass of his breath against the cut, her core warmed, that familiar need rising within. She inhaled a deep breath as she watched his mouth.

"How's that?" Alarian slid a finger along hers.

Curse. Him. "Better." Her throat was dry as he reached for the kit.

He removed a bandage. Carefully, oblivious to the war in her own body, he wrapped her finger, checking to make sure that it wasn't too tight. "These are moments I wish I had the ability to heal others and not just myself."

She didn't have anything to say to that. Not certain if she could trust her own voice. When done, he placed a kiss against the injury. Her breath caught in her throat. It was gentle, kind—but in that moment she was completely aware of the all-encompassing want that pulsed through her body.

"Why did you do that?" It was all she could think to ask.

He gave a half grin as he let her hand go, then cleaned up the mess he'd made. "A story Meira always told me growing up about a youngling with the power to heal through her kiss. I think it was how she got me to stop crying when I had an injury."

"I have a hard time imagining you crying." Felicity shook her head as she focused on that image instead of the way his throat bobbed. The shift of muscle as he carried her kit back to her pack. "Tears don't seem your thing."

Alarian chuckled. "It might surprise you, but I cry plenty. The other younglings would make fun of me. Even now, Sloan recently caught me and all he did was toss me a handkerchief, told me to talk to him when I was ready then walked away."

"When was this?"

Alarian seemed to consider if he should answer. "The night all those younglings and rebels were killed." He tossed the gauze he used away. "It was hard not to feel responsible for every single one of their deaths. I wondered if I hadn't started the rebellion, what would have happened? If it was a waste and had cost more people their lives than saved them." His movements had slowed, gaze pinned on his hands.

Felicity resisted reaching out to him. Thought about the nightmares interrupting her sleep. How the deaths on her hands had been a choice made in the name of loyalty. For him, it was something else that plagued him. "It's not easy. I don't think it ever will be. But their memories live on in those who are now free because of their sacrifice. Because they offered hope in dark times."

"Hope is fickle. It can change within a breath. Dread. Doubt. Those are easier feelings that can become overbearing. I've realized that even if I occasionally lost hope, at least the rebels had initiative." He looked up and stared into nothingness, his gaze desolate. "Chaos wouldn't have gotten the proper message across. Especially to many of the nobles we were attempting to persuade to our side. And Kellan. He might not have been willing to assist if we weren't an organized group."

At the mention of her brother's name, Felicity looked towards her bandaged hand. "Sometimes I wonder what it would have been like if the three of us had worked together."

"I have too." Absentmindedly, he brushed a strand of hair behind her ear. His finger grazed her cheek. The movement was so familiar. Yet...

Felicity stood, tossing the whetstone into her pack. "We have an early morning tomorrow." She stared at that bed. Shit.

"I was wondering if you wanted to train."

There was hope in his voice. As if he could see everything she was attempting to cover up. "No."

"Oh."

She didn't look his way, instead categorizing what she packed to wear to bed. The last time they had shared a bed, she'd slept in very little and he had been gentlemanly. That had been before the kiss. Before they were friends.

She removed a pair of loose-fitting pants and an oversized shirt. They had been meant for layering clothing in colder weather, but it would do. She reached for the hem of her shirt then stopped, peeking over her shoulder. "Turn around please."

Alarian did one better as the shadows drifted up between them and darkness shrouded her body like a cloak. While she appreciated the privacy, his magic reminded her of so much more. The cool caress of the touch of his shadow when he held her close as they traveled. The training ring and the way their magic had intermingled in wisps and starlight.

With a shake of her head to force herself to the present, she slid off her clothes. It was after she pulled her last leg through the pants that she cleared her throat. "I'm decent."

The shadows dissipated, but she didn't move as she felt his presence behind her. Close. Yet not close enough. "How do you want to do this?"

Heat pooled. A warmth spread. Suddenly her skin was aware of the fabric brushing against her. The smooth curl of his breath against her ear. How the hell should they do this? And what was this but a test of her fortitude?

"Like you said, we've shared before." Did she just say that out loud? "If your uncomfortable—"

"No." He didn't give her a chance to finish her sentence. "It's fine."

She turned to find him also in loose pants and, thankfully, a tunic. His gaze darkened as it slid slowly over her body. His mouth a thin, stubborn line. A furrow in his brow. The light from the bedside lantern illuminating the dust of freckles.

Her heart was about to pound from her chest. She knew it. "Rian."

His eyes flickered at the nickname, then pinned to her mouth. On an instinct of its own, she licked her lips. Heat flared in his gaze and Alarian swallowed. "Yes, Starlight?"

"Why do you call me that?" She needed him to talk. Needed something to fill the silence charged with electricity.

His gaze moved from her lips to her eyes. "Because it suits you. A light in the darkness."

"I am the darkness. A weapon." It felt like a lifetime since she'd thought that way.

"Are you?"

His question dropped the world right out from under her feet. She shook her head and turned towards the bed. "Remember, stay on your side." She curled under the blanket, trying to shut out the static that coursed through her blood.

He chuckled and the bed shifted as he climbed in. "I wouldn't dream of crossing the line you've put between us." He was careful not to touch her.

She reminded herself that he'd pulled away from their kiss. And she didn't need to know why.

A pillow pressed into her side, and she turned to find him grinning. "You know. Barrier. In case either of us need a reminder of which side is ours."

Then he turned away, his back to her as he nuzzled into the bed. No comeback came to mind.

Chapter 10

Alarian

The following morning, Alarian spent time downstairs among the same three battered patrons that had been in the tavern the night before. They looked a little worse for wear now, nursing hangovers in an otherwise busy establishment. It seemed breakfast was when the place shined. He ate a puffy buttermilk biscuit and dubious-looking eggs scrambled with onion, peppers, and potatoes while he afforded Felicity the privacy to take a bath.

And gave himself a moment to breathe without the heaviness of her presence. The knowledge of his feelings and what they meant felt like a wall between them and keeping up their *friendship* was more difficult than he'd anticipated. Not when she'd look at him and he could see the heat rise in her cheeks, the way her body would brush his when she passed—Alarian wondered if she was even aware of what she was doing.

Was she as drawn to him and aware of it? Or completely oblivious? The emotions he felt from her in waves were jumbled. He needed to learn control. It wasn't fair that he had this insider information on her when she wasn't aware. But to tell her—he wanted to live through this excursion. Not die by her blade.

When he returned to their room, his heart nearly stopped as she straightened from her sitting position on the bed. She wore a loose-fitting linen shirt tucked into skin-tight pants. It wasn't anything out of the ordinary, but it immediately brought back memories of sessions in the training hall. She was pulling her thick, wavy mahogany hair up into a ponytail.

"Ready?" She grabbed her pack and tossed it over her shoulder.

He nodded, not trusting his words.

They walked in silence and Alarian was surprised at the energy he felt in each step. He had slept well. Better than he had in weeks. No nightmares plagued him, no visions of the rebel children he'd found brutally murdered. Nothing about his parents stabbing him in the back. Or a recent addition to his library of fears—Felicity's throat being torn open by his mother's magic while he just stood there.

He liked to think if it were her, that he would move. That he wouldn't have a delayed reaction as he had that day Felicity sliced through his father. He was still angry at himself for pausing a breath longer than he should have. His mother may not be free right now if he had reacted.

"Do we knock?" Felicity jiggled the locked door of the Fios. "Or are we too early?"

As if the door heard her question, it clicked open and a female with curly brown hair peeked through the crack. "Hello, can I help you?"

Felicity cleared her throat. "We are looking for Miss Illith. I'm Felicity."

Alarian felt for the note from Kellan in his pocket.

"Oh!" The door widened revealing the female in full. She grinned at Felicity and dropped into a curtsy. "Miss Illith is my aunt and told me all about you. Please come in. I'm Cara." Then she looked at him, meeting Alarian's gaze. "Oh, it's you." Her eyes widened and a grin played at her lips.

Alarian held his breath. Damn, he knew her. And not in a way he should. Well...fuck.

He remained impassive as his insides tightened. Not the best alternative. Cara had been meant to be a means to an end. It had backfired. Completely. Her willingness should have been clue enough. "Yes, it's been a while."

Cara's eyes sparkled. "I didn't think I'd ever see you again, but I'm glad to be wrong." She opened the door wider. "Please, come in."

He suddenly wanted to bury himself in the ground. Felicity sliced a glare in his direction as they moved past Cara into the Fios.

Cara's arm brushed against his as he passed and Alarian took a small step away—right into the doorjamb. He winced and the female blushed as she led them towards where Illith stood behind her desk. He remembered her too—for different reasons. The matronly female smiled up at them and stilled, her gaze locked on Felicity with wide eyes. "Princess Felicity."

She rushed around the desk towards them. Illith was a little taller than Felicity and had a darker complexion and hair—which must have come from Kellan's mother's side. Lanky arms wrapped tightly around Felicity—who remained ramrod straight and unmoving.

"It's been decades. Too many to count. Look at how you've grown. More than a youngling now for sure." She pulled back, looking over Felicity with tears in her eyes. "You probably don't remember me—"

Felicity shuddered. A slight movement that only Alarian noticed. "Sorry."

"You were so small, I doubted you would. When I received my nephew's letter, I could only imagine you as a babe. How you would toddle around the gardens after your mother. My sister would have been proud of Bastien and Kellan for finding such a suitable queen in her stead." Her eyes glistened further. "Your mother was a treasure—I'm so sorry."

The mask Felicity often wore slid over her face. "It was a long time ago but thank you." She stepped away from Illith, attempting to control the emotions he could feel nearly submerging her. He needed to intercept this conversation.

"I'm glad to hear you received Kellan's letter." He removed the missive from his pocket and held it out. "We need some information that's of a sensitive nature."

She nodded. "He mentioned that." She tilted her head. "I remember you too. You've been here before. More than once." Illith peered quickly at Cara. "I hadn't thought I would ever see you again. Not after your last visit. And certainly not with the princess."

Felicity's brow rose in his direction but kept her impassive expression in place. Only he could feel each spike of annoyance—and a twinge of jealousy. Maybe. He knew he shouldn't hope that was the case. "Alarian has been working against his parents for some time. We need information to stop his mother. Which means we need your help to find it."

"Hm." Illith stared at Alarian for a beat longer than necessary. Shit—maybe the letter wouldn't be enough.

He extended out the missive further, the seal intact. "From your nephew."

A brow lifted and Illith took the parchment and snapped open the seal. Her firm mouth finally moved into a small grin. A chuckle. She peered at him from over the letter for a moment. When she was done, she folded and slid the parchment into a pocket. "Well then, let's see what we can do. Follow me and I'll set you up at one of the corner tables."

Illith noticed Cara moved in beside Alarian as though invited. "Cara, please ensure the last of the stacks are organized before we open the doors. I know a small pile still needs to be put away."

Cara opened her mouth but sighed instead, turning on her heel in the opposite direction.

Illith shook her head. "She's young. Well, about your age, Felicity."

Felicity's mouth twitched, and Alarian was certain she didn't appreciate being compared to the other.

The cylinder shape of the interior of the library was much like its façade. On the ground floor, cushioned chairs sat around coffee tables while wooden chairs surrounded square tables for research. Multiple levels of shelves with walkways curved around the edges were reachable by two sets of spiral stairs that disappeared into the stacks above.

Illith stopped at a table already piled with books. "I had these pulled and ready once I received the first letter. These are more generic texts regarding the veil. Now that I know more specifically what you're looking for, I'll search the older texts. This will give you a good start though, and I have a few leads." She paused. "The library might make it difficult."

"What do you mean?" Felicity's brow furrowed.

"The Fios chooses what it deems appropriate to be discovered. Books have a power all on their own. The knowledge they contain can decimate civilizations or introduce someone to an entire new world. It must consider your character, and it doesn't take such decisions lightly." Illith looked over her shoulder for a brief moment. "I will place a silencing bubble around your table so you can talk freely. Only Cara and I will be able to pass through."

"Thank you." Alarian took a seat. "We appreciate your discretion."

"Come only to me with any direct questions." Illith stepped back. "Good luck." She waved her hand and a hum of air magic surrounded their space.

Felicity watched in utter curiosity. "I didn't know that someone could do that."

"She is well suited for her position. Air Fae can do more than rush wind about." Alarian reached for the first book from the stack and dragged it in front of him. "Kellan probably can do something similar."

"I don't think he's one to use his magic often." Felicity took the next book.

"It doesn't help that his magic had been at about a third of its ability for fifty years. I assume he's not stretched those muscles in a while. Speaking of which, did I wake to find you in your glamour?" It jarred him to see the curved ears and softened curve of her jaw when he'd woken at dawn. She'd turned as she woke and kept her back to him. The glamour was gone when he saw her face again, and he couldn't bring himself to say anything.

Felicity glanced at him from the corner of her eye. "It helps with the illness."

"I see. Instead of training?"

That was obviously the wrong question. She glared, turning away. "You keep bringing it up as if there's a problem. Stop poking around for something wrong."

A brush of discomfort that pulsed to life in his head told him of the hurt she felt. He had to look away so to not reveal he could sense her emotions. Felt what she tried so hard to hide. "You're not exactly being your usual self."

Felicity sat back, the chair groaning under the sudden pressure. "Listen, we both are learning to trust each other, but that doesn't mean you need to pretend to know who I am. There isn't time for that. Right now, we have a mission to concentrate on."

Mission. That sounded like the old Felicity—almost. "You do realize that you get to define how all this goes? This 'mission' as you call it, will have a better outcome if we work with each other. Or did you forget one of the reasons why you came along?" Alarian felt the shift in her again, so he wasn't surprised to find her expression blank. "I just want you to know that you can be yourself around me. And that I'm here to help."

She opened her mouth, then snapped it shut. Her attention fell to the book in front of her.

He wanted to push the subject further but now wasn't the time. Not here. If—when she was ready, he would be there.

They worked in companionable silence for the next few hours. Illith came by with another stack of books. Others streamed by from time to time as they researched, but with the barrier in place, worked uninterrupted.

It was nearing noon when a click of a tongue drew Alarian's attention upward. Cara had stepped into the barrier and stood over him, shaking her head. "If you don't take a break, you're going to pass out at the table."

Alarian peered at Felicity from the corner of his eyes, noting her attention pinned on the book in front of her. "We're doing fine here."

Cara sighed dramatically. "Well, I'm famished. Would like to go eat? Sustenance is important with all the concentrating going on."

He'd been such a stupid ass in the past. Why had he thought a roll in the hay would give him a chance to look closer at the archives? Illith had told him to either leave or look at the tomes at the lower levels. He'd known he wouldn't find the topic he needed there. Judging by the coy look on Cara's face, she hadn't seen through his blatant attempts to get what he wanted.

But he could be polite. Or he should be if he wanted to remain in Illith's good graces. "You're probably right. A break is a good idea." Alarian reached for a piece of parchment to place into the book he was reading. "Felicity, did you want to get something to eat?"

She didn't look up. "I'm going to keep at it. You two have fun."

Her lack of reaction irked him. He needed to bring her back to herself. Alarian leaned over the table, his arms on either side of the book she was reading. He waited there, unmoving, until she looked up. "Come have lunch with me."

Felicity's gaze blazed to life. "You already have a willing participant."

There was a bit of the sass he'd been missing. "But it wouldn't be the same without you." He gave her that half cocky grin—one side of his mouth rising a little—that she pretended to hate.

Felicity bit her bottom lip, then turned back to the book. "I'm fine. Enjoy."

"Please?" he whispered.

Her expression softened. Hell, he couldn't wait until she accepted the emotions brewing inside of her. Any of them. Allowed them. She met his gaze once more with a small smile—one he could tell was forced. "I'm not hungry." Now the stubbornness...

Alarian nodded. "Suit yourself." He couldn't force her. Wouldn't. "I'll bring something back for you."

"Don't bother."

It was a mistake to leave with Cara, but what was he meant to do? He needed to move and eat. They had been researching for hours without luck. The books Illith had found hadn't given them new information. There had to be something on those shelves. If only he could speak to the Fios and beg for its help. That wasn't how it worked though...

Cara led him out the door and then scooped her arm through his, a grin etched on her face. "It's chilly."

It was a little brisk, but the female wore a shawl. If it had been another time, he would have welcomed her advances. Flirted back. But now, there wasn't an inkling of interest or desire to make him turn away from what he left behind.

"So, what is it the two of you are researching?" Cara leaned into his side. The scent of honeysuckle tickled his nose making him wonder if she had been wearing it earlier or had added the perfume.

"Classified, I'm afraid."

"Oh, I see. Then how long do you plan to stay? I hope a few days." She batted her lashes at him.

Alarian moved away from her, removing his arm from her grasp. "Not long." He kept his answers vague with half-truths as she peppered him with more questions about himself. When she bored of his half-responses, she began to talk about herself. He hoped she would get the hint without him having to be too forward or rude.

They purchased stew and ate their lunch at a table outside the pub down the street from the Fios. Children played at a lawn across the way, a few flying kites that dove and swirled by the breeze and enhanced by air magic. Cara found any excuse to touch him throughout the meal. From taking his extra fork after dropping hers, to asking for assistance in wiping a stray crumb off her cheek. He obliged as much as possible to be polite. When the meal was over, he offered to pay his half, but she turned him down. "Can't have that, now. You're a guest in my realm." She winked as she handed the server the necessary coins.

Alarian winced. "Even though we're just sitting here as two acquaintances?"

Cara waved him off. "For now."

Polite wasn't going to cut it. "Cara, I apologize if you had expectations but beyond lunch, nothing else is happening between us."

She tilted her chin down, pushing out her chest. "You didn't feel that way on your last visit. Don't you find me attractive?"

He was used to the bait and switch. The game of guilt she was attempting to play on him. She wasn't the first. "Finding someone attractive and being willing to sleep with them are two completely different things." He stood up. "I will pay you for my lunch, but I'm going back to the library now."

Cara huffed as she stood, crossing her arms. "Your loss."

"For someone, it very well will be. But for me, it would be a grave mistake that I couldn't come back from." He stood to leave.

Cara caught up to him. "You can't be serious. I'm no one's mistake. Is it *her*?"

The way she added an insinuation to the 'her' made Alarian's skin crawl. He turned on Cara and she fumbled to a stop. "It's about respect. Be careful how you speak of her." He leaned in, his voice low and gaze sharp. "And it's Your Royal Highness Princess Felicity to you."

The female trembled, her eyes searching his expression. "I'm sorry."

Alarian's cursed under his breath and turned on his heels. He was careful not to bump into anyone as he stalked back down the two blocks to the library only to enter and find her chair empty. The table was still piled with books. A glance around the room, a quick scan for her emotions, but Felicity wasn't there. He rushed to Illith who was looking over a ledger at her desk. "Where is she?"

"The princess needed to stretch her legs. She seemed quite upset." Illith gave him a questionable glance from head to toe. "Cannot, for the life of me, figure out why."

Alarian knew she was tense. Could feel the sensation against his skull, but it wouldn't tell him where she was. He started for the door. "We'll be back." Before he exited, he turned back to Illith. "Where is the nearest training ring?" Felicity would have found it in no time, with or without directions.

Illith smiled at his question. "You do know her."

He kept the impatience from his voice. "I do."

"You're not the same young male who came before."

He gave a single nod. "I hope I'm meant to take that as a compliment."

"You are." She smiled.

After Illith told him where to go, Alarian followed the directions easily. Once he reached the double doors of the small wooden building, he inhaled deeply before sauntering inside, hands in pockets. The rectangle space was empty except for her. He needed to play this right, otherwise it would all be cursed before it started.

Felicity stopped her regiment as he made his way into the center of the open space filled with the scent of sawdust and two training dummies on either side.

He grinned. "I thought I'd find you here."

"Seems I'm as predictable as you are." She spat out the words like one would rancid milk.

He chuckled, his shoulders hunched and dug his hands deeper into his pockets. "Or I just know you well enough to realize you're upset."

"What would I have to be angry about?" She turned her back on him, going through a series of jabs and kicks. She moved with certainty and force. Angry was an understatement.

"I didn't say angry. I said upset." Alarian called upon the shadows, curling them around his fingers. "You've been holding back. It's not good for someone like you."

She stopped, dropping her hands to her side and glared, her feet in a fighting stance. "Holding back what?"

"Everything. All the emotions you feel. Even your training sessions." Alarian twisted his fingers, manipulating the shadows to move around them. "Why?"

She watched his hands carefully as Alarian continued walking circles around her, creating a wall of shadows that blocked out the light. He was waiting, painfully patient, for her to react.

"Emotions are a weakness. Do you know what my memories brought back? Feelings. And with them came lessons that have been drilled in me from the beginning. Feeling something, anything, can be your undoing. Only anger will keep you alive."

"But you're not just the spy or assassin. You were never *just* those titles. They have always been a part of you. But emotions don't make you weak. Nothing happened you need to get all stabby over."

"We're on a mission," she scoffed. "That's what this is. It's not lunch dates or flirting with buxom maidens. It's us trying to protect the realms. One of us has to keep our head on our shoulders and think straight. And to do that, I need to concentrate." She started up the movements he'd watched her run through so many times. Hell, it was intoxicating. Felicity acted like the shadows weren't there.

Alarian shook his head. "This is a mission that we're both taking very seriously, but there is nothing we could have done differently."

"Aer's heartstone," she hissed. "We could be looking for it. Maybe I should leave you here to research with Cara and—"

Alarian laughed. "This is only one town in a realm that has miles of plains and villages. Tell me, Felicity, without the research we're doing, how do you expect to find the stone? Have you found any information that is worth our time yet or that could lead us closer to our destination? By all means, please share it with me."

"You went to lunch with *her* instead of concentrating on the task at hand." She punched the dummy straight in its straw jaw, sending its makeshift head flying off the post.

Alarian dug his fingernails into his palm instead of closing the space between them to kiss her. It was a step, even if she was yelling at him, in the direction he so desperately hoped for. To break the wall she was attempting to put up. "Yes, I did. Because food gives the ability to think and fuels our bodies. You know that as well as I do." He stepped closer, bringing in the shadows tighter. "But it's more than that. It's not that you think I was being lazy. It was because I went with Cara."

Rage consumed her and he could feel every sharp edge trace down his spine. It shouldn't excite him as much as it did. In fact, the smart move would be to immediately protect himself. But he couldn't help but bait her—he enjoyed it far too much. To see the moment when *she* reappeared. It was like a drug—intoxicating.

She was in his face within a breath. "You want it to mean more, don't you? That there is something deeper. Well, there isn't. One of us is doing the work—the other would rather play."

Alarian breathed a small sigh and tilted his head, his gaze roaming over her flushed face, those piercing amber eyes. His eyes momentarily flickered to the rise and fall of her chest as she tried to catch her breath, then back to the wisp of hair that had fallen over her brow. He stopped before he brushed it from her face. "There are other games I would rather play." Then he leaned in closer, so close he could smell the mixture of perspiration that only heightened her wildflower scent. "And I would only ever want to play them with you." He pulled the shadows around him. "I'll be at the library when you're ready to get to work. Take your time."

Alarian concentrated on his location, not allowing himself to think of her or he'd go nowhere. The temptation to close that distance between them had already been too great. Thankfully, the shadows responded and dragged him away even as her pulsing confusion followed him.

Chapter 11

Felicity

Felicity seethed as she walked back to the library. She had only stayed for a little longer, and while the walk was undoubtedly good for her, it gave her too much time to curse the male who had left her behind. Insinuations. Accusations. She blamed the heat he had left in his wake on the fuel of her anger and not anything more. Because she couldn't go there, but it was sometimes hard to remember why she must resist him.

She stormed into the library, attracting more attention than she planned as heads turned with annoyed glares at the disruption. She didn't care. Even if one of those looks was from Cara and another female whispering with their heads close together and glancing at Alarian from Cara's desk.

Alarian sat at their table, a book opened in front of him. She dropped into the chair across from him, grabbing a rather thick volume from the stack titled *Myths and Legends of Talamh's Magic*.

"Did you have a nice walk?" Alarian didn't look up, but she could hear the smile in his voice.

That only frustrated her more. "You left without an offer to transport me back."

"It seemed like you needed some time for yourself. Did I misinterpret?"

She was thankful that the barrier that Illith had placed around their table stifled the sound of their conversation because her voice rose. "You shouldn't assume. Maybe I wanted to return quickly."

He looked up and met her gaze, his smile vanishing. "Then I'll make sure to offer in the future. Now, if you don't mind, I think I've found something useful, but I need to read further."

She snapped her mouth shut, hope aligning with agitation. If, after her speech, he was the first to discover helpful information she would scream. Felicity perused the book in her hands, hoping that something would appear that could rival his possible success.

Alarian chuckled, the sound nearly a whisper and she looked up for a moment only to find him still reading. What did he find funny? She stuffed her nose back into her book before she could ask. With his attention diverted, her gaze lifted and slid over his broad shoulders. His inquisitive brow. Those emerald eyes filled with mischief. The freckles that danced across his nose when his mouth...he was smiling. Her gaze met his and his smirk lengthened. Her teeth clenched, her cheeks flushed, and she pinned her attention back to the book.

He stood, walking around the table to place the tome beside hers. "It's not much, but it could help us." Alarian pointed to an excerpt and Felicity leaned over to read.

A heartstone's connection to the realm requires it to be closest to the element in which it fuels. To create the magic, it needs to funnel that energy to the earth where it resides.

"That could have multiple meanings." Felicity sucked her bottom lip between her teeth and worried it.

"If my prediction about Domhain's heartstone is correct, this could be a necessary lead," Alarian added.

"Are you going to fill me in on this prediction?" Her words came out sharper than she intended. He actually enjoyed research. There was excitement and seriousness alight in his expression. Her anger softened along the edges.

Damn—she'd messed up. Let her feelings get in the way. He was being proactive, and her jealousy had triggered her reaction.

Jealousy. *Curses.*

She hoped to ignore that he was right about her in some way, but he must have seen it. Must have noticed the spite that she tried so hard to deny.

And she hated that the workout had felt good. Even if she had kept it short, the familiarity hadn't seemed an unnecessary habit like it had following the discovery of who she was—it had been the necessity it once had been.

Alarian sat down in the chair next to her and she met his gaze. A mistake. He was too close again. His addictive rainy forest scent surrounded her. She sat back in the chair to put some distance between them.

"I've seen the previous location of Domhain's stone. It was a decade ago, before the Fomorians moved in. I went back to decipher if there were any clues that I may have missed, but the rock trolls interfered. My prediction is that Domhain's stone was originally in catacombs within the depths. Almost like a plant's root system that powered the realm."

Felicity considered his observations. "So you believe that we will find the stones within the depths of each realm? We just need to find caves and caverns?"

He shook his head. "Not necessarily. Domhain's heartstone fed the earth because that was their magic."

She blinked. "And other realms are connected to different elements. In other words, you think that Visce's stone may be in the water?"

He nodded. "It would make sense. Our magic is fed by nature."

"Then what about Dorcha and Éardrom?"

Alarian's brow scrunched in concentration.

Felicity rubbed her temples. "Dorcha is always cold, usually dark and covered in clouds...you said that Sloan knows the location of their stone?"

"Yes, he's never told me where it resides though, only that it's safe. They have always limited knowledge of their heartstone's location, so I don't know if his family will show us. It won't hurt to ask. Especially if it could give us insight in finding the location of the unknown stones." Alarian turned back to continue reading out loud.

Felicity listened intently, but the rest of the passage was information they had already had—lore of the stones and what they meant to the realms. Not a hint of their use.

She stood, walking out of their barrier to Illith. She stood beside Cara at the desk, the latter stiffening when Felicity approached. She ignored the younger female and met her step-aunt's gaze. "While these books have helped, we need more."

Illith tilted her head then nodded towards their table. When they were safely back within their bubble, she looked at the pile they had gone through. "I understand your topic is quite secretive, but what exactly are you looking for?"

Alarian glanced between the two of them and gave a brief nod.

Felicity rolled back her shoulders. "We need to know how the heartstones can affect the veil."

Illith balked, catching herself with the chair. "What? I didn't know that was possible."

"It's knowledge that not many know and for good reason," Alarian replied.

"Do you think someone wants to break down the veil using the stones?" Illith's brow bunched together but neither answered. "If that's the case, then you'll need more information on the veil. I'll ask the Fios, but I can't guarantee that it will part with such important information. It might not deem it necessary to allow anyone that knowledge."

Her step-aunt was going to ask a magical building for help? The concept was foreign to her, even after the magic she'd done and seen. Felicity swallowed. "It doesn't hurt to try because we believe others already have that information and without help, we may all be doomed."

Illith nodded. "I'll give it an attempt."

She stepped out and Felicity watched as the female called upon a burst of air that pushed her into the abyss that was the library's upper levels. Illith nearly disappeared from view.

It felt like hours as they waited. Felicity looked at Alarian more than once to gauge his expression. He was watching Illith, and while she felt the dread of failure, she couldn't help but note the hope in his eyes. The opposite of her own trepidation.

Illith landed with a thump a few minutes later. She entered the bubble and sat down at the table beside them. "The Fios has agreed to hear your request. Tonight, at the time the moon is highest, we'll need to return for the ritual. Do you agree to give what some hold dearest?"

Felicity's brow rose. Illith smiled. "It's a drop of blood. 'What some hold dearest' sounds so much more exciting though, doesn't it?"

This time Felicity couldn't ignore her words. "What do you mean that the Fios agreed?"

Illith's expression softened. "History questions are my favorite." She grabbed one of the leather tomes and opened the page to a map of Talamh. "There were once towers in every realm. They housed the heartstones of their element. These stones are like the fruit of a great root system that spreads through the entire continent, connecting the elements of each realm. The heartstones were housed within towers—air was within the topmost point, in an alcove that captured the wind and caused it to curve around the stone." Both Felicity and Alarian glanced up. "In Éardrom, it had been held in a spire for the sun to catch it. Before Domhain had lost their stone, or even before the realms were united, enemies came to our shores to steal the magic of our continent. When the towers were targeted, the continent came together to unite under one banner."

Felicity's eyes widened. "Under my grandmother," she whispered. She'd read about this war in one of the history books Kellan had given her but hadn't known that the enemy had been after their magic.

"Correct. Your grandmother led this continent for centuries. And one of her first orders was for guardians to hide the stones in safer locations within their respective realms. Hidden, and in some cases, forgotten. Many were terrified of what that would do to the realms but instead of the magic weakening, it thrived."

Alarian glanced down at the map. "Who was the enemy?"

Illith pointed to the northernmost corner of the map. "They traveled far to reach here. Attempted to enter through Éardrom until they discovered that the sides of the cliffs were too dangerous to scale. They came through Saol and found many who were easily manipulated by their promises of glory and power."

"Humans," Alarian stated matter-of-factly. "This was when then veil was closed between our worlds?"

"That's the story. Over time, many of the towers have been removed. History forgotten. I honestly haven't been asked about heartstone lore in many years." She peered over at Alarian. "When my curiosity was piqued, I searched the records to see who asked prior. Before you both, it was a young woman. She left empty handed. There is a note of only one other. The log showed that shortly after the veil was closed, a young girl arrived asking about them."

Felicity and Alarian shared a look. "No name?"

Illith shook her head. "At that time, it might not have been such an uncommon request. But they felt it was important to note that her goal was to save her mother."

"If that's true, could it be the girl from the children's tale?" The one about a young girl who had stolen Domhain's heartstone to heal her ailing mother. In the end, she had saved her but only long enough for others to come and take the stone. The mother died and the stone was lost. "If she wanted to save her mother, why would she choose the Earth Realm's stone instead of the Life Realm?"

"A question only that girl could answer. Or maybe the young woman who came decades later." Illith sighed. "Either way, if you want the information you seek, tonight you'll need to come back and prove to the Fios you're deserving. As the guardian of such knowledge, I can only assist you—the library must deem you worthy."

"We don't have a choice." The muscles in Alarian's jaw flexed. "Either way, we have to give it our best attempt."

"In the meantime, would you like to come home for dinner?" Illith closed the book and added it back to the stack at the end of the table.

"You don't—" Felicity was cut off by the female's sharp look. "Thank you. That would be nice."

"Good. Now, will you take these to Cara for me?" She pushed a stack of books that they had first started with towards Alarian.

Felicity clenched her hands into fists as he nodded and made his way across the space towards Cara.

She needed to let her jealousy go. They were meant to be friends—and currently working together to save the continent. He could flirt with whoever he wished.

Yet, as he put the books down on the table by Cara's shoulder, a sour taste filled her mouth. She forced her attention back to Illith.

Her step-aunt smiled. "I can't wait for you to meet Thomas."

Chapter 12

Alarian

Illith led them to a house with a bright purple door squished between other brick buildings. She opened the door to a cozy entry with a long hallway and a sitting room to the left. Brightly colored masks and paintings of landscapes hung on the walls.

"Beautiful home." Felicity entered first, Alarian a step behind her.

Illith smiled over her shoulder. "Make yourselves comfortable. I'll be right back." She left them in the sitting room with two sofas and four multiple-colored overstuffed chairs adorned with an abundance of cushions. Candles sat on the mantle of the fireplace with a large clock hung over it that ticked each second.

Felicity looked around the sitting room, Alarian watching as her fingers grazed over a thick wool quilt that sat over the nearest chair.

"What are you thinking?"

"She invited us for dinner. As one would invite their family."

"You *are* family, Felicity." If anything, he was the interloper. An interruption who should be kicked out. His parents were why they were in this hell of a mess in the first place.

Her gaze flickered around the room, and he could sense trust mixed with instinct to search for the unseen enemy. He knew they were safe here and not only because Prince Kellan trusted his aunt. He leaned in and brushed the hair from her shoulder. "When you were young, did you ever think about leaving the Tower and settling down? Or was it always the next mission?"

She stiffened. The question had the opposite than intended effect but at least she was no longer searching for the quickest escape. "The next mission. Always. Settle down for what?"

He shrugged. "Some younglings dream of marriage and such. Plan out their weddings—"

"Are you assuming because I'm female that I would be picking out dresses and centerpieces?"

Alarian snorted. "No. But now I want to see that."

"I didn't even like dresses until after I became an initiate. Before that, I never had a chance to wear them and thought they were gaudy and looked like they would only be in the way."

He shrugged. "I thought about it."

"The rakish ex-prince thought about settling down?"

A squeal and grind of gears had them turning to find a male rolling himself into the room on a chair with wheels. "So, this is the Princess Felicity and the ex-prince Alarian." The laughter in his eyes put Alarian at ease despite his matter-of-fact words. "Excuse me for not giving a proper bow, but unfortunately I'm unable to."

Felicity's eyes widened. "I would never—"

"He's kidding." Illith appeared from around the corner and thumped her husband in the back of the head. "His first instinct is to state the obvious—then use sarcasm to disarm you."

"It worked," Felicity murmured.

The male chuckled. "Illith knows me too well. I'm Thomas. Welcome to our home."

"Thank you for having us." Alarian cleared his throat. "If you prefer, I could leave. I wouldn't take offense considering—"

"Don't you dare." Thomas grinned. "If our princess and my wife trust you, then I must." He nodded towards Illith. "I'm in the middle of preparing dinner. Why don't you come to the kitchen and we can chat while I finish."

"Can I assist you?" Alarian moved in beside Thomas as the male used his hands to turn a smooth gear which propelled the wheels forwards.

"Are you asking because I don't look capable or because you want to help?" Thomas' brow rose.

Alarian snorted. "You and my nana, Meira, would get along well."

"Aw." Thomas added, "Is she also in a chair?"

"No. Though I'm impressed by this contraption."

Thomas went down the hall and entered a wide-open kitchen with a few areas of lower counter tops so he could reach from his seat. "It was helpful after the injury. Not much else to do but sit in one place when your legs no longer work."

Alarian glanced behind to see Illith and Felicity talking, the former smiling from ear-to-ear while Felicity timidly attempted to keep up with the female's robust energy. He heard Kellan's name and knew it was best to let them catch up, so he made his way to the sink and washed his hands. "What are we having?"

"You cook? A prince with skills? Unheard of."

"Ex-prince, remember? And don't let Felicity hear you say that. She already questions her capability." He kept his tone even.

"Ah, I see." Thomas peered over at the two females. "Illith is elated she's here."

"She seems to be."

"I felt it as soon as she received Prince Kellan's letter and even more so when she saw Felicity this morning."

"Felt it?" Alarian snapped to attention at the choice of words. "What do you mean?"

"My Cridhe." Thomas winked. "Or have you never heard of the heart bond? I know many think it a myth."

Alarian shook his head. He'd heard of the bond between two individuals, but the term itself wasn't commonly used. "Many believe in the bond to some capacity. They just think it's impossible to achieve." He swallowed and kept himself from looking towards the hall. "My parents were bonded. Two friends of mine are as well."

Thomas' mouth pursed. "Well, the Cridhe bond isn't impossible, but it isn't given by Magic lightly."

"I've never heard of the term Cridhe before?"

"It's the formal name for the heart bond. Most don't want to give it a name, but it is as old as Magic itself."

"What do you mean?" He'd only ever heard tales and stories of the bonded. He never considered asking his parents. Partly because he hadn't wanted to consider the concept before. If Magic offered something so precious to them, then was it worth it?

Thomas grinned. "Grab those tomatoes. The rolls are ready to go in the oven and if we time it right, we can have a delicious stew to go with our meal."

Alarian didn't hesitate to comply. He needed more information on the bond to understand what was going on between him and Felicity.

"Cut the potatoes while I talk." Thomas pointed towards the knives where a stack of potatoes sat. Alarian got right to work, and Thomas watched him for a few moments before he was satisfied with what he was doing. "The bond is an offering from the magic of the earth itself. Magic is a part of the land, and since we are fed by the earth, it is connected to us. It cannot be forced, tricked, or made into existence."

"But why are some offered it and others not? So many I know are madly in love and never had Magic connect them in such a way."

Thomas laughed. "You would make a great romantic scholar. I'd know. I am one."

"Do you work at the Fios?"

Thomas shook his head. "No, I don't, but it's where I met Illith. The Fios is the collection of knowledge. It doesn't collect scholars."

"So, you're the writer of books."

Thomas grinned. "Particularly on the subject of the bonds created by Magic."

Alarian stilled. Could this male have information on their cause as well as answer the question to why he sensed Felicity's emotions?

He reined back his excitement. They needed to be careful as leaving a trail of their search could be dangerous. So far, he didn't think anyone was following them but that would not always be the case. "Go on."

"A bond between two fae is a connection that Magic recognizes. It's believed to be offered when love appears against all odds. If everything is stacked against love, then Magic sees them as a true match and therefore offers the bond. It doesn't look at an individual's morals. Villain or hero." When Alarian stopped working and listened to the male, Thomas grinned. "It doesn't give you more power over others, no matter how one might believe it. That's not the meaning of the bond."

Alarian thought of his parents. As much as they both were evil, their love had been impressive, and he knew their bond had been deep. Against all odds though? "How does it decide if love is against all odds?"

"It depends on the progression of the relationship. If there were personal or outside forces making it near impossible for them to be together and yet they found a way to each other, Magic recognizes it."

"What are the effects?" He wondered why he felt Felicity's emotions if the bond wasn't in place? But that was a question he shouldn't ask aloud.

"Usually there is a sensation of emotions and feelings—a connection of sorts. If the bond is taken by both parties, then a second gift will often appear that is personal to the two of them. In my case, Illith and I are able to find each other no matter how far the distance between us. I believe it's because she found me after my injury. She was the one to nurse me back to health." Thomas placed the quartered tomatoes into a bowl and reached for the root vegetables.

"If one feels the other's emotions, but there isn't a bond offered, do you know why?" Alarian whispered, his gaze darting towards the hall for a moment. Well, it seemed he couldn't keep his mouth shut after all.

Thomas paused and stared at him. "That's rare."

"Meaning?"

"That only one of you has accepted your feelings and connection with the other. Magic realizes that too and is prepared to offer the bond if the other member comes to the same conclusion."

Alarian breathed a long sigh. "So, it could stay like this forever?"

"You don't sound like you have hope that they will pick you."

He didn't know how to reply. It was bad enough he spoke the question out loud. There were too many variables. "I wouldn't force her too. Is there a way to block it?"

Thomas nodded. "It takes practice and concentration. You must imagine a barrier between her emotions and yourself. You also have to want it. If magic doubts your intentions, it won't block the bond. It will take time, so practice often. Just be glad you know that Magic agrees you're meant to be together." Thomas put down the knife and reached across the counter, resting a hand on Alarian's arm. "Don't give up hope." His eyes crinkled at the sound of his wife's laughter. "Besides, I think you'll see that stubbornness can only last so long."

"When it comes to her, I don't doubt her ability to hold back." Alarian finished the last of the potatoes, hoping that he hadn't made it obvious that he was speaking of Felicity. "Thank you. It helps to understand. You should write a book on the Cridhe."

Thomas snorted. "And deal with the ramifications? There are books within the Fios that are restricted to those who can read them. People have been searching for the answer to love for eons. If they knew achieving a bond would require a challenge to their love, they would create it in an attempt to trick Magic. There are fanatics out there. Let them learn as they go. Some things are not meant to be read but discovered on their own."

"How did you learn all of this?"

Thomas chuckled. "Curiosity."

The next question—he had to be careful how he worded it. "How about the way that Magic bonds with each realm?"

Thomas' brow furrowed and he tilted his head. "Have you heard of the beating heart of the realms?"

He nodded, uncertain if he would tempt fate and speak.

"They are what power the realms and keep the magic flowing. Without them—well, I'm certain you've seen Domhain? The stories don't lie. The heart-stones are important to each realm since they feed the continent."

"And why would people take the risk and remove them?"

"It would be a selfish or desperate individual who covets power beyond what one or even a group should control. It's funny what people will grasp onto out of purely self-centered reasons."

"I agree—but what if they have other uses for the stones?"

Thomas blinked. "What else is there to do with them beyond to protect, heal, or connect us to the element's magic? Dorcha's stone can cover someone in darkness. Domhain's helps someone grow and heal. I don't even want to imagine what Saol's could do."

It looked like they didn't have a choice. If they wanted the knowledge, then the ritual was their only choice. "Thank you. You've—"

Felicity moved in beside him, holding two goblets of wine. She held one out for him. "It smells good."

"It should." Thomas nodded at the glass. "Illith, where is mine? She walks in and hands one off to her beau and—"

"Thomas," Illith warned.

Felicity's face brightened to a level of red that Alarian hadn't seen before. He couldn't help but chuckle even as she handed over the glass and said, "We're friends."

"For now," Thomas mumbled.

Felicity brightened further.

Chapter 13

Felicity

They arrived back to the Fios a little before midnight. Thomas had stayed behind to allow them privacy for what needed to be done. Illith unlocked the large door, the creak of wood echoed through the entrance as it was swung open. A chill ran up Felicity's spine.

"Go to the center—I'll meet you there," Illith ordered over her shoulder as she stalked towards her desk.

Felicity and Alarian shared a glance before doing as they were told. She took the time to take in the expansive shelves of books that surrounded the walls of the tower's circular structure. When they reached the center of the library, it was unsettling how never-ending it seemed. "It really is impressive."

"That it is," Alarian breathed.

Illith sighed loudly as she appeared carrying a small wooden bowl, a bottle of ink, a quill, and a piece of parchment. "Let's begin. We are on a bit of a time crunch. You'll need to write your one request for information here. Then you both will speak it aloud, place it into the bowl, then add a drop of blood from each of you."

Felicity reached for the parchment and froze. "What do we write?"

"Be as specific as possible."

Alarian took the ink and quill. "We can do it together."

Felicity nodded, uncertain where to start. She had so many questions but to narrow it down to one seemed impossible.

"Remember, we must have this done by the time the moon is over the Fios." Illith peered at the large clock that sat above her desk near the entrance. "You have until the next toll of the bell. Half an hour at the most."

Felicity and Alarian made their way to the nearest table. "How are we meant to come up with only one request?"

Alarian dipped the quill in the ink. "Let's start with what we need. Information." He wrote the word down on the parchment.

"The heartstones use in the opening of the veil."

"We need to be specific. Should we mention the veil to the human lands?" He added a few more phrases to the list.

Felicity glanced at his scribbles. *Open veil. Necessities. How?*

"What if there are other veils that can be opened?"

"I feel like Fiadh is the key to that answer, but I don't know why." Alarian dipped the quill again.

"Why Fiadh?"

Alarian shrugged. "Why else is she a part of all of this? I understand my mother wants power—control. I can only imagine why. But what is Fiadh's motive?"

She hadn't considered what the witch wanted. Only the ramifications if they succeeded. There were so many unknowns—but the wants of the traitors couldn't be answered by the Fios.

After some bickering, words were crossed out, others added, and they finally had their request written down.

They headed back to the center of the room. "We're ready."

"Good." Illith held out the bowl. "You both need to hold onto the parchment and read the question aloud before you place it into the bowl."

Alarian's fingers brushed hers and they both read clearly. "May we be deemed access to texts that will inform us on the heartstones use to open the veil so that we may protect the continent from harm?"

"Good. Drop it in."

They simultaneously let go, the paper dropping into the bowl. "Now a drop of blood."

Felicity removed the dagger at her hip and pricked the tip of her finger. She pinched, until a drop of blood fell onto the parchment. Alarian mimicked the movement in quick succession so his skin didn't heal before it dropped.

Illith began walking away with the bowl.

"What do we do now?" Felicity whispered after the departing female.

"Wait. I'll return with an answer." Air wrapped around Illith and she rose up to disappear into the unending darkness.

It felt like hours as they waited in tense silence, but the bell had only tolled once by the time Illith returned with one book held against her chest. She placed the tome on the table beside Alarian while Felicity continued pacing.

When Alarian reached for the book, Illith stopped him, placing her hand over the cover. "The knowledge granted is for both of your eyes only. The library has deemed you acceptable, but only for your cause to protect the realms. Nothing more. Do you understand?"

"We will tell no one what we discover," Alarian vowed, and Felicity nodded in agreement.

Illith breathed a long sigh.

Felicity took her seat. "Thank you. We appreciate your silence on the matter."

"Of course. The library wants as few as possible to know this truth. It's dangerous in the wrong hands. You should know that if anyone finds out you're aware of what this book contains, it could put your lives in danger."

"We understand." Felicity glanced at the book, then back to her. "How is the library enchanted?"

Illith smiled, her body relaxing. "By the heartstone. And before you ask, no it isn't here. Hasn't been since before my appointment as Guardian of the Fios." She turned. "I'll give you some time to read before I return the book."

Felicity and Alarian both stared at the tome in front of them. He inhaled. "Are you ready?"

"As I'll ever be."

Alarian opened the book, and their elbows brushed as they huddled together. Felicity's jaw dropped. *Shit.* They turned the pages, scanning each one with a sinking heart. "I can't...can you read this?"

Alarian rubbed a hand over his jaw. "No."

Felicity signaled Illith over. "Do you understand different languages?"

Illith perked up. "Which one?"

"I don't know."

"Or it's a code." Alarian ran his finger over the lines of text. "This doesn't make any sense at all. It doesn't follow any linguistic structure I've come across. Many of these symbols don't seem to have context."

Felicity was about to push the book towards Illith when she remembered. "Can you see if you recognize it?"

The female shook her head. "The Fios didn't grant me permission."

"Can we ask it to?" Felicity glanced upwards into the darkness. "I know we can't take the book with us. It wouldn't be safe, but we don't have enough time to sit here and try to decipher the meaning either." It wasn't a large volume, but they didn't have weeks to spend here on this text. She eyed the unintelligible manuscript again—weeks was being generous. She wasn't a scholar.

"It won't allow me. I'm a Guardian. The Fios sees me as such, and I'm meant to protect the information, not read dangerous volumes." She breathed a sigh. "Besides, it is too late now. Another request cannot be made until the next phase of the moon."

Damnit. "How long until then?"

Illith's brow furrowed. "Three days' time."

"Thomas." Alarian's jaw worked. "He's a scholar, correct?"

Illith swallowed. She closed her eyes for a moment then nodded. "Yes, he is."

"Do you think he could decipher this if he had access to it?"

The silence was deafening. Felicity resisted begging, something that, in this instance, wasn't beyond her. But she could see it in the female's expression. The impending reality battling with the need to protect someone she loved. If anyone discovered Thomas had such information, it would be dangerous. But the fate of the continent—

"He probably could, yes." Illith stood. "The Fios would grant him access. It has in the past, especially since he has authored tomes within the very location where this book came from."

"We need to talk to him. Ask his permission." Alarian closed the book. "And then, if you're both comfortable, come up with a way to share what he finds with us."

"It's for the good of the realms." Illith took the book. "I'll return it to where it belongs for now." Her shoulders were slumped, concern marring her expression as her magic propelled her upward.

"Why couldn't the library have given us a way to decipher the words?" Felicity shook her head. "This only puts more people in danger, and we don't have time."

Alarian reached out and squeezed her hand. "There is only so much Magic can do."

"We pretend like it's infinite. All powerful." She felt the sensation of his skin against hers. Maybe it was the wine they consumed that was befuddling her mind. That had her concentrating on his touch more than the problems before them.

When Illith appeared, Felicity expected Alarian to pull away, but he didn't. Instead, he wrapped his fingers through hers.

"You're welcome to our home tomorrow morning for breakfast. We'll discuss plans with Thomas."

"And ask—" Felicity started but the female shook her head.

"He will do it. I know my husband." Illith straightened with a small smile. "But I will ask this—we will never share that you have this knowledge. Can I expect you to do the same for him?"

"Yes," Felicity and Alarian said in unison. She felt the sensation of the scar against Alarian's palm. An oath the two of them still shared.

Felicity bit her bottom lip. "Do you want a blood oath?" Alarian's hand flinched.

Illith smiled and shook her head. "The fact you offered is enough for me." She glanced at their joint hands. "I trust you both. Maybe that's foolish, but I do."

"Thank you." Alarian gave her hand one final squeeze, then let go and headed towards the door together.

"See you tomorrow." Illith nodded after she locked up, then turned in the direction of her home.

Felicity and Alarian walked in silence. The evening was quiet, revelers already home after a long day at the Inventors Fair. Felicity wrapped her arms around herself to fight off the chill while she tried to think of something to say. "What were you two talking about?"

"Who and when?" Alarian's brow rose. He removed his jacket and without a word, placed it over her shoulders.

She gripped tight to the fabric, trying to ignore his scent. "You and Thomas before we joined you in the kitchen." Felicity peered at him from the corner of her eye.

Alarian opened the door of the inn for her. Felicity watched him as she passed, waiting for his answer.

There was a battle in his expression, but she didn't press. "We were discussing bonded partners. He'd studied the concept."

Felicity paused on the step. "What? Why?"

"He and Illith are bonded. Besides my parents, and Lian and Dimitri, I hadn't met anyone else who was bonded before."

Felicity considered the response, moving again up the steps. A creak sounded and she smiled to herself. Even though he was raised among the shadows, he still sometimes was heavy footed. Alarian grimaced when the wood groaned under his next step.

"Interesting." The topic made her smile. "I asked Kellan about it once. Your mother said that she and your father were attempting to marry you off to ensure you were bonded as soon as possible."

"That's because she thought she could control a connection that's given by trust."

"I mostly remembered that Kellan had a small panic attack when I asked. Now I understand why—he didn't want to explain it to his little sister."

Alarian chuckled. "I would have loved to overhear that conversation. The way he doted on you as a child, I can only imagine that the idea you were a grown female must have been difficult for him to comprehend."

"He did?" She stalled at the door, staring at Alarian.

"Did what?" He blinked in confusion.

"How did you know he doted on me?"

Alarian cleared his throat, running his hand through his hair. "When my parents called me to Éardrom, I'd met Prince Kellan and, for a brief moment, you."

"You did?" Felicity stared at him. "How could you have never mentioned that until now?"

"It was short lived. A meal, that's all. Even with your memories, I doubt you'd remember me. It was in celebration of your tenth birthday. Once the dinner was over, I went to Koselig for the rest of the visit and didn't see either of you."

"Oh." Felicity bit her lip, her head beginning to ache. There was no reason to try, but she attempted to grasp the memory that wasn't there.

Alarian sighed and seemed to realize the direction of her thoughts because he changed the conversation back to their previous topic. "As for the bond, I guess it's difficult to find books on the subjects."

She bit her lip. Why was he curious about the bond? "I think I'm going to get up early tomorrow and head to the training ring before we meet Illith and Thomas," she said instead of asking what was really on her mind.

Alarian's expression warred with a smile. "Mind if I join you?"

She faced him and leaned against the door. Part of her still wasn't certain if there was a reason for her to train, but she couldn't deny that the few moments in the ring that afternoon had helped. With an inhale, she met Alarian's gaze—his scent of a misty forest surrounding her. So close. One step and he could have her pinned against the wall. She swallowed. "Yes, you're welcome to come."

He inched a little closer. "Magic or no magic?"

She lifted her chin to look up at him as he stopped a half step away from her. "Magic," she breathed.

"Why the change of heart?"

There was no answer to that question. Not truly. The word had just slid from her mouth because she had forgotten how to think when he was this close. Magic, yes—that. She had it. Should use it. "I need to be prepared. We don't know what's to come."

"Good." He reached for the doorknob. Her body stilled as his arm brushed hers. A rush of electricity raced through her body as she stood frozen. He grasped the knob and turned it, the door opening. She straightened just in time before falling back. "Ready for bed?"

Her heart raced as she stepped backwards into the room. He followed, their eyes locked on one another. Felicity stopped when her legs touched the edge of the bed. Shit—did he want to touch her as much as she wanted him to?

Her eyes widened as shadows rose and curved around his body, and Alarian disappeared from view.

Her gasp was audible as the shadows cleared, a pile of clothes surrounding a fox. "You're turning into the fox? Really?"

He tilted his head innocently, green eyes the only sign that it was him amidst the gray coat.

She sighed, trying hard to ignore the annoyance that had settled in her stomach. He was probably right. They had a long journey, and to ruin their relationship with whatever was hanging between them...

"Fine. Goodnight, Alarian."

Then, without turning around, she removed her cloak and let it pool at her feet. Even if he had made a choice and she agreed with it, she couldn't help it. She reached for the waist of her pants. There was a small growl behind her, and Felicity peered over her shoulder to see that Alarian had turned to stare at the wall.

She couldn't help but smile to herself.

Chapter 14
Kellan

*B*lood pooled at his feet. Murky gray against the white marble floor. His arms were chained behind his back. He'd been here before. Was well versed in this type of pain and torture. Just enough to keep him compliant without breaking their agreement with his father.

His father. Who had been swept out of that room. Still chained. Screaming. Gone. It felt like weeks had passed since, but it had only been two days. A blink of time.

The witch was placing different objects around his prone form. She didn't mind his blood. Not as she took some of it for whatever hell she was creating. Kellan had heard the word muttered. Knew what she was capable of. What her gift could do. He didn't see it as a gift. Not when it was planned to be used on him by his captors. The same two individuals who had exiled his father. Had risen a coup and sent assassins after his half-sister and stepmother. All while he had bled here on this cold stone floor, a healer sent to ensure he remained alive. And somehow, just conscious.

"Is it done?" Heeled shoes click clacked across the marble, the sensation rumbling in Kellan's head.

"Almost."

"You must hurry. There is only a matter of time before the people revolt. We need to ensure they don't know what they are revolting against. In the end, everyone will understand that what we have planned is vital."

The witch stilled. "And what is that again?"

Marquette—even her name made Kellan want to scream—whirled around to face the witch. "Are you having cold feet?"

"I'm giving my life. I might need a reminder as to why I'm doing this."

Darkness inked into his peripheral again. It did that sometimes. Beckoned him to a release that usually was interrupted by prodding fingers and a painful rush of magic. He willed himself to remain awake. For whatever this *was.*

Kellan felt more than he saw Marquette turn her attention to him even though she wasn't speaking to him. "Your kind will finally get what they deserve. What they need. And so will we. You know our plan. What we shall do with your sacrifice is fix all that has been wrong in this world for decades. At least since the death of my parents. So many unnecessary losses."

"And this is the only way?"

"They won't fall into line if they think we're the villains. The curse you enact will solidify our rule and allow us to move forward. The final opportunity to rise up and do what you've always wanted. In your name, we will succeed. And you will be there in the end to see it done. Correct?"

The witch didn't hesitate. "Yes."

"This is for them. Those who died and suffered unnecessarily. For your parents. Your daughter."

The witch moved with a renewed fervor as she walked around muttering incantations and drawing symbols he couldn't decipher. Not with the hair in his eyes. The limited viewpoint on this floor. Just a week ago, they had celebrated his sister's tenth year here. It had been a joyous celebration. Now the memory was darkened by what followed.

He tried to fight the pain. To grasp onto his consciousness. To find the magic that had been drained away by the iron at his wrists.

Marquette laughed at his attempts, the clank of the chains more like a tinkling bell than a fight for freedom. "Pitiful. There will be nothing of you left, Prince. Soon, you will be nameless. Erased."

***

Kellan pinched his eyes closed, rubbing his temples. It had been another long night, and his only reprieve was Avyanna reminding him she knew his name. Was there for him. Kellan stared at the pile of papers in front of him. All the notes. Considerations. Ramblings. The door creaked as it opened and Avyanna entered. "How's it going?"

The sun had set just an hour before. Tonight, he was hoping for a letter from his sister. It might not be there until morning. The wait was painful, and he couldn't stop himself from worrying about her.

"It's going." He rubbed the back of his neck.

Between his sister, father, the people he was supposed to protect, the seemingly never-ending trials, he kept looking for signs of the realm weakening without the stone.

Avyanna took a seat in the chair in front of his desk and held out a letter, the seal already snapped.

Kellan reached across, taking hold. But it wasn't a seal he recognized. "What is this?"

"My parents finally got a letter to me."

His brow furrowed and he unfolded the missive. "And?"

She nodded towards his hands. "You can read it."

He skimmed—then reread word for word. Paused. Read it again. With a blink, he looked back to his fiancée. "Shit."

Avyanna crossed her arms over his chest. "They caught sight of Fiadh. I have no doubt that it's true. The offer though..."

The witch was rarely far from Marquette, but that didn't mean she wasn't present in the realm on the traitor's business. She'd been an enigma, a dangerous one since her gift was mind reading. Thankfully, it didn't work well if multiple people were in one room.

That wasn't as shocking as what followed. An offer from her parents to be their spies. The dangers that could possess—the sacrifice it might be. "I don't want to put this on them. On you. It's way too dangerous."

"They know."

"This letter could have been intercepted and someone may have already found them out." It didn't outright state their intentions, but the insinuation was enough. There was an attempt at a code but since he was able to decipher it with one glance, so could anyone curious enough. "I can't..." He shook his head.

Avyanna straightened. "If they want to, then we should find a way. We need someone with insider information, Kellan. I know you're aware of it as much as I am, and I can't go with my current patient load. There are few we could trust within the fortress. But my parents are in the center of it all. We can guide them on how to be discreet."

Kellan covered his face with his hands, his expression tight. No. It was a simple word to say—but the truth rang through. They didn't have a pick of spies, and they needed to know if Marquette was also present and if Fiadh stayed. "They are only to respond if they catch sight of Fiadh or Marquette. Nothing more. It's too dangerous otherwise."

Her features were rigid, but she nodded. "Fine. Did Sloan's letter come last night? Any news on your father?"

"I received word but no news on my father. They reached the first small group of islands. It might be a few more nights before we hear back."

She stood and came around the desk. "Felicity and Alarian?"

"Nothing yet."

Avyanna sighed and he noted the notch between her brow was indented, the only sign she'd allow of the stress she felt. The same he did. "They're all right."

He nodded. "Word would have come otherwise." Maybe not that quickly, but he told himself the lie anyway.

"There is something else I needed to discuss with you." She removed a piece of parchment from her pocket.

"Since when do your dresses have pockets?" His brow rose.

"I saw Felicity's and had the pattern copied for my own." She slipped her hand into another pocket and withdrew a dagger. "Figured I might need access to this."

The blade made him smile. "Practice has been good for you, I see." They had started to train together. He showed her how to disarm an opponent, twist out of holds—self-defense that may become necessary. She hated the idea of killing anyone—a healer through and through—but they had both agreed she may need to defend herself. But he hoped she would never have to use it.

She handed him the parchment, and he unfolded it. A list of names was scrawled upon it. "What is this?"

Avyanna gestured for him to turn the page over and he found a crude drawing of a leaf-heavy tree, but instead of roots it was the twisted bare branches of a dead tree reflected beneath. "It looks like the tree of life—but also death?"

Avyanna cleared her throat. "Every single one of the surviving and dead prisoners had this branded on their skin above their hearts."

Kellan's brow furrowed, and he brushed a finger over the ink. "But what does it mean?"

Avyanna slumped into the seat across from him, tucking a strand of hair behind her ear. "They were forced to repeat words as it was burned in their skin. If they didn't repeat the words, they were tortured. Some died from it, but they were still branded with the tree."

"What the hell—"

"Exactly." Avyanna wiped a tear from her face. "I'm trying to find out the exact words used. So far, many don't remember much beyond the pain. Others don't know word for word. I have more to ask."

"All of them?" It seemed monstrous on its own but if all of them were forced into such an agreement, what did it mean?

"Yes. I hadn't realized right away. Many hid it, others didn't think to mention it over their other illnesses or pain. I just realized today there were multiple brands. Then I was told the story." Tears slid freely now.

"Shit—Avyanna." He pulled a handkerchief from his pocket and stood, moving around his desk to kneel beside her.

She took the square and dabbed under her eyes. "They would be dragged into a shack. Forced to repeat an incantation as they were tied naked before the hot coals. Fires—" She shook her head, trying to form words. "It would be so hot, but they wouldn't realize why. Two humans led the ordeal while guards stood over them. Those with magic would already be wearing manacles to weaken them. Salt would be added to ensure it remained on their skin."

He shuddered at the implication. "Humans? You mean witches?"

Her jaw clenched. "I believe so."

"Why would they do this?" Maybe it would uncover what they were attempting to do in that ravine. A horrifying thought occurred to him. "Wait, the children too?"

"Yes." Avyanna trembled. He quickly wrapped her in his arms. "I asked to see some of the bodies preparing for the funeral pyre. Those that families had yet to claim. They all had this insignia in the same spot. It was on all of them."

Kellan pulled her into his arms, cradling her, unwilling to let her go. She had witnessed so much. A healer. His fiancée. Sure, he knew he couldn't always protect her but that didn't mean he wouldn't try. No one should ever have to see the atrocities of the world. "I'm so sorry."

"It was nothing you did."

"I know. I just wish I could have stopped it sooner. All those people..." He trailed off for a moment. "So many dead and lost."

"But so many saved." She kissed his cheek. "Remember that darling. Even through it all, so many were saved. You couldn't do more than you have."

He pressed his eyes closed, waiting for the pain to ease. Hoping it would. As usual, it didn't. But this wasn't about him. "What do you need from me? Extra hands? More supplies?" He would never ask her to step away and let others handle it. Healing was her passion. Always had been—and she'd been so excited at the opportunity to do what she loved.

"No. We have the supplies we need." She closed her eyes, taking a calming breath. "We are doing everything we can. All of us."

Kellan kissed the top of her head. "I love you."

"And I love you." She nuzzled into his chest. "I think we both need to rest."

"But Felicity's letter—"

"Will be waiting for you in the morning," she intervened. "It might be hours until it arrives, and I know you've been having difficulty sleeping as it is."

He couldn't deny that. The nightmares—they had been filled with unbidden memories, as though his subconscious was searching for clues within his past. The witch's face remained unseen. The spell unuttered. "I'll try." Avyanna slid off his lap, dragging his hand with her. He stood, following her willingly down the hall.

"About the letter to your parents..."

"Tomorrow." She squeezed his hand. "That can also wait until tomorrow. Tonight, I just want you to hold me."

To feel safe, she didn't have to say. Kellan pulled her to his side while they walked.

Chapter 15

Felicity

Felicity looked at the passing landscape with the familiar pang. Domhain had always made her feel useless. Since the first time she'd entered the realm on a mission years before, the idea that the land had shifted and changed from a glorious green and bountiful harvest to a rock garden was frustrating. That it was likely due to someone's selfish desires made it unfathomable.

Alarian pulled his mount to a stop and Laochra did the same, shaking her head with impatience. Since they had entered the realm, the mare had been uneasy. "Which town are we staying at tonight?"

It had been two days of travel since the Fios. After they set up camp, they would challenge each other in training sessions that she had actually looked forward to, then slept under the stars on the rocky ground. The nights of discomfort usually left her battling anxious thoughts and sore muscles, so a soft place to rest sounded wonderful.

"Vaen—one of the local outposts."

She nodded. She had been there on a few occasions for Tower missions. Alarian had said he didn't trust most of the outposts since his father had been from here. But a contact—a friend—he called him, had a place for them to stay before they reached the center of the realm where the stone was said to have been stolen. He told her how his recent attempt to garner information had been thwarted by the Fomorians. She wasn't looking forward to dealing with the stone trolls.

At least it would be a distraction from the waiting. They had left their letter for Kellan early in the morning before leaving the inn at Aer to update her brother on their unsuccessful trip to the Fios. Thomas and Alarian had agreed upon a location to leave a letter after they confirmed if Thomas had been accepted by the Fios. They just had to wait. And hope—which was becoming more difficult each day they didn't have something to show for their hard work.

"I should warn you, Braum can be a bit much at times."

Her brow rose. "Oh?"

"Relentless flirt. Loud." Alarian looked her way. "But harmless and loyal to a fault. Just be prepared for him to try his luck. It's almost like a second instinct for him."

"Hm. Sounds like someone I know." She stared forward, careful not to look at him as she was reminded of their last night in the inn when he'd turned into a damn fox. After he'd built the fire within her, he put as much distance between them as he could. And for some reason it stung. "How do you know him?"

"We spent a lot of time together when I left Éardrom. I liked the idea that I was hiding right under my father's nose." Alarian shrugged.

"Oh—so he would have some embarrassing stories to share?"

Alarian winced. "No."

She laughed. "I'll have to ask."

They reached the outpost and headed towards the small lean-to where they tied the horses out of the relentless sun. Even with the chill, it was currently stagnant—the air dry and uncomfortable. They took care of their horses, Felicity glancing about to see if anyone else was present. "One horse. That means everyone here is local."

Since food was scarce, there was usually only one horse at each outpost. They would call an alarm if necessary—but with the towns spread apart and no easy access to resources, there was little they could do if there was an attack except send out a warning by rider.

"That's a good thing." Alarian finished untacking his gelding.

She glanced over her shoulder at the half-built homes, thatched roofs, stone outlines in the ground making up a semblance of a wall to an otherwise ramshackle space. There were only seven buildings total and most had drapes for doors and fabric along the edges for privacy.

Alarian led the way down the path and Felicity inhaled deeply as he came to a stop in front of a home in the center of the outpost across from the only shop. A crimson curtain hung in the entryway of the all-too-familiar building. "Well, this is going to be awkward."

Alarian's brow rose but a voice called out before he could ask. "Linny?"

Braum must have heard them. Felicity pinched her eyes closed as a tall man pulled aside the blue curtain he used as a door. "To hell and back—it is you." He grinned, leaning into the wooden doorframe as he brushed his blond hair from his tan face. When he noticed Alarian, his grin widened. "Well, isn't this a coincidence—Rian, you're back."

"Linny?" Alarian glanced at Felicity. "You two know each other?"

"Of course we do. Well—a version of her." His grin lengthened at the pointed ears and other features she'd kept hidden for years. "The voice is the same and of course she's gorgeous as always. Nice to see your true colors there, Lin."

She swallowed. "It's—" She hesitated. Linny had been her alias for so long, it was hard to let go of it. "Full disclosure, my name's not Linny." She nodded to him. "Just like your name isn't Haven."

"Figured." Braum winked. "Linny didn't fit you."

"Haven didn't fit you either," she murmured.

"Aw, honey, don't wound me. You know I'm always willing to be your haven."

She rolled her eyes, even as Alarian growled. She ignored them both knowing it would get them nowhere if they started a pissing match. "Can we come in?"

Braum grinned. "Of course. Welcome." He stepped aside to allow Felicity in, Alarian a step behind.

The house—if that's what you could call it—was one of the lucky ones. Three full walls, the fourth was made from two stacks of stones, with a long board across the top to allow the thatched roof over a portion of the home and a woven drape to create some privacy. There were two rooms, the bedroom separated by a gauzy blue curtain. "Your letter arrived yesterday, so I didn't get enough food for three."

Alarian dropped his pack on a table and removed a few dried and fresh goods. "Brought along some supplies. Figured we could cook tonight."

Braum brightened. "Please and thank you. I know Linny here isn't much of a cook."

Alarian paused what he was doing, cleared his throat. "You didn't say how you knew each other."

Felicity took a seat at the table. "He was one of my informants."

"I thought you must have died. It's been months since I heard from you last. Glad I was wrong." Braum tilted his head. "And seeing as you're with the ex-prince, what does that make you exactly, Linny? Care to share?"

"No." She thrummed her fingers against the table.

"Always so secretive. Like this one." He nudged Alarian before eyeing the provisions. "You got enough vegetables for something tasty. How about I get some bread from the shop? I'll be back in no time. There are usually a few loaves ready for tomorrow morning."

Felicity got to her feet. "I can get it if you like?"

"Naw. You've been traveling." He glanced at Alarian who was glaring daggers at their host. "Seems you two have a few things to chat about. Might want to make sure he doesn't kill me." His grin widened. "Maybe figure out who is taking the bed. Room for two there."

He laughed as he left, and Felicity shook her head at his familiar humor. "I should have known."

"Informant?" Alarian asked, steel in his tone.

"Yes. Had a lot of missions here. He gave me intel when necessary. Haven—well, Braum—was my contact. Obviously, we both thought he had valid information. I didn't know he was permanently based since I've met him in different parts of the realm."

"And you two...like each other?"

She removed three apples from the pack. They could make for a nice dessert even if she preferred to give them to the horses. "You mentioned his antics so I think you can decipher that he likes just about anyone."

"You didn't mention you'd been to this particular outpost."

She shrugged. "Didn't think it was necessary. I've been to a few of the outposts around here."

"Oh—so you knew where his home was?"

Another shrug. If he wasn't going to outright ask what he was insinuating, then she wouldn't answer. Just like she didn't want to know how much had been between him and Cara.

Alarian sighed. "You mentioned in Aer during the solstice party that the stories weren't about you."

"What?" She paused, tilting her head.

"I asked if the stories I heard about an assassin and spy could be about you and you said no."

Felicity's brow furrowed. "I was in Saol. You never came there, and I certainly didn't travel as far north as Éardrom."

"But those stories I head were from Braum." His brow lifted. "Which then would mean—"

"That he probably had multiple contacts." Her small grin couldn't be fought back. "And there is a chance some of them are about me."

Alarian chuckled. "I knew it."

She glanced up, searching absently about the space, wanting to change the subject. "Do you think it's safe now to check?"

Since they left their missive to Kellan, they hadn't had a chance to check for an update. Alarian did not trust checking through shadow magic in plain sight. And even now—

"I wish I could. I don't know if it's safe. We can inquire from my aunt's house."

Wait... "Your aunt? We trust her?" Was it the same aunt Felicity had ensured her husband's death? Advisor Gullist hadn't been faithful to her, but would she care if she lost a male she loved?

"I trust her with my life. The only family member I ever would." Alarian sighed. "Besides, if we wait until tomorrow, we should have a lot more details to share. Maybe even two letters from your brother."

All she could think to do was nod. "I suppose." Her thoughts trailed off.

"You want to know about your father." There was a softness to his voice. A soothing lilt in the way he spoke.

"I'd like to reach Saol and find out why I can't remember him in the first place." Felicity tried and failed to keep the tension from her voice. It didn't work and she knew it.

He must have realized it was best to change the subject. "So tonight?" He gave a pointed look toward the bed.

Her gaze thinned on him as he grinned. Alarian stepped across the room, pulling aside the drapery that separated the two rooms. The bed was a decent size, obviously meant for Haven—oops, Braum's—many guests. The other option was a quilted sofa that sat two but would be uncomfortable to sleep on.

Alarian watched her. "I can't—"

"I know." She wouldn't ask him to give up his secret and shift into the fox. It was a vital piece of information that could harm him if others knew.

Not that she had asked him to shift the other night...

There had been a warmth—a draw between them. It was easier to blame those emotions on the wine consumed that night. Especially since he pulled away from her over and over again.

Heavy footfalls on the stone entrance pulled her from her thoughts. She ensured that there wasn't more than one set. Old habits certainly die hard. She doubted Braum would betray them with their history, but one couldn't be too careful.

He entered carrying a canvas bag and removed a jug of ale and a loaf of bread. Alarian turned his attention to the pot. She glanced between the two of them. Braum waggled his brow. "So, any big decisions made, Linny?"

Felicity rolled her eyes. "I get the sofa." She turned back to cutting the apples, ignoring Braum's laughter and the desire that coursed through her at the thought of Alarian's body pressed against hers.

It would be so much easier if she could figure out how to compartmentalize these emotions. Sooner rather than later.

"Did you hear that—she'd prefer the sofa over either of us." Braum nodded at the pot over the fire. "Let's get this stew started. And since you don't want my company in bed—though I think you and I have proven it could be fun—I've got myself an invitation elsewhere tonight."

"You *just* asked about the sleeping arrangements." She cast a glare in his direction.

"To see if I had a chance." He winked.

Alarian, on the other hand, stood stock-still in the corner, his shoulders taut. There wasn't a hint of humor in his expression and Felicity couldn't ascertain why. Was it because they would be alone? Again.

"Is there somewhere I can get a good workout in?" Change tactics. Probably best to use the pent-up energy elsewhere.

Braum hissed between his teeth and glanced at Alarian. "Does she always make it this easy?"

Alarian just glared at the male.

"What's your problem?" Braum shook his head and turned back to Felicity. "Don't know if you got a good look around but we can see for miles if we try hard enough. Flat lands of rock. There aren't enough resources to make a training ring."

She nodded. "Figured." That would make anonymity difficult. They were already on display, and she'd stand out going through her routine. The familiar ache in her muscles urged her to do what she had grown comfortable doing again during the past few days but—

"So, who are you really, Linny?"

She plopped root vegetables into the pot over the fire, about to answer when Alarian slid in between them. "She's a friend of mine."

"Oh, but she must be more than that. You and I go way back and any female with a good brain was sick of you within a few days." He peered at Felicity from the corner of his eye. "I know you have a good head on your shoulders. So how did the two of you connect? The rebellion?"

Felicity's side-eyed Alarian who snorted. "Kind of."

She had questions of her own. "How many others knew of your involvement?"

Braum sat at the edge of the table, answering for Alarian. "There was a small group of us who were aware. Sloan acted more as messenger, liaison, and informant. He'd pass the information to the rest of us who oversaw different groups throughout the realms. That way Alarian's identity was kept close-knit, but everyone knew what was going on."

"Besides Sloan and Braum?" Felicity looked expectantly at Alarian. "Who else was aware?"

Alarian shrugged. "Dimitri, Lian, and Sloan's father."

His two friends from Aer. The visit to their manor had been more than a celebration of the season. It had been a chance for him to have a meeting with rebels. And she had never known nor considered. She'd been such a fool.

"He had us all organized. I was impressed. Most see the laziness as a dead giveaway, but Rian here could have three separate females—"

"We do not need to go there." Alarian shook his head, grabbing the loaf of bread Braum had purchased and a knife. "You—"

"Oh no, we can't just stop there." Felicity gave a saccharine smile. "Please, Braum, continue. I want to hear the best and worst stories you have about Alarian."

Braum opened his mouth but paused when he noted Alarian's stony glare and the knife in his hand pointed in his direction. He chuckled. "I see now."

Felicity's brow furrowed. "See what?" She glanced between the two of them. *Wait*...was Alarian jealous?

Alarian got back to work without looking at either of them, pulling Felicity from her twisting thoughts. "If you want to hear a story, then you can tell her about the time in Aer. Where you almost got me caught."

Braum was still smiling as he tossed a few herbs into the pot. "Oh, that had been a crazy night." He shook his head as if that would bring back the memory. "There we were, playing a friendly game of cards. Stupid me had one too many drinks. Alarian had already passed on the packet to me, but I'd been an idiot and put the satchel beside me. He always said to keep it on my person, but I didn't think twice. Someone had grabbed my bag halfway through the game. We had to track them down."

Alarian shook his head. "If only you listened to me then we would never get in those messes in the first place."

Braum laughed and poured himself a tankard of ale. "Same thing he said that night." He took a gulp then nodded his glass towards Felicity. She shook her head, and he continued. "We went down a piss-coated alley. One of the assholes jumped out at us and poor Alarian got stabbed."

"Because you got in the way," Alarian grumbled.

Braum ignored him. "Thought he was going to bleed out because I don't know what to do except how to bandage a cut and the nearest healer was a huge supporter of his damn parents."

Felicity stared at Braum. The pieces coming together. She could feel Alarian watching her reaction. "And?" Although she knew how this story ended, she wanted to know how it had started.

"He said there was one person he trusted from his traveling party. I dragged his heavy, slightly intoxicated and incapacitated ass back to some inn. Couldn't use his magic because, of course, it had been an iron tipped blade. I dragged him up two flights of stairs to a damn door that was locked. Had to pick the lock, then literally dumped him against the wall and got out of there fast. First time in a long time that I was jealous of magic."

"Only one person you trusted, huh?" Felicity glanced at Alarian, but he was focused on slicing the bread. She asked the only reasonable question, "Why didn't you stay with him?"

"A lot more to explain if he'd stayed," Alarian answered. "I may have trusted you to keep me alive, but you also still worked for my father. You had made it abundantly clear when we reached the celebration that the mission was important. Otherwise, I would have introduced you to Braum at the party."

"You were there?" Her eyes thinned on the bulky male. "How did I miss you?"

Braum blinked. "Shit. You were the spy. Alarian warned me someone would be watching so I had to stay clear of him. You know me—I keep out of sight. Thought I saw you once but excused it for a trick of the light." He grinned. "Well, now I know who you are—"

"Don't go there," Alarian warned. "Secrets can carry on a breeze, and you know better. We are already out in the open enough but if the wind chooses to betray her..."

Felicity glanced between them. After all they had shared, her identity was where Alarian drew the line. And the way he spoke, the glare—was protecting her?

"Sorry. You're right." Braum nodded.

Felicity tried to organize her thoughts as she spooned stew into bowls and passed them around before settling down to eat. Alarian steered the conversation to lighter days when he and Braum had traveled together and soon laughter overtook the tense atmosphere. Braum wouldn't stop marveling about the fresh food. When they finished, he poured the leftovers into separate bowls. "Gonna pass this out to the others if you don't mind."

Felicity and Alarian quickly got to their feet to help. "Of course."

Once the last of the food was placed into bowls, they helped Braum put together a bag with some of the other provisions they shouldn't need, keeping only the necessities for themselves. Felicity longed to help pass it out but knew it was best for their mission to keep a low profile. Besides, it had been Braum's idea.

"I'll leave you to it then. The sheets are clean—surprisingly." He chuckled. "Sofa available if necessary. I'll see you in the morning before you go." Braum winked. "Don't do anything I wouldn't do."

"We aren't trying to kick you out of your house." Felicity placed a cloth over the food and handed him the basket. Alarian moved in behind her, and she felt his presence like a warm blanket. Shit—how could he smell so good after sleeping on the forest floor for days?

He cleared his throat.

Braum looked over her shoulder at the male behind her. "Naw, trust me. I'm going to be just fine." He waved as he headed towards the doorway. "Just remember there is no privacy here."

The drape dramatically whooshed back into place as Braum left and suddenly it felt like the air had followed him out.

When she turned around, Alarian seemed to hover over her. She didn't remember him being that tall before. He sighed. Cleared his throat. "Your past doesn't mean a thing to me."

Her brow furrowed. "All right?"

"And I shouldn't care." He swallowed. "But what did Braum mean when he said you two have proven being together is fun?"

She glanced over his entire body. The way the shadows curled around his feet. The fact that his breathing was faster than usual. He *was* jealous.

"It might be the same way you balanced three females." She tilted her head, and he shrunk a little. "Or maybe like you and Cara."

He ran a hand over his face. "Fuck." Alarian stepped back, shaking his head. "Braum spoke out of turn."

"We all have pasts, Alarian. We haven't known each other forever. I don't know what you want from me." That last part was true in more ways than she cared to admit. "And I don't think you do either."

"You think I'm confused?" He blinked at her, his hands falling to his side. "Have I really not been transparent?"

She rolled her eyes. "You turned into the fox. Remember?"

"Because you've made it quite clear you're not interested. Or ready."

"I don't plan to be another notch on your bedpost." The words came unbidden, and she snapped her mouth shut.

He shook his head, his mouth drawn into a frown. "We need sleep. I'll take the sofa."

Alarian started to walk past her, but she stepped into his path. "No, you haven't been clear. You flirt—trust me, I'm aware. But it seems you flirt with everyone. And you're the one who stopped us that night at the *Rose & Wisteria*."

His gaze thinned. "You were after one night and one night only. Don't deny it."

"I won't." She raised her chin. "By all the stories I've heard so far on our travels, one night hasn't been a problem for you before."

"Jealous?"

She laughed, the sound more viscous than she planned. "Right back at you."

"Yes, I am."

Felicity stopped laughing.

His eyes searched hers and she couldn't turn away even if she wanted to. Not as he stepped into her space. Looked down at her with an intensity that she could feel to the tips of her toes. "You're right—that was our pasts. But since you're confused, then let me enlighten you." He took a step closer, and she shifted back. Her breath hitching. His gaze settled on her lips. "You wouldn't just be any notch on my bedpost, Felicity. You would be the last mark and there would be no other. I want you. Completely. Every part of you. So, when you're ready" —he leaned in until his lips brushed the tip of her ear— "all you have to do is ask."

With those parting words, he walked around her and grabbed a blanket from the back of the sofa.

"Then why are you walking away now? Again?" Her heart hammered against her chest.

He didn't face her. "Because I don't think *you* know what you want."

Her magic swelled within, heating her skin. She bit back the desire to call his bluff. To challenge him. Either sounded perfect right now. Just to see what he would do.

Except she knew what he said was true. And although she still wanted to know why he had broken off their kiss that night, she was frightened of the answer. "Alarian?"

He paused.

"Take the bed. There's more room."

He glanced at the sofa. He would fit but his feet would hang over the edge. It wouldn't be fair if he slept there. He didn't fight her and dropped the blanket back in place. "If you change your mind or want to sleep on the bed, that's fine."

She heard the disappointment in his voice. They had been careful to give each other space. But his words—he said he wanted her. She realized she wasn't brave enough to take what he offered. Felicity pinched her eyes closed at the realization. She was afraid...

"Thank you," she whispered.

She almost admitted that she and Braum hadn't slept together—other things—but not sex. Like she said, it would do neither of them any good to share the parts of their pasts that didn't matter anymore. She needed to remember that too.

He nodded. "Goodnight."

"Goodnight." And she watched him walk away from her for the second time.

Chapter 16

Alarian knew it was preposterous that he was so wrapped up in someone he had only a small taste of but couldn't let go. This was why he had meant to do this damn mission alone. To clear his mind of her.

Thomas' words rang in his head. The bond was there. She just needed to realize it. Well, if that gave him hope, last night did not.

He'd laid his feelings out and she hadn't said a word of her own. Not a single damn word. Even if he could sense her want, stubbornness had won out. It shouldn't hurt as much as it did.

Until reality hit like a hammer—he hadn't proven himself. How could she care about him?

They woke before the sun rose and packed up their things. Well, he'd tried to sleep as he tossed and turned between nightmares. Braum appeared before they left, his hair a mess, his shirt half tucked in, and a lazy grin mixed with his half-asleep expression.

Silence had never felt so deafening as they actively avoided looking at each other. Once the dilapidated signpost with the faded worn carvings signaled the canyon was ahead, he was on high alert. According to Braum, there were more Fomorians in the center of the realm. He wouldn't be caught off guard this time and they should arrive a little after midday, when the sun would be near the highest point in the sky.

For a moment he'd considered turning around, but they only had speculations for the location of the remaining heartstones and needed more substantial proof. Dorcha could offer more information but not every realm knew their stone's location. Éardrom was a prime example—they had missed out on a pivotal opportunity.

He knew Scáth's heartstone often exchanged hands and locations to keep it safe. Only the keepers of the stone knew its secrets. That could be said about some of the other stones as well. They needed to have as much intel as they could if they wanted to stay ahead of his mother.

He peered at Felicity's stoic form from the corner of his eye. There was no chance he was entering the Shadow Realm. They didn't have time to deal with the ramifications—that was a problem he would deal with after. One week had passed since they left the palace and there was still so much ground to cover.

Domhain was their best chance at finding clues to pinpoint the other heartstones' locations.

"I didn't know the Fomorians live in civilizations. I had only ever seen a few on their own—never a group of them." Felicity's voice broke him from his reasonings.

"They don't make it long without their hoard so those must have been outcasts. Fomorians have a very strict chain of command and if you step beyond your rank, it means death or eviction." He sighed. "We will have to rely on our magic."

She flinched beside him as he knew she would. She had removed the dampener clasp and chain from her ear. The one that had silenced her for too long. But he'd found her glamour falling from her again this morning. What had happened to the determined female who was training to master her magic? It's as if she stopped moving forward altogether. At least she had started training physically every night. She didn't always include her magic in the rotation though.

There was nothing in sight beyond dirt and the occasional remains of a tree. No person, town, or sign of life. Not even a breeze, just the blazing sun.

"They fear light, correct?"

He nodded.

She breathed a long sigh, her fingers reached up and grazed the crystal at her neck. "Understood."

"We should have a good viewpoint once we reach the next ridge. Since they aren't out in the middle of the day, we won't be able to see within the cavern, but we can make a plan."

Felicity nodded. "Agreed. You'll need to hold onto your magic. If it's as bad as you say, you might be our only way out."

"And you could be our only way in."

The silence returned, and he couldn't help but stare at the thin line of her mouth a beat too long. He closed his eyes, forcing himself to turn away.

When they reached the ridge, both dismounted. Their horses were agitated, a few snorts and nervous feet dancing against stone. Felicity shushed them as she stroked Laochra's neck. The mare gave a nervous whinny and buried her nose into the crook of Felicity's arm.

"Where should we tie them?" she asked as she took in the barren land.

This was where the death of the land originated so many years before. Rock was all that remained except for that one fossilized tree he'd left his mount on his previous visit.

"That tree." He loosened his gelding's saddle. "As long as we can reach near here once we get out." He pointed to where a piece of rock stood out and curved over the ground, creating a shadow underneath. "That's where we'll return."

Felicity nodded. "All right. We know our exit strategy and escape location." She loosened Laochra's girth while she spoke. "Now it's just figuring out how we get in."

He tossed a few carrots onto the ground near the tree and the horses' noses ruffled through the treats. After all the traveling, he doubted the animals would go far. "There will be plenty of shadows to draw on once we reach the caves." He walked towards the outlook and stopped. He turned to find Felicity staring where Laochra chomped a carrot, a smile tilting her lips. He cleared his throat and she looked up, her expression going blank. "But from this vantage point, we have no idea how many are inside. I don't have the cave pathways memorized, otherwise I could shadow us right in."

Felicity ran a hand over the horses who stood nose to tail, heads low and relaxed. Whatever reassuring touches she gave must have been enough. "We can get close. Use our stealth to move around them. How close do you think we need to get to the location itself?"

Alarian closed his eyes, trying to remember the details from his previous visits. "Close. If memory serves, the path to take is the third to left since the caves down there are quite numerous. But I believe there were specific markings etched into the walls around where the stone had been. I can't remember enough to replicate them." He shook his head. "I should have taken copious notes. I didn't know better."

"That would have taken some impressive forethought." Felicity fumbled with her pocket and removed a second pendant. This one was a clear crystal unlike the red one around her neck. "You should wear this?"

His brow furrowed.

"Like the lanterns you had me practice on, I can direct the light towards the pendant, and you can adjust it for an attack. Just a precaution."

"Have you practiced?" Alarian took the crystal and hung the chain around his neck. It was warm from her pocket and the residual heat radiated as soon as it touched his chest.

She glanced at the caverns. "No. But I won't miss."

"I trust you."

She worried her lip, and he couldn't but help watch the movement. Resist the want to brush his thumb against her mouth. He swallowed and turned away. "Ready?"

"We don't have much of a choice."

He went through a mental checklist of what he knew about the Fomorians. "Silence will be key. Since sight is not their strongest asset, they rely on hearing. They should be sleeping since they are nocturnal. We need to stick close together for a quick escape if necessary."

She nodded and began the uneven descent towards the caves, scaling down the rocky incline to the entrance. As they walked, Alarian pointed to the southwest. "My aunt lives in that direction. Near the Balla Mountain Range."

She frowned. "Why are you telling me this?"

Alarian faced her. "Because if anything happens to me, she is our next destination. Find a way to get word to your brother, then head to the Tower."

A wave of turmoil crashed in his mind, but Felicity didn't show any of it. "Nothing will happen to you," she said the words vehemently—as if she had control over his life and death.

"Just in case."

When they reached the entrance of the cave, both stopped.

"Shit," they said at the same time.

The entrance to the caves was a maze of rolled stones spread out amidst bare bones and old armor. Fomorians. They looked like boulders that breathed. But when they unfurled, that would all change. At their tallest they could be at least twice his width and tower over him, seemingly impenetrable. And they were sleeping at the entrance and as far as they could see into the cave.

Felicity's magic would be helpful to distract or repel them. Their weak spots were the cracks and fissures in their bodies, depending on how deep those points went.

A few snored. Some breathed heavily. If one had a more sensitive sense of smell than another, they were doomed.

He held out a hand and pointed ahead, conveying his meaning without words—travel by shadow to the farthest point he could see. There wasn't much space, but the two of them would have a better chance than moving around their sleeping foe.

Felicity nodded but ignored his hand to wrap her arms around his waist and pressed her front against him. He momentarily stilled, lost in the feeling of her body against his. Ignoring his racing heart at the sudden contact, he concentrated, his gaze thin slits on their destination. The shadows whispered against their skin as he called for them. The sensation of the ground disappeared, the sudden jolt as they landed but this time she didn't falter on impact.

He grinned down at her, though he doubted she could see in the darkness surrounding them. He'd made his mark. The entrance of the path they were meant to take appearing as his shadows dispersed. There was only a little light from the entrance, so it took a moment for his eyes to adjust to the dim surroundings.

Felicity remained ensconced in Alarian's arms, and he looked at the minuscule space between them and the few snoring stones. Close—too close. Just a shift in the wrong direction and they would touch the beasts. Alarian squeezed her arms, drawing her attention to him. He nodded towards the cave, darkness encapsulating with each step they took from the entrance.

Felicity started to glow. She kept the starlight dim, enough to give them sight without being a shock if the Fomorians opened their eyes. Hopefully. Felicity moved from his arms, but he slid a clammy hand into hers—an anchor. She was careful not to even touch the walls of the cave, and he followed suit, stepping only where she had first.

They made it deeper, the cave inching in closer to their bodies. The air became thicker as they continued, his lungs slow to fill. There were fewer trolls here, the space too small for their larger bodies. He relaxed the farther they went, but the grip Felicity had on his hand didn't lessen. He squeezed once in reassurance, and she paused to look over her shoulder at him. In the limited light, he gave her a half smile and her magic fluttered, brightening for a moment. He chuckled quietly, and she bit her lip.

Alarian looked up and paused, causing Felicity to halt. Her scowl softened when he pointed towards a path to the left. There wasn't a moment of hesitation as they headed in that direction, her leading with her light. The tight space forced her to move sideways as she edged against the walls and Alarian didn't let go of her as he did the same.

Once they reached the end of the narrow path, they entered a small cavern. The space had little divots cut into the stone. The largest of the divots must have caught Felicity's eye because she brightened her light, carefully looking about the space. They were lucky that the passages were too tight here for even the smallest of the Fomorians.

She picked up the pendant and directed her magic upon the intended divot. As soon as the starlight touched it, faded veins illuminated, casting out from the divot and into the stone and earth surrounding it. "Alarian, do you see this?"

He squeezed her hand. "Yes."

"What do you think it means?" The lines disappeared the higher she cast her light.

"The magic is weak, but this is where the heartstone used to be. Deep within the earth it fed. If there is that little power left, I don't expect the realm will last much longer." He shook his head in disappointment. What would that mean for Domhain? Would they have a future without their heartstone? And what of the fae who lived here?

Felicity bit her lip. "What do you think will happen when it runs out?"

Alarian shook his head. "I don't know what the lasting effects will be."

"Your fox?"

He didn't want to think about that. Would a part of him cease to exist? Or would it slowly slip away like the power of the heartstone?

He reached forward, the wall warm and smooth to the touch. Would younglings no longer be born with the magic imbued from the earth? It would be catastrophic if the loss of Magic changed the makeup of fae for future generations. Or would earth magic become extinct?

"How long since the stone was taken?"

He traced the veins. "There isn't a date. That story has been shared since before my time." He paused. "Your brother has been on this continent for over a century, so he may know of its origins."

He pulled on his magic. Felt the fox rise in summons, but he didn't let it consume him. "It looks like roots."

He placed his hands into the alcove where the stone had once been and closed his eyes, bowing his head. A wisp of magic pulsed from his skin, causing the roots to brighten, expanding just a little further into the earth. As though it was feeding off his magic.

"What are you doing?" With her hand still in his, she tugged gently. "Careful."

He winced, lightheaded as he stepped back and dropped his hand from the stone. "It wants the power. I think...it drew it in."

He saw the implication of that light in her eyes. "Do you think that's a possibility? That Earth Fae can help it?"

"Maybe."

He wanted to try again but Felicity's grip tightened. "We still have to get out of here. Can't have you drained." She looked over her shoulder.

He dropped his hand from the stone, annoyed that he couldn't do more to assess and help. The light remained in the roots, just a little brighter than it had been but not by much. "If access remains dangerous as it is right now, it won't be easy for the fae to help. But it's an alternative to consider. It might not heal the realm, but it could sustain it." He stared at the wall for another moment before looking her way. "We have a lot to share with your brother."

She looked towards their way back. "We have to get out of here first."

He nodded, then they headed towards the exit, this time he was in the lead. They fell into silence as they moved through the narrow passage. Once they reached the first of the wider corridors, Alarian caught a movement in the corner of his eye. He stilled, pulling her to a stop. "Shit," he breathed in a whisper.

There was movement up ahead, a shift in a large stone—the Fomorians were awake.

"Shit," she echoed.

Alarian glanced about. "Expand your light."

"What?"

"Create a shadow I can use. I can at least get us to the entrance of the catacombs. Then we can see where the sun is so I can get us to the horses." Alarian pulled her in close as the grumbling creatures grew closer.

Felicity adjusted her pendant and covered it with her hand. "Ready?" she asked in a whisper.

A roar sounded. They hadn't been quiet enough. The thunder of heavy feet echoed against stone.

Felicity moved closer to Alarian, and the shadows enveloped them. When they landed near the entrance, a roar was heavy in the air. Before they could react, she and Alarian stumbled face first into the stone. He realized she'd been pushed from behind, unbalancing them both.

He ignored his aching back as he fumbled upright, heart in his throat when one of the beasts grabbed Felicity's shirt, tearing her from him. The Fomorian glared at her, face to face, then bellowed, spit and saliva coating her skin. She brightened in response, starlight blinding, letting the heat waft from her, the sensation grazing Alarian's skin as he was forced to close his eyes. The Fomorian dropped her with a yelp, one of her limbs thumped Alarian in the stomach forcing air from his lung.

As Felicity's starlight dimmed, Alarian opened his eye to see her rushing to her feet. Alarian called on the shadows to hide them from view.

Felicity's magic shuttered. "Alarian," she called, searching for him. Another troll appeared beside her.

Alarian growled and launched himself to push Felicity out of harm's way when a stone arm knocked him from the air. He landed with a grunt, barely catching his bearings. Head ringing and vision altered, he barely saw the Fomorian's fist coming for his skull.

He rolled to the side, the skim of knuckles causing his jaw to shudder. Fuck, that was close.

Healing magic coursed through his body, clearing his vision and he sent wisps of shadows into the first crevice he saw—the beast's mouth.

It sputtered, unable to breathe as his shadows slid into its nostrils, cutting off all air flow. He expanded his magic, the troll falling to the ground in a clump, just in time for Alarian to dodge another attack from the side.

He needed to get to her. Others were coming. Heavy footfalls. The rock walls shook. Their only saving grace being the light ahead. So close. They were so close.

He whipped shadows around. "Felicity. Light," he ordered.

She called the starlight to the pendant, sending it shooting at beasts and their weapons, trying to break the metal with the heat of her magic, but it only caused them to clatter to the ground as it burned the palms of their wielders. An arrow flew past her before she sent a flash of light towards the bow, slashing the wood into pieces. The Fomorians didn't care about the light now—not with the battle rage.

Shit, shit shit...

Alarian darted around two of the Fomorians, letting his magic do the work. He was so focused on getting to her, on holding the shadows at the ready, that he didn't see the spear coming down.

Not until it was too late. He tried to whip around, but his movement was too slow. Uncalculated. The shadows faltered—he faltered. His eyes widened as a mane of mahogany hair whipped in his face.

There was no time to react as the blade sliced through Felicity's shoulder and out her back. As her pendant hit to the ground and the light sputtered. No time to hear her scream over his own. Not when she was on the ground, her head hitting stone, and blood—her pinkish blood—puddled upon stone.

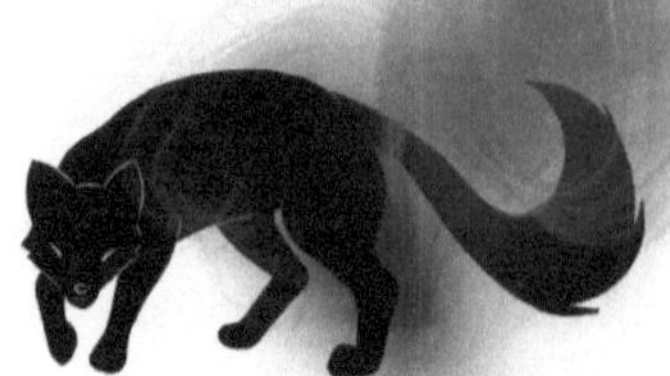

Chapter 17
Alarian

Alarian roared, his magic twisting out of control from his body. Wisps of shadows turned to sharp angles that plunged into the creatures' weak points. They screamed, clawing at their throats and armored torsos.

Alarian grabbed Felicity's prone body and scooped up the surprisingly unbroken crystal. The last sounds he heard before the shadows took him away were the sputtering gags of the Fomorians as they choked on his magic. Then he forced the shadows outward, the creatures' bodies expanding from within.

Alarian's jaw was tight. As he shielded Felicity's body with his own, he called the shadows out through the cracks in their bodies. They didn't have a chance to yell as they exploded, bits of stone-like bone and muscle scattering around them. Alarian stepped into the open, concentrating on the horses, the location of the sun informing him where shadows would be near the rock.

His heart raced as they landed. Blood soaked his hands where he held her but the wound on her back was the least of his concerns compared to where she landed headfirst into the stone. "Damnit. Fuck, Felicity, why?" Not for him.

He hated that he couldn't heal her. That his magic was of no use right them. He looked up at the sky, then back to the horses. There was no way to transport her just yet. His magic was too weak after the attack.

A small moan broke through her lips, and he brushed the hair from her face, cradling her tighter against his chest. He searched her for any other visible injuries but found none besides the still forming bump on her head and the spear wound that had gone through her shoulder. Too much—she had done too much for him. Put herself in harm's way on his behalf. He got to his feet, knowing he needed to hurry and get her to a safe place immediately.

The sound of the Fomorians were behind him. Night wasn't far off, and he knew that they would come for them. Search for their prey if he remained too close. They held grudges. All he could do was run. With a quick brush of his lips to her forehead, he laid her down on the ground and made quick work of tightening the tack of both horses. He stuffed the two pendants into his pocket before putting both packs on Laochra. After he moved the gelding until he was in the shadow of the rock outcrop, he used what he had left to transport them into the saddle.

With Felicity held firmly in his arms, he reached for the mare's reins. She would follow, he knew that, so he tossed them over her head and turned the gelding towards his destination. With a heel to the gelding's sides, they took off and Alarian urged him faster until the only sound was their galloping hooves against stone. His aunt could help. Would help. He just had to reach her.

***

The first signs of swaying grass signaled they were nearing the perimeter of the realm and close to their destination. When the house came into view, Alarian sighed in relief. Felicity's breathing was labored, and she hadn't stirred, forcing him to ask more from the horses who were already giving their all. When the covered porch of Leana's two-story home came into view, he called on whatever magic he could muster. The sun had slipped closer to the horizon, but the structure gave off small shapes of shadow. Somehow, the shadows congregated, and with the horses still running, his magic took them away, landing heavily on his aunt's doorstep. Without knocking, he pushed the door open.

"Help," he called.

A maid gasped, her body pressed against the wall, the folded laundry she was carrying tight to her chest. With Felicity in his arms, Alarian rushed to her. "Where's my aunt?"

She pointed towards the doorway on the other side of the entryway, and without a word, he ran in that direction, Felicity limp in his arms. His aunt met him halfway and paled at the sight in his arms. "Alarian, how?"

"Please." He didn't take the time to explain, barely registering a hello. "Help her."

She didn't need to be asked twice. His aunt stepped aside, gesturing to an ornate sofa. "There—put her down."

Alarian had to force himself to let go of Felicity, but he stepped back immediately, knowing he would only be in the way. Aunt Leana crouched over her, salt and pepper hair dangling over Felicity's body. Alarian trembled, staring at his blood-stained hands. "Please," he repeated.

Leana's brow furrowed as she found the injuries, magic called to the surface and a light glowed between her palms and Felicity's skin.

Alarian stood frozen in concentration—and fear. Curse them all if he lost her. He'd tear the Fomorians apart one by one. "Her head. She hit it hard."

"Don't worry, Rian. My magic is doing its part." She spoke with a healer's voice, with the years of experience of one who had seen and done so much. Who had calmed masses of injured and their loved ones. It felt like an entire day had passed when she finally sat back on her heels, running her hand over a sweaty brow. "I've done what I can. She's stable, but I'm forcing her to remain asleep for a little longer. Her body needs to catch up with the healing I've done."

Alarian nodded, unable to voice his thanks. He'd been practicing blocking out her emotions but now he wished he could feel anything from the unconscious female. Reassurance that she was all right.

"Your Cridhe will be safe, my boy."

He shivered at the title being spoken aloud by another. "She's not—"

Leana glanced between him and her. "Oh?"

"No." He shook his head. "She doesn't feel the same." Thomas' words came back to the forefront of his mind. *It is offered when love appears against all odds.*

His aunt looked down at Felicity with a tilt to her head. "How did she get these injuries?"

"The Fomorians. She saved my life."

"Hm." Leana placed a hand on his cheek, drawing his attention away from Felicity. He took in his aunt's frizzy red hair in a loose bun at the nape of her neck. The casual blue dress and cream apron she wiped her hands against. "I can sense the beginning of the tether between you while I healed her. It's there. The option. You must be special to each other."

He kept hope from his expression, not wanting to speak on Felicity's behalf. He only had his intuition to guide him, but that didn't mean he would assume Felicity would make the same choice. "Maybe."

"In my experience, the vacancy of a one-sided bond leaves you wanting." Her expression softened, her thumb brushing his cheek, wiping away a tear he hadn't known had fallen before she dropped her hand.

"Graham? You were bonded?" Her first husband had died unexpectedly. Ankus takes as death wills.

She smiled, though it didn't touch her eyes. "Yes, most who enter the bond don't talk about it. Feels personal. After his death, I looked in the wrong places for someone to fill the void."

Alarian shook his head. "That was more on my father than on you." Roald had forced his sister into an advantageous marriage, or so he had called it when he'd announced her impending nuptials to Lord Gullist. But Alarian had known the truth then as much as he did now—it was his father's way to attempt control over Leana. Alarian hadn't been close to his aunt until he ran from his parents after the coup. That was when he learned just how much power the matriarch had. Roald hadn't been able to stifle it.

"I've only heard the term for the heart bond recently. Most just call it a bond."

She winked. "As a healer, I see truths a bit more deeply than others might."

"What do you know of the Fomorians?" He changed the subject to something he felt he could control. Away from Felicity, who lay listless on that sofa. Away from the desire to curl up beside her.

"Oh yes, they have been a problem as of late. But first, let's get the princess into a bed so she can rest comfortably."

Alarian's gaze thinned on his aunt. "You knew?" He hadn't meant to make Felicity's identity known.

She rolled her eyes. "Of course I knew. I still have my informants. Those who stood at Lord Gullist's side are more loyal to me than they ever were to him. Once the curse was broken, one returned and filled me in on what happened." She turned towards the door, but Alarian didn't move, not willing to leave Felicity's side.

"She'll be all right."

He growled in protest.

His aunt chuckled. "It's about time you grew up. Took you far longer than I would have liked. The last time I saw you, your hair hung to your shoulders, a wild look about you. I always thought you'd prove to be more than my ignorant brother expected. I'm glad to be right." She grinned. "Again."

She called for the maid that had been in the hall earlier. "Prepare the second room on the left for our guests. I'll escort them up when it's ready. Then please ask the cook to prepare a meal for him and broth for her."

Alarian's shoulders relaxed. "Thank you. Now the Fomorians—"

"Can wait until tomorrow." She shook her head. "You need rest."

"No—"

"Yes, it can. It will not result in immediate change. I've been on this plain much longer than you, my boy. Tonight, you rest. Tomorrow, we discuss problems."

The maid returned. "It's ready miss. I'll go speak to the cook."

"Thank you, Olivia." The maid curtsied, casting a furtive glance at Alarian before she walked away. Leana turned to face him. "Be careful with her head."

Alarian did as commanded, gently curling Felicity's body to his, her head pressed against his chest. When they reached the room, he laid her down while his aunt adjusted the pillows to cradle Felicity. "She should be much better after some rest. Now, let's take a look at you."

He stiffened again. "I'm fine."

"Bruises, a cracked rib, and a deep gash on your arm. Those beasts are not known for their gentle demeanor." She pointed to an overstuffed chair in the corner.

"If you have magic left, then use it on her. I have my own."

"You know it doesn't work that way. Besides you're exhausted." She twisted her fingers, her earth magic forcing the wooden planks of the floor to pop up then down one after the other like piano keys moving the chair beside the bed. "Her body needs to catch up with what I've already done. Too much healing could have repercussions. So, sit down and listen to me."

Her forceful tone was enough to make him sit. He sighed as his aunt shifted to a crouch in front of him. "Lift your shirt a bit so I can see which ribs are cracked."

He did as asked and her gaze narrowed. "I thought you could heal yourself."

"I can. Just drained a bit in my haste to get here."

"I'm aware of your current reason, but why do you have a scar here?" She pointed to a slice of raised skin. "Whoever did the stitches did a crude job."

"It was dark, and she wasn't exactly a healer. Iron tip blade as well." Alarian ground his teeth. He could have allowed the gash to disappear, but for some reason he hadn't. Now it was a continuous reminder of a gentle touch, the bite of her protective tone...the first time he caught glimpses of a female who may actually care.

"I see." She got to work healing the ribs first, the sudden heat of her magic as it repaired bone forced a small hiss from his lips. When she was done, she moved onto his arm, cleaning the wound of debris before closing up the sliced skin. When she was done, she sat back, just in time for a warm meal to arrive. "Good." She patted his arm as she stood. "Eat. Sleep. We'll talk in the morning."

Alarian knew better than to argue with her further. He ate quickly, realizing how famished he was. Felicity didn't stir once, and if it wasn't for his aunt's reassurance, he would have worried. With his stomach content and his body healed, exhaustion caught up as the adrenaline faded. Safe. He would be by her side and keep her safe.

Chapter 18
Alarian

The bed shifted under Alarian's head. His groan was muffled, his back aching from his position. He'd fallen asleep with his head rested on his crossed arms against the mattress. It would take some time to roll out his muscles and sit upright—

He looked up abruptly, Felicity's eyes piercing his. Her face was still pale and her hair a knotty mess. But she was awake.

Without another thought, he sat up, ignoring as his muscles screamed at the movement. "How are you feeling?"

"A bit sore. Small headache." She closed her eyes for a brief moment. "Where are we?"

"My Aunt Leana's home. She's a healer. You—" He swallowed. "You saved me but were badly injured in the process." He ran a finger along her cheek. "Never do that again."

A small smile was her only response before she winced, her eyes pinched shut again. "The light hurts."

He hadn't realized that the sun had risen, shining through the wide-open window and enlightening her profile. He stood, closing the curtains. "Sorry about that."

"You did nothing wrong."

"I should have closed them last night. Didn't think about it." He'd woken to check on her and had spent some time looking out the window, taking in the starlit sky amid the peace and quiet of the darkness. It didn't compare to a clear evening in Dorcha, but it was calming. Enough to allow his mind to rest and for him to find sleep again.

"Alarian, seriously, it's all right."

When she started to move, he rushed back to her side, adjusting her pillows so she could sit up.

"Let me get some food for you. I bet you're starving." He started for the door. He also should ask for—

"Alarian?"

He stopped mid-step, looked back at her. She shook her head, a small smile on her lips. "I'm fine. Your aunt must have excellent healing skills. Now, are the horses all right?"

He chuckled, running a hand through his hair, his shoulders relaxing. Of course, she asked about the animals. "The horses were collected by my aunt's gardener and settled with food and water. Made sure to pass on two carrots from your pack." They deserved all the rest they could get after the hard pace they endured for her. For him.

"You shouldn't have risked yourself like that—" Alarian cleared his throat. "I was worried about you. If I hadn't gotten us here fast enough..." He shook his head, not wanting to consider the position they could have been in. What could have happened. With less hurried steps, he went to the door and asked a maid for food to be delivered and for his aunt to be made aware that Felicity had woken. He couldn't leave her, not now.

Not ever again.

He sat again in the seat beside her, eyes lingering on her face. "Besides the headache, how do you feel?"

"Tired, but otherwise fine. I feel limited pain despite being stabbed through the shoulder, so I'll have to thank your aunt for her mending."

He reached into his pocket and removed her necklace. "It fell when you did." He held the red crystal out towards her. "My aunt gave me a new chain for it. Yours broke."

She reached out and he placed it in her palm. "Thank you." She clutched it in her hand and held it to her chest.

He wanted to ask about it. Why this one was so special when the door opened to Olivia carrying a tray of food, Alarian's aunt a step behind.

"It's good to see you awake." Leana pointed to a table where the maid placed the tray before leaving, closing the door behind her. She removed the cover from the food, spooning portions onto plates. "I thought we could all eat together. I know Alarian has topics to discuss."

"I'm sorry. I mean—thank you." Felicity remained upright, her shoulders drawn back. Her concern and guilt spread in his chest.

Oh, shit. He'd forgotten to mention Leana's position on her late husband.

"Your thanks are not necessary." Leana smiled over her shoulder, her attention on Felicity as though tracking movement. "Don't worry. You're safe here."

Alarian looked down to see one of Felicity's hands bunching the sheets while the other splayed out—searching. He cleared his throat and pointed to the stash in the corner. "All of your things are waiting over there." He winked, certain she wanted her dagger close out of habit. The blade was a comforting trinket more than anything else. He gave a reassuring smile and she visibly relaxed.

Felicity winced and frowned at the nightgown she wore. "How did—"

"My maid and I assisted each other." Leana smiled. "We had to clean your wounds after the first round staunched the blood flow. You're strong. The healing did better than I thought it would."

Felicity blushed further. "Oh—"

Leana waved her off. "Now, Alarian, you had asked about the Fomorian problem."

He nodded, glad to get right to the point when his instincts begged him to climb into bed with Felicity. To ensure she was healed. "Their numbers are out of control. It seems as though they are congregating in one location. They usually aren't organized, and it's dangerous if they become so." If there was a chance that the fae could help the Magic, they would need the Fomorians back to their homes for easy access to the caverns. "I heard about a disagreement between the dragons and Fomorians?"

Felicity shifted, ensuring her back was against the headboard.

Leana grabbed a robe from a nearby wall hook and handed it to Felicity. "The Fomorians and dragons have never gotten along. It's only recently been worse. Even the dragons have been seen leaving the mountain ranges to fly over towns and other realms."

Felicity slid her arms into the sleeves and tied the robe closed. "Which isn't normal."

Alarian knew that numerous bands of Fomorians settled in different locations throughout the mountain ranges on the north and south side of Domhain. Sometimes they would pick battles with the dragons for territory, but it was rare they moved within the realms. Was the recent unease between the two beasts related to the dragon that was believed to have taken the heartstone in Éardrom?

Leana nodded. "My spies have informed me that the Fomorians were seen meeting with a certain Lady Fiadh and a Tine general at the base of Domhain's northern mountain range."

Tine. That made sense. His mother could use the alliances she had with the realm's leaders. "Why would the Fomorians side with them? They don't usually follow orders."

"Not orders, but if they are given ideas that benefit them, they might act in such a way. At first, we thought this might cause them to fight each other and lessen their numbers. However, whatever Fiadh promised must have intrigued them enough because our hope has not come to fruition." Leana handed them each a plate of apple pastries and eggs from the tray Olivia had brought. "Soon we'll be out of resources and if their numbers continue to grow, trade routes will close for the remaining communities and outposts. If that happens, we'll be forced to leave."

Felicity sat up straighter, the quilt pooling in her lap. "What can we do?"

"I sent a representative to your brother. You probably just missed each other." Leana shrugged. "Until I hear back, I cannot act further, or it would seem as though I'm working against the throne."

Felicity glanced at Alarian. He nodded. "Write a letter and I'll send it right away. This also confirms what we feared—a realm has sided with my mother."

"Worse. There is a chance your mother is using the Fomorians to gain more alliances. If my family is unable to protect Domhain, she could use that information to entice others to side with her. It sounds like she's already manipulated Tine. What impact could she have on the remaining realms to force them to her side?"

An army. Alarian was already thinking what Felicity didn't say. If the other realms sided with Marquette, then the continent would be split. Tine already was the muscle and soldiers. They had the weapons to back them up too.

They'd be more than cursed.

Alarian considered the question as he took a bite of the pastry. He swallowed, the food like lead in his stomach. "She'd never want Visce's loyalty, so they are out of the question. She broke too many ties with Scáth, and I know Saol wouldn't side with her. I think she's aware that Domhain and Tine will be her strongest supporters if she can force their hand—but it might be enough to make Aer and Dorcha question who holds power. I didn't realize until now how important it was for your father's return. I'm sorry."

"Nothing we can do about it now." Felicity was halfway out of bed. She glanced at Leana. "If I could get some parchment and ink, we have a lot to inform Prince Kellan. Also, maybe you and Alarian should have a designated point of contact. He can keep you aware of what's happening and vice versa. It may be faster than a messenger."

Alarian and Leana looked between each other. "It wouldn't be a bad idea." He smiled at his aunt. "If you don't mind."

"Of course I don't mind." She took a sip from her mug. "I would recommend that you take another day to rest, but I doubt that you'll agree."

Alarian stood, knowing that time wasn't on their side—and judging by the fact Felicity was already getting to her feet, she agreed. Each day that passed was a day closer to war. "We wish we could but there is too much at stake."

"There is more you aren't telling me, isn't there?" When he didn't answer, Leana sighed. "I figured. I had my doubts that you would be passing through the realm just to see me." His aunt stood, crossed the room and wrapped her arms around his shoulders before pressing a kiss to his forehead. "You should visit more."

He chuckled. "Once this is all taken care of, I'll make that a priority."

"If you need a place to call home, you know you can find your feet here." She patted his shoulder and then picked up her plate and cup. "I'll leave you to it. Olivia will come by soon to assist you with a sponge bath. Let me know when you're ready and I'll do the final round of healing." She gave Felicity a warm smile from the doorway then turned to Alarian. "Make sure to say goodbye."

When she was gone, Felicity cleared her throat and Alarian looked at her. "What does she mean a place to stay?"

Alarian shrugged, trying not to over-complicate the truth. He knew exactly what his aunt meant. "I don't exactly have a home right now."

"Oh." Felicity looked at her feet. "I'd never considered that."

He wanted to assure her that he could never leave her side...but the truth was that they had made no such promises to each other. A tentative friendship was all that was between them, and he didn't expect her to request he remain in Éardrom.

But he knew one thing—after what had transpired in that cave, he was done holding her at arm's length. He had admitted he wanted her, but that wasn't the same as saying he cared about her or proving his worth. And he wasn't going to resist his feelings anymore. But now wasn't the time to bring things up. He still had things he couldn't speak of. Secrets.

A knock interrupted his thoughts, the paper and ink arriving.

They worked in silence, Alarian packing their things—a satchel of supplies arriving with the writing tools—while Felicity wrote the letter. When she was finished, he opened the portal to the location, placing in the missive and retrieving a small piece of parchment. "There's a letter here for you." He held it out towards Felicity.

While she opened it, he created another shadow opening and reached his hand in, a small paper in his clutches when he pulled it back out.

"Thomas?" she asked as she unfolded her brother's letter.

He scanned the parchment. "Thomas has been accepted by the Fios and he's working on deciphering the manuscript. He doesn't know how long it will take, but he will spend every waking moment on it."

She sat upright and began to read the letter from her brother. After a quick perusal, her shoulder slumped. "No news yet about father. There is—" Her mouth parted and she looked up at him. "You need to read this."

There were so many unsaid words in her expression that he hesitated for a moment before taking the letter. It started out simply. Concern etched in the curves of Kellan's writing. Then...

"A brand? An agreement?" His stomach churned and by the time he finished the letter he thought he was going to be sick. He looked up at Felicity, shadows spiraling in waves. "And a sighting of Fiadh in Tine. That confirms that they have remained my mother's ally."

"What do you think the brand means? Any ideas?" Her mouth was taut, her brow furrowed.

Alarian shook his head. It didn't make sense. "No. My parents never let me in on that information. I don't even think their advisors were aware."

He held the letter out for Felicity who took it. She scanned it again and Alarian softened as worry lines etched across her face.

"You know I'll understand if you want to return. After Saol, you can go back to Éardrom." It ached to say the words, but he needed her to know he'd support her decision.

Felicity shook her head. "I'm where I'm meant to be. Without a doubt I know that to be true."

He tried not to read too much into those words. But his heart couldn't help it. He knew she didn't mean it the way he hoped—that she was where he was always meant to be. But he'd prove otherwise. That he was worth more than his past.

Chapter 19

Felicity

Leana arrived after they wrote and sent a follow up letter to Kellan and Felicity had a bath. To give her privacy, Alarian had gone to check on the horses and ensure they were ready.

"Let me check the last of your injuries, if you don't mind. I didn't want to stress your body."

Felicity swallowed, fists gripping the robe. She schooled her emotions until a tight knot formed in her chest. It wasn't guilt for Gullist. Or for Leana's brother's death either. She didn't regret killing either one of them. It was guilt that Felicity's choices had caused Leana pain of any sort. "You don't have to trouble yourself."

The matronly fae tilted her head, observing her and Felicity knew she was using her magic to ascertain the level of her injuries.

Leana gave a small smile. "You're near healed but one wrong move or another run-in too soon and you could bleed out and reverse all the work I've done. Do you want to leave with that knowledge?"

She bit her bottom lip. She considered it, but she'd be foolish not to take the healing. "No. But only if you're sure."

"Why wouldn't I want to help you?" Leana smiled and it warmed her in a way it shouldn't. Friendly. Inviting. Trusting.

"Because I killed your husband. Your brother too." The words tumbled off her tongue, her heart pounding and chest tightening.

The female's breath caught. Her eyes welled. Felicity almost reached for her dagger to defend herself if Leana reacted. Kellan had filled her in on Gullist's part the betrayal. He had vouched for Roald and Marquette to her parents. Invited them to the Light Palace. Gave them the layout of the castle. Handed over whatever they would need to raise a coup.

They had deserved to die for what they had done. But the guilt clung tight and wrapped around her lungs. This female had healed her. Housed her. And Felicity had killed her family.

Leana closed her eyes and brushed a tear from her cheek. "You killed a vile man who I never loved. Who was forced upon me. And my brother wasn't a man worth saving anymore. He'd made his own decisions that I could never understand." She opened her eyes, her body shuddering. "In your own way, you saved me."

Felicity clenched her teeth, her own emotions rising. The knot expanded as she tried to control it all. "But—"

"No buts." Leana gave a wobbly smile. "My true love died long before my marriage to Gullist. Now, others might not feel the same way about your previous job title but for me your involvement in his death was a blessing. And even if Roald was blood—he had to pay for what he'd done. The brother I used to know and cared for had been poisoned to become the male you knew and there was no saving him."

Felicity blinked in surprise. "You don't hate me?"

"No. I don't." Leana gave her a small smile. "I thank you."

Air stilled. The world closed in on her. Sounds became mumbled. "How could...?"

Leana spoke but Felicity couldn't decipher any of it. Her brows furrowed as she tried to catch her breath. To catch herself.

"Sweet..." The rest of the words disappeared as the female reached for Felicity's face.

Her breathing sped up and her heart along with it. Images flashed through her mind.

The blood. Clear mixed with red.

The head rolling on the floor.

The intestines hanging.

Air was gone. Darkness edged her vision.

The taste of metallic on her lips.

Her reflection with splattered blood on her clothes and face.

The sound of her dagger slicing through skin.

The screams as her light blinded.

Darkness almost had her. She welcomed it. The silence. The opportunity to forget again.

"Felicity." Arms wrapped around her. His voice breaking through the tortures of her past.

Her body shook uncontrollably.

"I'm here." A hand brushed her hair from her face. "Slow your thoughts. What happened?"

She couldn't hold onto words to even attempt to talk.

The smell of burnt skin.

Words no longer register. So far away.

Eyes pleading for freedom.

The feel of her dagger pressing through muscle.

Blood coating her hands.

Trying to wash her skin.

Stained in vibrant colors of fae blood. Green for Domhain. Blue for Visce...

Something cool was pressed against her forehead before warm coffee and mint-scented breath brushed her face. "Starlight. Breathe."

It wasn't a request but an order. Another shudder instead. Curses, it felt as though her body, her mind, wasn't her own. She was going to pass out. The darkness beckoned, but him—

"You're smart. You're strong," he whispered the words like a prayer. "You're a gift." A pause. "My everything."

She gulped air.

"That's right, Starlight. Breathe." A hand against her chest tapped a beat, slow and steady. "Now with me." A long inhale.

She listened to his voice. Pinched her eyes closed against the images of flashing light. The sounds of screams. The sensation of her blade plunging through skin and muscle. "I can't—"

"You will." He tapped his fingers against her chest and pressed her hand against his. "One. Breathe in. Now."

She did as he ordered.

"Two. Breathe out. Think of Loachra."

The mention of the horse's name had her image snap into Felicity's head.

"Good. Now three. Breathe in. The brush of the wind as it slides against you when you ride."

The sounds of her surroundings began to settle again. The tapping of her hand against his chest, his against hers.

"Think of how happy you were when we raced through the field in Aer."

She blinked in surprise.

"The smile on your face was infectious."

The world came into view. Had he been watching her while they rode?

"How content and free you felt."

Was she so transparent?

New images passed over her—the memory of dancing with him in Koselig. How he had held her so timid and careful as if worried he'd scare her away. The training ring when he'd let her use him as a training dummy and didn't pull away from her beatings. His hand held out, asking for her to choose him.

Her gaze fell on his.

"There you are." He smiled, leaning in and resting his forehead against hers. "Slow breaths while you catch up."

Even with the steady tap, her heart continued to race. She kept hold of his gaze, her breathing attuned with his. "Rian," she whispered the nickname.

"Thank goodness. I hoped you wouldn't pass out," Leana sighed, reminding Felicity they weren't alone.

For a brief moment, she and Alarian remained frozen in each other's gazes before he dropped his hands and slowly straightened. "Is that better?"

All she could do was nod.

"Good." He stood and Felicity hadn't realized she was now sitting on the edge of the bed, the sheets tangled around her, some of them still wadded up in her hand. Alarian swallowed, then finally broke their gaze to look at his aunt. "I'll step out so you can do a proper—"

"No." Felicity shook her head. "Stay. I assume I don't need to remove my clothing?"

Leana hid a smile. Felicity was certain of it. "Might just need to shift things a bit is all."

She turned to look at him and his expression softened. "If you're comfortable, then I'll stay."

Felicity nodded, then turned back to the female. "How bad is it?"

Leana chuckled as she began to wave her hands inches away from Felicity's body, scanning for injuries. After a few moments, she pulled back. "Your shoulder is together but definitely taking its time to heal. There was a lot of blood loss, so you'll need to eat plenty of vegetables and protein. I'd also recommend rest, so try not to push your body to exhaustion. Don't go looking for trouble."

Leana reached up again, and Felicity hissed as heat and strain pulled against bone and muscle. "Good." Leana grinned. "A few more minutes."

She winced, but then Alarian's hand covered hers, and the world shifted again. She closed her eyes, trying to concentrate on his touch over the ache of the healing. One might think that it wouldn't hurt to be magicked back together. Felicity remembered when she'd broken her leg, and the Tower healer told her that it would be a rush of heat and nothing more. A lie told to younglings that had ended in her screaming. She'd learned how to bite through pain after that.

She ground her teeth together as the last of her injuries healed. When it was done, sweat clung to her brow.

"You did great." Leana reached for a rag and basin of water. She took the wet cloth and pressed it against Felicity's heated skin. "How's that?"

"Good." The cool water felt wonderful. "Thank you."

"No thanks needed." Leana stood, brushing a hand over her own forehead. "I was able to make some improvements. The worst of it was able to be done while you were unconscious yesterday. I hope you're able to sleep in a bed tonight. I'll worry less."

"We might be able to." Alarian squeezed her hand. "Depends on how quick we can ride."

"Please take one more hour to allow the rest of your muscles to heal." Leana headed towards the door. "I'll see you both downstairs then." She didn't leave any room for disagreement as she exited.

Alarian didn't move, as if afraid to do so. Didn't speak or look at her.

"Thank you," she whispered.

"Anytime. You should rest. I'll grab the provisions and make sure our packs are ready." He gave her hand a final squeeze, before standing, loosening his hold. She gripped tighter and he stopped, looking at her with a question in his eyes. He swallowed, his throat bobbed. "Do you want to talk about it?"

Every instinct that was trained into her for years told her to shut her mouth and pull away. "She forgave me. For killing her husband. For killing Roald. While I don't regret their deaths, I guess after all the shit I've done without question..." She shook her head.

"You needed someone to tell you it didn't matter?" The softness of his voice startled her.

All she could do was muster a nod.

He gave that damn smirk. The one that she had tried so hard to hate. The cocky grin he wore as armor. He lowered to his knee in front of her and looked up into her face. "Your past may have molded you, but it doesn't define you. You get to choose who you're meant to be. Not by the part you think you're meant to play but the person you want to be. Not as a spy. A weapon. Or a princess. Just as you are. As Felicity. Because the world won't be ready for the impact you can have on it if you embrace yourself."

She almost leaned in to kiss him—to melt into his arms. But she didn't move, stunned into silence. Stared at the freckles that dusted his nose. The fiery dark red hair that hung over his brow, shadowing his green eyes. Those broad shoulders...

She considered asking him to stay, but that would be too much right now. She'd been weak enough. Vulnerable. Emotions swirled in her mind, and she couldn't put words to them.

He slowly stood, pressed his lips to her forehead before leaving the room. She was thankful when he walked away because she was afraid of what she might say.

Chapter 20

Kellan

Kellan sat at the desk in his private study. His father's private study. A candle flickered on the edge of the table, wax skimming down the side and puddling at the base.

A gentle knock caused him to look up. Avyanna didn't wait for his acknowledgment to enter. "Here you are."

"I didn't mean to wake you." He leaned into the chair and sighed. "You should be sleeping. It was a long day, and you'll need your strength for tomorrow."

Most of the injured were healed as much as they could be physically. Mentally—that was another layer of their needs she wasn't educated enough to help with. Avyanna had not only interviewed patients about the incantation and brand but found them a specialist they could speak to about the atrocities they had witnessed or had done to them.

Avyanna ignored him. "Another dream?"

He pinched his eyes closed. "Yes."

"Which one this time?"

This time it had been the witch. Fiadh had arrived with Marquette. Looked over the symbols that had been erected around him. Nodded then glared at him and grinned. The unknown witch had waited for their perusal, cowering nearby in uncertainty. To die. Their sacrifice—for a curse that would take his identity away. He'd lost so much. The pain of his family's death and banishment still fresh. He felt it as if he was living it all over again.

Then Roald had arrived. Grimaced at the sight before him. *"Is it ready or not?"*

"It is." The unknown witch nodded. Her hands fidgeted. Kellan tried to see her features. To make her out. Roald had strutted across the room, blocking his view. Claws had elongated from his fingers. He looked down at Kellan. Stared. *"Pitiful. Your father would be disappointed."* Then with one hand, he tore Kellan from the ground, kept him dangling in front of him like a fish on a hook.

He had been exhausted. Wanted death. Wished for it, even. If only it was a chance for his father to be free. Roald's other hand rose in the air. Ready to maul. Maim him.

Then—

Kellan opened his eyes and stared at his fiancée. "The curse." He swallowed. "Again. It's like my subconscious is trying to tell me something, but I can't figure out what."

Avyanna came around the desk and settled herself between his legs. She bent over and kissed him. And for a moment he relaxed under her touch. "You're worried about your father. Your sister. I can only imagine that all of this is bringing back traumatic memories."

"Spoken like a true healer."

She shook her head. "This is beyond me. Harder to touch. But do you want to talk with one of the specialists who are helping the others?"

Kellan considered. "Not yet. But I will."

"Did you receive another letter from your sister?"

He glanced at the place where the letters were meant to arrive. It had only been two days since the update that the Fomorians were causing trouble in Domhain. Information that wasn't new since a messenger had arrived from the realm. But with further information about the unrest with the dragons and the meeting between the stone faeries, Fiadh, and McGrath—Tine's general, Kellan couldn't ignore the pressing need to deal with the beasts. Then there was the waiting for information from Thomas about the heartstones.

Not like there wasn't enough to deal with judging by the tension in his temples and the strain in his shoulders. He was stressed anyway as the days passed by. Samhain looming closer. "No. Not yet."

He and Avyanna hadn't spoken that evening. She had been asleep by the time he'd returned. "Any luck on uncovering the words of the bargain?"

"I have enough records now that I think I can decipher the most common phrases. Everyone's memories have twisted the words."

Kellan pinched his eyes closed. "You think it was more than an agreement?"

Avyanna nodded. "It seems that way."

"And what have you ascertained so far?"

She sighed, staring at the letter in her hand. "An oath of fealty. To what extent, I don't know. There are a few individuals I hope to talk to soon. They are most likely to give me the clearest accounts. Even if they don't know it by heart, they might be the most insightful."

Kellan nodded. "What do you need me to do? Maybe I should come." He felt stagnant. Continuous political matters had kept him sequestered in the palace for days. Finalizing the new guard retinue, finishing the last of the trials, and working on relations not only with the current realms in attendance, but in Saol and Scáth as well. He hadn't gotten very far. Scáth, in particular, had been quiet. A representative had arrived shortly after Felicity had left, but he hadn't attended any meetings and had only observed during social events. Any attempt at conversation had been thwarted.

Then he seemed to have disappeared. No word. No explanation. Just vanished. It didn't bode well.

"My parents sent a letter," Avyanna said as she sat down in his lap.

"Are they all right?" He still didn't like the idea of risking their lives. It felt like a perilous mistake, and he didn't want Avyanna's family in danger. He'd only met them once, but they had proved to be kind and caring. Even if, at the time, they had been under pressure by Tine's advisor to use their daughter as a bargaining chip. They trusted Avyanna's judgment when she chose to come to the palace, and to stay when the two of them had started their secret relationship.

"They are." She played with the collar of his linen tunic. "It seems they're being left on the outskirts when it comes to court matters. Fiadh comes and goes quite often with the general. Where to—they are still trying to find out. Marquette has made an appearance, and they believe she's taken the role as leader of the realm in an unofficial capacity. They aren't hiding but aren't present either. Some members of court have voiced concerns, but they're doing so behind closed doors. With the general backing the traitors, many are too frightened to do anything."

Avyanna held out the letter. "And there is one more very important item to note." He took the parchment, preparing to read but Avyanna whispered, "They *do* have a dragon."

"What the actual—"

"I know." She shook her head. "What could this mean and what do they plan to use them for?"

"Cause hell is my guess." Kellan stared at the paper, the only word he concentrated on was *dragon*, as if it would give him all the answers he needed. "How did they get them to agree? Dragons and faeries don't interact." The letter only mentioned that they had seen one a few times. The same green tinged dragon and always with Fiadh. "We need to let Felicity and Alarian know."

"There was another missive." This one was still folded and sealed shut. "It's from Sloan."

Kellan breathed in. He took the letter, opening it quickly. With each line he read, the words began to bleed together, and it wasn't until he wiped his eyes that he realized he was crying. "He found him." He looked up and smiled at Avyanna. "My father."

Chapter 21

T hey had left for Dorcha about midday and arrived at a small inn on the outskirts of the realm. Alarian had ordered her to rest while he purchased supplies and attire suitable for the freezing elements. She had been too exhausted to fight him about being left behind and instead had fallen asleep within minutes.

The following day she'd found a fox curled up at her feet. She didn't remember waking, but her aching muscles told her she had spent the night tossing and turning—on edge. She realized, looking at the gray fox as he stirred, that she wanted contact. A sensation that she'd never considered before. But despite the feeling, they said little to each other as they packed. She didn't know how to respond to his confession that night at Braum's. *All you have to do is ask.*

Or his soft words when he coaxed her out of the panic attack. She reminded herself that they had a mission. An excuse to ignore whatever was between them. Alarian, on the other hand, was more concerned that she got the rest she needed to finish healing and was nothing but caring and patient.

Why was it so hard to allow herself to fall for him? Maybe if she did, she could relieve herself of these thoughts—cravings. It had only gotten worse since his aunt's house. Now there was a continuous need to have him touch her.

Once outside, the chill of upcoming autumn mixed with the promise of Dorcha's ice and snow. They would keep the horses in town, leaving by shadow to a spot a mile from their destination. It was the closest Alarian could transport before the wards would stop them. Then they would have to brave the elements on foot for the remainder of the journey to the fortress.

Alarian held out his hand towards her. "Ready?"

She swallowed, stepping close to him and pressing her body against his. Alarian met her gaze, his entire body still. Felicity gave him a half smile. "Ready."

He drew in the shadows, his grip tightening around her waist. His heartbeat quickened. His misty scent encompassed her, the chill of the shadows a contradiction to his heat. She shouldn't want this—want him. Not with the fate of the realms in the balance. It was selfish.

The sensation of her body being lifted from the ground went ignored, her concentration solely on the press of Alarian. The feel of his arms wrapped around her. His breath against her cheek.

When they landed, she hadn't realized he'd lifted her slightly from the ground until he gently placed her down. Neither stepped away, the shadows evaporating to make way for a cold like no other, urging her to move closer to him.

Air caught in her lungs. A gust of wind caused bumps to rise on her skin. Alarian loosened his hold and pulled her hood over her head, tucking her hair within, his gloved finger grazing her cheek. "Come on. We have a walk ahead of us and we want it over as soon as possible."

His hand slid down the sleeve of her cloak and wrapped around her gloved hand. She let him lead, catching her breath, calming her heartbeat as she tried to push the sensation of his touch from her mind. But it was imprinted now. A part of her.

"Alarian?" The question was left in the balance, but he must not have heard her over the howling wind that fought to tear them apart. Maybe that was for the best.

She tripped on a jagged piece of ice—a reminder to concentrate on her surroundings. Alarian moved in front of her. Either to act as a guide or to block her from the chill. Cold, so cold. It beat at her skin, her face stinging from the elements.

Alarian peered over his shoulder and pulled a piece of wool over his nose, a signal for her to do the same. She'd forgotten about the scarf he'd given her. In

Saol, the weather held only a hint of what came from over the mountain peaks separating the two realms.

They walked in silence, unable to converse had they even wanted to. The only warmth she felt was where his hand gripped hers. It was nearly dark, the high mountain peaks blocked the sun earlier, but she was thankful there wasn't any snowfall—yet.

Felicity saw a faint glow of light in the distance. She nudged him and pointed. Alarian glanced over and his grip tightened, speed hastening towards the beacon. A thick stone wall at least six times her height expanded in view, the light just beyond it.

He reached out his hand, releasing hers. With swift movements, he removed one glove and pressed his palm against the stone. His teeth grit together, and Felicity instinctually placed her gloved hand over his bare one. Then there was a shift of stone, and Alarian pulled his hand away as an opening appeared between the cracks of the wall. A guard stood on the other side, sword at the ready. "Names?"

"Alarian and Felicity—Princess of Talamh."

The initial hesitation at hearing him speak her title aloud didn't grate as much as it had in the past. There wasn't time to dwell though since the guard immediately returned his sword to his scabbard. "Follow me. You've been expected."

Once they entered through the wall, the winds stopped, and a warmth slid over her. Felicity inhaled, the sting of her skin from the sudden heat a welcome reprieve to the numbness. The opening behind them snapped shut as the stone shifted back into place.

She took off her scarf as they passed guards in training leathers, with weapons at their sides, chatting as they passed. Others walked in formation, repeating chants from a sergeant.

"This is more than a fortress. We're in the middle of nowhere," Felicity whispered.

Alarian removed the cover from his face and stuffed his gloves in his pocket. "It seems that way. The realm feels like a desolate ice storm, but the mountains are just two miles to the west of us. They are the highest peaks in all the realms. There is a small pass where an attack once came from outside invaders. They hadn't been prepared for the freezing conditions though, but since then, there have been other attempts. A fortress was a good idea. Especially when it's filled to the brim with Night Fae."

Felicity nodded. Some of this was repetitive, she knew that the realm had the strongest and stealthiest warriors. When you had night on your side and conditions most would balk to train in, then you became hearty and strong in your own right. The information about the attacks was new to her. "Can they see in the dark?"

He shifted his pack on his back. "Yes. All Dark Fae have the ability to see in the dark, but only to the same distance as we do during the day. Some of the other faeries within the realm though...they are the monsters that parents speak of to scare children to stay in their beds. Not exactly friend or ally."

She knew the dangers of traversing through Dorcha, but she had only been sent on one mission here. Usually Dorcha had their own means to deal with any transgressions within their realm and didn't have a need to hire outside sources. Any mission that sent the Tower's recruits to Dorcha were probably hired from outside of the realm over some dispute or another.

The guard led them around a building to a home near the center of the fortress. Felicity recognized the light within a glass tower that rose above the structure as the beacon that had directed them here. Alarian moved in closer to her. "You're about to meet Sloan's family. His father is the general and his sister lives here as well. We can trust them."

Felicity nodded, understanding what he was insinuating. The guard knocked on the door before turning to them. "Welcome to Dun Brig," he said before he turned and walked away.

The door opened and a young fae stood there, the feminine version of Sloan with the same shaved head but maybe ten years younger than she was. Felicity knew immediately this must be his sister.

Her face lit up. "Alarian," she squealed, jumping out of the door and into his arms. "It's really you."

Alarian laughed, squeezing her tight before placing her back on the ground. "Good to see you too, Letia."

The female glanced at Felicity, her gaze narrowing. "Who's this?"

"The princess of the continent." A thick voice sounded behind her. "So be respectful."

A male stepped in behind her. Same midnight black skin as both of his children, his head was smooth, the beard on his face well groomed. Strong shoulders that Sloan had obviously inherited from him held insignias braided into the sleeves of his uniform. The only difference was Letia and Shale's eyes were pale blue, nearly white, to Sloan's deep brown. "Come in." He pulled Letia from Alarian's arms, the door opening wider. "I'm Shale. Glad to meet you, Princess Felicity."

She stopped herself from correcting him, swallowing the words. "Thank you." She stepped in with Alarian behind her.

Shale called to the retreating guard, "Care to join us, Macmillan?"

The guard turned, and Felicity noted Letia turned a shade of crimson at the invitation.

"No, thank you, sir. I assume you have much to catch up on." Macmillan continued on his way, his posture more rigid than it had been.

Shale chuckled, closing the door. When he caught Felicity watching, his expression softened. "Family is fun."

"Is he family?" Felicity didn't see a resemblance.

As Alarian reached out to remove her cloak, Shale shook his head. "Well, not exactly."

With the extra layers off, Felicity and Alarian followed them further into the stone home. It had a very masculine feel with antlers hanging upon the wall, sharp corners, and little decor. But it was comfortable. Thick blankets settled over leather sofas and cushioned chairs stood sentry by the large fireplace.

Letia clung to Alarian's side, talking to him in hushed tones that Felicity did her best to ignore. Even if the urge to growl at the female was increasing each moment the young female leaned in closer to him. It wouldn't be right for Felicity to claim someone who wasn't hers from a female obviously excited to see him. This was, in a way, Alarian's extended family. He'd spoken of them with a familiarity and fondness that he never showed for his own blood—excluding Leana.

Shale led them towards a grand dining room which looked larger than the entire house from the outside. Instead of one large family table, there were many of them spread throughout the space. Shale went to the one in the center and with a wave of his hand, food appeared on plates.

"Cloaking magic." He winked at Felicity's wide eyes. "Can't imagine what it must be like to see magic like this for the first time. I heard you were raised among humans?"

"Honestly, I have seen such magic used before, but not usually for domestic tasks like uncovering a meal. More often it was used to hide objects or nefarious dealings." Felicity took the seat Alarian pulled out for her.

"Sloan shared a bit about your upbringing. I could imagine it would be intriguing to see the less shady use of some magic. In this case, the cloak helps keep the food warm." Shale gestured towards the plates. "Dig in. I can only assume you're starving."

Letia took the seat between Alarian and her father. "So, we have a princess in our halls. Can't remember if that ever happened." She lifted her chin and pushed back her shoulders. Felicity wondered if she was attempting to look older. Though still a youngling on the cusp of adulthood, not much younger than Felicity, but there was a lack of maturity in her gaze. Or maybe that was admiration Felicity was picking up on—not flirtation. She couldn't be sure.

Shale sighed. "You're too young to know, but Felicity's family has been here—a few years before she was born, in fact." He nodded at Felicity.

"Oh?" Felicity leaned forward. Alarian shifted in his chair beside her.

Shale passed a bowl of greens. "That was when Sloan and your brother first met. Your mother had just learned she was expecting you."

At the mention of her mother, Felicity felt the need to change the subject. She glanced at Alarian. "And when did you meet him?"

Shale laughed, a hearty sound that hinted at mischief. "You haven't shared that story?"

Alarian cleared his throat, and Letia bounced in her chair beside him. "Can I tell?"

Alarian groaned. "If you must."

She lifted her chin and grinned larger. "They met in a bar. Both of them were losing money at the tables. Sloan had a bit of a streak going of shirking his duties and, from what I've been told, Alarian was running away from his."

Felicity glanced at him. "That sounds about right."

"It gets worse..." Alarian grumbled.

Letia giggled. "They woke up in the same bed. My bed." Her smile widened. "I was traveling with my brother, and the drinks had gotten out of hand—even for them. Their counterparts dropped them in our room, but in my bed instead of Sloan's. They woke the following morning shirtless and spooning each other. I wish I could have painted a portrait—it was so funny when they woke. They were drooling and everything."

Alarian buried his head in his hands. "At least we had our pants on."

"Trust me, I think Sloan was disappointed you did." Letia winked. "I know I was."

The growl rose in Felicity's throat unbidden. Letia turned towards Felicity, although the sound hadn't been too loud, and gave her a once over. If the others heard, they ignored it.

They ate, Alarian and the others catching up on each other's news. It wasn't until the berry compote was served that Alarian got down to business. "We're here to check on the status of your heartstone and to ask to see its location." There was a moment of silence before he continued, "We need to see if we can retrieve any information on the whereabouts of the continents forgotten stones and hope you can help."

Shale sat back, his fingers steepled in front of him. "I received your letter. We put in the order to double the guards and heighten the alerts, but Advisor Heavin wouldn't hear of it. He said we don't have the resources right now."

Heavin. That name was familiar beyond being an advisor of the realm. Felicity tried to remember why.

Alarian continued, "Even with the request coming from the acting king of the realms?"

"With the vagueness of the request, unfortunately we couldn't go above him. I don't know."

Alarian shook his head. "Sometimes he's more stubborn than the Dorcha fae he used to sit beside."

"You know he feels the need to prove his worth whenever he can."

Felicity ground her teeth. "Do you have guards on the heartstone regularly?"

Shale nodded. "At all times. They change shifts every five days. The new guards will be stationed tomorrow. If you choose, you can join them."

Felicity and Alarian shared a quick look. "Yes, please," she said.

"Father, can I go too? You said it was time for me to go up there."

Shale pinched his eyes closed. "Macmillan is going too."

She inhaled deeply, looking from Alarian to her father. "I'll think about it then."

Felicity was confused by the female's sudden frown, but Letia moved further away from Alarian in the process. Not that Felicity wasn't appreciative.

Curses. She needed to work on controlling that emotion.

Alarian stood then. "What time do we need to be ready?"

Shale wiped his face with his napkin before placing it beside his plate. "First thing. The cailleach will be ready for you then."

Felicity's eyes widened, and she pushed to her feet. Callieach. Giant lynxes with wings—the very creature she remembered ogling in Aer only months before. "We'll ride those?"

Alarian smirked. "We can ride together since it will be your first time."

"You've ridden them before?" She swallowed with a mix of excitement and anxiety.

Shale stood then. "Yes, he has. The change in elevation has been difficult for some and after your travels you should get some rest. Let me show you to your quarters for the night."

They were placed in their own rooms side by side. After a quick goodnight, Shale promised everything they needed would be ready for them in the morning, and then she was left alone.

She should sleep. It had been a long day. Very long. Her injuries no longer bothered her and even after the biting winds and a long walk, she wasn't tired. It was pitch black outside the window though she wondered if it was considered the night hours since it was the time of year that Dorcha was leaning towards perpetually dark no matter the time of day.

A giddiness settled into her that she couldn't ignore.

At the sound of fluttering paper, Felicity turned to see a note near the foot of the bed. She bent to retrieve it, and her smile brightened.

Want to train?

-A

She didn't look for ink or a quill to respond. Instead, she put her boots back on, glad she hadn't yet changed out of her clothing, and trotted to his door.

"Yes," Felicity whispered when he answered it. "I need to train."

He chuckled as he held out his hand towards her. "Let's go."

Then the shadows wrapped around them.

Chapter 22

Felicity

"I thought we couldn't travel by shadow within the fortress?" She looked around the space, taking in the stone walls and the dirt floors. There was the tell-tale musty scent of sweat and soil.

"Once we're in the fortress, we can. But we can't use it to leave the fortress itself."

"Interesting." She rolled back her shoulders, stretching her arms in different directions.

Alarian stretched his neck, watching her with a smirk. "Is it now?"

She nodded. "Of course it is. It's not very often you learn the inner workings of a fortress." She paused. "Wait. You told me that only the royal family can shift from one location or another in the castle grounds and yet you did."

"Correction." His smirk lengthened. "I said only the royal family and those the palace has deemed loyal to them. Seems it has proven my mettle without me having to do a thing."

"Oh, so you are loyal to my family?"

Alarian stalked towards the stack of training weapons. "To you, Felicity, I am. Didn't know I had to say so out loud. Haven't my actions proven such?"

Her heart fluttered, and he seemed to know because he straightened and stared at her. She cocked out a hip and he chuckled. "Magic or non-magic?"

They hadn't trained in the past few days after the attack in Domhain. And not once when they had trained prior to that had he asked her that question. But the experience with the Fomorians reminded her of something very impor-

188

tant—it might feel good to settle into her routine again, but she was ignoring one of her biggest assets.

"Magic," she answered assuredly.

That grin again. "Good." He reached into his pocket then tossed her an object.

She caught it and glanced down to find the clear second prism. "Keep it." She tossed it back to him.

"Are you certain?"

She swallowed. It had been a few days since the attack, and she'd always worn her pendant. It made sense for him to have one too since they were working together. "Yes."

Alarian placed the prism over his head and stuffed it under his tunic. He rolled back his shoulders. "How about we play a little game?"

"What do you have in mind?" She continued stretching, doing a little jog in place to loosen her muscles.

"If one of us bests the other, then we remove—"

"No." Heat rushed to her face, her eyes wide.

A corner of his mouth lifted. "Look at you, you flirty little thing."

Hell, she was paying too much attention to his mouth.

"What I was going to say was that we get to remove one of each other's weapons if we land a hit. Count them as a point system."

She appraised him for a moment, considering how many blades he might have hidden on his person. He'd surprised her before. "How do we know we are carrying an equal amount?"

The other side of his lips rose—a full smirk now. "Part of the fun, don't you think?"

"Only magic?"

He smirked. "Mostly. We don't want to maim each other after all. But we have to use our magic to best the other but...hits count. And the challenge is to use your precision. Are you game?"

She lifted a finger to her lips and tapped her mouth with a smirk. "Let's do it." Then she called her light.

Alarian was ready, gathering the shadows to him. His magic expanded, darkening the cavern until it was only her that glowed.

He disappeared. "Come find me."

She'd done this before. Worked within the darkness. Trained to rely on her other senses when one was blocked. It had saved her life more than once.

She pivoted just in time to miss a left hook but wasn't fast enough to dodge the jab that landed on her chin. She winced, but she missed her counterattack, only hitting a wisp of shadow with a slice of light.

"One point for me." He appeared beside her and reached for the dagger at her hip. "I'll start with the obvious choice first."

Before he could disappear again, she swiped his legs out from under him and he fell onto his back. He laughed between gasps for breath. "You don't play fair."

"Who said it had to be fair?" She bent down and removed the dagger at his forearm. "Tied."

She stepped away, into his shadows, diminishing her light. Felicity calmed her rising heartbeat. Listened.

Precision. He said he wanted her to practice. She inhaled, closed her eyes, and tried to picture the space prior to Alarian's rising shadows. The stone walls. The weapons on display...including the shields.

She grinned as she mapped out the layout of the room and figured out where she was in location to what she needed. But she'd been turned around too much.

A hit to her back had her sprawling against the cold earth. "You're sidetracked," he said and leaned down to trail fingers over her side and waist as he removed the blade at her thigh. She fought back a gasp, wishing clothes weren't between them. "Get back on task. You won't like my gloating."

As he stepped away, Felicity grumbled a few choice words as she got back to her feet. With a deep breath, she called the light. She knew this would draw attention, but for her own benefit. She spread her magic from her pendant to break through the rising shadows. The darkness attempted to combat the starlight, but it was forced to part. There it was. The shields.

She sensed him, like a tether connected their magic. She let it lead her, and she began to move. Quickly. Crouched low to catch him off guard—his attention on the lights reflecting off the shields. It had worked.

Her light went from her pendant reflected off the shield, and pinpointed his chest, radiating enough heat that he paused and looked down at the small pinprick against his shirt. "Impressive."

She stalked across the room and as she reached for his dagger, he grabbed her arm, attempting to twist her to the ground, but she parried and pinned him underneath her instead.

That damn grin played at his lips, and she froze. The rapid succession of the rise and fall of his chest matched her own. A sudden warmth curled around her, binding her further to the male underneath. She wanted to taste him, wanted to ignore all the reasons why she shouldn't want to touch him. Feel him. They were gone now, and it was just the two of them. "You tried to cheat."

"Did I?" It would be easier if she hated that grin.

She reached for the blade she knew was at his other forearm but stopped.

He leaned up on his elbows as her hold on him loosened, confusion playing at his brow. Her arm fell to her side. Alarian reached up and brushed a strand of hair from her face. "What's wrong, Starlight?"

Slowly, carefully, giving him every opportunity to stop her, she leaned towards him. He met her halfway, his hands sliding into the hair at the nape of her neck, tangling his fingers within. Her lips met his, warmth permeating from the touch into her core. She pressed into him, and he met the challenge with his own, tugging her slowly to him as she gasped against his mouth.

His lips formed into a smile, and then he kissed her again. The taste of him—it was unlike before. This kiss was pure temptation and heat. Lust and want. She couldn't think anymore, could only concentrate on what she needed at that moment. More.

She reached for his shirt, pulling it free from his trousers. He deepened the kiss, his tongue sliding into her mouth, and she welcomed it with fervor. Her hand rested against his stomach and grazed the defined tautness of muscle. Felicity moaned as his lips moved down to the hollow of her neck, pushing aside her collar to gain access to her skin.

"Alarian," she gasped his name, knowing she didn't want him to stop. "Please. I'm asking. Just for tonight."

His lips stopped their trail, his movements stiffening. Felicity pulled back slowly, her eyes sliding over his features. "What's wrong?"

He closed his eyes, his chin dipping. "I can't." Alarian rested his head against her shoulder for a moment before he lifted her from his lap and placed her on the ground beside him. "I can't just do tonight."

The chilly air against her damp skin had her shivering. "What? You do one nights all the time. Is it because we're friends?"

"Yes—but also no." He stumbled to his feet and held out a hand towards her.

She stared at his offer but didn't take it, getting up on her own. "What is it then? You can't—" Her eyes widened. "Oh." She shook her head. Felicity brushed off the dust from her pants, making her way towards the exit as her cheeks reddened. "Sorry, of course. I understand." She was a fool. A complete and utter fool for even thinking or considering.

He studied her. "No, I don't think you do."

She stopped, turning to look at him. "I think I do. We're friends, and just that. I must have misunderstood when you said all I had to do was ask."

The shadows shifted in front of her, and he appeared less than a step away. "We are friends, but—"

"Good," she snapped. He pursed his lips, and she rolled her eyes. "That's all we're meant to be." She removed his daggers from her body and tossed them on the ground between them. "Here." Then turned on her heel to storm out. She reached the door and opened it, and the chill of the evening air hit her skin.

"Running away? How original."

The words stung, hitting their mark. She paused. "Not like you have more to say on the matter so why should I stay?" Damn the cold. Damn him. She would use the chill to bring her back to reality.

"Because it can't be one night for me."

She stopped mid-step and peered over her shoulder. "Why?"

Shadows drew towards him, causing her to turn to face him. "You're not going to like my answer."

The reason he pulled away. The question she left unasked for weeks. Her heart stuttered. Was it to protect herself or because she didn't want to know the truth? "But I need the answer. No more secrets between us." She hated the vulnerability in her voice.

"I don't have the luxury to make promises that there aren't secrets between us. No matter how much I want to." He broke the distance between them and the expression on his face had her inhaling. His drawn brow, flushed cheeks that highlighted his stubble and freckles. There was no smirk, his mouth tight. "One night wouldn't be enough. Not for me. Not ever. When we kissed—it was just a taste, and I was already intoxicated."

With his close proximity, his words, she swallowed and stared as he continued, "But if there was ever more—than I'd be addicted to you. And I couldn't walk away like you want me to."

She didn't move. Hell, she didn't even know if she breathed. "What?"

"You would be my beginning and my end. I realized it the first time we kissed. That's part of why I stopped it. Because I knew I wanted more and couldn't bear the pain of having you walk away from me. So, this is it. This is all I can offer you. We can be friends like you asked. But I cannot do *just* one night. Because I want all the little things, and the big things. I'm laying myself bare—and giving it all to you and only you can decide what you want to take, Starlight."

He leaned in then, pressed his forehead to hers. Instinct had her nearly melting into his touch. To break the final distance between them and kiss him again. Yet—she didn't move. Just stared into his eyes.

"You were the one who asked to be friends," she whispered.

"Because I saw it. You hesitated. You're trying to find your place and I can understand that." He cupped her jaw and leaned back to meet her gaze. "When you realize who you are, who I know you are." His finger brushed her cheek. "If you're ever ready, and I'm deemed worthy, all you have to do is say so. Because letting you go will break me. And right now, I can't break. Not when so much is at stake."

Her limbs were like lead. She didn't know what to say. Where to begin. Their conversation on that bluff the day he was freed replayed in her mind. When he'd brushed a strand of hair from her cheek, and she stilled. Turned away. She had been thinking it would be safest to call him a friend and then he'd said the word. Offered the chance to hide from her confusion longer.

With him looking at her this way now, it would be so easy to allow herself to fall into him, but his last words reminded her of their mission. The importance of keeping her distance and avoiding distractions. This was the reason why she had kept herself under control for so long.

A tear stung—the sensation foreign, but she forced her resolve, straightening her shoulders. "Then we understand each other. The mission, protecting the realms, must come first." She was a coward. An utter incomprehensible coward. And she knew it.

He shuddered, then drew himself up, becoming the male she hadn't seen since that moment on a cliff many moons ago. When he'd lost so many to a cause he hadn't thought they'd win. The façade of strength and fortitude—the pain behind it all hidden. "We should head back. I think we both need a good night sleep in preparation for tomorrow."

She didn't question him as he called on the shadows. Nor did she when he didn't hold her as close as he usually did. And not when he took her straight to the entrance of her room.

He kissed her forehead and stepped back. Suddenly, he was gone, only the wisps of shadows that brushed against her skin were proof she hadn't imagined it all. She knew if she knocked on his room, he wouldn't be there. He had gone somewhere she couldn't easily follow.

A fissure in her heart cracked open. And knowing that she caused him similar pain made her entire body ache. Felicity entered her room and curled up in her bed, her legs pressed into her chest and arms wrapped around them. Although the tears didn't come, inside she was falling apart. She'd made her choice, and it felt like the wrong one. But how could it when the entire continent needed them to stay on task?

Or when he offered her everything when she only felt lost. She pinched her eyes closed and began to count before the fear and darkness could edge in. The thoughts...

Spy.

Princess.

She inhaled a long breath and held it, counting.

Mission. This was one thing she could concentrate on. That she knew how to do.

Alarian had said so himself—too much was at stake. He was a distraction—a weakness—in a time she couldn't afford one.

A sudden clatter sounded, and Felicity sat up to find her weapons by the door. Each dagger he had removed. She couldn't bring herself to get up and collect them.

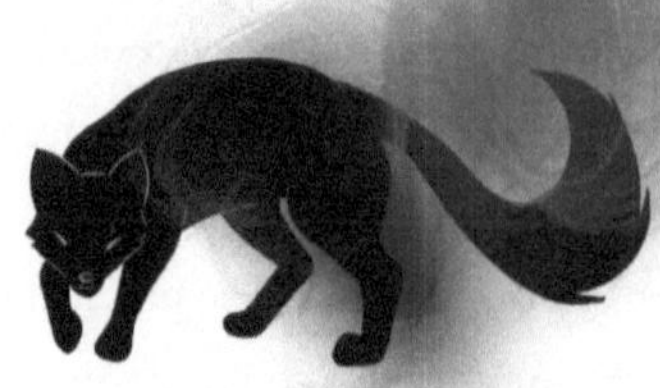

Chapter 23
Alarian

The previous night had been a new kind of torture for Alarian. He had been on the precipice of breaking. Rushing to her room and taking it all back, one night or not.

He knew he was right, though. Knew that if he went to her as badly as he wanted to, that one night would tear him apart. And she said it—said that she didn't want him. Not then. Not now. He wasn't important enough for her to put aside their mission.

And why should he be?

His family was the reason they were in this mess. Decades of pain and suffering that he'd never been strong enough to stop. Never been capable of pulling off on his own. He had the chance to take his parents' lives, to put an end to the suffering of an entire kingdom, and he'd never taken it.

He needed to make things right and ensure she knew he was still her friend.

When he left his room the following morning, Felicity met him in the hall and looked just as worn around the edges as he did. That didn't make him feel better. Guilt built in his chest, pressing against his lungs.

"Morning." The word gruffer than he planned.

She glanced up at him and then quickly away. "Morning."

Her tone was stinted. His stomach plummeted further. "Listen, Felicity—"

"There you two are." Letia rounded the corner. "Ready?"

Felicity looked up and he immediately recognized her expression of indifference. The hurt, confusion, and embarrassment. All forced behind a blank gaze and fake grin that he could feel within the bond. It made a part of him ache further.

"Yes, we're ready." Felicity adjusted the pack on her back. A small rush of excitement brushed through her and he hid his smile. The cailleach—of course she'd find joy in the animals and what was to come.

"Good. Come on then. My father's waiting." Letia continued past them.

Felicity breathed a sigh and finally looked at him. "I'm fine, Alarian. We have a job to concentrate on." A crooked smile, one he could see right through. "We're still friends."

He almost called her out on the lies but stopped himself. Right now, what would that do? It was true that they needed to concentrate on the task at hand. He'd talk to her about all of this later. Whatever was between them, he refused to lose. Even if it was just friendship. Besides they had days together on the road while they traveled to Saol and Visce, before heading to Éardrom. Each day that passed was one less they had to stop his mother. And less than sixty days remained.

When they reached the dining room, a meal was laid out with an abundance of food that Alarian barely touched as they waited for the guards who would escort them to the stone's location.

"I see you decided to go, Letia?" Shale sipped on a mug of coffee from his chair.

Letia lifted her chin. "Yes, I did. Figured it's one thing to fly up, but wholly another to come back down."

"Is this a one-day trip?" Felicity asked. She was looking over the packs piled up on one of the tables.

"No." Shale shook his head. "You will fly up about two thirds of the way today. There is a cave on a mountain ledge where you will camp for the night. Then you will arrive late morning tomorrow. Coming back is much faster though. It's just a lot on the cailleach to fly upwards with the elements and elevation change. While some of our mounts can make it in a day, if we don't have to force that upon them, we don't."

Felicity sat down, Alarian taking the seat across from her, and picked at her food. He didn't comment as he realized he was doing the same.

The guards arrived, Macmillan among them. Letia quickly looked anywhere else. Alarian had noticed the interaction yesterday and wondered who they thought they were fooling. Shale even shook his head at them, obviously aware that something was going on.

It was time to leave, and after they had donned extra layers to protect themselves from the harsh icy elements, Shale walked them to the door. They were halfway to the stables when Letia took Alarian's arm and pulled him to a stop. "Can we have a moment please?"

He noted Macmillan's rigid posture at the request. Alarian shrugged. "Of course."

Felicity didn't spare them a second glance as she followed the other guards out. Alarian sighed, turning away from her to give Letia his attention.

She bit her bottom lip, glancing at him nervously. "I'm sorry, Alarian."

His brow furrowed. "For what?"

Letia swallowed. "I've fallen in love with someone else."

Alarian rubbed his neck. "Um." He glanced up to see that Macmillan was waiting at the door, his face unreadable from the distance. But why was she—then he remembered and tried to hold back his grin. When she was much younger, she'd made a playful remark about wanting to marry him. He'd been able to carry her in his arms then and had thought nothing of it. Obviously, she had.

Alarian salvaged what he could of his reaction. "Well, that's understandable. We have a friendship to consider after all. And the distance. I'm not surprised that you have met someone." He glanced at Macmillan and then back to her. "I'll only be all right with this though if I know he is treating you well."

"He does." She blushed, playing with the end of her braid. "If it makes you feel any better, I think the princess may be interested in you. Just know that you're free to see whoever you like."

Oh, to be young and naive. It was both a blessing and curse. "Thank you, Letia. I'll cherish our time together."

She reached for his hand and he let her take it. Before Alarian could react, she pulled him closer and kissed him straight on the mouth. He was too shocked to react. A growl broke them apart and Alarian turned to see Felicity at the door standing behind a vengeful-looking Macmillan. Fuck—if Shale had seen—but Felicity was bad enough.

Felicity's fingers were wrapped around the hilt of her blade. He didn't have a moment to react before she dropped her hand and turned to go inside without a second glance. Alarian didn't know if it was Macmillan or Felicity who had audibly reacted. Either way, it couldn't get any worse.

When they entered the stables a moment later, Letia trotted over to Macmillan. The young guard cast a death glare at Alarian as she bubbled over with excitement in a high-pitched whisper.

Alarian got to work on preparing his mount when the other guard, Murray, arrived at his side. "Here's the tack you'll need."

He looked over the supplies. "I'll need another strap for Felicity."

Murray swallowed, looking over his shoulder and then back to him. "The princess has asked to ride with me."

He bristled. This would be her first time riding on the cailleach, and he'd be lying if he hadn't looked forward to sharing this experience with her. But what could he do now? Alarian couldn't force Felicity to ride with him. Especially not after what she witnessed. He hoped she knew it hadn't meant anything to him, but after last night—

There wasn't time to consider the ramifications because Murray was already assisting her on his mount. With patient and calm words, he went over where to put her hands and how to grip her thighs—the details Alarian had wanted to teach her. Reality ached in his chest. She'd made her choice and he would respect it. But that didn't make the sting any less.

Alarian mounted his cailleach. The lynx shook his gray and white head, peering at Alarian over its shoulder before seeming to resolve itself. Macmillan urged his winged lynx beside Alarian. "I apologize for my coldness towards you."

He fought not to bury his face in his hands at this point. It was too early for any of this. "It's quite all right."

But Macmillan wasn't done. "I had thought you wouldn't understand. Or worse, that Letia would change her mind once she saw you again. You're a lot more formidable than I remember."

Remember? Did this male know him? Alarian grimaced, ducking his head to hide his expression. "I just want Letia happy." The two of them were perfect for each other, because neither seemed to be able to catch the obvious cues that Alarian wasn't interested.

"I do apologize that she kissed you. I don't think she realized that the princess was watching. Maybe Letia should—"

Oh no. There was no way he was about to let that happen. "No. Felicity and I are friends. Just extra protective of each other because we've been through a lot together."

"Oh, understood." Macmillan cleared his throat. He glanced around before settling on the lynx, clearing his throat. "Your cailleach is named Gaoth. He prefers to be scratched behind his left ear, not the right, and he banks fast. Just so you know."

"Thanks." Alarian patted the beast on the shoulder. Gaoth shook his head—the lynx hadn't warmed to him yet.

They headed out on the mounts into the yard. The others started to fix gloves and thick covers over their faces. He attempted to catch Felicity's attention and ask her to reconsider, but she didn't look in his direction once. A growl of possessiveness caught in his throat. He had no right to hate the way the male's arms wrapped around her body to hold the reins. Nor how she was settled close to him to fight off the chill. How could he have made the situation so much worse? And why had Letia felt the need to kiss him?

"Ready?" Macmillan glanced about the group.

When the riders nodded, Macmillan nudged his cailleach and the winged lynx leapt off the ground. Felicity let out a yelp of excitement that he felt in a prickle along his back when her mount did the same. Alarian urged Gaoth to follow and the cat let out a hiss before taking a few meager steps, stretched out his gray feathered wings, and then pushed from the ground in annoyance. It seemed it would take some time to get the beast to like him. Reminded him of a certain female...

Macmillan sent a flash of darkness into the sky and an opening cracked through an invisible barrier. Already the chill of the outside hit Alarian but once they passed through the crack, his muscles locked up for a moment, reacting to the sudden cold. He pressed himself closer to the cat, trying to loosen himself up so that his body didn't cease further. A heavy wind bit at their faces. Flurries attacked, ice and snow mixed with a wind that brought the temperatures below freezing. Shit—they hit a storm and had to fly right through it.

The others didn't seem to note the weather, flying ahead while remaining close. The cailleach couldn't care less, their flapping wings along with their thick coats were warm enough to ward off the chill. Alarian was thankful for the layers, especially Gaoth's speed picked up to clump in with the others.

Cailleach didn't commonly stay within groups, but they were smart when it came to battling the weather. A glow of light caught his attention. Felicity's pendant shined and she sent the heat of her magic ahead of them to carve through the chill and light their way amidst the limited visibility. Even Letia seemed impressed by the white light.

They evened their ascent, and although Alarian could barely see in front of them beyond Felicity's light, the Dorcha fae had no issues seeing in the dark and leading the way. They flew in silence, the distance too far between them and the air too thin for talking.

When they reached a location the Dorcha fae seemed to know on instinct, they urged the cailleach into a steady climb upwards. With each passing moment, the darkness encapsulated them within the turbulent snowstorm. Time felt like it stood still. Before he knew it, they were flying upwards in almost a straight vertical climb. Alarian's calves ached from keeping a grip on Gaoth, his body pressed as close to the beast as possible to allow an easier flight. Gaoth flew as if Alarian wasn't even there, not at all deterred by the extra weight.

It wasn't soon enough when Murray called back that the cave was in sight. They landed, Gaoth letting out a groan as they passed through a barrier. The others were laughing as they dismounted, two guards chuckling about the snowstorm.

Letia, given her experience with the weather, looked tired but giddy. She rushed to Macmillan and jumped into his arms, letting out a whoop of excitement. He laughed as he twirled her around, the two celebrating something Alarian didn't quite understand. Even Murray looked more annoyed than ready to join in. While Letia regaled the experience, Murray began to take care of his mount. Felicity mimicked his movements with another lynx while Macmillan and Letia went further into the cave, leaving them behind.

Alarian remained silent, listening as Murray guided Felicity through the steps of untacking and caring for the cailleachs. He tried to ignore the quiet words, the occasional chuckle, the easiness he felt from Felicity as Alarian took care of his and Letia's mount. A moment later, he was certain he heard his name and peered over his shoulder to see the guard nod, walking into the cave and leaving them alone.

He cleared his throat, turning to face her, unwilling to let the moment pass. "You know I didn't want or try to kiss her, right? It was unexpected and—"

Felicity shook her head. "You don't have to explain it to me, Alarian. I know there isn't something between you and Letia."

"And never was. For one she's my best friend's sister. And there seems to have been a misunderstanding. You see—"

She reached over and covered his mouth with her hand. He stopped talking immediately.

"Truly, there is nothing to discuss on the matter of the kiss."

"Then why didn't you ride with me?"

Felicity's jaw flexed and he blocked out the emotions he saw battling in her eyes. "Honestly? I was a bit embarrassed."

His chest felt as though his heart would beat from his chest. "I never intended to make you feel embarrassed. We should talk about this."

She looked down to the ground between them. "I chose not to ride with you because I needed a moment to collect myself. That's all. I'm sorry if I upset you."

He wanted to say that it only made him utterly jealous, but he bit back the words.

"We're still friends, correct?" She peered up at him beneath her lashes. Damn, that only made him want to continue what happened the previous night. To curse himself until the end even if that meant he'd break.

"Of course we are. I'm not trying to pressure you and if you feel that I am—"

"No." She shook her head. "It's not that. I need to not talk about this right now though. But soon."

"Of course."

"Good." Felicity gave him a cautious smile. "Again, I apologize."

"Forgiven. Not that you did anything wrong." What game were they playing? He wanted to tell her the truth. About the bond forming between them, about his feelings—but it wasn't only fear that held him back. It was part of what was keeping him together. The unknown. Even if she could ever feel as deeply for him as he did her, she was still figuring out her own identity. And while that broke him a little, he could accept it. He never wanted her to feel that she didn't have a choice. Whatever happened between them must be because she wanted it to.

She headed to follow the others. "Want to help me get the food and water? Murray told me where we could find them."

After he assisted her, he followed her deeper into the cavern to where the others huddled. They ate around a fire that warmed the entire cave before curling up on mats in a circle. Felicity laid only a few feet away, but the distance felt like it was growing by the moment.

The nightmares came that night. Ones he hadn't had in some time.

He jerked awake at the third one, his heart racing like a caged animal and despite the chill in the air, his skin was clammy to the touch. He stiffened as a warmth curved against his back, fingers trailing soothing circles along his shoulder. Concern oozed from her—not pity but understanding. The sensations soothed him and this time when he slipped off to sleep, he dreamt of her.

Chapter 24

Alarian

The storm had blown over during the night. It was still cold the next day, but the sky was layered with thin clouds and a dim light broke through. The guards grumbled a bit at the lack of darkness, and Alarian could understand missing the easy access to their magic. Murray extinguished their fire since he was also of Tine heritage and had a touch of their magic.

"It's a requirement," he explained. "One of us must have another magic to call upon otherwise without darkness, there isn't a way to protect the stone. It's a safety precaution."

Alarian was glad they had these considerations in mind, although a sense of dread had settled within him the closer they neared the heartstone. It might be that they were nearly flying straight up, or maybe because he could see just how high they were in daylight. Felicity had chosen to finish the ride with him, and although he held her close, he was worried he'd fail and they'd both plummet to their deaths. Gaoth wasn't that keen on him, but he would at least save Felicity.

The cailleach had quickly taken to her. Maybe he should take note of the treats she used or the spots she scratched behind his tufted ears because he had a feeling Macmillan may have lied to him.

When they broke into clouds, Letia squealed loudly in excitement. Even Felicity's quiet emotions spiked with joy.

"We're almost there," Macmillan called out to them. "Just have to go through the cloud layer."

Wisps of clouds surrounded them and Alarian actually looked forward to the thick cumulus that were ahead. He hadn't realized until now that he might have a fear of heights and actually missed the clouds blinding him from how far he was from the ground. Or maybe it was just that he'd never had time to consider it since he hadn't spent much time climbing mountainsides on a flying lynx.

They reached the threshold of the clouds. A heaviness wrapped around them, condensation soaking their clothes as they entered. Alarian closed his eyes, trusting his mount—even if the beast didn't care a lick about him.

Felicity chuckled, the sensation reverberating against his chest.

"What?" he grumbled.

"Are you frightened?"

Alarian shifted. "What makes you think that?"

"I don't think I've ever felt you so stiff. Your knuckles are white on the reins, and your legs haven't relaxed once. No wonder Gaoth isn't sure about you." He could hear the smile in her voice.

"Oh? Relax my legs? Why would I do that if that meant I would fall?"

"Your legs are in front of his wings. You're probably pinching the muscle he's using to fly. Add in the fact that you are obviously holding on for dear life, Gaoth probably assumes you don't trust him." She placed her hands on top of his. "Relax just a bit. Grip with your thighs, but the death hold isn't necessary. Lean forward to keep with the momentum instead."

Alarian did as she said, and he was almost annoyed when he felt Gaoth relax underneath him. "I've flown plenty of times and haven't had that problem before." There was a defensive note in his voice.

"Maybe it's the ascent. It made me nervous too. Murray talked me through it." Felicity's fingers began to graze circles on top of his.

With the sensation of her touch and the warm press of her body, he relaxed enough to ignore the frequent mention of the guard's name. Almost.

Gaoth purred, the sound echoing through the clouds surrounding them. But just as quickly, the cat's body stiffened beneath them, a growl vibrating.

Felicity inhaled, the sound and movement like a second skin to him. "Do you feel that?"

He really needed to stop concentrating on her. He forced his attention to the task at hand and glanced around. There was a scent in the air, intentions thick...this couldn't be good.

An order, incoherent but the tone demanding, sounded from ahead. Gaoth shifted left, the sudden movement catching Alarian off guard that he forgot Felicity's words and his grip tightened on all fronts. A cave opened ahead, stone jutting off like a cliff from the mountainside. They landed abruptly, the lynx shaking its head in irritation. Felicity and Alarian undid the straps and jumped off Gaoth as Murray rushed back to them, having landed first.

"They're dead," he gasped out the words before he turned to the side and vomited. The scent of bile mixed with the heady smell of burnt skin and blood.

Felicity and Alarian glanced at each other and then ran into the cave. The sensation of the remnants of a barrier tingled against his skin. They stopped once they entered and Alarian ran a hand through his hair as he took in the grotesque remains of the guards' charred bodies slumped against the cave wall. Felicity gripped Alarian's arm and pointed with her other hand. He followed the direction and saw an alcove within the wall at the highest point of the cave.

No stone remained. It's former resting place similar to that of the alcove in Domhain.

"Dragon," Macmillan hissed the words, glancing about at the ash and bodies. "It must have been. There were sightings of one recently, but we heard about the trouble in the Balla Mountains. Knew the beasts and the Fomorians were fighting. We didn't give it a second thought."

Alarian straightened. It was worse than he imagined. "It was more than a dragon." He walked across the space, looking at where the heartstone was meant to be. The letters written in blood underneath them. A warning flagged in stone: *I know.*

He whirled around, heading towards the cave. "We have to get back."

Letia rushed to catch up to them, Felicity at his side. "What is it?"

"Marquette stole the stone," Felicity answered on his behalf. "We need to warn your father."

Macmillan and Murray rushed to catch up, the former a step behind Letia. "We need to stay here and take care of our comrades. Warn Shale." There was a catch in his voice.

Alarian mounted Gaoth. "I'm sorry for the loss of your friends."

Macmillan shuddered and then glanced at Letia. "Take them back safely."

She jumped onto her cailleach. "Let's go."

Their flight down was much quicker, the cats aware of the urgency. Alarian's stomach rose in his throat at the speed, but he fought it down.

Felicity urged Gaoth with Alarian concentrating on not getting in the cailleach's way. Letia created the pathway through the barrier of the fortress much quicker than Alarian had expected. They landed in front of Shale's home late in the evening. Letia had her harness unclipped and dismounted in one fluid movement. Alarian was not as lithe, and although Felicity probably could dismount just as nimbly, she waited for him as he took a moment to catch up. Assistants rushed towards the cailleach to take them back to the stable, worried glances following Letia and their urgency to the house.

"Father," Letia bellowed, flinging the doors open wide. Alarian and Felicity caught up as Shale rushed to the entryway wearing his general uniform and confusion marring his features.

"They're dead," she gasped out the words.

Letia fell into Shale's embrace. He looked at Alarian and Felicity for the answer to the question swimming in his eyes.

"The heartstone is gone." The words nearly stuck in Alarian's throat. "The guards are dead. A dragon—it looks like my mother has a dragon."

Shale squeezed Letia tighter. "Where are the others?"

"They remained behind to collect evidence and bring back—the bodies." Felicity's gaze lowered to the space between them. "I'm sorry. So sorry we weren't here in time."

Shale shook his head. "It must have been within the past few days. And with a dragon, there was no way we could have been prepared. If you had been here sooner, there is a chance you would be dead now too."

Alarian fought back the protectiveness bubbling up within him. He'd make sure his mother was dead long before that ever happened.

Shale cleared his throat. "We have another problem." He peered over his shoulder. "A visitor arrived this morning. I've kept him entertained, but Advisor Heavin isn't easily distracted. It seems he wanted to check on the status of our patrols. He'll be here any minute."

Felicity and Alarian shared a look. This couldn't be a coincidence. He stepped forward, ready to deal with the male. If the advisor was here, it was because he knew something. Felicity grabbed his arm and held him back. "I will take care of it."

Alarian's expression tensed. "I'll be right there."

"No." She glanced at Shale. "Has he mentioned mine or Alarian's presence?"

"He's only hinted that he's aware I've been in contact with Prince Kellan. Nothing else."

Felicity squeezed Alarian's arm. Before she spoke, he could sense what she was going to say. "Don't let him know you're here. I can handle this."

He grinned. "I know you can." Pride had his grin lengthening as she turned to Shale.

"Keep him entertained for a little longer. I'll be right there."

Shale nodded and walked away, whispering words to his daughter as he went.

Alarian remained quiet. Felicity breathed a sigh. "We need to leave as soon as I can get this taken care of. With the information we have, we might be able to find Visce's heartstone before her. We must."

Letia returned without her father. "The cailleach. They travel much faster than horses and you can save time instead of going back. We'll have supplies ready for you by the time the bell tolls the hour."

Felicity still hadn't let go and he used her touch as an anchor. The reality of how cold he'd been battled with the warmth generated from the barrier. He hadn't even realized it, a shock to his system, as had everything that had happened within the last few hours.

"Thank you," he murmured.

Letia nodded. "Come, Alarian. I'll pack up the princess's bag for her. If you don't mind?"

Felicity thanked her and Letia walked towards the hall.

Alarian put his hand over where Felicity's still rested over his arm. "Do you know who he is? What you're dealing with?" Advisor Heavin was here for a reason and there was a good chance it was on his mother's orders.

The smile that she gave him was vicious. "Yes."

"You know you shouldn't kill him." Explaining his sudden demise to the other Dorcha councilors may make things messy for her family. Not a headache they needed right now.

"Shouldn't?" Her brow rose.

"I trust your judgement."

She chuckled. "Good."

With one final squeeze, she let go and removed her layers of clothes until only her training leathers were exposed. She handed him the clothing, then turned on her heels, shoulders drawn back, head held high, a swagger in her step.

Alarian smiled to himself. *There she was.*

Chapter 25

Felicity

She remembered who Heavin was now—a name on the list her brother had given her months before. One of the remaining individuals she hadn't been able to frame. At least not in a way that would have appeased Roald.

She opened the door and a pale male with a pointed chin turned towards her. The sneer, because it definitely wasn't a smile, that spread made Felicity's palm itch for the dagger at her hip.

"Well, if it isn't—"

"Princess Felicity." She walked up to him, looking down her nose at him. "Lord Heavin."

He made a pathetic attempt at a bow. "I didn't expect to find you here."

Her brow rose, but she ignored him to turn to Shale. "I've got it from here. Thank you."

Shale nodded, giving a respectful bow Felicity knew was to prove a point.

Once he was gone, Felicity turned her attention back to the advisor. "I've been tasked with checking in with our allies. Especially those who have left others in their stead to advise my brother. While we appreciate Sloan's attendance and loyalty, is there a reason you chose to ignore your summons to your post in Eardrom?"

That sneer disappeared. "What are you insinuating?"

Kellan had told her why he was on her list. How he had planned Marquette and Roald's invitation to her birthday party. Had offered his station as a steppingstone to gain the traitors' favor.

What promises had they made to him? And was he still their ally now?

"No insinuation. Just a question. You weren't there when the trials were required for all the previous leadership's council."

"So your brother sends out his sister—the spy, the assassin—to do his dirty work?"

She smiled. And it all settled something within her. The duty. The part she was meant to play. Or even better, be. "I only have to get my hands dirty if you don't comply."

The male chuckled. "I see. Well, I will make it a point to visit the kingdom soon. With the upcoming change in seasons, it's a hassle to travel. As I'm sure you're aware."

Felicity could hear the callousness in his tone. It wasn't the change of season, but a change in leadership he was expecting. Felicity trailed a finger upon the edge of the high-backed chair as she walked closer. "I'm aware."

"Then you understand my hesitancy for attempting to make my way across the entire continent."

Her blade was in her hand, at his throat, and the male squealed as he fumbled backwards into the desk, arms sprawled to hold himself upright. "You can't—wouldn't—"

"What?" She tilted her head, considering him. "Slice your throat open right here? Leave your body on the ground as you suffocate on your own blood?"

"You—" His throat bobbing against the blade. "You don't have a reason for this."

"No. Which is why I won't be ending your life. But, if you don't return to Éardrom within five days—and trust me I'll know if you don't—to stand trial, I guarantee that I will find you and then yes, you will have my blade embedded in your chest."

"Why would I go when you're just going to assume the worst and kill me there?"

"Funny—not a single person has died yet after a trial. If you don't go though, then we'll assume you are not only assisting those who are a danger to the continent but aiding them while disobeying a direct order from your princess."

She watched him. Tracked the shudder that worked through his body. "And therefore, deserve to die."

He stood stock-still. Whether it was fear or something else that held his tongue, she didn't care. "Do we have an understanding?"

"Yes," he hissed.

She removed the blade from his skin but remained in his space so that he didn't dare move. "Kellan, your prince, will expect you in five days."

"It takes five days to travel to the capital from here."

She stepped back and turned towards the door. "Then I'd be sure to hurry if I were you."

When Felicity exited, Shale was waiting for her. He glanced from the door back to her. "Is there a mess to clean up?"

She smiled. "No. At least not yet. Come, we have much to discuss. Would he leave by magic?"

Shale shook his head with a wry smile. "No, there would be no attention if he did that."

They spoke in hushed voices as they walked together to the hall where her and Alarian's rooms were.

"Have one of your best follow him. Or if there is someone he trusts that you trust even more, put them in his employ to track his movements. I have no doubt Heavin is heading straight to Marquette."

Shale nodded. "May I ask why?"

She didn't have to ask what he was referring to. "If I killed him, then it wouldn't send the proper message. He may lead us straight to others that have allied with Marquette. Besides, we have more pressing matters to consider right now."

Shale nodded. "I think Letia packed your things but check to ensure you have everything. I'll get a tail on Heavin before he leaves and then can see you both off."

"Thank you."

Felicity arrived at her room and closed the door, staring at the bags ready on her bed. A scan of the room informed her that Letia had done a thorough job.

There was clatter in the room beside hers. Alarian's room. She bit her bottom lip, made her way to his door and knocked.

The sounds stopped before the door opened. Alarian stood, sweat glistening on his bare toned torso. He blinked, his cheeks reddening as he leaned against the doorjamb. "How did it go?"

Felicity had to force her gaze away from him for a moment. Collect herself. There was so much she wanted to tell him. How she had felt when she walked into that room. Had warned—neigh threatened—Heavin. But in his current state of undress, she was already feeling the draw and distraction of his body. The fine lines of muscle. The sprinkle of freckles. The perspiration glistening on his skin. "May I come in?"

"Oh, sorry. Yes." He stepped aside and closed the door behind her.

She glanced around the room. It was much like her own. Simple and comfortable for guests. His bags were also packed on the bed, ready to go, but his shirt sat folded beside it. The only thing out of place was a coat rack that was toppled over on its side.

"I asked Shale to have someone trail the lord. Either Heavin will do as I told him and go to the palace to await trial or, the likely alternative, head straight to Marquette." She had noted how the use of 'mother' caused him to withdraw and stopped using the word as he'd respected her about the title she cowered upon hearing.

"I knew you could handle it."

She faced him now. "Alarian?"

His head jerked up, meeting Felicity's gaze.

"You need to talk to me. What's going on in that head of yours?" she spoke in a whisper.

He ran a hand through his hair before he reached for a towel. "Nothing. Just considering our options."

"And?"

He wiped his face. "After Saol, we may need to visit an old friend of yours."

Her brow furrowed. "Who? I don't exactly have *old* friends."

"Someone from Visce who would be likely to help. Someone who would know the area well and can point us in the direction of the deepest lake or swamp. Because I think we both know that's where we will have to search for the stone."

"And if we know that, certainly your mother will too." She bit her lip, glancing at the door. "Is that information you think we can't get from someone else. Anyone else?"

She couldn't help the trepidation bubbling up in her stomach. This could be a very bad idea. It's not that she didn't like Lady Molyle, it was more that the female enjoyed a good story—and loved spreading them more.

Alarian ran the towel over his hair. "No, at least not someone we can trust. Dark Fae won't have that information—we need someone close to the realm itself."

Felicity groaned, running a hand over her face.

"She invited you to visit, I assume."

She peered at him between her fingers. "Of course she did. It's not that. I just know she will squeal in excitement that I'm a princess..."

"Probably. But in the best possible way." Alarian chuckled. "By the way, that's the first time you've used your title so easily."

She waved off his observation. It didn't seem that important with everything else. "I like her. It's just that she has more energy than I could ever fathom. You're going to have to explain why we're there to Lady Molyle. Good luck with that."

Alarian chuckled.

"That doesn't explain this." She gestured to his shirtless, sweaty torso then the horizontal coat rack.

Alarian winced. He rubbed the back of his neck with the towel now and her eyes may have lingered on the way his biceps flexed. How every bit of him had become defined again after being out of those manacles.

"I was distracting myself."

"From?"

"The fact that my princess was talking to a male that deserved to be torn apart, and I couldn't be by her side."

Her brow rose and lips pursed, resisting the shudder at the way he claimed her. Could she get used to that? "I can handle—"

His hand rose to stop her. "That's not what it was at all. I had every desire to be in that room and watch the interaction without intervening. The fact I couldn't be there, though, I didn't exactly like that." He tossed the towel to the chair. "It's instinct—I can't help it. And I'm so damn proud of you."

She was taken aback, her heart began to race while her breathing momentarily stilled.

He smirked. *Her* smirk. "You sauntered in that room, and I saw it. Saw you."

Now she couldn't help but smile. "It felt right." She bit her lip. "For once, it felt right."

"I saw it. And hell, I wanted—" He reached out to touch her but stopped himself, his hand falling to his side.

"I'm trying to figure myself out." She stared at that hand for a moment. After admitting her embarrassment, she had kept one thing from him. One thing that felt impossible to say, but he deserved to hear. "I'm scared."

"What?" He didn't sound surprised exactly. More shocked that she actually admitted it aloud.

Felicity reached for his hand, unable to meet his gaze. "Of what I feel for you. It's not fair of me to keep that to myself. But I don't understand it all yet."

She looked up and he was staring at her, dumbstruck. Was he breathing? "I'm terrified that if anything happens between us, and it all goes to hell, that I'll fail. This mission. My brother. The continent. Too much is in the balance. So maybe it's selfish, but I can't risk it right now."

He tore his gaze away and stared at his hand in hers. Then stepped a little closer. Pressed his forehead against hers. "I won't push you, Starlight. But I meant it. You say the word, and I'll be there."

She wanted to kiss him. To seal his words with a vow. The scar on her palm tingled. That reminder of their connection. Sometimes it felt that the promise of a dance had grown. That there was more between them, tying them together. "Thank you," she whispered.

"Are you ready to leave? We want to beat the cold and be sure that Heavin has left."

"Yes." She swallowed, stepping away. "Let's eat to give some distance between us and Heavin. I promised if I saw him again, that I'd kill him for disobedience. Don't know if that would really fix our current problems. I also don't want him to know we're traveling together."

Alarian's jaw worked. "If you're right, which I bet you are, then he's running to Marquette and Fiadh. I wonder what he was promised to gain such loyalty."

Felicity shrugged. "You said those abducted people were forced to mine for gems and treasures to pay off their allies. Could it be as simple as that?"

"I don't know." He turned away, removing his hand from hers and grabbed his shirt. "Maybe whoever is following him will find out."

"Maybe."

Either way, this was information she needed to share with Kellan. "We need to check if Thomas or my brother has another letter for us too. I should probably write to Kellan."

He nodded towards the desk. "There is ink and parchment there. Grab what you need."

She took a seat and considered the past few days. Dorcha's stone was gone. A dragon was confirmed to be within Marquette's control somehow, and they had run into a potential enemy. She hoped Kellan would have good news because things were looking rather dim.

Chapter 26

Kellan

Well, shit.

The letter Kellan received from Felicity hadn't been filled with the news he'd hoped for. Thomas had yet to break the code of the book. Dorcha's heartstone was another loss. Already here at home, clouds began to accumulate—not weather the Light Realm was used to seeing for a few days on end. They had intermittent rain from time to time that matched their coastal landscape. But the current promise of storms was new, and Kellan was certain they were linked to the lack of their heartstone. With so many missing from their rightful homes, would the entire continent start to react?

It was a question that he never wanted answered. Even if he had doubts before, now he couldn't ignore that Marquette was searching for what he had hoped to be nothing more than a myth.

But that wasn't what he needed to include in his newest letter to his sister.

Felicity was headed towards Saol, and the truth was he was worried more than usual. The idea of her returning to the Tower only brought trepidation. More so than knowing she was traveling with Alarian. He hated to admit that he had become less concerned that they were traveling together. Maybe it was because his sister's letters didn't allude to any nefarious acts by the male, even though she wouldn't tell him otherwise.

"Deep in your thoughts again?" Avyanna nudged his side and kissed the bicep draped over her shoulder.

It was a rare moment they were taking advantage of. She'd come home early from the town. With more assistants, she wasn't out for long hours, and they had settled into a semblance of a balance that he clung to. Something he needed while he waited for his father's return and attempted to keep the peace.

"Something just feels off."

She peered up from her spot against his chest as they curled up on the sofa—her with a book of medicine, him with his sister's letters.

"It's quiet? Usually means we just don't realize what's wrong."

"You feel it too?"

She shrugged. "I never know anymore."

Kellan sighed. "I'm sorry. Maybe I should just enjoy this moment."

Avyanna nuzzled into him. "Is it the letter?"

"No. I mean, there isn't anything else I've garnered from it. I am tempted to go assist Thomas. I haven't seen them in so long and maybe I could gain the Fios' discretion and trust."

"With your father coming home soon?"

With the shift in weather and change in the seas, Sloan hadn't given a definitive timeline. But she was right. He already knew it, but it was nice to hear that she thought similarly. His place, right now, was here. "I know. It just feels like I could do more—besides a bunch of meetings. Felicity is actively helping. She even has one of Marquette's allies being followed. I wonder if Advisor Heavin will show his face or not."

"Only a few days will tell."

He reread Felicity's words. "It sounds like she is doing better though. That could be the problem."

She frowned. "What? Didn't you want her to feel better?"

"Of course I did." He folded the letter and put it aside. "I just wish home—that I could have helped her. Not him. Not being somewhere else."

Avyanna chuckled, the sensation warming his chest. "I think you're seeing this all wrong. She's going to come back and have purpose. Doesn't mean she won't stay. And if she doesn't, we will know it's for good reason. She left for answers."

He leaned his head back against the cushion. "That's part of the problem. There is something about the Tower. I hate that she has to go back there."

He snagged hold of a stray thought and bolted upright, Avyanna almost sprawling to the floor before he caught her. "Oh no."

"What?"

The memory came full circle.

The witch bent forward and grabbed hold of his arm. Kellan fought but he was so tired. Drained from the manacles and the torture. His hair was plastered over his eyes, and he pinched them closed against the tears as she speared a dagger into his forearm and dragged it down to almost his wrist. Blood. So much of it gushed forth.

The witch smiled as she dipped her fingers into his wound. He screamed against the pain. But she did it again and again, painting bloody symbols that matched those on the floor against her forehead. Her cheeks. Her chest. She stood naked in front of him and drew more symbols on her stomach, each of her wrists, and the tops of her feet. He couldn't see clearly with the hair in his face, sweat stinging his eyes. Words he couldn't understand slipped from her lips. An incantation.

Roald cut off his limited view and grabbed Kellan's arm. He hissed, roared from the pain. Roald laughed. "Can't have you bleeding out and dying, can we?" He pressed a hard, calloused hand to Kellan's wound and the heat of healing magic fused together veins and skin until it was closed. The witch was moving behind him, limbs flinging in jagged twists and turns.

Roald dropped Kellan's arm, ran his hand over the prince's clammy forehead, moving the hair from his face. "Watch, boy. Watch as the world forgets." Then he left the circle. Kellan stared at the witch.

The spell, his blood, glowed. The symbols set off an iridescent light. He tried again to fight. To move. He didn't know what the spell was truly meant to do, but he knew his positioning in the center was vital somehow. Kellen screamed to get the witch's attention. Could he make her doubt herself? What she was doing? Why she was doing it? "Don't," he yelled. "You don't have to do this."

He sounded so weak, even to his own ears. He hated to beg.

The witch stopped. Turned and stared at him. Dark hair hung wildly past her shoulders. She was coated in his blood and her sweat plastering strands of hair to her cheek and throat. But those eyes. That strong jawline. And on her chest was a symbol that stood out among the others. A tree. His blood turned bright red, fire and light glistening off the drawings on her skin and the floor.

"I can't stop it." She grinned, the sight feral. "But I'll be back."

She fell to her knees and screamed. Heat streamed from her body. The light of all the symbols surrounded them both, he in the center of the largest. The circle of fire was hot but didn't burn him. He screamed right along with her.

Then the world snuffed out as the witch fell to the ground and everything went dark.

Kellan drew in a ragged breath. A shiver ran through his body. Avyanna held his face in her hands. "Kellan?"

"The Countess." He squeezed Avyanna's hands. "The witch that made the curse. She looked—she is the Countess."

"What?"

He stood, pulling her with him, to the nearest desk. Quickly he removed parchment and ink from drawers and began writing. "The Countess. The Tower. The witch. She told me she would be back. The one that had enacted the Nameless Curse."

"But what does this have to do with—"

"It was her."

"What?" Avyanna gasped.

"It's worse. The brand that the prisoners had. She had it too. On her chest." He tried to stifle the sensations of the pain. The memories he desperately wanted to forget. "I have to warn Felicity. She could be walking into a trap."

Avyanna peered over his shoulder and read as he wrote. "But how? The Countess—wasn't she at the Tower when Felicity arrived?"

"We don't know. Not without Felicity's memories. Maybe that's why they're gone." He crossed out a sentence and began writing again. "There must be an explanation, but she needs to know."

"But they aren't meant to check in for a few more days. Won't they already be in Saol?"

He stopped. Stared at the parchment before him and swallowed. "I have to hope that time is on our side."

She nodded and urged him to keep writing.

When he was finished, he took it to the corner where all the letters were picked up and then sat and waited. Staring. "I'll send out a messenger. Check in with the other contacts. One way or another, we will get word to them."

Avyanna sat next to him and took his hand. "You remember it all?"

The trauma, the pain of that day had hit him hard, but not as much as the knowledge of the witch's identity. "Yes." He'd pushed back that experience as far as he could. Didn't want to recall what had happened. The sensation of feeling his existence erased from his tongue. Stolen from the minds of all who had been close to him. Unable to utter his own name. And never to hear it for almost fifty years since.

"Kellan."

He inhaled a shuddering breath, pinched his eyes closed against the sting of tears.

"Your name is Kellan."

He nodded, eyes remaining closed.

"And I love you."

"I love you so much, Avy. To hear you speak my name. That you know who I am now—it was something I thought I could only wish for."

She kissed his cheek, and he met her gaze. A warm, soft smile. Kind eyes. Hell, he loved her. Avyanna kissed his lips this time. "I always knew you, Kellan. With or without your true name."

He nodded. Tried to anyway.

Then he turned back to that letter. Hoped it would disappear. That luck and fate were on their side. For once.

But the parchment didn't move.

Chapter 27

Felicity

Felicity stared at the gate that surrounded the Tower. It looked different somehow. After years of it being her only home, one she'd never wanted to leave, she'd outgrown it.

And a sense of relief settled within her at the thought.

They had left the lynxes, Gaoth and his mate Reóta, at a nearby grove of citrus to hunt. Shuffled footsteps caused her to draw her attention to the male beside her. She breathed a sigh. "It feels strange to enter this place without my glamour on."

He smiled. "I won't judge you if you need to do so, but I think you and I both know you're past that."

A cool evening breeze ruffled her hair. They had flown throughout the day, arriving once the sun had set. Alarian had asked if she preferred to find somewhere to sleep for the night and make a fresh start in the morning. While she appreciated the offer, she declined. It was time—and knowing the Countess, the woman would be expecting her.

Felicity walked to the gate and knew it was futile to ring the bell. The guards, hidden in the shadows, already knew they were there. "Let the Countess know that Felicity has arrived."

Alarian cleared his throat, and Felicity couldn't help the smile. He was right—she needed to own it—even if she was presumably speaking to the darkness. "Princess Felicity and her escort, Lord Alarian."

"Just Alarian," he whispered, but she ignored him.

He had wanted to be the one to announce their arrival, but by the giddiness in his eyes, she knew he would make it a spectacle. This was their agreement—her title had to leave her lips. *Own it*—he'd said. Even though it annoyed her, the pride in his expression made it worthwhile somehow.

Someone stepped from the shadows, only their eyes visible between the black cloth wrapping their face. "It's very presumptuous to assume the Countess would ever want to see *you* again. The lies you weaved. The secrets you kept." The woman hissed the accusations as though she were judge and jury.

"It wasn't just her." Another stepped into the dim moonlight. "The Countess had made those choices as well." The voice was familiar, and Felicity recognized his gray eyes. He'd been friends with Garder—the assassin gone rouge who had attacked her and Alarian. She had killed Garder, not knowing then that he had turned against the Tower. Alarian had filled her in on this tidbit on that bluff after he was freed. He'd made a visit to the Tower shortly after the attack on the road to ensure it wouldn't happen again. The Countess had promised they weren't involved. But it was another reason to be on guard. The man sniffed. "Go tell the Countess. I'll wait here."

"But—"

"Go."

The first must have been a newer recruit still learning the rules and pecking order. She harrumphed but did as she was told.

The man lowered the mask from his mouth. "Garder deserved what he got. Doesn't mean I like you though."

At least he got straight to the point. Felicity shrugged, knowing a response was unnecessary. She didn't expect that the Tower would have changed overnight. Very few had liked her, but most had respected what she could do.

When the woman returned, she crossed her arms. "Come along." She turned without waiting as the man unlocked the door, allowing them in. He grumbled under his breath when Alarian followed Felicity. She tracked their movements. Although she didn't expect them to attack, to assume otherwise was a death sentence.

When they reached the entrance, another figure stepped into view, bustling down the hall. He slowed, a small misstep forcing him to a stop. "Felicity?"

Her heart did a flip in her chest. The last time she'd seen Harrison she'd yelled at him. Blamed him for the Tower barring her return. Abandoned her. He'd only been the messenger then. She hadn't yet understood and still didn't. With the sight of his graying hair, the few wrinkles under his eyes, the memories of many nights spent together came to the surface. Whispered promises that could and would never be. At least not how either of them expected. It was words said between two young ones in love with hope still in their hearts. Before love had been trained out of Felicity and a new reality had set in.

"Hello, Harrison."

He grinned, suddenly looking ten years younger. "The Countess is unavailable, but I'm certain she will want to meet with you as soon as possible. In the meantime, come. I'll show you both to rooms for the night."

Felicity wanted to argue and demand a meeting with the Countess now, but the reality of her exhaustion had settled over her as soon as she'd stepped through the door. Even if she was healed, they had been through a lot the past few days with little sleep. They both deserved rest. "Thank you."

"I hope your old room is acceptable." He turned towards Alarian. "We also have guest quarters for you."

Alarian stood rigid, his stance squared—ready. With a glance at Felicity, he rolled back his shoulders. "I'd appreciate it."

They made their way down the hall, the path muscle memory for her. When they reached her room, she stared at the door for a moment, uncertain what she'd expected to find on the other side. Harrison cleared his throat, unlocking the door and sliding it open a bit before stepping back. "See you in the morning."

"Wait." The words were out of her mouth before he could turn away. "Can we talk? Tomorrow?"

Harrison's warm smile held a touch of relief. "I'd be happy to."

"Good."

He nodded, then turned back to Alarian. "Ready?"

The male nodded, forcing himself back a step. She noted the hesitation in his eyes. *Be nice*, she wanted to say.

Alarian breathed a sigh, picking up her unspoken message. With a wink over his shoulder, he followed Harrison down the hall.

Felicity opened the door the rest of the way and entered. It looked exactly the same without her things. No trunk at the end of the footboard, the bed made with the same thrown quilt, the wardrobe empty. It had never been full, but back then it had been home. She bit her lip, closing the door behind her. She went around to the other side of the bed and sat down against the wall as she had done so many times before. With a thud, she dropped her pack beside her and opened it. She pulled out a few stray crumbs from the small lunch they'd eaten on the road—a crust of bread that had been easy enough to pluck and put aside for later.

The hole in the wall was still present, but there was no sign of the little mouse who she had once befriended. Felicity placed the remnants on the entrance to the hole in the wall, waiting patiently to see if a pair of curious whiskers emerged. When her eyes had grown heavy, she finally pushed to her feet and shuffled to the bed. Exhaustion took hold and she took off her boots and pulled the quilt over her body.

The garden was filled with bountiful colors that ranged from shades of reds, greens, blues, pinks and purples. The flowers and leaves bent gently in the breeze. Felicity inhaled the fresh scent—familiar yet so far away. The garden at the palace. Her attention drifted towards the white picket fence that Alarian had fallen over. That she'd stood and spoken with Avyanna and Kellan on multiple occasions. And the figure that sat overlooking it all. Air caught in her lungs as she slowly made her way towards the female. Except her features were distorted. Wisps of hair that looked similar to her own, yet different—straight and cut to her shoulders.

"Hello, my darling."

Felicity inhaled, drawing in a long breath. "Mother? How? I can't remember you."

"Your memory might be fuzzy. It might be taken, but there are still parts of me that are embedded in you and can never be removed. Those are the parts that matter. The things you hold onto through it all."

"I'm trying—" She swallowed. "I'm trying to find you both."

"You will. When it's time. But I'm always here no matter what."

"This is a dream." Felicity couldn't make herself turn away though.

"Perhaps."

"That wasn't a question." She was on guard. Ready for the shift. The running. The sound of hoof beats on the chase. The nightmare that usually visited her.

"Oh, my darling. We're safe here."

"No." Felicity was aware that wasn't the case. That was not how these dreams went. Her heart sped up, hands began to fidget.

"Yes, you are. He's nearby."

Felicity blinked. "He?"

"Our protector—"

Felicity woke with a gasp. The blanket wound tightly around her, she extracted herself from within its grasp. The room was dark. Pitch black. No light coming in through the small window. It took her a few moments to remember where she was and why.

A knock sounded and she shuddered. Pinched her eyes closed. Another knock, a little more hurried. "Felicity. I'm about to come in if you don't open this door."

The tone held a warning and worry she didn't want to ignore. Felicity padded across the stone on bare feet and opened the door. "What are you doing here?" she hissed at Alarian.

"I—" He swallowed and looked away. "I couldn't sleep."

A lie. She could tell. Was he checking on her?

"And I was worried."

"Everything is fine here."

He ran a hand through his hair and nodded. "I'll leave you be. Sorry."

When Alarian turned to head down the hall, she reached out for his arm. "But—"

He met her gaze. Didn't move. Gave her the option to turn him away. Did he know she had a nightmare? "Come in."

"I could go. It's all right."

Protector. That's what her mother had said. Had it been a message? Her head ached in the attempt to disconnect reality from the dream. "Please come in. I…" She didn't want to be vulnerable again. But sometimes it was tiring to hold it together all the time. "I had a nightmare."

He didn't wait for any further coaxing but stepped into the room, closing the door behind himself. "What happened?"

"Not a nightmare exactly, but I kept expecting it to turn into one. It was about my mother."

Alarian ran a hand through his hair. "Do you want to talk about it?"

She couldn't believe she was about to do this. To ask for his help. "No. But could you hold me?" It was selfish after what she'd said or rather left unsaid. But in his arms, it was safe. She knew that to the deepest part of her. And she wanted this. Not just for one night.

The realization nearly stole her breath away.

Alarian's finger brushed her chin, and she hadn't realized she'd looked away until he coaxed her to meet his gaze. "If that's what you want, Starlight."

She didn't say a word. Just curled up into the bed, patting the spot beside her before adjusting the blankets.

At first, he didn't touch her. She didn't know how that was possible on the small bed. It barely fit two. Felicity pressed back gently and found his hand to pull his arm around her waist. His chest brushed against her back as he breathed. She reveled in the way his hold felt protective and comforting. She nuzzled into him until her body was flush to his. So close. Where she could feel every ridge and line. Every muscle and bone.

A groan sounded in her ear. "Careful." A small shimmy of her ass had him growling. "What game are you playing?"

"Maybe I'm realizing that it's stupid to ignore what's happening between us." Hell, he smelled so good. This felt right.

"Don't tease me."

"I'm not."

He pulled her onto her back and bracketed his arms on either side, staring down at her. The predatory eyes of a fox found hers in the darkness—seemed to glow in anticipation. Need and want.

"What do you want? I need you to spell it out for me."

"Simple. I want you." Just saying those words aloud eased a weight from her shoulders. She reached up and cupped his cheek. "You, Alarian."

His lips crashed into hers, and her hand slid around his neck, pulling him in deeper. Closer. Their mouths parting to allow the other to explore.

Alarian pulled back, searched her face. There was hesitation written in his expression and she realized he was looking for the moment to break. For her to take it all back. She wasn't sure which. "I see you," she whispered.

He closed his eyes and that smile of his appeared. Hell, she always wanted him to smile at her like that. She ran a hand over his arms. A squeeze to the fine line of muscle at his biceps as her core warmed. "Rian. Touch me."

He sighed, nuzzled into her neck. Kissed her collarbone. "I want to explore every bit of you."

"Then do it." She arched towards him.

His mouth left a heated trail below her ear, his stubbled cheek grazing her throat, and she shuddered at the sensation against sensitive skin.

"I need you to be completely certain. I meant it—I'll become addicted to you." A kiss to her jaw, heat spreading from her core. "So, if you want to explore this. Each other. Then we need to do this slowly."

She groaned as she slid her hand under his tunic to feel the planes of his stomach and chest. "No."

He gripped her wrist. Stopped her movement. "Please, don't make this harder. You've mentioned on multiple occasions that you don't know if this is a good idea. I need you to be certain first. Mission or no mission."

She found his gaze in the limited light. The intensity and yearning battling within his expression. All the parts of her she kept hidden from him. Mostly out of stubbornness. But also because she hadn't seen him. She didn't owe him anything. But he did deserve her to prove that she was in it for more than one night. She kissed him then and he didn't pull away as her hand curled around his waist, the other trailing down the side of his torso. The memory of his bare chest from the previous day came unbidden, the sweat clinging to his skin.

"But slow isn't your thing," she teased.

He chuckled against her lips. "I've rushed everything and you—I don't want to rush you. I plan on this being forever, and I need you to understand and know that. The only way out of this is if you tell me we are over, and I never want to hear those words. Besides, there are some things that I haven't told you. Can't tell you." His nose brushed her throat and then he kissed the curve of her neck. "Because of this alone, I need you to be certain that I'm what you want."

She closed her eyes, trying to control her breathing and the rush of her heart. She wanted to ask what he kept from her, but she heard it in his tone. There were things he couldn't say. And right now, she had other things on her mind.

"I want to court you."

She blinked. "What? Why?"

"Because it feels right."

She raked her fingers through his hair, grabbed hold and gently pulled his head away from her neck to meet his gaze. "You know what also would feel right?"

Feral. That was what she found staring back at her. His green eyes shined bright with mischief. The shadows accentuating the angles of his face, casting him half in darkness. She noticed the strain in his muscles. The bulge at his trousers. This was taking all his self-control. "This is important to you, isn't it?"

"You're important. And I want you to know that. Feel that. And, then if you still want me, then I'll happily oblige."

Her hand relaxed its hold. "All right." She kissed him, sealing the deal.

His shoulders relaxed and he settled in beside her, pulling her close until her back was flush with his body. She was tempted to test just how much control he had, but she resisted.

For him.

Chapter 28

Felicity

A knock woke her. Felicity sat up, stifling a yawn and stretching her arms over her head. Alarian stirred beside her, and she smiled at the sight of him. Crap—she was smiling about this. Was that normal?

With heavy feet, she made her way across the room and opened the door a crack. Harrison stood with a tray in hand. The smell of thick bacon, biscuits and eggs welcomed her, and she couldn't help the sigh as her stomach grumbled. "I thought we were meeting with the Countess?"

"Food first. I hope it wasn't too forward of me, but I wondered if a chat over breakfast would be all right?" Felicity looked over her shoulder at her unmade bed, the male stirring within it. There weren't exactly places for them to sit. "Don't worry," Harrison said in a rush. "Figured this might be our only chance."

"It's not that." She considered stepping into the hall. Even if she and Harrison had been together—it had been over a decade since their relationship had ended. That didn't mean she wanted to throw anyone else in his face. With a sigh, she opened the door, allowing him to enter. "It's just that now might not be the best time."

Alarian was already out of bed. Harrison remained in the doorway, looking between the two of them. Protectiveness flashed in his gaze, but he met the male's eyes without hesitation. "I don't have a meal for three but you're welcome to join us."

Felicity bit her lip as Alarian stuffed his hands in his pockets—giving off that air of ignorance she'd seen many times before. A smirk played at his lips as he moved in beside Felicity. For a moment she thought she felt the protectiveness radiating off him, but just as quickly it was gone. He cleared his throat. "Thanks for the invitation, but I'll give you two time to catch up."

Harrison nudged the door closed behind Alarian with his foot. Thankfully, he didn't comment on Alarian's presence and instead nodded towards the tray in his hand. "Is this all right?"

"It is, but there isn't much room."

He laughed. "Don't you remember similar meals like this? We made it work then."

She blushed, eyes widening at what he was alluding to. "I—"

"That's not what I meant. We were friends once too, you know." He placed the tray on the bed and pulled the stool out, dropping onto it.

Felicity paused, watching the familiarity of the movement as the memories settled. So many nuances forgotten over time. Moments she'd overlooked when everything went back into place. But it was more than that—now she was used to having places to host guests. To talk to friends. This room wasn't a location for discussions. She'd changed more than she'd realized in such a short time. Became familiar with comforts she hadn't always had. It was...unnerving.

He removed two plates from the tray and handed her one. Her jaw momentarily clenched. "I'm sorry."

"Why?" Harrison took a bite.

"For the way I treated you the last time we spoke. You were the messenger, and I was ready to put your head on a spike." She tore a piece of bacon off between her teeth. "It wasn't your fault."

"No, it wasn't. But as difficult as it was, I'm glad I was the one there. If it had come from Bishop..."

She visibly cringed, and Harrison chuckled. "Exactly. It was meant to come from me. Otherwise, we probably would be down a liaison."

"Not that it would be a bad thing," she grumbled.

"There is a lot you don't understand yet. Some things I don't even know. But I didn't come for an apology, I came as a friend." His eyes sparkled, the familiarity within them causing her own chest to feel heavy.

"I—" She didn't know how truthful to be. Harrison had always been a safe haven. Even back then. A confidant. It wasn't until now that she realized that she'd missed him. And not just because a part of her mourned losing him—but because they had been friends. "I'm adjusting. I'd be lying if I didn't say it's been a lot. That's part of why I came though. To try to figure out what's missing."

Harrison chuckled. "Missing? Felicity, even when you didn't have all your memories, you always knew what was and wasn't true. Now that they are all back, has that changed?"

She looked down at her plate, breaking a piece of her biscuit into her hand. It made her think of Squeaks. The little mouse had been a friend too. A quick glance told her the crumbs were gone. She smirked. "It's not that it's exactly changed. I just thought I'd feel drawn back here. Now I'm trying to find a balance between what is expected of me and what I expect of myself. They don't exactly match."

Harrison sighed. "Do you feel like you're meant to come back here?"

She shook her head. "I wanted to before. This was home. But I just realized that it isn't anymore."

"You haven't belonged here for a long time. I know it wasn't easy, Felicity, but you were ready for the next step. It was time. You're meant for more than this place. Hell—even this realm."

"What about you?" She bit her lip. It was time to steer the conversation away from her. The Countess had too much to answer for first before she delved deeper into her own emotions.

He smiled, resting his elbows on his knees. "I'm good."

She bit her lip. "I'm sorry I left you in such a way. That I couldn't change who I was for you. You deserved better."

"It's not that I deserved better, Felicity. It's that we both had different paths. I'll never regret the time we had. You helped shape me into who I am. And I've always been proud of you because the decisions and roads you were on were never easy."

Felicity sighed. "I loved you. A part of me always will. You showed me what it meant to be loved in a time when it was hard for me to comprehend it." It was easy to speak to him. To be candid about it all. Even if it was in the past. "Thank you for caring for me."

He reached out and took her hand. "I always will. Honestly, you have your memories back helped me too. I was able to finally connect with someone else. I always harbored a sense of guilt for what had been done to you and my part in it. Even if we couldn't be together, I wanted you to be happy. I've always cared about you—no matter how confusing to do so, but I've also moved on, Felicity."

She hadn't loved him that way for a long time, and it was reassuring to hear his words. "Were you ever angry with me for choosing the Tower over you?"

Harrison folded his hands in front of him. "There were moments I felt selfish about it, yes. But that's all it ever was. I wish you could have chosen me, but the truth was plain and simple. I wasn't the one who was meant to be by your side. You're meant to have someone outside of me. I knew it then, and I see it now."

"See what now?" She took another bite of bacon.

"You and Alarian."

She felt the heat rise in her cheeks. Guess he was going to go there after all. "We are still figuring things out."

"Did you know he came after the attack by Garder?"

"He mentioned that." Felicity thought back to the moment on the bluff after Alarian had been freed. When they decided to be friends. "He said he came to ask if the Tower had sent him."

"Ask?" Harrison chuckled. "He showed up and had both Bishop and I pinned to the wall with these shadow things demanding information. I haven't seen the Countess talk so soothing and so quickly before." He took a sip of coffee. "I knew it then—he'd fallen for you. The way he arrived, knocked out four guards, and didn't even once mention himself. He would have taken us all out for you."

She didn't have a moment to comment. The door suddenly flung open, shadows dispersing throughout the room. As if the mention of his name had called him, Alarian rushed in. "Felicity." He held up a missive, casting a furtive glance at Harrison.

She stood and met him at the door. Felicity unfolded the letter to find her brother's writing. And read. Then a second time, not believing the first.

Before she could respond, footsteps Felicity would have known anywhere sounded in the hall. Her mask of indifference hid the pulsing desire to react to the information she just learned. With a look over Alarian's shoulder, she met Bishop's steel-eyed gaze. "The Countess is ready to see you now. If you'd follow me."

He seemed shorter somehow. His sharp chin a contrast to his stubby frame. Bishop turned on his heel without waiting for them, expecting her to fall in line as she always had. For some reason, it didn't bother her now as it had for so many years. She handed Alarian the letter. "I need to dress first."

Bishop turned and glared. "You have five minutes."

"I have as much time as I need." She didn't wait for his response but went back into her room.

Before she closed the door, Harrison chuckled as he bustled past her, the tray of food in his hands. "I'll see you soon."

With a nod, Alarian folded his arms and leaned against the wall beside her door. His smirk in place as he watched Bishop. A sentry.

She changed into her training leathers and fixed her hair into a thick braid while considering her options. If Kellan was right, the witch was more dangerous than they had originally thought. There was a chance she had cast the curse. Was it possible? Doubt and suspicion circled her mind. She thumbed the dagger's hilt at her side. A reminder. When she emerged, she wore the impassive expression of the spy. Alarian moved in beside her, and she could almost feel pride bubbling off him.

Bishop gave an exasperated sigh, then continued down the hall without a word.

"Be ready for anything," she whispered. He brushed a finger against her hand in silent agreement.

Bishop led them down a familiar hall to the meeting room she'd only been once before. Where all of this had begun. Her hand slid along the sheath at her hip. Felicity inhaled deeply, pausing at the entrance when her eyes collided with the Countess. The woman straightened, a familiar movement mimicked on more than one occasion.

Alarian rested a hand on the small of her back, urging her forward. She walked alongside him and swallowed as he pulled a chair out for her before sitting beside her. A united front. It felt strange to sit here in this position—but right. As if it all led to this.

"We are happy for your return." The Countess gave a gentle smile. "Princess Felicity."

Anger mixed with melancholy. "Why?" It was the only word that jumped to the forefront of her mind amongst the chaos and anger. They'd be ready and she'd get to the bottom of Kellan's allegations but first she had questions that needed answers.

"You may need to be more specific. Where would you like me to start?"

"The beginning." Felicity held the Countess' gaze, something she had never done before. Even now, it was intimidating and took will-power not to cower.

Bishop cleared his throat from his place beside her, but the Countess ignored him. "We should begin by stating that none of the decisions we made were ever easy. Many were done with a heavy heart. I know I'll never be able to explain everything, but I'll do my best."

The door opened and Harrison walked in, taking a seat on the other side of the Countess. "I apologize for my tardiness. What did I miss?"

Bishop crossed his arms. "Nothing of importance."

"She's going to tell me why my memories were removed." Felicity washed away all emotion from her expression.

"More so, why her identity had to be kept from her when she had a right to know," Bishop grumbled loud enough for them all to hear.

The bitterness in Bishop's tone had Felicity glancing toward the man. He'd usually saved that disdain for Felicity. Or about her. It almost sounded like he understood her.

"Which I shall get to." The Countess drew her shoulders back. "But the beginning is the most important place to start."

Alarian straightened beside her as the Countess continued, "We all know of the powerful curse—a Nameless Curse that forced the memory of a great king and his family to be forgotten by an entire continent. But it's never spoken of where that curse came from."

Felicity's hand slid into her lap. If this was where the Countess wanted to start...

"It was a witch." The Countess lifted her chin and folded her hands on the table.

Felicity and Alarian stilled beside each other. Her magic slid through her body.

"We know," he said slowly. "Some believe it was you." The reality that she could be a witch wasn't as surprising as it would have been months before. Felicity didn't glance at him but felt the cool lick of shadows at her feet and calves. He was ready too.

"That is not where my gift lies, but it might as well have been." The Countess inhaled. "It was my sister."

Air stuck in Felicity's throat. She gasped, her eyes widening. "Sister?" Her muscles tightened like a spring. Wanting to react. She glanced at the others from the corner of her eye. Alarian and Harrison looked just as shocked as she was. Only Bishop remained cool and collected. She pulled herself together. Waited.

"Yes. My younger sister. This curse was so powerful it took her life with it. Drained her."

"How do we know if this is not another twist of the truth?" Felicity asked, her magic beckoning to be used.

"Roald and Marquette ensured all of this remained a secret. You see, there is always a way to counter a curse. They didn't want that easily discovered. My sister sent a letter to me. A letter that arrived only a few hours before you did on our doorstep."

Felicity swallowed. "What did this letter say?"

"That only a member of the royal family could remember the prince's name and somehow, one of you had to survive. I think my sister regretted her choices but felt she couldn't back out. She told me that I'd remain immune to the curse, so I could use that knowledge to the best of my ability." The Countess sighed and she looked to the men beside her. "It's difficult to share pivotal information I've kept to myself for years. I'm a witch, given the gift to see pieces of the future."

Harrison shifted beside her. His teeth ground and Felicity knew that he also had not known the truth of her heritage until then. Bishop, on the other hand, didn't seem flustered or surprised at all.

"I knew what I needed and couldn't share. While your memories were taken, I was tasked with the job of protecting a fae orphan and to keep secrets from everyone I know." The Countess shot Harrison a look. "To make decisions that others didn't agree with, but to ensure the pieces moved in the direction that led to this point right now."

"I'm more curious of what's to happen next. If you can see the future, then what's to come of my mother and Fiadh?" Alarian grumbled.

She shook her head. "There are some things I'm not meant to tell because it can change the outcome. The gift of sight is only beneficial to a point. There are many paths that can be taken." Her careful expression relaxed and softened slightly. "I kept your identity a secret to protect you from the outside world. When I saw the different paths the only one to keep you safe was to conceal your heritage—which also meant hiding the magic you contained."

"From me?" Felicity swallowed. "I thought it was a secret I possessed on my own and yet my memories revealed otherwise." She didn't realize she had gotten to her feet. "That I was being dampened by a band on my ear."

The Countess didn't move or react as Felicity continued, "I had given my life to you. My loyalty. I was working and struggling toward a future as a Dearmadta. But all I received in return was secrets and manipulations."

"It was to prepare you for who you are now. Are you angry with this outcome?"

Felicity glared at the Countess' patient tone. "I don't know who I am." Fists tightened at her side, her nails digging into her palm "My memories were taken for a reason I didn't know or understand. My identity hidden. I was ostracized by those around me. My magic was withheld when I could have practiced and mastered it long ago. And now I am meant to say thank you?"

Harrison stood, walking around to Felicity's side. "Explain it to her. As you did to me all those years ago." He reached for Felicity's hand, but she stepped away.

The Countess closed her eyes for a moment then breathed a long sigh of her own. Felicity sensed anger radiating around her and glanced at Alarian, his calm façade gone. His hands gripped the arms of his chair, the wood cracking under the pressure. To know he was upset on her behalf made her lift her head higher.

The Countess opened her eyes and calmly glanced between Alarian and Felicity. "I wished to do otherwise. What I foresaw..." She shook her head. "Your identity was hidden because otherwise, in earlier years, you would have been discovered. Found. Murdered. I couldn't let that happen. Because of my sister's letter, I knew who you truly were. But the usurpers did too and at the time they thought you dead. Even though their memories shifted over time, if we had taught you your magic, once you arrived at the castle, the king would have uncovered the truth—he'd have killed you in your sleep like the coward he was."

Tears welled up in the Countess' eyes.

"If your memories remained, then Garder would have manipulated you, and turned you in to the king out of jealousy—or turned on you himself—and succeeded."

Felicity's eyes widened, sickened that Garder could ever have the upper hand. She sat—her legs weak.

The Countess dabbed her cheeks with the back of her hand. "You were important to me and as much as it pained me to make or enforce certain decisions, it was always for a good reason. Your life. This continent. To give the future a chance to outlive the outcome Roald and Marquette so badly want."

"Then if you returned her memories, why can't she remember anything before the Tower?" Alarian's grip had only loosened slightly on the cracked armrests.

Harrison glanced between Felicity and the Countess. Bishop stood then and met Felicity's gaze. "Because a deal was made with the one who delivered you upon our doorstep. They are the only one who can return your memories to you..." His tone was matter of fact and it made Felicity's stomach churn.

The Countess nodded. "It was an agreement that reflects a decision that either will benefit or be a detriment to this continent."

"To think you train us not to have biases, and yet it seems the Tower has more hands in the political climate than the crown," Felicity ground out, her magic curling along her limbs.

The Countess actually smiled at the accusation. "It isn't for the crown. Politics do *not* have a place here. It is for the realms of Talamh."

Alarian tilted his head. "What does that mean?"

Her smile turned mischievous. "Harrison and Bishop, we need the room, please."

Bishop got to his feet and gestured for Harrison to follow. Felicity grabbed Harrison's hand before he could pass and gave it one final squeeze before he followed the liaison out the door. A thank you.

The Countess stood, making her way around the table until she was in front of them. She sat down in an empty seat. "I know what you seek."

"Of course you do. If you foresee the future, that could be surmised," Alarian muttered.

Felicity's head ached from all the information. "What do you know about it?"

"That the heartstone of Saol has been well protected for hundreds of years." She removed a notebook from her pocket. "There is no safer place it could be."

They waited. Stared at the Countess. With a few muttered words Felicity couldn't discern, the notebook shimmered and, as though it had been covered by a cloak, the notebook peeled away to a red stone in her palm, a bag in her other hand.

"Is that...?" Alarian gasped. "How?"

Felicity took a step forward and the Countess' grip tightened around the heartstone. She paused and met the matron's gaze.

The Countess sighed and shoulders relaxed. "I apologize. It's a habit."

"That's why you look like you never age. It's always on you?"

The Countess shook her head. "Yes and no. It is the reason for my long life, but I do not always carry it on me. Even with the protection spell, I'm not naive. It would be unwise to carry the stone."

"Can I see it?" Alarian whispered.

The woman's head tilted, taking him in. "You've searched for many."

"And found none," Felicity added.

The Countess held out the stone and Alarian inhaled as it fell into his palm. "It's warm."

"It's life. Life is warm."

He held his flat palm outwards for Felicity to look it over. Jagged edges. Deep red like blood. She grazed a finger over a corner. "It looks like it broke here?"

"It did."

"Where is the piece? Do you have it?" Alarian handed it back to the Countess.

"It's in a safe place." She removed a pouch from her pocket and while muttering a few words, she sprinkled a powder over the stone before sliding it into a bag. The cloak of the notebook slid over the stone again. "And I have sequestered a spell for you to protect the other stones—but know that this journey will be fraught with challenges, more than you've so far seen. That, as cliche as it sounds, it's important to follow your heart." Her gaze was settled on Felicity during that last sentence.

Felicity turned away from her scrutinizing gaze. "Who gave you access to a spell that will protect the stones or even one that contains memories? I've never heard of a witch that had more than one gift."

"I cannot and will not claim to be able to. That doesn't mean that I don't know others who are capable of such magic."

Felicity's chest ached. So many secrets had been kept from her.

The Countess inhaled. "I wish that you never felt lost, Felicity. I think you've found more truth than you ever bargained for. But mostly you have found yourself. I meant it when I said this mission would define you."

"That mission is over."

"No." The Countess shook her head. "It's not yet over. The first stage is complete, but there are many more to come."

Felicity slumped back into her chair. "So, you claim the stone is safe, memories I still don't have are with someone else, and I assume you cannot or will not tell me who they are?"

"They will reveal themself when it's time. Just remember to open your heart when it's questioned. It will make things easier." The Countess tilted her head. "I know you're still confused, filled with even more questions. I knew who you were, what you were meant to be—a savior. I hope you're able to see that in yourself soon."

Another title she didn't want. Weapon. Assassin. Spy. Princess. Savior—she wanted it to be much simpler. Not when so many of those descriptions contradicted the other. She wished that there was a way to make the Countess talk, but what would it be worth?

Alarian stood then. "Unless you have further information, I think we're finished."

The Countess looked upon him, a sense of gratitude in her expression. "Have some lunch. Supplies will be packed for you and the spell delivered to your room."

Felicity stood. "I want my thirtieth star." She hadn't expected the words, but they fell from her lips easily.

The Countess nodded. "It will be done."

Chapter 29

Alarian

N o wonder Felicity had difficulty trusting anyone. With all the mind games that had been played since she arrived at the Tower, Alarian couldn't blame her for her doubt. But he knew exactly who she was. Had seen those pieces start to click into place. How she dealt with Dorcha's advisor had been a tipping point. He knew telling her wasn't enough though. She had to see it for herself and all he could do was try to help her along the way.

It had been hard to sit there today. He'd wanted to tear that room apart on her behalf. Maybe he should still consider walking away, but the attack—almost losing her in Domhain—told him exactly what he already knew. He could never walk away. If she moved on with another, he would have to leave. He didn't have that type of self-control even if they promised to remain friends. It wasn't possible anyway. With the bond creeping between them, he needed to allow her to make her own choice. When she decided, he'd know what to do.

A knock at the door stopped him mid-step and he realized he'd been pacing the small guest quarters while he waited for Felicity to say her goodbyes to Harrison. He hoped he had been able the ever-present desire to tear the man apart and claim Felicity as his. But she would never forgive him for that.

He expected it to be Felicity when he opened the door, so was taken aback when it was the Countess. "What are you doing here?" he growled.

She didn't wait for an invitation inside but pushed past him, then nodded at the door to be closed.

"I'm not one of your lackeys." Alarian winced, realizing that Felicity used to be loyal to this woman.

"I didn't think you were."

He closed the door and folded his arms, leaning against it. "What do you want? You should be in her room, apologizing."

"I've tried but until she has her answers, apologizing will get me nowhere. I wish I had more to give."

"Your sister is the cause of a curse that tore her family apart and you never thought to tell her on your own? She had to come all the way here to find out. And things could be different if you were honest with her." He ground his teeth. "Does she even know your real name?"

The Countess tilted her head, considering him. "You watched as a name broke a curse strong enough to spell the entire continent. Names have power and I'm not going to beseech the future with knowledge that can only be an undoing. And you and I both know that one should never be blamed for the fault of their blood. Or maybe you are still learning that to be true."

Alarian glared. "No wonder she can't forgive you. You don't trust—"

"Don't you dare finish that sentence." The Countess seemed to grow as she stood before him. "I trust her with my life. Even now. This is as much for her protection as it is my own. Don't diminish what or who I am to a name." She stepped back then, considering him. "The love you have for her is obvious."

He blinked at the change of topic. "So?"

"She hides so much that she feels, but it's there. Don't give up."

"Are you giving out fortunes now?" Alarian knew he sounded snide, but he didn't care.

"No. Just facts."

He kept his gaze pinned on her, because through it all, he wouldn't turn his back on the witch. "Why did you come here?"

The Countess cleared her throat and straightened once more. "Because I have something for you."

Alarian watched as she reached into her pocket and air caught in his lungs as he suddenly forgot to breathe at the sight of what she held out in her hand. "What is this?"

"Don't worry. You won't need it now." She gave a reassuring smile. Something in his gut told him he should be worried anyway.

Chapter 30

Felicity

The following day they landed in Visce, to a small town on the outskirts of a partially frozen lake. Felicity was near dead on her feet.

The stable master snorted at the sight of the cailleach, a grumble in his throat as his short stature was dwarfed by the mounts. But with a few extra coins in his pocket for his troubles, he said little. "Lucky you have them over horses. Land animals are easily grabbed by the water demons in these parts."

Felicity's eyes widened at the gruff nature, none of the members of the community particularly warm. In fact, any who did cast a look in their direction held piercing stares and questionable sneers.

When they met the proprietor of the inn—a building held above the ground on stilts—Felicity wasn't surprised when an undine, a water nymph with webbed feet and iridescent green scales led them up the stairs to their room. She didn't offer them a second room, her actions saying she didn't care what they wanted and that they would be happy with what was given to them.

She gulped down a glass of water she held—enough probably to keep her alive on land as they spent more time within the rivers and lakes—then trudged away muttering to herself.

Since sleeping outside in the mist and water was the only other option in the vicinity, Felicity didn't comment. She hadn't slept a full night in days and was certain Alarian was having the same difficulties.

The male in question was currently eyeing the small bed with rapt attention. Since his announcement that he wanted to court her, and her agreement, all that had happened was an occasional kiss, a brush of skin, and then he'd hold her as they curled up for warmth amidst fallen leaves and pokey twigs.

"It looks comfortable maybe?" He tried to smile, but she could see the exhaustion in his posture and the fake smile he attempted. Felicity didn't take the time to change. Didn't consider the opportunity of teasing him to test his fortitude. Her body ached from sleeping on the ground the past two nights.

Alarian dropped his pack beside hers, and they both curled up into the bed and burrowed under the blankets for warmth. To fight off the chill that sunk into her bones. The warmth he emitted was enough. It wasn't long until his breathing turned heavy and sleep found them.

They ran. The grass brushing against skin. Terror bit at her gut and Felicity's hand tightened in her mother's.

"Faster, Starlight."

Felicity tripped and fell to the ground. Her mother bent over to assist her up. "You don't call me that."

Her mother blinked, eyes widening. The trampling of hooves echoed, and the earth shook underneath them.

"Up. Keep on going." Felicity was dragged to her feet and the Tower came into view. "There."

Felicity shook her head. Knew what would happen if they went there. "No, Mama." She tried to drag her mother away from the looming building.

But her mother froze, as if made of stone, her feet planted. Felicity felt so small. Her fear mixing with her desire to run in any other direction. "They're coming. We mustn't go there. This way." She tried again.

It was no use. Her mother turned her head, and a sad smile brushed her lips. "Don't worry, my darling."

"Mama, no. We have to run. This way."

Her mother pulled Felicity close. Kissed her forehead, ran her hand over her head and tightened her grip. "No—this is the way it must be." Another squeeze. "I love you."

Then her mother was torn from her grasp. Darkness engulfed her body, but although her mouth was open before she disappeared from view, it was Felicity who was screaming.

"I've got you."

Alarian had her wrapped in his arms. The room was ablaze in a white light. "It's a dream, Starlight."

Felicity gasped. Realized the light was her—her magic. She snuffed it out. Shuddered and a sob stuck in her throat. She gripped his arms, reality dragging her to the present. His arms were scabbed, the sensation of his skin rough to touch.

"Shit." She let go and attempted to pull away. "Rian—no, I hurt you."

He didn't let her out of his hold. "I'm healing already. Don't worry."

Another attempt to break from his hold, but he only tightened his arms. "I'm all right," he repeated. "It will be gone in no time. Just try to breathe."

She swallowed around the tears that threatened to fall. Bit them back. The pain of a loss that dreams attempted to replicate. Hell, at this point she wanted to cry.

When it was silent for some time, Alarian loosened his hold. "Do you want to talk about it?"

No. That was her first instinct. But it felt right to share this with him. "My mother. I have dreams with different versions of her death. This one—" She swallowed. "This one was different."

"How?"

She shook her head. "She stopped running. Didn't fight anymore. Almost like she had accepted her fate even though I was trying to get her away from the outcome. "

He kissed her hair. "I'm sorry, Starlight."

The mention of the nickname—the fact her mother had used it in her dream. She pinched her eyes closed, willing tears that wouldn't come. "It's not your fault." Felicity wrapped her arms around his and nuzzled into him. "Thank you for being here."

He kissed the tip of her ear. "If you need to talk more, I'm willing to listen."

Fatigue mixed with trepidation. And something else. Especially when he spoke that way to her. His raspy whisper caused her body to want other ways to be sidetracked. "I—will you just hold me?"

He nuzzled in closer. "Whatever you need."

She pinched her eyes closed and did something he'd asked of her before. "Tell me something. Anything."

His hand pressed against her stomach, splayed out over her tunic. "I keep thinking about how if we weren't traveling, that I'd take you to my favorite tavern for dinner. Just the two of us. No stress. A chance to sit back, and talk."

She closed her eyes. Considered her next words. "Oh—are you saying you're too busy to court me now so instead we should..." She turned and kissed him, a small groan slipped from him as she opened her mouth, her tongue tasting, his exploring.

His fingers grazed over her side and gripped her shirt, before his palm slid down to her waist. Heat expanded, desire scouring her body. She deepened the kiss, relishing the moment.

When they separated, he ran his hand through a lock of hair and pushed it behind her ear. "I like the idea of getting you to the point where I make you beg."

"You know..." She trailed a finger against the curves of his muscles on his chest. "There are other things we can do."

He growled low in his throat. "Oh, are there?"

Felicity grinned. "You know there are."

"And what is it you had in mind?"

"You said you wanted to explore my body." Felicity reached for the buttons of her tunic. "I've seen your shirt off. Only seems fair."

He watched as she slowly unbuttoned one at a time, then paused her movements when she reached the fourth one. "Felicity—this, maybe..."

She grinned as heated emotions flashed through his expression. This could be fun. "No good reason for me to stop?"

And she let the fabric fall open. He inhaled. He stared at her, his gaze sliding over her skin, her bare stomach, the brassiere covering her breasts. "May I?"

She reached for his hand and placed it at the edge of the lace and satin. "Yes. Please."

Alarian's growl was more animal than male. He leaned over and traced his mouth along the edges of brassiere, following the peak and fall of the fabric. He inhaled against her skin, and she shivered as he gave the exposed flesh a gentle kiss. He groaned as she arched into him, the sound making her skin prickle in anticipation.

The sudden squeak of someone's bed. The banging of a headboard against the wall next to them. A roar and scream of a name.

Alarian paused, their eyes met. And Felicity couldn't help but laugh as someone yelled out profanities.

More banging on the wall and another voice began to count, loudly.

The second individual began to fight with the first, all while the headboard, or what they assumed was a part of the bed, continued to hit the wall with loud smacks.

Alarian laughed with her. His forehead rested against hers. "I think these walls are too thin."

So close—but the moment was broken. The noises from their neighbors continued. At least someone was having fun.

He pressed a kiss to the spot above her heart, and then rested his head on her shoulder, arm splayed across her body as he pulled her in tight. She curled into him. "Goodnight, Starlight. Sleep well."

And she did. The rest of the night, she didn't dream at all.

***

The following day, they flew until the sun was hovering midway in the sky. They arrived at a large wooden home settled on the outskirts of a town, where other small shanty-like buildings stood above the water on stilts.

"It's for when the water rises," Alarian had explained. "They don't have to worry about flooding this way. They might enjoy the water and marsh landscape but don't want to deal with the maintenance of a flooded house every season."

When they landed on the small patch of reeds outside of the home, Felicity's feet had barely touched down on the squishy earth when a squeal sounded behind her. There was a chance the exclamation could have been carried through the entire realm by pitch alone.

"Felicity." She turned to watch as Lady Molyle rushed from the steps, racing to meet them. "You're here. Finally."

They'd sent a letter to inform Lady Molyle. In hindsight, it may have been better to have just surprised the female.

"My father was pleased that you took me up on my offer. Please, come inside." She grabbed their packs, ignoring as a male came and attempted to take their things. "Come, come. Truly, I'm so excited you're here." Molyle glanced at Alarian. "And you too. Imagine my surprise when I heard you were together."

She, as usual, got right to the point. "Are the two of you engaged? It would make sense—the chemistry between you two was impossible to ignore. There was no way anyone could fake the draw you two have to each other."

Felicity lifted a brow at Alarian, and he shrugged. "Not everything can be a lie."

That wasn't an explanation at all. "We aren't engaged." A simple answer and the easy way out.

Before Felicity could comment further, Molyle squealed again as they walked up the stairs into the house. "So exciting. We're throwing a ball in your honor. Don't worry, it is a small affair, but it must be done. It's not every day that a princess comes to call."

With how quickly she spoke, Felicity was having a hard time keeping up, and she had to bite back a frown when the words registered. Damn. They definitely should have surprised the female with their arrival. "We appreciate the gesture, but truly…"

"Nonsense," Molyle interrupted, not letting Felicity continue. "We're thrilled to have you here. Visce has been ignored for years. It would do good for your family to gain allies within the realm." She cast a glare at Alarian. "Nothing personal, but your family was horrible at realm relations."

There was no way around it. If Molyle had told everyone of their presence, then it certainly wouldn't look good on her family if she was to disappear—or cancel the ball. "May I ask, when is this ball?"

"Tonight, of course. After you mentioned you could only be here for one night, I was sure to send invitations out immediately. Let me tell you that rounding up proper decorations and attire at such short notice was a headache at the very least, but for you, it was worth it."

"We hoped not to draw attention," Alarian added.

Molyle grinned. "That's why it's a masquerade. No one will know who you are because I went with the full mask motif. Only your mouth will be left uncovered." She winked, as if allowing them in on a secret. "I commissioned one for each of you and didn't tell them where you were lodging, only that you wanted to celebrate among your people. They ate it up."

"We didn't actually bring attire for such an event." Felicity gave her last defense.

Molyle waved them into a sitting room where a maid waited with out-stretched hands for their cloaks as they passed. Two overstuffed sofas in pink florals with lace decorative pillows awaited them. A small coffee table was settled between them had tea waiting. "It's all been taken care of. In an hour, a seamstress will arrive and finalize your measurements. Now, come take a seat so we can catch up."

Felicity needed rest, not a meeting with a seamstress. That and food. Or some peace and quiet. Maybe all the above. But Molyle was excited and characteristically oblivious to their mood. When a male entered—his features older but with a similar dip in his nose and round face as Lady Molyle—she jumped up from her seat and rushed to his side. "Papa, I want to introduce you to Alarian and Princess Felicity. This is my Papa, Lord Cormac Molyle."

He bowed.

Felicity resisted the usual shudder at the title as she stood. "Thank you so much for giving us a place to stay."

He gave her a timid smile. "We don't have as much space as an inn, but Fiona assured me the two of you would be comfortable sharing a room. I hope that wasn't presumptuous on her part."

Lord Molyle looked between the two of them, Alarian clearing his throat first to answer. "If there isn't an extra room, we will make do. We're just glad to have a place to stay. Your daughter was telling us about the party she planned. It sounds like a big event."

Her father chuckled. "I've never seen a masquerade planned in such a short period of time. I can assure you that Fifi has it all figured out. It should be a lot of fun and the realm loves the idea of not knowing each other's identities."

"It will." Molyle giggled before a knock sounded and a woman entered carrying a tray of food. She placed it down on the coffee table and left. "Oh goody, food has arrived. Let's eat and then I can show you to your room."

They ate a quick meal of bread and cheese with a spread of different fruits, enough to sate their hunger. Afterwards, Molyle led them up a grand staircase and stopped at the second door on the left. "Here you go. The seamstress will be by soon. Until then, get comfortable and let us know if there is anything you need."

She slid the door closed behind her, whistling a tune as she walked down the hall. Felicity and Alarian looked at each other and then both diverted their gazes to look around the room. Cushions were everywhere. On the chair that sat under the window overlooking the view of swamplands and moss-covered trees. Upon the settee on the end of the four-poster bed that was also filled head to toe.

"It's comfortable at least." A pitiful attempt to keep the distance between them. They agreed that they would need to be on their best behavior. Molyle would spread word like wildfire, and now with a masquerade to prepare for, if they crossed any lines there would be no way to stop the female from gossiping.

They moved around the room in a stagnant silence. There had been the rush to reach their destination but now it was as if they were forced to face the impasse of the previous night. While alone. In a room. With a bed. Besides, he wanted to court her. Last night they almost rushed things. The idea made her heart flutter.

Then there was the fact that the title—princess—one she'd heard more of in the past few weeks than had been uttered within the palace walls surprisingly didn't bear the same weight as it once had. But the fear of the responsibility, to be more than the weapon she'd been molded into at the Tower, still lingered. Out here, she was actively participating. Had a purpose. More than a title and pretty clothes. How would it be when she returned home?

"Felicity?"

She was drawn out of her thoughts, realizing her scarf was threaded through her fingers. By Alarian's tone, it hadn't been his first attempt at garnering her attention. "Yes?"

"What's going on in that mind of yours? It's almost as though I can see the wheels moving." He reached out, gently taking the scarf from her before folding it. One night—that was as long as they could stay, so unpacking made little sense.

Felicity considered her words carefully. "This ball isn't a good idea."

Alarian sat down, his leg brushing against hers. She wanted to lean into the touch. To pick up where they were rudely interrupted the night before.

"I don't know Visce well. I never spent much time visiting and since they didn't like my mother, I wasn't exactly welcomed. She hadn't hidden her disdain well and it's not really my cup of tea with all the wet and marsh. The towns are spread out because there aren't many dry areas to settle in large groups. Those Lady Molyle invited haven't seen each other in a long time and aren't likely to recognize one another, let alone us. But I think, if anything, the masks will help."

"But the implication that your mother or Fiadh could already be here or have found the stone. I'd hoped we would get the information then be gone early."

And they have a dragon, she almost proclaimed. The idea was still incredulous to consider.

Alarian shifted, his hands tightening on the scarf. "We have to hope we're a step ahead. My mother already knows what we mean to do, so all we have is time on our side and the information that Thomas is attempting to uncover...and Molyle has the knowledge we need. I trust that."

Felicity remembered the little of Visce she learned from her studies with Kellan. At first, he had started with trade routes and resources. It wasn't until later within their time, as trust had blossomed, that the books he gave her took on a wider range of topics. Visce was known for coming up with water inventions to help with crops, irrigation, plumbing but their prices were either exorbitant or they weren't willing to share beyond their realm. Not unlike Scáth, the people of Visce kept their resources and secrets close. There wasn't trust among them and they wouldn't give information willingly, especially to outsiders.

Not a reaction she could blame them for, specifically with the ex-queen's disdain for the realm. It was easy for them to hide since not many outsiders knew of the trails and paths to follow through the realm and most of the inhabitants lived within the water itself. That was why this stop was necessary—why trusting and speaking with Lady Fiona Molyle was a priority they couldn't ignore.

"I do have a question though."

She paused from loosening the straps on her vest to face him. "Yes?"

Alarian rubbed the back of his neck. His head low, he looked up at her between wisps of hair falling over his brow. "Would you go with me to the masquerade?"

Felicity swallowed, pulling her bottom lip between her teeth. "Who else would I go with?"

"Not like that." He winced slightly. "I'm messing this up."

A small smile played at her lips. "Actually, I don't think you are."

"So, yes?"

She closed the space between them and kissed his cheek. "I couldn't imagine going with anyone else."

Chapter 31

Felicity

There was a knock at their door. When Felicity opened it, a squat man and a sprightly female walked in beaming with excitement, the former's arms laden with clothing.

"It's true then—we are meant to dress royalty." The female grinned widely and rushed to Felicity's side. "I cannot believe it. When Lady Molyle told us, we were in such awe. She speaks so highly of you. Sometimes her stories are a little exaggerated, but it seems these were more than brusque dreams."

Felicity's brow rose and she mouthed *brusque* at Alarian who just shrugged, trying to hide his smile from his spot on the settee. The gentleman was already lifting Alarian's arms up, forcing him to his feet, before taking a step back and pushing out his bottom lip, eyes narrowed as he tapped his chin. "With that hair, dark brown might be best. Although a deep green could be intriguing."

"Oh, the one with a bronze or copper trim," the female beside the man added, mimicking his stance.

Felicity stifled a laugh, glad not to be caught in their crosshairs and certainly not wanting to draw attention to herself. She stepped into the corner of the room.

But it had the opposite effect as the female whipped around. "My princess! Let's see what we have here. There are three dresses we've been considering." She rushed to the pile of clothes that the man had placed on the bed, pushing fabric aside until she removed a pale pink gown. "This might be too elegant for your sharp features. You need something fierce, and this fits more for a wall flower that needs to stand out."

Felicity swallowed, surprised at the description. There had been times that she had heard clothes being described to accentuate certain attributes, but always in line with the mission she'd been on. Even at the palace, most were chosen for the occasion—whether it was a ball or times at tea where they needed her to look prim, proper, and relaxed. But this—this wasn't about the event. This was about her.

"What's your name?" Felicity probably shouldn't ask. Sometimes that brought on more curiosity than she wanted.

The female grinned, her cheeks flushing. "Modiste. I know—seems picked from a fashion book, but it just may have been. My mother chose it, and she was a seamstress before me."

Modiste grabbed a second dress. "Hamish over there thought this one up. I questioned his design at first, but I think this is just what we need." Deep crimson red that looked like it would mold to her body with a slit visible up to her mid-thing. "This is a dress some would put on and it would wear them—in this case, you would wear *it*."

Felicity had no idea what she meant, but Modiste didn't give her a chance to decipher before she was dragged behind the privacy screen in the corner of the room. Modiste ordered her to remove her clothes, handed her undergarments that would be commonly found at a brothel...

Although once they were on, Felicity wondered if she could keep them. The buttery pieces of dark red lace and satin shimmered in the candlelight and were soft against her skin.

The dress came next. Modiste assisted her into the garment and fastened the pearl buttons up her back. When she was done, Modiste stepped back to take Felicity in. "Perfect," she whispered. "Just as I suspected—you make this dress."

Felicity gestured to pass but Modiste wouldn't hear it. "This will knock him off his feet. Save the reveal for later," she whispered as she held up Felicity's clothes. "Change back for now. I need to make some minor adjustments."

When she reappeared, Alarian was already back in his clothes, Hamish taking care of the last pins on a pair of trousers. "Well, that's all we need. We will return prior to the ball with the outfits and masks. A stylist will assist you with hair and any cosmetics, Princess."

Felicity swallowed back the desire to refuse their assistance. When they left, it was only a few moments later before a tray of food arrived. It seemed Molyle was certain to have them well fed and cared for. "Baths will be ready a little after noon. Please feel free to take a tour of the grounds. Lord Molyle is downstairs if you would like for him to show you around."

After a quick meal, they walked the yard, both borrowing heavy boots to protect themselves from the sloshy water. Lord Molyle led them on a tour, discussing the structural aspects of the houses and how they made adjustments in the different seasons. Currently, they were preparing for winter and the ice and chill to freeze the land before the spring showers brought floods. Houses were built to withstand the elements but required a lot of maintenance to handle both variables—a mixture of magic and technology.

"Our realm has been ignored for years and left to our own devices. Some of us have had to make connections and sacrifices to ensure Visce's prominence in Talamh. When we're drawn to water, it's hard to leave our homes, even if other locations appeal to us. And not many come to visit us since flash floods aren't the only danger within our waters. We've had to learn to adapt. Mostly for protection. If our houses were in the water, like a boat, then many of the creatures of the realm could enter. They are not a welcomed guest—dangerous."

Felicity took that as the warning it was. Stay clear of the water. Damn—that wasn't going to make finding the stone easy.

They caught up with Lady Molyle when they reached a solarium built down a long corridor off the main house. It was a large circular room with glass ceilings and walls that made the space look like a giant fishbowl. It was decorated to fit the aesthetic of the landscape. Green moss was fashioned among white lilies. Birch wood for tables and chairs—cushions made of deep greens, vines hung from the ceiling, bulbs glowing alongside them casting a faint light that added to the motif. It was as though they brought the outside in.

"It's enchanting, Lady Molyle." Felicity turned in a circle, taking it all in.

The female clapped in excitement, walking over to them. "I'm so happy you like it. But please, call me Fiona."

"It's very impressive." Alarian grinned. "Did you plan all of this yourself?"

Her cheeks pinked. "I did. Planning and decorating events brings me joy."

She tutted at an assistant, asking them to move one of the tables a bit to the left.

Felicity glanced from Alarian to the female. "It's a pity we don't have time to visit since we have to leave tomorrow." Tonight would not be the ideal time to have a conversation where anyone could overhear.

Fiona stopped mid-step. "Oh my, I apologize. Let me finish up the last few things here. We can sit and chat for teatime before we get ready. I'll hold off on baths for a little longer if that's all right with you?"

"Yes, that would be great." Alarian reached for Felicity's hand and as their fingers entwined, Molyle let out a little squeak.

"You are just so cute. I'll meet you when the bell tolls one."

Lord Molyle gave a small smile as he led them back towards the sitting room. "She wouldn't stop talking about you when she met you at Advisor Boister's ball. I'm glad you took her up on the offer to visit."

Guilt settled in Felicity's gut. They were using her. Their hospitality. All of it. She'd make it up to the female.

They made their way back to the main house, and Felicity didn't realize until they were halfway down the main hall that her hand was still in Alarian's. She didn't pull away. The walls of the long corridor were covered in art and paintings. Lord Molyle occasionally paused to discuss some of the acquisitions but from how he talked, it was the late Lady Molyle who had a love for art.

"She dreamed of being a painter but didn't have a knack for it." He stopped at the last painting before the double door to the main house. "But this was one of her best."

It looked more like smudges, but the colors swirled until a child was present within the swipes and swirls of paint. "Fiona?" Felicity asked in a whisper.

"Yes."

"It's beautiful. I've never seen art like this before."

"She wanted it to look like water. They might not be everyone's taste, but I could never part with them."

"I'm sorry she's gone."

Lord Molyle glanced down the hall, his gaze hooded. A long, slow sigh. "Thank you," he whispered before continuing down the hall without stopping. Felicity noted his countenance. The way he spoke of his home. There was something nagging at the back of her mind, but she couldn't think of what it could be.

Fiona met them shortly after the bell had tolled. She ordered tea immediately, asking for cookies to be brought before she sat, stuffing one of the many cushions at her side. "Well, what brought you to Visce? I'd love to think it was to see me, but I know there must be other reasons."

Right to the point. Molyle was smart, observant. They needed to be careful with their words.

"I haven't been to Visce. It seemed important to learn about the realms I'm meant to help rule over. With our father missing, I'm trying to be as helpful to my brother as I can." Felicity smiled as the female's grin widened. Just a touch of information shared. Breadcrumbs for a story that she would weave into a more elaborate tapestry for her guests and all who would listen. "The chance to visit here with you—it was a bonus."

"What have you seen so far? Did you go to Dorcha? It isn't common for cailleach to come into the realm."

Observant, for certain. "Yes." Alarian leaned back, giving off a relaxed air. His arm draped over the back of the chair behind Felicity. The persona Fiona would expect—and eat up. "I have friends there, so it seemed like a good place to start. Most of Felicity's previous visits had only been near the outskirts." Truth that could be confirmed by their advisor if he deigned to speak about her threat. "They offered the cailleach for easier travel."

"Flying is much easier. We have boats, but if you don't know the canals well, it's hard to traverse without a guide. Especially with the creatures that live within the depths." Molyle sipped her tea.

Felicity took a bite of a sugar cookie and wiped the crumbs from the corner of her mouth. "Do you have any places you recommend visiting or staying away from on our way through the realm?"

Molyle tilted her head, her lips pursed in thought. "Not really. Well, beyond the main town. It's the largest in the realm—where you can see many uses of our water inventions. It's near the coastline and the only beach we have. From the sky, you can tell you're nearly there when you reach the remains of a tower."

Another tower. Could they be so lucky? It was doubtful that Visce would have their heartstone on display—or out of the water. "Which direction would we go?"

"Stay along the coast as you fly, and you won't miss it. At one point the marsh turns into sand." Molyle grabbed a cookie.

"We'll have to head that way. What about any lakes?" Alarian asked. "We wanted to see some of the large bodies of water the realm boasts about."

She paused her chewing, her brow furrowed in thought. "We only have one lake. Not much boasting going on about it though. It's near the center of the realm and the creatures there divert any travelers. I don't recommend going that way. It isn't even safe for those native to Visce." She reached for a drawer in the table beside her. "Speaking of which, you will need these tonight."

She held out fabric towards each of them and it wasn't until they were in their own hands that Felicity realized they were gloves. "What are these for?"

"The selkies," Molyle said it so matter-of-factly that Felicity froze her perusal of the silk elbow-length gloves. Molyle took another cookie from the tray. "The selkies live within the water and can take the form of others that they touch. Don't let anyone touch you without gloves. It's with skin-to-skin contact only that they can transform. For the most part they are harmless, but more than one has taken advantage of the unsuspecting."

She sipped her tea primly, as if nothing were amiss. Like she hadn't spread the word about their arrival and then placed them in danger.

Felicity glanced at Molyle's bare hands for a moment wondering if there was a chance that this wasn't her friend. "How well, or long, do they keep another's form?"

"Depends on the strength of the selkie. When they become another person, they would have to learn a lot about their mannerisms to pull it off over a long period of time. The masks will make it more difficult for them to decipher whose identity they stole. Security will be present. I wouldn't worry."

Felicity was going to do just that.

Chapter 32

Felicity

Felicity had asked that they keep her cosmetics light with only a touch of kohl around her eyes and rouge to her cheeks and lips, hoping it would be a good contrast to her dress. A second divider had been put up for Alarian to change while Felicity did the same with Modiste's help. A slit now extended up her left thigh, playing peek-a-book with the stars and moon tattoo. The shape of the neckline dipped slightly between her breasts. With the fit of the gown, Felicity was thankful for her undergarments holding everything in place.

Alarian finished first. The sound of Hamish bickering with Alarian to fix his hair beckoned Felicity to steal a peek, but Modiste pulled her back, stopping her.

The female finally was happy when she handed Felicity a copper lace mask that matched the color of the gold and brown gloves with sequins and strategically placed gems. Together, it gave the effect of a wolf.

She thought of the Tower's insignia. The wolf in the center of two snakes knotted together, eating their own tails.

She lifted the mask to her face when Modiste stopped her. "Don't put it on yet. Just before you leave the room but not before."

"Why?"

"So that he sees the full affect." Modiste winked, then stepped out from behind the screen. "Everyone ready?"

Hamish grumbled a response and clapped his hands twice. "Come out, Princess. I want to see my creation on you."

It felt too formal. The idea of being on display like this. Being watched after decades of hiding in the shadows. She bit back the rising panic that settled in her chest, breathing in and counting to ten like she'd done before, and stepped out from behind the privacy screen.

Hamish and Modiste grinned widely, Alarian's back towards her. "You look absolutely stunning," Hamish gasped. "Modiste was right—that gown was made for you in mind."

"I appreciate you letting me borrow all these nice clothes."

Hamish shook his head. "Borrow? No, Your Highness. They are yours to keep."

She almost turned down the offer—they only had so much room in their packs and needed to keep provisions light—but how could she deny an artist's gift? She moved towards the mirror, her eyes on Alarian's form. He still hadn't glanced her way, and she tried to ignore how finely the deep brown suit fit him, the way the copper trim accentuated the color and matched her accessories' embellishments—how it hugged his body to the point that she could see the fine lines of his broad shoulders and the corded muscle she knew by heart.

She stopped before looking in the mirror, suddenly frozen in trepidation. Alarian turned and met her gaze. His eyes widened, breath hitching as his mouth parted. A step. A pause. Air stuck in her throat. He'd shaved, and she kind of missed his stubble. But the colors of his suit accentuated his green eyes. He was exquisite. Truly. Yet she couldn't move. Speak.

His gaze sharpened as he straightened, glancing at the others. "Thank you for your time and assistance. You've done a wonderful job. You're dismissed." It was a prince's tone. One she hadn't heard from Alarian in some time.

Modiste glanced between them both, and Felicity's heart began to rush faster. Fear.

The tailors glanced at each other, and then back at Felicity again.

She turned to face them. "This dress is beyond what I could even imagine. Thank you." Somehow, she spoke without her voice cracking, the words thick and heavy on her tongue.

Modiste and Hamish smiled, the latter giving a small bow before they left. Felicity almost collapsed as the door closed behind them. Emotions welled, battled within her. She couldn't grasp onto one. Alarian had her in his arms before she could comprehend what was happening. "What is it?"

Panic spread. The fear of looking in that mirror and seeing who looked back at her. Would she recognize herself? Why did this exact moment suddenly seem so pivotal? So important?

"I don't—" She shook her head, unable to form words.

He led her to the chair, sitting her down, before kneeling in front of her. "I thought it was their presence—too many eyes. But then your face went pale. What are you thinking?"

Fear. A word she hated. It made her weak. Incapable. Froze her with indecision. An emotion she couldn't use in her line of work. But that was it, wasn't it? She wasn't a weapon anymore. Once she returned—would her father order her to remain within the castle walls where it was safe? Would Kellan risk losing her again? Would she be expected to dress in gowns, play a part?

"Please. Trust me. You shouldn't be afraid, so tell me why?"

How did he always seem to know what she was feeling?

"All of it." Her body shook. A weight made it difficult to breathe. "Modiste kept saying that I wore this dress—that it didn't wear me. But I don't understand? All of it is so confusing. Who I am—" She shook her head. "I feel like I take a step forward and then just as quickly stumble back."

Alarian took her hand and placed it against his chest. He took a deep breath. "Breathe with me, Felicity."

He brushed a lock of her wavy hair behind her ear. "It's confusing. I went from being a citizen of Scáth, to suddenly a prince under duress, and then I was lost. For a long time. You're handling this a lot better than I did."

"How?" Her chest contracted.

"You're realizing it. That's a big step. It took me years to recognize that I could do something. But it was never because I was a prince. I had purpose. Like you do. Give yourself some space to accept that you don't have to have it all figured out. Right now, you're doing exactly what you need to do."

Her palm warmed under his touch, and the shadows grew around them as Alarian held her hand tight against him. She took him in. The way his hair curled over his brow. How his emerald eyes glittered in the dimming light. The way his finger patted against her hand with the beat of his heart. She concentrated on that movement. On him. Saw him.

A gasp broke from her lips, and he nodded. "Good. Again. Slow and easy. Breathe in and out." But he'd misinterpreted.

Like she had misinterpreted him. His words no longer confused her. She felt them fully as she looked into his eyes. The truth was there as he held her hand in his.

As her breathing evened out, Alarian tilted his head and scanned her face. "Now, do you want to talk?"

She swallowed deeply as sincerity and concern flitted over his expression. The words tumbled out. "I don't know who I am."

Alarian reached up, cupping her jaw. "Oh, Felicity, but I think you do. I've always seen you, and you were yourself many times during this trip. I think you know it, and it scares you." He stood his hand still holding hers. With a small tug, he pulled her to her feet, and she swore her heart jumped a beat.

He led her away from the chair and she balked, but only for a moment, when she realized he was taking her towards the mirror.

Alarian settled her in front of it, remaining behind her, his hands at his sides. Leaving her wanting his touch, for him to hold her. He leaned in, his head nestled near her ear. Shadows dimmed their view of their reflection. "Do you know why I wanted them to leave? Why I didn't turn right away?"

She shook her head.

He smiled. "Because I heard Modiste—she wanted a reaction from me." He whispered, "This dress—it's beautiful—you look absolutely gorgeous in it. It does fit you perfectly and you make it better. But only because I know who you are."

She swallowed back the tears. No, she wouldn't cry. Not now. "And who am I?"

"You're Felicity. You're not defined by titles or pretty gowns. You're not signified by a tattoo on your hip or the crown you wear. They aren't what make you who you are."

"But I can't ignore the title of princess." She shook her head. "Or the responsibilities that come with such a word. Not when I've been raised as the complete opposite. And what if my father cannot accept me for that?"

A lump swelled in her throat. She hadn't even considered that before she said it aloud. Her father. The male she couldn't even remember. The king of the continent in disarray. Would he be all right with who she was now and able to separate the youngling he used to know her to be? The shadows slowly cleared.

"He will. Because I have no doubts he loves you. Even after all these years. But, as I've told you before, you're the one who defines those titles placed on you. Not the other way around. You don't have to fall under a specific category to fulfill your duties. You get to make them. Mold them to you. Just like when you dealt with Advisor Heavin. That was all you."

True. That had been a moment she was proud of. It had felt right. She looked herself over in the mirror, surprised at what she saw. Herself. Completely who she was. "What if I can't live up to other's expectations?"

"For what it's worth, you've already surpassed mine. As for any other's expectations—they can fuck off. You know who cares about you. Only those who truly support you matter. And they won't have expectations if they deserve to be in your life. Kellan, Avyanna, your father..." He swallowed. "Those at your side doesn't get to put that pressure on you. Remember that."

There it was. That truth again. Love. No wonder he didn't rush it. He had been waiting for her to catch up. Or so he hoped. Hell, could she feel that for him too?

She didn't concentrate on that emotion—not now. Not when he was so close, when temptation was the beating heart under her palm. When the want had only been growing. He was right to assume she might soon be begging.

Air caught in her lungs again as the shadows dissipated. But for a completely different reason. There he was, at her back, speaking words to build her up. "You look handsome tonight, Rian."

He grinned, that familiar tilt to one side of his mouth. The smirk she loved. He reached around waist and squeezed, giving her a kiss on the cheek. "Thank you, Felicity, but look in that mirror."

She realized her gaze had pinned on him in the reflection. As she took herself in, Alarian stepped out of the frame, no longer in her sight. It was all her. The deep red dress that accentuated her curves and matched the pendant she always wore. Highlighted her hair and amber eyes. The dress wasn't fierce—she was.

"Thank you." She met her gaze in the mirror after taking in the entire image in front of her. "For seeing me."

"Anytime, Princess Felicity."

This time she didn't balk at his words. In fact, as she took the mask that he held out to her, she smiled.

She glanced at him, remembering his aunt's offer to return to Domhain once all of this was done. Would he leave even if they were courting? Part of her knew she could find herself on her own. But he had been right about so many things—she needed to learn to accept help for what it was. It wasn't doubt in her abilities, but how someone showed they cared. And she cared about him.

She slid the last glove on. "Are you ready?"

"Yes, let's go have a good time." He put the gloves on and then strapped the mask to his face.

Felicity turned away, lifting her chin, ready to show the people of Visce exactly who she was. She'd deal with the possibility of him leaving later. A room full of curious fae was the first on her list of things to deal with.

When he reached for the door, she stopped him. Alarian frowned, concern written in his expression. She slowly took two steps towards him and saw the light shift in his eyes before she pressed him against the door and her lips were against his as she explored the taste of him, her hand around his neck. A small growl broke from between his lips. Before he could deepen the kiss or she'd be tempted to undo all the seamstress' work, she pulled away.

"We can't be late."

Alarian groaned. "Damnit, Starlight. Really?"

The corner of her mouth piqued, and she nudged him aside to open the door. "We have a party to attend."

Resting his hand at the small of her back, he moved in beside her and whispered in her ear, "You will send me to an early grave if you keep that up."

"What is it you said to me once?"

His brow rose.

"You couldn't decide if threatening your life took all of the fun out of flirting? I guess now you know your answer."

"I'd test fate every day for you."

Chapter 33

Felicity

Felicity arrived at the ball on Alarian's arm, and a few cast assessing glances. Unlike the continuous mass of fae who flocked to royalty's side at most events, their haughty and disinterested looks were discernible even behind their masks before they returned to their conversations.

Felicity shook her head. "Maybe I should move here."

Alarian chuckled. "Would you be able to handle Molyle at every waking moment? You know she'd request to move in with you."

His breath caressed her cheek, and her heartbeat quickening again.

A fae female Felicity recognized by posture alone trotted over to them.

"You both look lovely."

"Thank you. As do you Lady M—"

"Hush." She stepped in closer. "No names here. First rule of a masquerade in Visce."

"Then how do you get to know each other?" Alarian's gaze glinted.

"This isn't the time to get to know each other. This is a time for dancing, food, and fun." Molyle's mouth twisted into a smile. "Enjoy yourselves. No one here will know it's you unless you want them to." She tapped Felicity's arm with her gloved hand as a subtle reminder before disappearing into the crowd.

"Would they have even known we were here if Lady Molyle had spread the word?" Felicity whispered.

Alarian grinned. "Possibly not." He nodded towards the crowd. "Either way, it's enough you're showing interest in their realm. More than my parents did."

Felicity followed his gaze to find a few guests huddled together, chatting in a half circle, and staring directly at them. She turned her back to the group to face Alarian. "Maybe I shouldn't move here. I'd be exhausted with everything she'd have planned."

"It wouldn't be the same without you."

Felicity lifted her chin, unable to look at him as she said, "It sounds like you won't be in Éardrom. Your aunt offered you a place to stay."

Alarian's voice was a caress against her neck. "All you have to do is ask."

She blushed, turning away.

The dim rays of the setting sun illuminated the stone and algae decorated the room. Candles lit tabletops and the perimeter of the space with the shimmer of an air barrier protecting them from being knocked over. "She really does know how to decorate for a party."

"She does. Might want to consider asking her for assistance with any future events. Your brother's wedding, maybe?"

Felicity shifted. They didn't even know when that would take place. "They deserve a beautiful wedding. I'll have to make recommendations. Modiste and Hamish could design their clothing."

The sound of wind and string instruments filled the room. A haunting melody that ebbed and flowed as others began to pair off and dance. She noted that Alarian ensured no one without gloves was nearby, as did she.

"Would you like to dance?" Alarian held out his gloved hand.

Felicity smiled at him. "Yes."

His own smirk lengthened into a grin. She moved into his space until her body was just a breath away from his. Alarian wrapped his arm around her lower back, the other still holding her hand.

He leaned in and whispered in her ear, "Does this count as the final dance for our oath?"

A shiver ran down her spine at the rumble of his voice so close. His breath heated the skin at her throat. "Shouldn't I be asking you that?"

"At this point I feel like we need to agree."

The scar on her palm warmed against his hand. A reminder of what was still between them. One final connection and agreement that drew them together. "Not unless you want it to be."

He pulled back and met her gaze. "I thought I made everything perfectly clear. I'm willing to wait."

It had already been difficult to wait. But they still had so much to accomplish, and their time was running short. There hadn't been any word from Thomas. The most recent note from Illith said he was working day and night. Finding the stones and stopping Marquette was beginning to feel impossible.

The world tilted as he dipped her. "Al—"

He shook his head. "No names." A small grin—but it wasn't a real one—as he brought her back up. "We're just dancing. Let me pretend for a moment. Please?"

His words broke her open. Emotions she repressed for so long. A mix of heartbreak, empathy, desire, longing...did he know what he was doing to her? His expression softened, and he rested his chin against the side of her head and swayed to the music. As if he knew exactly what she needed.

Instead of overanalyzing, they danced. Held each other close. The only sounds were the music, the shifting of feet and chatter. All she could see was him. Everything else a blurred.

As one song ended and another began, she worried someone else would interrupt them and ask for a dance but that wasn't the case. So unlike home.

She missed home.

The word hit hard in the center of her chest. Kellan, Avyanna, the gardens, and ocean view. A lone willow tree among the plains. She missed it. The idea should have terrified her, but instead it made her heart swell.

She had a home.

And when the music turned into the intoxicating animalistic cadence, Alarian led her to the side of the dance floor. "Ready to call it a night?"

She nodded despite being tempted to see what would come of it if they stayed. Alarian's hand moved to the curve of her waist. Pinpricks curled along her spine, spreading from the warmth of his gloved touch. Involuntarily, she moved closer to him. A group crossed in front, drawing her and Alarian to a stop. When his grip on her waist tightened, Felicity leaned further into the touch.

"Starlight." It was a breath at her neck. A caress she couldn't ignore.

"Hm?" Her fingers grazed his forearm.

"We can walk again." His lips brushed her skin. Not exactly a kiss—more of a taste.

"Oh." She had closed her eyes, let herself become lost in the moment and forget everything around her. But him.

When they reached their room, his hand rested against hers—as if he couldn't resist touching her. The gloves were warm, but she wanted his skin. To feel him.

She walked inside and stopped in the center of the room. As Alarian closed the door, she caught her reflection in the mirror. Saw him move behind her. Remove the coat and hang it on a hook by the door. Begin to take off the gloves and place one on the table.

"I don't want to resist anymore," she whispered the words aloud.

Alarian stilled, caught in mid-movement of removing the second glove. "What?"

She turned slowly to face him, the dress twisting dramatically around her feet. This wasn't a game she was willing to play. Not if it would hurt him. He'd seen more pieces of her than she'd ever allowed anyone, and he hadn't balked once. Not at her anger. Her frustration. Her anxiousness.

His expression was unreadable as he glanced down at his hands and removed that final glove.

Her chest cracked open at the civility in his movements. She wanted him to say something—anything. "Alarian, I want everything from you, but I'm still scared."

He shook his head. "I'm scared every day."

She blinked, her arms wrapping around her mid-section. "Of what?"

"Of not being enough for you. That I won't prove I'm worthy when you are so much more than I'll ever be." He inhaled, his chest expanding. "Of admitting that I've fallen for you and may never have the chance to hear you say you have feelings for me too."

She bit her bottom lip but before she could respond, he continued, "I want to court you properly. But I desperately want to—"

Felicity couldn't wait for him to finish his thought. She was across the room in a heartbeat, her arms round his neck and kissed him. Felicity clung to him, wishing that she could say all the feelings that were difficult to put into words. That this kiss would be enough—but it couldn't be. For him, she had to say it.

She broke the kiss, and he stared at her as she brushed a finger against his cheek. "You're worth everything. That's what scares me the most, Rian."

He shuddered, his mouth twitching into his half smile at the nickname. "What are you saying, Starlight?"

"You're going to make me spell it out, aren't you?"

"I've been waiting a long time." His grin widened, his chin lowering until his gaze was level with hers.

She resisted rolling her eyes as she saw the hope blaze to life in his. "I see you. I choose you."

A growl slid from his throat as his mouth retook hers, his arms wrapping around her body to pull her tight against him.

She gripped his bicep, muscle flexing under her touch as she deepened the kiss. The damn gloves were in the way of what she wanted. Needed. She wrapped her arms around his neck again and pulled off the elbow-length gloves. His chest brushed against hers and desire spiked through her entire body. She needed to feel all of him, touch him everywhere. Have him touch her.

Felicity reached for the hem of his shirt, but Alarian's hands clasped hers. Another low growl. "Damnit, Starlight."

"What?" She barely recognized her own voice. Heady with need and breathless.

"We can't. Not here."

A wave of want. Her eyes widened as he groaned against her mouth.

"What do you mean we can't here?"

"I've waited a long time for this." He kissed her cheek, brushing his mouth down her neck to her shoulder. A small nip at her collar bone had her arching her body further into his. "But I can't do this right. Not here in Lady Molyle's house where everyone can hear. Because we're not going to be quiet, Starlight. Besides, I'm still working through things. We both are."

Heat pooled at her core, an ache she needed satiated. "I don't care who hears." Let them all be damned as far as she was concerned. "And we will figure those things out. Together."

He chuckled, the sound and sensation vibrating against her neck. A tease. He was a tease. "I've wanted to hear you say that for far too long." He pulled back enough to press a kiss to her nose. "And in that waiting I've also used my imagination for exactly what I'm going to do with you. For you." That damned grin appeared. The one she was learning to love. "I've had to be patient." A brush of his lips against her jaw. "Now it's your turn. I said I want to take this slow. I've never done that before and this, for us, feels right."

He stepped back, shadows appearing, and she grabbed his arm sharply. "If you turn into that damn fox right now, I'm going to kick you out of this room. Don't you think we've waited long enough?"

Alarian smirked as the shadows dispersed. "Yes. But that's part of it. I've gotten to know you. But I want to learn those places you love to be touched in passing. Want to discover who we are together first before we go there. Besides, I have a vision of how this is meant to be and here in Lady Molyle's guest bedroom is not that. You can wait one more night."

Her gaze only sharpened. "Fine—you want to wait. I can accept that. But I've just admitted things that aren't easy to say. Not for me. So, you're going to hold me close tonight and live with your decision. Understood?"

The shadows dissipated and he stepped back into her space. "I was only trying to make it easier." He winked. "For you."

"Shut it." She turned on her heel and stopped at the entrance to the divider and paused. If he was going to show constraint, fine—that didn't mean she had to play fair. Felicity peered over her shoulder at him. "Will you help me with the buttons?"

He licked his bottom lip, the sound he emitted was feral. "You play dirty."

Felicity slid her hair over her shoulder, exposing her toned back fully to him. "Always."

His movements were slow and methodical as he made his way to her back to undo one button after the other, starting at the space between her shoulder blades to the curve of her hips. His fingertips brushed against her skin, and more than once she caught her breath at the jolt of heat from his touch. It was as though his lust mixed with hers.

On the third time, he chuckled, and she steeled herself for any other 'accidental slips,' aware then that he was playing his own game. When the last button was done, he stepped back. "Finished."

Felicity let her hair fall against her back and then reached for the straps of her dress. As the fabric fell at her feet, she heard his inhale, the grumble under his breath as she stood in the lace underthings that Modiste had given to her. With her heeled shoes still on, she stepped from the dress completely and moved around the divide slowly. Adding temptation with every deliberate movement.

"Unfair," he grumbled.

"I hope I'm worth the wait."

"I know you will be. That *we* will be."

She caught her breath when she was behind the divide. Now that his eyes were no longer on her she waited for the emotions to overcome her—that she would start to regret everything. But she didn't. Instead, she smiled. She wanted him, yes. But she could play this game. Anticipation, somewhat foreign, prickled her skin. When she came around wearing only a long tunic, her bare legs on display, she paused as her eyes took him in.

Oh, this was going to be a fun game...

"Where is your shirt?"

Alarian stood before her with only loose-fitting trousers hanging low on his waist. "Where are your pants? Don't you think you'll be cold?"

She made her way to the bed. "I expect you to keep me warm."

He smiled, and she couldn't help but enjoy how his gaze roamed over her body.

See me.

She saw him now more than ever. And she knew that there could be so much more if she wanted there to be. One step...that's where she was at. One step at a time.

As she laid down, she pulled the cover up, leaving a leg out. He stood over her. Staring. "Are you coming to bed or sleeping elsewhere tonight?"

His steps were predatorily fluid. Slow and deliberate. He sunk under the covers, pressing his front to her back. His hand caressed her thigh. He inhaled, a slow breath tickling her throat. She sighed as he pushed her hair aside and his lips trailed kisses from below her ear to the curve of her throat.

"Rian," she whispered.

"Yes, Starlight?" He played with the hem of her tunic.

"I thought you wanted to wait."

He groaned at her throat. "I do." His clever fingers skimmed a trail at her inner thigh. Her skin pebbled in its wake. Her entire body igniting with need.

"But like you said, there are other things..."

His touch moved to her hip. A small chuckle rumbled against her back as she arched into him. His trailing fingers stilled. "Starlight...are you not wearing any undergarments?"

She smirked, reached for his hand, and placed it at the lowest part of her belly. Right above where she wanted him. He nuzzled into her neck, his kisses warm, her skin becoming feverish. She wanted so much from him. *Everything...*

"Touch me." She ground into his hardened length. "Please."

He didn't wait, but obliged, his fingers slipping between her legs. A gentle touch against her folds. She shuddered, and he nuzzled her throat. "I like that, Starlight. I can't wait to hear you beg." He kissed her ear as his hand splayed against her body. One finger tauntingly moved in circles.

Not only had it been too long, but she had wanted this for months. It had been the most deliciously slow back and forth, but she was over it now. "Yes," she hissed.

"Good." His hand inched lower. "Is this what you want?"

"You." She bucked as his finger slid within her again, teasing that sensitive spot. "I want you."

His chest rumbled against her back. "I like this control I have over you. That you allow me control."

Felicity moved her hand behind her back and palmed the bulge in his trousers. She curved at the waist, pressed her body further into his, her hand pinned between them. Alarian inhaled and let out a long, deep breath. A chuckle. "Yes, Starlight—you have that same control over me."

She preened from his words as her hand slipped within his trousers and gripped him. They moved against each other, her hand keeping pace with the friction he built between her legs. Soon the only sounds were their heavy breathing, her body rocking against his as she neared the edge, a stifled purr of release as she came, and he followed shortly after. They lay together, him holding her tight as their heart rate slowed.

After they cleaned up and changed, Alarian kissed her slowly. "You're it for me, Starlight."

Felicity nuzzled into him. "I think I could get used to that."

Felicity appreciated the feeling of his body against hers. Even as his breathing shifted to something heavier—a half snore—she realized how content she truly felt.

Neither of them had nightmares that night.

Chapter 34
Kellan

After Kellan had walked through the make-shift hospital Avyanna had ordered constructed after the curse had been broken, he'd returned to the palace and called a meeting with the advisors to start the process of planning a proper building for the sick and injured. Thankfully he'd had no difficulty in convincing them and they got straight to work.

He'd had little sleep since the arrival of Felicity and Sloan's missives two days prior. Partially because he was concerned for Felicity in Visce. Thankfully, the Countess hadn't been the immediate danger, but the witches were involved more than he'd originally considered. If the Countess was a sibling to the witch who created the curse, then what part did Fiadh have in all of this? And why?

He'd done some digging but couldn't find much information about her. No family tree. No history. She didn't appear from thin air. They were always told she was from Scáth and that was how she and Marquette had connected. Now, after thinking on that, it didn't make sense.

Then there was Felicity. He knew it hurt her that her memories were still not intact. Whoever had that vial of her past needed to be found whether or not Felicity considered it a priority. But he noted a change in her writing. Less urgency in her script and a more elegant twist in her letters. He didn't know yet what that might mean, but he hoped she had found whatever it was she needed. Even if he still couldn't let himself consider Alarian to be that *thing*.

As for Sloan, they would reach the mainland any day now—with his father. It was enough to keep him up at night, trying to prepare but uncertain who would return. Sloan said little about his father's actual health and wellbeing. The letter he left for Sloan in the designated spot still hadn't been retrieved, so he was left waiting and hoping for an update. Worrying, if he was honest with himself.

Then there was the oath between the prisoners and the traitors. His dreams hadn't been of any help to connect the puzzle pieces of the oath the survivors had taken. If only Felicity and Alarian had considered asking the Countess. Though, with the vague answers she gave, he had doubts she would have been forthright with any information. He picked up the first letter he received from Alarian and Felicity, reading it again.

He needed another book. Another question to research. Something to make him feel useful beyond signing papers, running trials, and appeasing a council. Kellan stuffed the letter back in the breast pocket of his vest and headed towards the library where he found Avyanna pouring over a book at the first table. A quick glance towards the desk at the entrance told him they were currently alone. He took a seat across from her and stared at the text she was pouring over.

"What are you looking at?"

She jumped, her hand to her chest and the table bouncing from her legs hitting the edge. "Kellan, you scared me."

He winced. "Sorry."

She rubbed her thighs and leaned back. "Probably not all your fault. I wasn't exactly paying attention."

"Helpful?" He gestured towards the book.

Avyanna rubbed her temples. "Maybe. Yes. Ugh—I don't know. Probably not."

"What is it about?"

"The tree. I found a reference to it. But it doesn't exactly spell out if it is just a symbol or more."

He held his hand out and she obliged him, turning the book towards him. "See here." She pointed to the top page.

There was an illustration of the same tree. Sprouting and healthy on the top, and the bottom where it should have roots was dead and bare. He began to read. "What did it say that doesn't seem right?"

"That..." She swallowed and glanced around the room. He paused his reading, glancing at her. She met his gaze, her stare holding him still. "Ankus."

"What?" He blinked. "That can't be..."

"Life and death. The tree of life is connected to the tree of death. If you look closely, you can see a symbol within the roots and branches."

He peered closer. The twists and turns of the branches took on another shape. "Is that...are those snakes in knots eating their own tails."

"I think so. See the diamond and stripe patterns on the back of those roots and they are embedded in the connection of the earth between the two trees. Like they are intertwined. Kellan—are you all right?"

He couldn't believe it. Here was more proof of a connection between the Tower and all that was happening. "Because...the Tower's insignia is a wreath of two snakes knotted together, eating their own tails. And in the middle is a wolf's head."

Avyanna blinked. "There are no wolves on the symbol. Do you think it correlates? There were accounts of wolves within Domhain before, but I've only ever heard of them in Scáth now."

"I would usually consider it a coincidence but with the Countess' involvement and manipulations, and with her sister being the cause of the curse, I have a hard time thinking of it as chance."

"The Tower is in Saol—the Life Realm. The tree of life. Could it be a symbol to the realm that we aren't aware of?"

He stared at the drawing. "What did you find out about the oath?"

"Just that they swore their lives to Marquette and Roald through life and death."

He leaned back in the chair and crossed his arms. "That seems like a lot of work for such a simple oath."

There was a sudden clanking in the hall and Kellan was on his feet, his magic swirling in one hand, his other hovering at the blade at his hip. Avyanna also stood, a dagger out at the ready, when a guard slid to a halt upon entering. "Your highness..." He gasped for breath, his gaze sliding between the two of them.

"I apologize for interrupting, but there is someone—" His eyes widened. "The king. Your father, he's—"

Kellan didn't give him time to finish that sentence. He ran, brushing past the bewildered guard as he headed down the hall. He heard Avyanna ask where and the guard's answer. He didn't wait. When he reached the double doors of the throne room, he paused. Stared at the handle. Avyanna caught up and came to a halt beside him.

He didn't move. Just stared. Caught his breath. Considered who might be waiting on the other side.

"He's here," she whispered.

"Fifty years, I've been waiting."

She reached for his hand and squeezed it. "So has he."

"I didn't save him. He didn't come back and—" *Save me.* He didn't finish the sentence on the tip of his tongue.

Another squeeze. "I doubt he blames you. And, just like you, I can only assume he has the same guilt. Talk to him. But first, just see him again."

Kellan gave her a peck on the cheek. "Thank you."

"I'll be right here."

"You're not coming with me?" His eyes widened.

She smiled. "Not yet. This part you need to do on your own."

Kellan swallowed. He wished Felicity was here. That she remembered. That they could walk into this room together and be reunited as a family. Soon. It would be soon. Then he pushed the door open, stepped inside and stared.

A male waited at the bottom of the dais and looked upon the thrones that sat there, his back to him. Kellan walked silently. But he'd never been as good as Felicity in that regard and the first scuff of his boot had his father's shoulders shifting back, his spine straightening as his posture went rigid.

He was much thinner than the last time Kellan had seen him. Auburn hair, similar to Felicity's, hung to his shoulders and was now peppered with gray.

Kellan couldn't bring himself to speak, his throat suddenly dry. What was there to say when there was a lifetime of unspoken words?

The king turned and Kellan watched the shift in his body. The way his feet moved slowly. How there was a small tweak in his left knee. The scar from his wrist to elbow. The way his cuffs were folded to his forearms and although they once would have been fitted around thick, muscular biceps, now hung loose.

Then he made it to his father's face. The beard he'd grown. The wrinkles that clung around his eyes and in his brow. Their eye color—besides build, Kellan had his father's eyes. And even with the changes time constructed against them, he recognized him. Saw his father in the tremble of his bottom lip. In the curve of his nose. In the tears that mirrored his own as they streamed down his cheeks.

Kellan didn't know who moved first, but suddenly his arms were around his father, Bastien's arms wrapped around him. Their heads buried in each other's shoulders as they sobbed. And as he inhaled a scent of sunlight on a plain—a scent he'd never thought he'd find again—they held each other tightly. No words spoken. All of them inconsequential now.

King Bastien was home.

His father was home.

Chapter 35

Felicity

That morning she'd woken but didn't move. Instead, she embraced the feel of Alarian's body wrapped around hers. His arm bent under the pillow, cushioning her head. His other hand rested against her stomach, splayed out in a possessiveness she didn't think would excite her. He was curved around her back, his misty forest scent surrounding her. Comforting her. And for a moment, she'd questioned why she had resisted the feelings she knew were growing within her if it meant she could have had more of this.

A small breath of a sigh, and she opened her eyes as he nuzzled into her back. "I could get used to this."

So could she. "Are you sure we—" She squirmed suggestively against him and couldn't help but smile at his deep guttural growl.

"You're not playing fair."

"I didn't know I had to."

He pressed a kiss to her neck, right below her ear. "The sun is rising. We need to get ready to go."

Now it was her turn to protest. "No. I'm going to stay right here."

Alarian chuckled. "I've wanted to hear you say that for a long time."

Movement outside the door, the sound of footsteps reminded them where they were. Felicity sighed. "I guess that's our cue."

***

The cailleach flew stealthily over the waters as the sun curved towards the middle of the sky. After very little deliberation, they chose to head in the direction of the deep lake in the center of the realm. Both she and Alarian thought it the most likely spot to find the heartstone. If they got there first.

Alarian pointed ahead. "I think that looks like it."

From this vantage point, the body of water below changed color drastically towards the center, from a shimmering blue to a deep navy. Her stomach plummeted. So far, she hadn't been able to figure out how they were meant to get the stone. It wasn't as if either of them could hold their breath over a long period of time. And they couldn't spell the entire lake to protect the heartstone. Especially if it wasn't there in the first place.

Alarian nudged Gaoth towards a dry spot on the edge of the lake. There weren't many of those and the great cat hissed when its tail slipped into the water on landing. Grass spots were surrounded by pink and purple flowers, sprouts of tall reeds, and with one step you could fall into water as deep as a knee. Felicity patted Reóta's shoulder, the lynx shifting underneath her in attempt to keep her paws dry.

Felicity dismounted, thankful for the waterproof boots that Molyle had offered them. She stared out over the water, her jaw clenched tight in concentration.

"Well, I have a plan. Do you want to hear it?" Alarian shifted beside her, the squelch of marsh under his feet.

"Am I going to like it?"

"You're to stay here. Watch our things and ensure that no creatures come up from the waters."

She glared. "So far I hate this plan."

"It doesn't get better." He sighed, running a hand through his hair. "It will take shadows, but I think I can create a version of an air bubble within them to help me swim to the depths. Don't know how well it will work, but the chance we have at befriending a helpful siren right now is even less."

Felicity folded her arms over her chest. "And if your air runs out?"

Alarian shrugged. "I'm going to have to swim my ass off either way. Who knows what is down there."

She was a strong swimmer, but she didn't hold any delusions that she would be able to hold her breath long enough. Her magic was of no use. There was little she could do—except...

"Do you still have my second pendant?" She fiddled with the red crystal around her neck.

"Yes?" He looked startled. "Why?"

"I'll place a bit of my own magic within to light the way. Can't have you blind down there." It was strange not to be able to do more, but at least it was something.

Alarian removed the clear pendant from his neck. "I don't like not being by your side. I know I'm not, but it feels like I'm leaving you defenseless."

Her mouth thinned into a line, brow furrowing. "I've been prepared for any of my targets to wield magic. I'm far from defenseless. If anything, you're the one in more danger."

He chuckled. "Point taken."

She concentrated, calling her magic to the surface and spreading it from her chest to her fingertips. The pendant began to glow with the calming white light of stars. "It should stay in there for you. But don't take your time or I'm coming for you within an hour."

She glanced at the touch of the sun's rays at the horizon, marking its location. When she turned to face him, Alarian held a flower out towards her.

"What's this?"

He rubbed the back of his neck. "Uh—I think it's called a rose mallow."

"I didn't mean what type of flower, I meant why are you giving it to me?" Her brow furrowed.

"Well, when someone sees a flower and it makes them think of another, they sometimes give it to that person. So..." He pushed it towards her. "It's for you."

With hesitation, she took it. "Is this part of the courting you spoke about?"

He sighed, shifting the pendant at his neck. It looked strange glowing from his chest. "I guess so. You have a lot to learn about being wooed. No one gave you flowers before?"

She blushed, searching her memory. "No."

"Not even Harrison?" There was a touch of pride in his voice.

"Not even him."

"Good."

She looked from the flower to him. "This better not be your own form of goodbye."

"It's not." He raised his hand in surrender. "I swear. Honestly, just saw the flower and thought of you. It made me smile and I wanted to make you smile."

A blush spread from her neck up to her cheeks. "Well...thank you."

He grinned as he made his way back to Gaoth. For a moment, silence lingered between them like a chasm expanding with the unsaid. That neither were brave enough to voice.

Alarian slid his cloak from his shoulders and laid it over the lynx. He turned his back to her, removing his tunic. The sight of the fox tattoo caused her breath to hitch as it bunched over his muscles while he worked on the laces of his boots. She twirled the stem of the pink flower between her fingers as he removed both them and his stockings until all he stood in were his pants. "All right then." Without facing her, he headed towards the water.

She thought about calling out for him back. Maybe even offering a word of support, but instead she watched him as he disappeared deeper into the water. Something at the back of her mind told her she should be paying attention to her surroundings, but all she could do was take in the view of the male before her as he slipped into the water, one step at a time before disappearing in a mist of shadows.

Felicity wiped her brow, vaguely aware that it was getting cold. A moment ago, she'd been warm. Hot even. She shook off the thought, taking in her surroundings.

A bird chirped. The brush of wind caused the reeds to slide together. The sounds of the misty marsh heightening with the rise of the sun in the distance. Felicity placed the flower in her pack, the head sticking out so as not to be squashed. She ran a finger over the delicate petals and smiled. He really did surprise her.

Then she paced, unable to settle in one spot. The sun was fully visible when the water bubbled—she stilled and stared. A figure broke the surface in the distance, and she recognized the shape of Alarian. His head was down, his hair dripping over his forehead, blocking his expression from view. With each trudging step from the depths, Felicity breathed a sigh of relief. Good, he was all right.

"Did you find it?" she called over the water.

He must not have heard her. The way the water moved around him looked as though it was attempting to drag him back under. She stepped into the lake, small waves lapping around her calves, pushing her towards land. "Alarian? Did you find it?"

When he was just an arm's length from her, she noticed too late—the flicker of scales along his shoulder that glistened in the sun. "Shi—"

She reached for her dagger, but the puca sprung at her and her blade fell into the water. Now, with its golden eyes on her, she could see the discrepancies. Features she should have noted had she not been too caught up with Alarian's wellbeing.

The puca pummeled her into the surf, water engulfing and surrounding her. It held her under, water filling her lungs in place of air, her hands scrambling for purchase to fight the beast off. Then, it was torn off her, and she rolled away and gasped for breath, spitting up water as she hunched over. Alarian was over her, pulling her to her feet. He ran a hand over her hip, a plop sounded at the sheath at her thigh, then he pushed her aside with a growl.

She whirled around to find Alarian and the puca that still looked somewhat like him fight for dominance. His movements were labored, slow, as he was forced to the ground. Felicity rushed forward and tackled the beast, the water only lapping at her feet now. She called upon her magic, letting it slide to her fingertips and burn. The puca hissed under her touch. Alarian dragged himself away from the water.

The beast cowered underneath her, screaming out a sound that forced Felicity to pause. She glanced over the creature. "Leave." She stood, stepping out of the water, her magic pulsing with every heavy breath.

The beast stumbled further from the shore. Limbs transformed into webbed appendages as scales spread over its body before it disappeared into the water.

"Noble of you." The voice was a hiss. And definitely not Alarian's.

Felicity turned slowly, reaching on instinct for her dagger, but there was no need. Her dagger was pressed against Alarian's throat by a male Felicity didn't recognize but had twice Alarian's bulk. It wasn't this stranger that had spoken though.

Felicity's jaw tensed as Fiadh tilted her head in consideration. "That creature will attack again. Why would you free it?" There was curiosity in the woman's gaze.

And then, as if to prove how much of a coward he was, Lord Molyle stepped out from behind the giant brute and sidled closer to Fiadh. She had to bite back the retort on the tip of her tongue. He wasn't the threat right now. Did Fiona know who held his allegiance? It wasn't as surprising as it should have been.

"Trying to understand me?" Felicity wished her breathing would even out. That the bile of salt and water hadn't risen to her throat.

"Pieces are still missing of who you are. I've been puzzling you out for a long time. You were raised an assassin—what made you free a beast that would have easily taken your life and even tried to?" Fiadh's lips pursed.

It was a question Felicity wouldn't answer. Not to her. "You do know that I can take on both of you." She waved to the male behind Alarian.

"You think I wouldn't come prepared?" Fiadh's grin widened when a shadow passed overhead, a dragon—larger than Felicity had ever seen before—landed a few lengths behind her. Wings pulsed air currents that nearly knocked Felicity off her feet. The female beast growled. She had glistening green and gray scales, and fire blazed to life within snake-like eyes.

Fiadh cackled. "We have a pet of our own."

The dragon growled and ground her teeth at the witch's words.

Whatever this was between the beast and witch, it wasn't loyalty. Felicity could see that in the dragon's piercing hate-filled eyes.

"A dragon. Impressive. Don't know if the sniveling male beside you is worth the time though." She glared at Molyle. "You're daughter in on this too?"

He shook his head, then glanced pleadingly at Fiadh. "Marquette promised to make Visce better for us."

Alarian laughed. "My mother used you and lied. She despises anyone from Visce." He hissed when the blade pierced deeper into his skin. Felicity tried to hide her desire to tear them all apart. Control. *Don't let the anger use you...*

"She made promises for our realm that your family hasn't made," Molyle spat from the safety beside the witch and brute. "That we couldn't guarantee you'd ever make."

Felicity had to fight back her reaction to seeing blood at Alarian's throat. He must be exhausted from the swim. From using his magic. Hopefully he had enough reserves within him. She glared at Molyle. "You put your trust in the wrong person. Has she kept those promises? Or is she still making you pay your dues?"

Fiadh laughed. "His daughter was invited to all of the important events and is friends with the princess of the realm." A smirk holding a deadly promise slid across the witch's face. "How do you think that came to be?"

The dragon growled, baring her teeth. Felicity could almost read the beast's mind. She was growing impatient.

The dragon's breath heated the air around them, smoke snorting from her nostrils. "How did you acquire a dragon within your employ? They would never willingly be kept on your leash." As she worked out this problem, she had to keep the witch talking.

"If you know what they want, then you can make anyone work for you. Just like now. Now, give me the stone or he's dead."

Felicity inhaled, glancing from Alarian to Fiadh. "I don't have it."

Her smile lengthened. It was all wicked teeth and sharp lines. "You didn't have the same viewpoint of your little fight as we did. Check your sheath."

Felicity looked down at the place her dagger had once been. Fuck—a glimmering heartstone in shades of blues and the size of her palm glistened in the depths of the leather sheath.

There must be something they can do. Somehow, she could get them both out of this. Her stomach dropped and teeth chattered from the cold water juxtaposed with the warm air from the dragon-heated air. With a glance around, she took stock of what was at her disposal. What she could use to stop this. Keep the stone. Save Alarian.

"You think it's smart to remove the heartstones from the realms? The entire continent will weaken."

Felicity had to keep the witch talking. Shadows attempted to draw towards Alarian but sputtered back with each of his ragged breaths. He needed as much time as she could give him.

Fiadh snarled. "Morals and empathy left long ago. Marquette will be a vital ruler. You won't get in our way, and neither will her wretched son. Hand over the stone—and you both can continue on your way."

She tried not to look at Alarian now. Regretted waiting so long to allow herself to fall. Nails dug into her palms. She would ensure they had their chance. The shadows began to pool at his feet, the only glimpse Felicity allowed in his direction.

"Why not just kill us?' It was a foolish question to ask, but Felicity had to know how serious the witch was. Her heart beat harder against her chest as Alarian shifted, but trying to loosen the male's hold only resulted in the dagger pressed deeper into his throat.

"Because Marquette wants you to suffer. To watch as she tears apart your world. You killed her love. She wants to see you lose it all and be unable to stop it. But him..." She flung her hand at Alarian. "He's a traitor to his blood."

"You're putting a lot of stock in the fact that I would damn the realms for him." And in saying the words out loud, she came to the realization that she would. Fuck it all, she couldn't lose him. She thought about the glove in her bag strapped to Reóta's back. The gift from Lian and Dimitri that shot daggers. The glove wouldn't have been useful against the Fomorians, and she hadn't considered putting it on now. She couldn't reach it now. A thousand alternatives came to mind, but with a dragon and a dagger at Alarian's throat, only two would work. If she could get close enough, could she manipulate her magic? But that dragon—she would be burned to cinders, Alarian too, and the heartstone would be lost. She doubted she'd be able to retrieve one of her hidden daggers without them reacting.

Felicity removed the stone from the sheath. Alarian growled, "Don't do it. Go."

The cailleach moved, as if on instinct, closer to her. Two steps and she could be on Reóta with the stone. The cailleach were fast, agile—they would be able to outrun the giant dragon, even if it would be close—the stone would be safe in the end.

Alarian nodded. Giving her permission. He was willing to meet his end.

But she was selfish.

She glanced at the stone again before looking up to meet his eyes. The dagger deepened into his skin, a trickle of gray blood...but Alarian remained proud, his shoulders drawn back. Their eyes met. She wished now that he could understand everything she was attempting to convey. Would he understand?

The corner of his mouth rose. That smile. *Her* smile. Somehow, he knew.

With a deep swallow, Felicity held out the stone. "Let him go, then I'll drop the stone."

"No, Felicity," Alarian ground out. "Don't do this."

She didn't spare him a glance. "Do we have a deal?"

"Toss me the stone at the count of three, and we'll let him go at the same time. You count."

"One." Felicity held the stone out on her palm. "Two."

Then she tossed it.

It plopped in the water and Alarian erupted the nearby shadows. They swirled around him, one small opening, and she smiled as she sent a slice of her starlight straight through to the pendant held out in front of him. He understood. The disgruntled and confused brute hadn't moved quick enough, and Alarian pivoted the pendant so that her light blinded the male. The dragon roared, discombobulated.

"Don't hurt the dragon," Felicity yelled.

Fiadh screamed, searching for the stone within the water. Alarian shifted the last of his magic towards the witch, the shadows rushing towards her in sharp, jagged lines she'd never seen from him before.

Felicity was already there. She swung out her leg, taking Fiadh down. Water splashed, Felicity grappling for the stone now within the witch's hand. Flames erupted and Felicity dove before the dragon's fire engulfed her, the water protecting her from being burned.

Alarian? Had he been in the dragon's trajectory. He couldn't be—

A look above told her that the flames were gone. She pushed to the surface, gulping air, and whirled around. Left. Right. Alarian was fumbling to the water's surface. She let out a breath.

Now Fiadh.

She turned where she had left the woman. But the witch was gone—with the heartstone. A cackling laugh was all that was left as the dragon flew away with Fiadh dangling from her claws.

"Shit. No." Felicity and Alarian ran towards the lynxes and mounted, leaving the blinded and burnt guard. Molyle cowered, shuddering in the water with his hands clutching his head.

They rose into the air, flying higher as Felicity urged Reóta on. But it wasn't enough. The dragon was faster.

"I wasn't worth it," Alarian shouted from his cailleach, the wind almost stealing his words.

"You are and don't ever say otherwise again," she bit the words out, frustrated with him. With herself.

That made him snap his mouth shut.

She pulled Reóta's reigns to slow down then veered towards the ground, landing right next to the Water Fae still curled in on himself amidst the charred earth. Felicity grabbed him by his tunic and pulled him to his feet. He whimpered as she glared. "How dare you smile at me, treat me as a welcomed guest, then plan with my enemy—with the continent's enemy—behind our backs."

Alarian landed behind her, the rustling of Gaoth's wings fluttering her hair. "I should kill you."

"No," Molyle cried. "My daughter. I'm all she has left."

Felicity snorted. "She's the reason I'll let you live. Because she has been a friend to me. But trust me, you're not all she has left. You're stripped of your title." She pushed him away from her. "Your daughter is now the lady of the house. You're coming with us."

"What?" he squealed.

"You have to stand trial for your crimes against the crown. You don't know what your betrayal caused."

Alarian dismounted, and without a word, tied Molyle's hands. It was obvious he wasn't a fan of flying because as soon as he was forced to mount Gaoth—who looked rather put out by the addition of the sniveling rider—the male burst into tears.

They flew towards Aer, Felicity's shoulders slumped in desolation. They had the stone. It had been in the palm of her hand. And yet, because she was weak—because *he* made her weak—she had cost the continent. Although she wouldn't change anything, she wondered then if she was becoming the villain of this story.

Chapter 36

Alarian

They didn't talk. Alarian led them towards Aer and his friends' home. They decided to stop at Lian and Dimitri's since the cailleach couldn't fly long distances with Molyle's added weight. Alarian was on edge, and with Molyle threatening to jump, he could feel the tension in Gaoth beneath him. Exhaustion bit at his bones. At his muscles. He was tempted to let them male fall like the coward he was.

Because of Molyle and the uncertainty of others like him and Heavin, they chose not to stop at the Fios again. If there was a chance they were followed, it would be too dangerous.

Which only had the scenario from that morning running through his mind. He couldn't thank Felicity for saving him. But he couldn't blame her. If their roles had been reversed, he'd have done the same thing. The conundrum only gave him a headache and made it even harder to concentrate on the task at hand. Thankfully, Gaoth only needed to be pointed in the proper direction.

Thanks to the flying beasts, it took less time to get to their destination than it would on horseback, cutting the trip from a day to hours. The stone manor came into view, familiar and welcoming. The windows were aglow in the darkness by firelight within. His friends wouldn't be expecting them, but he knew without a doubt that they would be welcomed with open arms. Especially since he was bringing Felicity along. On his last visit, they had requested her with comments that they would rather see the spy over him any day. It was meant in jest, but Alarian knew there was some truth to their words. He'd usually brought drama and trouble to their door.

As he was now.

It still surprised him that Felicity had chosen him. He didn't think she regretted it—or maybe she did. It was hard to decipher if it was anger or regret that caused the heaviness in his mind. The silence, though, was telling. He tried to close that connection between them. To give her the space and privacy she deserved, but her guilt pricked like thorns against his skull.

As they came in for landing, a flicker of resolve flashed across her features, and he turned away, realizing he'd been staring for far too long. Would this change her admittance from the night before? The words she finally said. That she chose him.

He should have known it fleeting. That there was a chance she could change her mind.

A figure broke from the house, illuminated for a moment by the light from within before the door smacked closed behind them. "Alarian?" Lian trotted over. "Is that you?"

Alarian dismounted, dragging Molyle with him and Felicity a step behind. He tightened his grip on his prisoner. "Hello Lian. Hope you don't mind some visitors."

Lian wrapped him tightly in a hug. The male had always been an act first, ask for permission later type of male. That's why he wasn't surprised when Lian enveloped Felicity in a hug next, the female rigid in his arms. Alarian couldn't help but chuckle as Lian apologized for his forwardness.

"Who is this?" He glared at the bindings on Molyle's wrists. "And do you need proper manacles?"

Molyle must have realized escape was moot because he didn't make an attempt to fight them. Even now, he shuddered at the mention of the manacles.

"Yes." He wasn't stupid. The male had tricked them with his easy-going manner once. He couldn't let it happen again. To warn the male to behave, Alarian's shadows twisted around the male's neck without pressure.

"McNaught?"

A female with a short bob of blond hair appeared. "Sir?"

"Manacles for our unwelcome guest. Then could you kindly get him settled within the cell. A meal maybe. Don't want to be uncivil after all."

McNaught grabbed Molyle's arm, removed a crimson pouch from her pocket and snapped a set of iron manacles on his wrists. Felicity nodded at the female, checking the manacles, before pushing the male to the guard. "Thank you for making him comfortable." Even though she said it with a sneer, there was no emotion in her expression.

"Come in. We can get you settled inside. It's been chilly these past few days, and I have no clue how you've handled evening flights." Lian continued, "And Dimitri will be home a little later. He was out checking in with the town magistrates on some security measures."

Felicity balked. "What security issues?"

Lian smiled and waved off any concern. "A little squabble among those who choose the outskirts and the others who prefer living in town. I don't know if you're familiar with the dynamics of our realm, but those who live on the plains sometimes feel as though they should have a say on what happens within the towns. We've always kept it separate before, but a few came in and threw eggs at the town hall. If the perpetrators return, they'll hopefully be caught and forced to clean up the mess."

Alarian bit his lip, trying not to consider the stench built up from a day of eggs cracked against stone. "Sounds messy."

"It is." Lian led them into a dining room. "Would you like something to eat?"

"We can wait for Dimitri." Felicity looked about the space as they entered. Probably noting the changes that had transformed the manor from a place of celebration to the warm home it was now. He'd wanted to show her this side of his friends for some time. For them to meet her under different circumstances and have a chance to get to know each other.

Lian paused. "He'd honestly appreciate that. I forgot, congratulations on the reinstatement of your proper title. I knew there was something special about you when we first met."

Felicity shouldered her bag and Lian gasped. "I apologize. Where are my manners." He flicked a finger and air wrapped around their packs, removing them from their shoulders. "Now, should I prepare one room or two?"

He noted the rise in his friend's brow. The information he wanted with that one question. Alarian bit the inside of his mouth to stop from answering, upset that he also wanted that same information. But if she needed space—

"Two please." Felicity looked at anywhere but him as she responded.

His shoulders drooped. Lian met Alarian's gaze, his brow rose in a puzzled expression. Alarian shook his head. Not even he knew how to interpret that answer.

Lian led them down the hall and pointed to two separate doors. "Why don't you make yourselves comfortable. Baths are available in each room, as are showers. I assume after your travels they will be appreciated. I'll let you know when Dimitri returns, and we can have dinner."

"Thank you." Felicity gave a small smile before she rushed into her room, closing the door behind her.

He glanced at his friend. "Thanks for everything." The bath, maybe even a quick nap—he needed them both. The sensation of the blade at his neck was still present.

"Is she all right?" Lian's voice was a mere whisper.

"She will be. It's been a testing past few hours, let alone days."

"And you?" He pointed to Alarian's neck. "There is some dried blood there."

"Like I said. It's been testing."

Lian nodded, a softness at the angles of his face. "Get some rest. I expect we will eat within the hour."

Alarian gave his friend's shoulder a squeeze and entered the room given to him. He'd stayed here before, but he had to bite back the chuckle at the door that connected his room to Felicity's. He vowed that he wouldn't open it unless she knocked.

He walked into the attached bathing chamber and breathed a sigh of relief at the pipes and plumbing. It had been some time since he'd had a proper soak.

Before he filled the tub, he took a quick shower to get off the grime of the lake, blood, and of sweat and dirt from their flight. His body shuttered when the warm water hit his skin. He rested his head against the stone wall, taking slow, deep breaths. The depths of the lake had been dark except for the light of Felicity's magic. Creatures left unseen had swiped at his legs, attempted to grab at him. When he had seen the stone, he had thought the worst was over. They'd finally had a win.

A ragged exhale, he pinched his eyes closed.

"Are you angry with me?"

His eyes flashed open, his body stilling. It was a slow movement, but he turned his head to face Felicity who stood in the doorway, her gaze pinned on the floor.

Alarian became extremely aware that he wore nothing at all. But the look that she tried to hide made him want to rush across the space and hold her.

But she'd asked him a question. "Why would I be?"

"I gave up the heartstone." She swallowed, still not willing to look at him.

"Yes, you did."

"I doomed the realms. Gave up another chance against your mother. For—" She bit her bottom lip.

"For me," he finished for her.

She nodded, wrapping her arms tighter around herself.

"What are you thinking right now, Starlight?" His words were soft, but his attempt to coax her to look up was unsuccessful.

"That I failed everyone. That, in the end, I'm just as bad as Marquette. I'm not fit to lead, because I can't make the hard calls after all."

He watched her jaw flex, and he could sense every one of her emotions—regret, disappointment, fear—brush over him even though he tried so hard not to.

"It's impossible for me to be angry when I'm still alive. But more so, I think that this just shows how much you've accepted the emotions you've tried so hard to hide."

"I'm weak." A whisper.

"Never. You are never weak. Your decision doesn't define you and it certainly doesn't make you a villain. I would have done the same for you. As would many in your position. Do you regret it?" Water pelted against his sensitive skin as he stared at her, scared and hopeful for her response. He wouldn't hold it against her either way.

She shook her head. "I wouldn't change it. I'd do the same exact thing." At her words, the prickle of her regret shifted to fear.

He turned off the water and reached for a towel. When he wrapped it around his waist, she finally looked up at him.

Curses, he wanted to take all her pain away. "What's done is done. I don't hold it against you at all. This isn't the end. No matter what, we haven't lost. We can still stop her. Visce won't feel the loss of the stone for some time, and we'll return it before they do. We just need a plan to get it back."

Her knuckles were turning white from the grip she had around herself. Alarian wished there was more he could do. More he could say. Anything to take her fear away. He wouldn't push her. Wouldn't force what she was trying so hard to piece together. But he'd be there when she was ready.

Felicity breathed in then let out a lung full of air. "Thank you, Rian."

Without another word, she turned on her heel and walked away, leaving him reeling.

Chapter 37

Alarian

Dinner was settled before them, wine in heftily poured goblets, and the comforting scent of roasted duck and greens wafted from filled serving dishes. Alarian shifted back in his chair, his meal half-finished and his body warm from the alcohol.

"So where have your travels taken you?" Dimitri sipped his own drink, a curious glance in both their directions. Up until then, they had detoured away from this subject, but it couldn't have lasted forever.

"Through almost all the realms." Felicity took out a roll from a basket. "I'd only visited border towns in most of Dorcha and Domhain prior, so it felt important for me to see the others."

"And Scath?" Lian asked, peering at Alarain from the corner of his eye.

He shook his head. "No. There isn't a reason to go there."

"Oh?" Dimitri rose one brow. "Is that so?"

"I'll probably have to go alone." Felicity took a sip. "Don't think Alarian wants to visit his childhood home."

"Yes, I suppose that's it." Lian nodded along, and Alarian cursed him under his breath. Not even they knew the truth. The scar hidden by the tattoo warmed as if reminding him of the long-ago oath. A secret not even he could speak unless he sought death. Thankfully, Felicity still seemed drawn into her own thoughts to realize his friends were baiting him. They were always curious as to why he hadn't returned to his home since his parents' summons.

Alarian cleared his throat. "How have you two been?"

Lian's grin widened, and he nodded at Dimitri. "We've got some exciting news. Sloan or you" —he winked at Alarian— "must have put in a good word for us. We've been asked to be on the Aer council and Dimitri will be the new advisor."

"Congratulations, Dimitri—well both of you." Felicity grinned. "I know Kellan has only heard good things about you, so I'm not surprised."

"I am." Alarian chuckled. "I thought for certain it would be Lord Chartow."

Dimitri smirked. "Honestly, so did I. Seems Lord Chartow will start as an advisor, but as he's given up so much to the cause and lost his wife, he will step down soon. I think Lady Chartow made him promise to take care of himself should anything happen to her."

"Did he meet with rebels at the brothel as well?" Felicity asked Alarian. "I remember there being talk about his presence there. If he's so devoted to his wife, that seems strange."

"Yes." Alarian nodded. "He met Sloan there, but he was faithful to his wife. His cover wasn't as easy to keep since he had been seen coming and going once or twice, so he had to drop the faithful husband persona within court. Lady Chartow was our main contact within the palace, but it was near impossible to correspond with her regularly. When we lost her..."

"I tried." Felicity glanced down at her place. "I tried to have Marquette look away from her. I never gave her name."

"I know." Alarian nodded. "And I'm appreciative of that. As are so many. Sloan made sure Lord Chartow knew that too. He was quite angry and heartbroken. We didn't know what he would do at first, but it seems that he decided it was easier to blame me."

Lian cleared his throat. "That's why he came to stay with us after the curse was broken. He needed time to separate his feelings."

"Then I think I know who may have recommended you to Prince Kellan, because it wasn't me." Alarian sat back in his chair, wine goblet in hand.

Dimitri snorted. "Chartow is a valid guess. Lian just has the romantic idea of you having pull. Seeing as you're here though, taking the princess on a tour of the realms, I assume you have some of our prince's confidence. Otherwise, I doubt he'd trust you anywhere near her."

Alarian couldn't help but chuckle. "Something like that."

Felicity shifted in her chair. "I needed to take care of a few personal things and seeing as Alarian was going to be traveling to check on the rebel alliances and how the people were fairing, it only made sense for me to tag along."

"That it does." Lian grinned. "Although I can't imagine you were just tagging along with the trouble he gets into. I *can* imagine traveling the realms is an adventure in itself. We were glad when we did it, weren't we, Cridhe?"

Alarian stiffened, Dimitri swallowing deep and glancing his way. Unfortunately, Felicity didn't miss the nickname. "Cridhe. Does that mean heart?"

Lian's grin widened, opening his mouth, ready to explain—Alarian's gut plummeted as he attempted to think of any way to interrupt. Unfortunately, Dimitri added to the conversation. "Oh, you're familiar with the bond?"

Felicity shook her head. "Not really. My brother told me a little about it. Not much, though. Is that a formal name for it?"

Alarian's heart beat faster against his chest. Would she mention if she had felt it too? He had his doubts. If so, if she sensed something between them, he needed her to know that it was a choice he'd never force her to make. It scared him. Terrified him. He knew he was only making things worse for himself by keeping his mouth shut, but any thought of discussing it with her was always interrupted.

Dimitri nodded along to Lian. "Exactly. It is a bond that can be rejected or accepted by either side."

"How does it start?" Felicity was purposely not looking at him. Alarian could tell.

"It's given by the magic of the continent. As for why some are chosen and others are not, we don't know."

Alarian needed to defuse this quickly. "Do either of you have a recommendation of somewhere we could visit that is close to the center of the realm?"

Felicity tilted her head, her brow furrowed and attention on him. He purposely looked away.

"Center of the realm?" Dimitri and Lian glanced at each other.

This was the one realm that neither Felicity nor Alarian could agree on where the heartstone could be found. It was unlikely to be floating in midair. More so, it couldn't be deep within the earth since the plains had no caverns or ravines. Nor up high in a mountain as the land was flat and devoid of anything beyond grassy knolls and rolling hills. The only other location they considered was along the craggy cliffs of the coast—but as they had flown alongside them for hours before turning inland to come here, there didn't seem to be a place that called for them to search.

"What is in the center of the realm you're searching for?" There was another question left unanswered in his words.

Alarian straightened, placing his untouched goblet on the table. This was taking a chance—but his friends were trustworthy. He hoped Felicity understood as he hadn't discussed this with her first. "Aer's heartstone."

Both males froze. The only sound was the tick of the clock in the hall. The mechanical gears were counting down the seconds as no one moved or even seemed to breathe.

Alarian held Dimitri's stare. Finally, the male let out a long breath. "I see. And what is it you want the heartstone for?"

"It needs to be protected." Alarian shifted in his seat.

Felicity folded her hands. "We plan to cast a spell around it to conceal it from Marquette and her followers."

"How does Marquette know about the stones?" Lian glanced between Dimitri and Alarian, then to Felicity.

"You know of them?" Felicity's fingers went to the pendant at her neck. "We haven't spoken of them with many, but we've learned some of the realms don't believe they even exist."

"Oh, we know they exist." Dimitri's jaw clenched. "Forget how Marquette knows, why does she want them?"

"To open the veil." Alarian didn't feel the need to keep this secret from his friends. The fact they knew about the stone was telling.

"Fuck." Dimitri ran a hand over his face. "They can do that?"

"It seems so." Alarian sighed. "We are still uncertain of the details but our best guess is they want to open the veil to the human world. It could be the reason for Fiadh's involvement." He and Felicity had considered different alternatives, but the enigmatic witch was one of the biggest question marks in the equation.

Felicity leaned forward, her brow furrowed. "Do you know where the heartstone is?"

Dimitri slumped in his chair. "Yes. It can't leave the realm though. Not allowed."

"We don't want to remove it from the realm. We know the repercussion of such a decision." Alarian sighed. "She has four stones. Éardrom, Tine, or so we assume, Dorcha, and Visce's. There is a dragon involved too—somehow."

"If she gets Aer's stone, then we're damned," Felicity added.

Lian nodded at his husband. "I think you can trust them."

"I know I can. I just never wanted it to come to this." Dimitri pushed himself up and left the room without another word.

Silence—for the second time that evening—spread through the room.

It wasn't until Dimitri returned, a bag in hand, that Alarian gasped. "How?"

Dimitri held it out towards Alarian. "I'm its guardian. Only a select few are aware of the stone. Lian, myself, and Chartow. If anything happened to me, then Lian or Chartow would be the first to act as its protector. That's why we do our best to never have all three of us be in the same place together for long—though it is unlikely anyone would notice."

"This is why I chose to decline your brother's offer to be on the council." Lian's shoulders drew back. "One of us needed to remain away from the others. For the safety of the stone. Chartow staying here for as long as he had was testing the guardianship and forced one of us to travel for portions of his stay."

"As its guardian, the role is passed down. My father was never given it—selfish male that he was—it had been my uncle's responsibility. My parents were never aware of it and no one else in the realm is either." Dimitri's jaw clenched.

Lian finished for him. "We have spells already protecting it, but if Marquette is searching, then we should take extra precautions."

Felicity nodded. "Then let's add our spell to the mix. Keep it someplace safe and hard to find."

"But keep it close. Just not on your person. I wouldn't want to lose you, friend." Alarian shuddered at the thought and shared a look with Felicity. A reminder of how much he didn't blame her for Visce. She looked away quickly.

"For the safety of the continent, I can be a sacrifice."

Felicity's shoulders drooped. Alarian wanted to tell his friend to shut it. Felicity didn't damn them all, as much as she feared otherwise.

"What do you need us to do?"

Alarian stood. "Let me get the necessities from my pack. I'll meet you in the sitting room." A sense of urgency and hope rushed through him. Finally, they were a step ahead. This was a win they needed.

After he collected the wording of the spell, the powder, and the pouch in which the Countess claimed would conceal the stone, he found them all waiting. Felicity was staring at the clock above the mantel of a large fireplace, transfixed by the movement of the hands.

Alarian sat down and laid out the bag and powder on the table. "The bag is enchanted with a strong protection spell." He repeated the words the Countess had taught them a few times to himself. "It should cloak the stone. If the wards are in place on your bag, then put it in here. We can do the spell to hide it further from view and you can put it in a place that you feel comfortable with."

Dimitri nodded.

"I want to see it." Felicity had shifted closer. "If you don't mind."

Dimitri smiled, pulling on the drawstrings of his bag. He removed what looked to be a regular piece of metal. Strange...

Then with a few uttered words, a glamour slowly slid from the piece, revealing a near clear stone with white wisps that curled within.

Felicity grinned as Dimitri placed it in her hand. "It's lighter than I expected. Almost like—"

"Air." Lian chuckled. "It *is* the stone that powers our realm."

"It seems impossible that something so small can hold so much power." Felicity turned it over between her fingers, glancing at every portion.

"It does, doesn't it? But that's what makes it even more special. It's a conduit. The heart of the power, but each and every one of those who contain air magic feed it. Every creature within Aer soothes it. It's how it stays strong, because in a way, it connects us all." Lian squeezed his husband's shoulder.

"Thank you for sharing it with me." She placed the stone back in Dimitri's waiting palm.

"Of course." Dimitri spoke the words to put the wards back in place before handing the satchel to Alarian.

He did the same, placing the stone and bag into the one provided by the Countess and uttered the incantation.

Instead of a notebook, this time the cloaking bag turned into a quill. Lian snorted as Alarian handed the quill to Dimitri who breathed a sigh of relief. "So much responsibility."

They tried to make small talk after that, but the heaviness of what they had discussed took all words from the room.

Felicity stood first. "I think I'd like to read for a little bit before bed. Do you have a library I could peruse?"

"Of course." Lian stood. "Let me show you the way."

Alarian got to his own feet after they left, stretching. "I'm going to try to get some rest."

"A good plan after all you've must have been through. If the heartstones are the *only* true reasons for your expedition, I can imagine the trouble that ensued."

"What?" Alarian lifted a brow at the warning note in his friend's tone.

Dimitri shook his head. "You better tell her soon. She's smart. And once she knows what that bond is—you could be dooming yourself before you even have a chance."

"How do—" He cut off his words and kept an unreadable expression.

Dimitri's chuckle bloomed into laughter, the sound reverberating in Alarian's skull.

"Then you're an ass—it's obvious Alarian. There's a draw that's evident between the two of you." Dimitri gripped his shoulder. "In addition, you changed the conversation to the stone over the bond...you had a reason to divert the topic."

Alarian's mouth drew into a thin line. "I'm figuring it out."

"It might hurt—but I think you've waited long enough. Tell her the truth. She will come around before you know it."

"Maybe I don't deserve her after all we've been through."

Dimitri shook his head. "Then you're fooling yourself. You're worthy of her and she of you. Even if I do like her a touch more."

Before Alarian could comment further, Dimitri patted his shoulder and walked out of the room. Alarian sat down again, staring at the fire in the hearth. Suddenly his mind was reeling, and the thought of bed was too much. There was something that told him he needed to wait. On telling her about the bond. And going to sleep.

***

Alarian didn't know how long he sat there. How long he stared at the fire as it lowered and blazed to life with a gust of air.

He jumped in his chair when Felicity entered. Her expression unreadable, her boots tapping against stone. "Training?"

Was that anger he tasted on the tip of his tongue. Tart. Sharp.

Alarian tilted his head, observing her. She already wore her training leathers. "Sure."

He got to his feet, and Felicity didn't wait for him but turned on her heel and started towards the foyer. It wasn't until they were outside that she slowed. "Do they have a training ring?"

"No. We'll have to go into the field. We haven't trained outdoors without light in a while. We should." Alarian tried to give her a smile, but she didn't even glance his way.

Felicity led them to the back side of the house where no structures were in the way. She stopped. "Magic?"

He considered. "You choose."

"None." She began pacing like a caged animal.

He trailed her movements, noted her tight fists. She needed to work off some aggression. He settled into a ready stance.

Felicity moved at a speed he hadn't expected. The first punch—well slap really—landed on his cheek. He stumbled a few steps as she attacked again, a kick that he barely dodged, her pace didn't allow time for him to counterattack. He was on the defensive and failing to gain the upper hand.

A whack to his back from her knee when he attempted a dodge had him falling forward. There was more than a need to let off steam—there was anger. *Oh no...*

"Can you sense my emotions?"

He stilled. "What?" His mind reeled. The library. He should have known—guessed. Now that he knew what he was fighting against, he changed his stance.

He didn't dodge the next punch to his stomach, keeling over at the impact. When she sent an elbow to his back, he fell to his knees. She pushed him back, sending him flat to the ground. "Fight back," she ordered.

This was familiar. The anger she encapsulated. The frustration evident in her expression. "No. I deserve this."

She paused above him. The reeds of grass waved in a breeze around his body. "How long, Alarian?"

He rubbed at his jaw. "Since the brothel." Alarian knew what she was asking. What she put together.

"That's why you stopped our kiss?"

A small nod was all he could muster.

"You created a bond with me, and didn't say a fucking word about it?" She threw the accusations at him. "That's bullshit—how could you not tell me?"

"I'm impressed you found a book. There aren't many on the subject and most books about the bond don't have all the information necessary."

She crossed her arms. Glared. "I didn't. At least not one that answered all my questions."

"What did you want me to say?" He was glaring now. He knew it but couldn't stop. "First of all, I didn't choose when to create the bond. Magic did. It hasn't clicked into place and offered itself either. I only learned that's what it was when I spoke with Thomas." He sat up and crossed his forearms over his knees. "You weren't ready and it hurt, Felicity. But I dealt with it."

Her knuckles were going white with how tight her fists were at her side. Why, even as she stood over him angry as a viper, was he still thinking how absolutely gorgeous she looked? "When was the right time? Should I have told you when you hated me for being related to my parents and you thought me the enemy? Or when you asked to be my friend—the first time you actually accepted that we could be allies? Maybe it should have been when you told me I was only worth one night to you. When you risked your own life to save mine? Or how about when you were meeting with your ex-lover to reminisce over old times?"

He hadn't been aware of how much he'd held back in the past few weeks—let alone months. "Besides, it hasn't solidified. It's not being forced upon you. You have a choice. I have already accepted mine."

She shook her head. "We have a continent to protect—"

"Exactly." He got to his feet, Felicity stepping back. "You just accepted who you are. I couldn't even consider adding to your confusion. You just accepted me. I don't deserve you and I'm sorry, I didn't plan for it to happen like this.

There is no obligation on your part. Nothing can happen unless you choose it. I have accepted my fate."

"So you regret it?" she hissed.

"Never." Alarian shook his head. "I could never regret it. No matter what. Even knowing that you may never feel the same, it won't change."

"Were you ever going to tell me?" Her shoulders slumped slightly.

He wanted to say yes, but was he? He knew he should have. "It would have been the right thing to do."

"That didn't answer my question."

Alarian's jaw clenched. "Probably. But I didn't want you to run away from me. Part of me hoped that the bond would ask you."

"How does it work?"

He explained everything he knew. The conversation with Thomas, what he understood, and even how he'd been trying to allow her the privacy she deserved. "How did you figure it out?"

"You asked me to see you," she grumbled.

He swallowed. "I did."

"I was paying attention. Some other comments you said." She shook her head then turned away, her back to him. "Then during the conversation with your friends, I started to wonder."

She sighed, her shoulders slumped. "There can't be anymore secrets between us if this is meant to work."

He considered the letter in his pack. The one from the Countess. The contents in that envelope. He wasn't allowed to open it until the night prior to their return to the castle. He regretted making that promise to the witch, but she swore it was for a good reason. Then there was the scar hidden by a tattoo. The secret that if he broke would mean his death. How could he make promises he couldn't keep? "Felicity—I told you there are things I can't tell you. I can't promise there aren't more secrets between us. If I could, I'd tell them all to you, but I can't."

"You did tell me that. That doesn't make this any easier." She stared at her feet. "And I would have run. You're right. I can admit it, but we can't keep things from each other."

She didn't move for some time, then peered up at him. "I understand I haven't given you much reason to trust my feelings—it has only been a few days since I've even been..." She trailed off, sighed.

Don't do it. He wanted to reach for her. To make promises he didn't know if he could keep, mixed with others he undoubtedly could. Would she turn away from him now? His own frustration mixed with the fear of losing her before he had a chance to love her.

"I can sense your emotions. That's it." He rushed ahead when she started to pale. "And I've been working on blocking them out. I've never used them against you, and I've wanted to figure out a way to tell you every damn day. The only one who had enough to share with me was Thomas and although he made assumptions, I never said it was you."

"You could sense my emotions since the brothel and knew why since the Fios?" She shook her head. "I need a little time. You kept this from me—held onto it when I asked questions. Sensed my feelings, understood them—but didn't consider how that information, in anyone else's hands when I was attempting so hard to comprehend them myself, might hurt."

He tried so hard to block her anger, but it was like a ship against a storm. The heartache. Not love—although he didn't know if she'd ever considered such a word to describe their relationship. "I never expected a thing from you."

A wave of disappointment washed from her.

"That's one of the reasons I never said anything. It wasn't to hurt you. It's because I didn't have any expectations."

She sighed, her eyes closed before she turned away again. "Understood. I just need some time." Then without looking back, she walked back towards the house.

Alarian remained outside, taking in a deep breath from time to time to try to clear the ache in his lungs. It didn't work.

Finally, he trudged back towards the manor. Once back in his room, he timidly pulled the envelope from his bag and held it in his hands. Tomorrow they would return to Éardrom. Their journey would end.

He promised he wouldn't tell Felicity about it. He'd been selfish that night in Visce. Should have stopped what had happened between him and her until he was certain what was in the envelope. But he wanted to show her. How much he cared...loved her. Even if it was in the smallest way possible.

And he'd had a deal with the Countess...

Not to open the envelope until the night before they returned. She said their lives depended on it. He listened. She'd asked him to join into a blood oath, but he was done with those. Up to that point on a night on a dark road, he had vowed never to take another blood oath again. He'd hesitated when Felicity offered it. But for her he would always comply.

He snapped the seal of the wolf head surrounded by two snakes in knots. When he turned over the packet, the contents falling into his hand only caused him to gulp back bile. Within his hands were two vials and on further inspection, one had his and the other had Felicity's name on it. A letter fluttered out, floating down like a feather until it landed on the bed.

He knew what this was before he even picked up the letter. Had hoped that he'd been wrong back then, but now with the information etched on the vials, he knew there was no longer doubt.

And he whispered a goodbye, tears welling in his eyes, as he unfolded the letter to read. A truth within the words—and the past within a vial.

This was it. His damnation.

Chapter 38

Felicity

The following morning, they rode the cailleach over the plains of Aer and into a hazy Éardrom in silence. Felicity glanced over her shoulder at Alarian. He'd been more withdrawn than usual—fake attempts at a smile, unwilling to look at her. She partially wanted to forgive him for withholding the bond from her but feared what precedent that would set. He admitted there were other pieces of himself, and he wasn't able to tell her what they were. Was trust enough? Her chest ached and home was looming on the horizon, the silhouettes of Koselig's buildings coming into view.

Aboard the flying cats, they were able to bypass another night at the inn in Cnoc and head straight to the palace. Part of her wanted to dawdle. Detour to that inn and discuss where *they* stood before they returned to her family. To ensure what they had was worth fighting for. It was bad enough that she didn't have her memories, and her father may be waiting—or would be arriving soon according to the last letter they had received from Kellan.

"We should make it before nightfall," Alarian called over the breeze. "And hopefully the storm."

Gray clouds thickened above. They flew below them, occasionally having to fight gusts of wind. Her clothing may have protected her from the bellowing air, but it wouldn't do much against the impending rain.

"Those clouds ahead look angry." Felicity nodded towards the dark gray that hung around the palace. As if warning her to turn around. Yes, they should have stayed in Cnoc for the night.

"We'll make it."

The grit in his voice had Felicity leaning over Reóta and coaxing the cailleach faster. The cats may deal with wind, snow, and harsh weather, but they didn't appreciate the rain.

The downpour began as soon as they landed in the stable yard. Assistants rushed forward to help as they dismounted, urging the lynxes toward the cover of the barn. "I'm sorry, Your Highness, we didn't know you were meant to arrive or we'd have prepared."

"Not a problem." Felicity followed them into the dry stable. "We didn't warn you."

The two of them assisted in drying off the cailleach and removing their tack. The staff watched the lynxes warily and although the stalls were large enough, they weren't prepared for the cats.

"We'll have the kitchen send over some food." Alarian patted Gaoth on the neck. "The horses should return within the next few days as well."

"And uh—what about these two? Are they to return home?" The youngest stablehand stared at the cailleach with wide, frightened eyes.

Alarian peered at Felicity. "No, they are meant to stay with us." He swallowed, gaze diverting. "With the princess. They are a mated pair, so open the doors to the pasture and they will fly off to hunt when weather allows."

Felicity sucked in a breath. "Really?"

"Hunting?" The youngling gulped at the same time.

The corner of Alarian's mouth lifted slightly, but any attempt at a grin disappeared just as quickly. "They won't hunt livestock. Don't worry. Cailleach understand more than we give them credit for."

He headed towards the door and Felicity followed. "I didn't know they were meant to stay."

"They may go back home during the summer months here. Would be too warm for them. But they are available for your use whenever you need them otherwise." Another near-invisible smile. "Remember, they're loyal."

She stared over her shoulder as the elder stablehand gave the younger reassuring words, his hand scratching behind the ears of Gaoth. When she turned back,

Alarian was already braving the torrential downpour. No sign of his shadows in an attempt to protect himself.

She jogged to catch up. "We need to talk."

"Felicity?"

Her head whipped around to find Avyanna at the door. "Hurry, you're both drenched." She paused and gave Felicity a meaningful look. "Your father is home."

All words escaped her. She glanced at Alarian, his emerald eyes dimmed. "Later tonight?"

He nodded.

Felicity rushed ahead, Alarian a few steps behind. Avyanna pulled her into a hug, uncaring that she was soaking wet. "I missed you."

For once, Felicity didn't pull away but enjoyed the feeling of her friend's arms around her. "I've missed you too."

Alarian gave her a half-hearted hug and then nodded at Felicity. "I'll give you time with your father."

She almost asked him to come but she considered what position that would put him in. It was best if she went alone. "See you later," she called after his retreating form.

Avyanna smiled. "Go clean up first. You look like you deserve a good bath. They will be waiting for you in the dining hall."

Felicity's heart stuttered in her chest. She made a mental list of what she should do. Bathe. What about her hair? What should she wear? Would seeing him jog her memory? Maybe she shouldn't make them wait...

Meira was already bustling about her room when Felicity arrived, the fragrant scent of lavender wafting from the bathing room. "Shall I pick out a dress for you?"

Felicity couldn't do more than nod, not trusting her words. She took a little longer than necessary to bathe, washing her hair and scrubbing her body until it was red.

Another handmaiden arrived shortly after and used air magic to dry Felicity's hair and assisted with styling it. The ties of a corset pulled at her body. Fabric from a dress she didn't recognize was assisted over her head. Buttons adjusted on her back while she stared at her reflection. By the time the sun had disappeared from the horizon, Felicity was dressed and ready.

"You look beautiful," the Aer handmaiden said as she eyed her handiwork.

She tried to smile, but breath caught in Felicity's throat. She closed her eyes, concentrating on words that Alarian had spoken. Reminders from Kellan to count. With each thought, each number, her breathing evened out and the panic with it. "I'm ready."

Thoughts vied for purchase as she followed the handmaiden out. Would she be what he expected? Was the dress right? Too little or too much? She wrung her hands as they walked, finding herself adjusting her skirts more than once and annoyed with the corset digging into her ribs.

Before she knew it, she was at the door to the dining room. An attendant reached to open it, but she shook her head. "Just a moment please."

She closed her eyes and considered turning around and hiding. The dress scratched against her skin. Felt tight and heavy. Maybe she should change? Excuses. Her father was not someone to run from. Alarian was right—he would accept her. Kellan had spoken of the type of male their father was—loving. Caring.

She finally nodded at the attendant who opened the door, and with her heart in her throat, she stepped into the room.

Kellan whirled around and rushed to her, blocking out the room as he wrapped her in a hug. He held her tight before holding her at arm's length to look her over. "I'm so glad you're home."

She closed her eyes, breathing in his familiar citrus scent. Before she'd always thought of home—of Saol—when she was around him. Now she knew why...he was her family.

"Are you ready?" he whispered.

Again, she nodded. "I think so. Does he—"

"Yes, he knows."

Of course Kellan would ensure their father was aware of her missing memories. Felicity gave him a weak smile as Kellan pulled away. "Father?" Her brother turned with his arm around her shoulder, holding her close.

King. Bastien. *Father.* The male who stood before her was familiar, but also not. Similar features to her brother—the shape of his nose and face—but the light that dared to emanate from him. That was all hers. Except, hers was like moonlight, while his was warm and welcoming like the sun. He stood with one hand on the back of a chair. Her training told her that his left leg was weak, not much muscle on his gaunt frame, but the build was there of a male who had once been strong. Stoic. Powerful.

He cleared his throat, his voice gravely. "I know you don't remember me..."

"But I want to." She made certain to have as much conviction as possible in her words, rolling her shoulders to relieve the itch of the gown. "I tried."

He gave her a small smile. Didn't move as she searched his face for something familiar. A feature to hold onto to put the pieces of her memories back together.

His throat bobbed. "It doesn't matter to me. I can remember enough for the both of us." He stepped forward, an uneasy step with a hand still gripped onto the back of the chair. "Do you want to sit and eat?"

"All right." She took a step forward, her heart speeding up against her chest. It didn't feel wrong, but it was awkward as hell. Why couldn't she remember? She moved from Kellan's hold and made her way across the room, trying not to pull at the stays at her back.

Her father paused and examined her from head to toe. "Are you comfortable?"

She frowned down at the dress. "Uh—yes?"

Bastien looked at Kellan. "Dinner has a few more minutes I think, don't you?"

"I assure you, I'm fine."

"Fine?" Bastien grinned and his features softened. "I would usually never compare the two females I was blessed to be with, but I learned that 'fine' meant exactly the opposite. You're accepted here, for you, Felicity. And if you love that dress, that's great. But if you prefer to change—"

Felicity glanced at her brother and Kellan scrunched up his nose and grinned. "You're fidgeting. You don't fidget."

She glanced over her brother's clothes—the usual dark tunic and trousers. Her father looked relaxed, despite the awkwardness, in a loose cream tunic. While she didn't know her father by sight or memories, she recognized him by the emotions visible on his face. Love. Pride. Adoration.

And she despised this dress.

Before considering her actions, she was in his orbit, arms wrapped around him and just held on. The scent of the Éardrom summer grass filled her senses. Bastien was timid at first. He didn't move as though worried he'd scare a young fawn. But then, when he realized she wasn't balking or running, he wrapped his arms around her shoulders and patted her gently on the back.

A sudden sense of relief curved through her. Her magic warmed in her body at his contact. Recognized him even when she didn't. With a deep inhale, she tried to drag memories that weren't there to the surface. Then she thought of new memories to be made. A chance to find each other again. To get to know one another. She was thankful for it.

"I'm glad you're home," she whispered.

He shuddered, his arms tightening briefly. "So am I, my darling."

The words reminded her of the dream of her mother. She opened her eyes to find Kellan standing in the same place with tears streaming down his face, watching them. Felicity beckoned him over and he made it to them in two large steps, wrapping his arms tightly around them both. Bastien chuckled and adjusted slightly to put an arm around his son. "I never thought this would be possible again. Had nearly given up hope."

Kellan sighed. "This is all I ever wanted. I just wish *she* were here too."

Bastien nodded against Felicity's head. "She is. In her own way. Both of them are. They loved you, loved us, so much."

Felicity pinched her eyes closed. "We have a chance to get to know each other again. They would have wanted us to be together. That's what is important now."

"That's right." Kellan pulled back first. "But if you're going to change, I need you to do so soon. I can't guarantee I can wait. All this crying made me hungry."

Felicity extracted herself from her father's hold and watched the two of them wipe their cheeks. She grinned. "I'll be right back."

She rushed out of the room, the corset constricting her lungs and making it difficult to move at the speed she would have preferred. The Aer handmaiden had tied it extra tight tonight. It wasn't that Felicity despised dresses. There was a time and place for them as she'd learned. And it was nice to dress up—like when she and Alarian had been at the ball. When she'd felt like herself.

Back at her room she pulled on her favorite pair of pants and a loose tunic before she returned to find her brother and father sitting at a small table, laughing at a joke she missed. At the sight of happiness and the sounds of family, the last of her fears evaporated.

After a delicious meal and a scrumptious pumpkin tart, Kellan brought up the past. Stories about her. The games they played. The trouble they had gotten into for those ten years of happiness that were far out of her grasp. It didn't hurt as much as she thought it would. The conversation was light, easy...

It was after the tenth bell when their father yawned. "Well, I'm not up to form yet, so this old male needs to get some sleep."

Felicity stood as they did, Kellan grabbing their father in a tight hug. When he stepped back, Bastien glanced at her. "I'm glad we get to do this again. Amidst all of what's to come, this will be one of my greatest joys."

She swallowed. Looked over to her brother and father. "I know you." Kellan and her father's eyes widened. "I mean, my memories haven't returned, but I do know you. I feel it deep within. Somewhere, there is a part of me that remembers." Felicity didn't know why she was saying all of this, but a part of her needed him to understand. "I'm not big on hugs, but Avyanna is working on that. She seems to believe I'm meant to like them. Earlier was a bit out of my comfort, but I liked it."

Kellan chuckled quietly.

"I'm still learning to understand my own emotions." She almost added that Alarian was helping in that area, but that was a conversation for tomorrow. When the outside world would break whatever spell was currently enacted for tonight. "And while I'm not always going to want them, let alone ask for one, yes—tonight I'd like a good night hug from my father."

Bastien's mouth wobbled before it fell into an easy smile. "Anytime you ask, I'll give one." He held out his arms and Felicity slowly stepped into his space until her arms could wrap around him. Gently, but firmly, he held her. Her head fit just at his chest, tucked under his chin.

He squeezed. "I thought you were gone forever," he whispered.

"I wish—"

"Hush now. If you wish that you could remember, just know that it never will matter to me." He pulled back gently, holding her at arm's length. "Understood?"

A nod was all she could muster.

"Good. I know that we have a lot to deal with now that we're all together again. Get a good night sleep." He patted her cheek and then gripped Kellan's shoulder as he passed. "I'm so glad we had this moment of peace. I look forward to many more."

When the door closed behind him, Felicity released a long breath.

Kellan nudged her on the shoulder. "Well, did I tell you?"

She chuckled, met his gaze. "You did. Smart ass."

"Smart big brother were the words you were looking for. It's all right though. You'll get it right next time."

Felicity rolled her eyes. "How does Avy put up with you?"

Kellan grinned, his cheeks reddening. "Oh, I could tell you, but—"

"Nope." Felicity covered her ears. "I can't hear you."

Kellan mimicked talking, his hands exaggerating movements that insinuated way too much while Felicity kept her hands over her ears. He paused long enough to open the door and almost walked right into Avyanna.

"Do I even want to know?"

Felicity bit her lip. "Well—he was just telling me about how you and he…"

"Oh shit, come on, Felicity." Kellan ran a hand over his face.

Avyanna glanced between the two of them. "Is this what I'm going to have to get used to? Where is Alarian to back me up?"

"He'd be in the midst of it, I assure you." Felicity bit her lip.

Kellan tilted his head. "Really? Is that so?" He glanced around the hall. "Where is he, by the way?"

They hadn't set a spot to meet, but Felicity had a feeling she knew where she was meant to go. With the anxiety of meeting her father out of the way, Felicity felt lighter than she had in a long time. Sure, there was still a war, heartstones, traitors, and so many other things to worry about but for a second in time, she was going to let her heart lead her. See what happened.

But she wanted to find out alone. "He's around, I'm sure." She walked away, taking a leather throng from her pocket and putting her hair up in a ponytail. "I'm going to get in a session. I'll see you both later."

Before they could say another word, she jogged down the hall. She thought she heard Avyanna chuckle. "It seems this trip helped."

Chapter 39
Alarian

Alarian's stomach tensed on instinct. He stepped back, trying to get into position, but Sloan seemed to know he needed this. A right hook to the ribs. Alarian grunted, curved over onto himself. His mind wasn't on what he should be doing. Protecting himself. Neither was his heart.

Sloan took a gulping breath of air and lowered his arms. Stared as Alarian fumbled into position. "What's going on with you? I haven't kicked your ass like this in months."

"We haven't sparred in months. And you have never kicked my ass like this." Alarian wiped his forearm over his forehead before sweat seeped into his eyes.

"What? The spy didn't give you enough of a challenge these past few weeks?"

Fists formed at Alarian's sides at the mention of her. His heart, or what was left of it, cracked a little more. He'd felt the bond between them. Had tried so hard to block out the emotions rolling off her in waves. The uncertainty followed by complete bliss. Whatever had happened between her and her father had gone well. A positive after the mess he'd caused. He'd been complicit in.

"Another round?" He spat to the side, lifting his fists and crouching slightly. It was the only way he could think of using his time while he waited for the inevitable.

Sloan blinked. Then stared. "What happened, Rian? Does it have to do with Felicity or is this something else?"

"Less talk, more action." Alarian feinted left then punched right, his fist meeting Sloan's shoulder. A weak attempt, and Sloan barely budged at the impact.

His friend shook his head. "When you need to talk, you know—"

He was interrupted by the door of the training room opening. Felicity walked in, a lightness in her step that tore his chest apart. Their eyes met. Hers shining with excitement. She wanted to talk. Was ready to talk. Saw it in her expression. This side of Felicity was what he had hoped for—until the previous night.

Alarian shifted a look at Sloan.

Felicity stopped outside the ring. "I didn't expect you both to be going at it. Can I jump in, or should I train elsewhere?"

Sloan chuckled, but Alarian turned, heading for his tunic and the pack that he'd left on the bench nearby. If their dinner was over, then the others should arrive soon. He needed to be ready.

He felt his friend's gaze follow him. "I'm good for tonight. Don't need my ass handed to me, but this guy might need another round."

Instead of tossing his tunic over his head, Alarian used it to wipe the sweat from his forehead and chest before he pulled the envelopes out of his bag. The contents of one shifted in his hands and he shuddered at the reminder of what was inside. Of what had been returned to him. Something he hadn't realized he'd lost and wished had never gotten back.

"Alarian?" There was an edge to her voice. Was that concern? For him? To have her attention had been a hope and a dream he'd only had a breath of time to enjoy. The ride back had been torture. He'd wanted to explain everything if only to take away her waves of trepidation and slashes of frustration. Now there was hope. Excitement that ran a shiver between his shoulder blades.

He turned to face her and silently trudged across the ring. "These are for you."

Felicity looked at the envelopes he held out between them. He couldn't look at her, knowing he'd regret it if he did.

"What are they?" She didn't reach for them.

"Last night I made a visit to Thomas. It was a quick trip from Dimitri and Lian's."

She gasped. "Did he..."

Alarian nodded. "Yes. This is the results of what he uncovered—for your eyes only. Remember that we swore to the library that this information wouldn't be shared unless it was used to save the continent."

Felicity glanced between Alarian, the envelope, and then towards Sloan before turning back to his hands. "All right, I can move past the fact you didn't tell me earlier. But—"

"And the other one" —he held the second envelope out further— "is from the Countess." A shudder stole down his spine. Air lodged in his throat. It took him a moment to gather himself before meeting her gaze. "And from me. I'm sorry."

"Sorry?" Felicity stared at him with a furrow in her brow. "I forgive you for keeping the bond from me. Why are you..." She trailed off as her finger grazed the broken seal of the wolf and knotted snakes, but didn't take it.

"The Countess? Why did she give you an envelope?" She swallowed, then her attention snapped to him.

Her sudden shock felt like a slash to his skull.

He wanted to confirm. Deny. Apologize. Speak. His throat bobbed.

Her mouth opened on a gasp for breath. Felicity shook her head. "No."

"Take them. Please."

She shook her head again. "No. I can't."

The door opened and four guards entered with Prince Kellan and Avyanna on their heels. "What is this about, Alarian?" The prince held up a letter. "Guards needed for an arrest? What happened?"

With slow movements, Alarian handed the packet to Sloan and slid his tunic over his head. It clung to him, dirt and sweat coating the fabric. Tears formed, but he blinked them back. Compared to Felicity, he didn't deserve to feel pain. He'd made a choice years before that he would regret for his entire existence.

Alarian faced her. "I'm so sorry, Starlight. I wish there was another way this could have turned out." He made himself look at her. To see what he'd done. He deserved it. Deserved to see the pain in her gaze, not just feel them from her emotions, as he broke her open.

Felicity wrapped her arms around herself, curled inwards. Prince Kellan rushed to her side. "What is it?"

Sloan moved between the guards and him immediately. "Someone needs to explain."

"Give her the envelope. She knows what it is. When she's ready, she will need it."

"Rian, what the hell?"

Avyanna gripped Prince Kellan's arm. "This needs to stop. Alarian—what is happening?"

Sloan pushed the envelopes towards Felicity. With shaking hands, she took hold of the second one. She met his gaze. "I don't believe it." Tears slid down her cheek.

Alarian felt the heat of his own tears. "I wish I could say differently. If I'd known, I would have never allowed any of this to escalate. I'm so sorry. Sorry that I did this to you."

Felicity grazed a finger over the broken seal on the envelope, then turned the contents over into her palm. Two vials fell into her hand. One full, the second empty.

The sob that broke through her, he felt it to the deepest essence of himself. It tore through that bond between them as she cried out.

Alarian's throat bobbed as a clock chimed in the distance, marking the hour. "There is a reason the bond is one sided." He spoke in a near whisper. Meant for only her to hear. No one else moved. Even Prince Kellan who had been about to reach for his sister had stopped.

Alarian's shoulders slumped, defeated. "The magic chooses to bond those who love one another against all odds. It chose me first for a reason. A punishment. It was never my intention to hurt you and if I'd known the truth, I would have done this sooner."

The guards stepped closer and Alarian turned to them. He held out his wrists. "I'm turning myself in."

Everyone reacted at the same time. Felicity clutched her chest. Avyanna gasped. Sloan froze as the prince crouched beside his sister.

Alarian met Prince Kellan's gaze. "For the murder of Queen Kaliana."

Chapter 40

Felicity

It was a lie. Had to be.

"No," she gasped out on a breath. "You couldn't have." Felicity looked up and met his eyes to find Alarian crying. Tears stung, her light rushing through her blood.

"The cloak—it was mine. Everything you need to know is there in your hand." His voice was far away, yet so loud.

No one moved, all seemed to be in as much shock as she was. Her light expanded off her.

Alarian's gaze softened. "I wanted you to have a moment with your father before I told you, and I swear I only found out last night. She…" He inhaled. "The Countess made me promise to wait to open the contents until the night before we returned to the palace. I shouldn't have listened."

Her heart shattered. Her body shuddered and she couldn't bring herself to move, even as Kellan tried to pull her towards him.

"I'm sorry. So sorry, Felicity. And to you too, Prince Kellan."

The guards were the first to come out of their stupor. One lunged forward and grabbed hold of Alarian—as if he was a fugitive on the run, even though his wrists were held out towards them, waiting. Of all the secrets that could have been left between them, this one hurt like no other. A stab to her chest. It was becoming hard to breathe.

Avyanna shook her head. "This must be a misunderstanding."

Alarian didn't turn away, his attention glued to Felicity as the iron manacle was fitted to his wrists. Felicity didn't move. React. Couldn't even fathom what to do.

"I always wanted to make you feel—to see all of you—but I never wanted to be the cause of your tears." He turned away and that's when the spell that had held her hostage evaporated. Her legs went out from underneath her. Alarian reached for her, but the guards pulled him back. Kellan had Felicity in his arms within a breath, Avyanna was asking questions Felicity no longer could hear. Not as the darkness edged in further. As her magic stuttered. As the world turned to ringing.

And the tears wouldn't stop.

***

Felicity groaned as she woke, willing her eyes shut as her body ached from the days of flying and travel, as if the past few weeks had accumulated to this moment and dragged her down. Lavender scented pillows and the comforting weight of her quilt told her she was in her bed.

Then the memory of what happened surfaced—of Alarian's admittance. No wonder he couldn't promise not to keep any more secrets from her. Although...she was keeping one too. One that she would have to live with her entire life.

He had killed her mother and somehow been involved with her arrival at the Tower.

"You awake?" Kellan whispered.

She stuffed her head further into the pillow.

"Felicity." Avyanna's voice softened—a healer's voice.

With a sigh, Felicity turned her head in their direction to find her brother and friend in the two chairs beside her bed. "How long did I sleep for? The way you two are coddling me, it's as though you sat beside my death bed."

"First off," Kellan grumbled. "You didn't fall asleep—you passed out."

The familiar memory of her lungs burning, her throat ragged. "Oh."

Avyanna squeezed Kellan's arm. "It's been at least eighteen hours. How do you feel?"

It was a question she would usually answer with a lie. But the two of them—they knew her well. "Where is he?"

They looked at each other, but it was Kellan who answered in a low voice. It didn't suit him. "With the crimes he claimed to have committed, we had no choice. He's in the prison, awaiting trial."

"And what will the trial decide?" She knew it was a mistake to ask.

Kellan swallowed and glanced between the two of them. "Well, once you return your memories—we figured it was your decision what fate awaited him."

"That's not fair." She sat up, her head aching at the sudden jolt. She hid her face in her hands.

Avyanna grumbled a few curse words that were muffled, before the bed shifted and her friend wrapped an arm over her shoulder. "You don't need to worry about this for the next few days. Or even weeks, really. The information he has on the heartstones and his mother can be useful. There is no point in making any further decisions or weighing his crimes until you're ready. For now—we need to concentrate on Tine."

She sat up straighter and took the offering of redirecting her thoughts. "What's happening with Tine?" She knew that Avyanna's parents were acting as informants.

"We haven't heard from my parents." Avyanna licked her lips. "Their letter is two days late."

"Shit." Felicity's head rang. She pressed her palm to her forehead to steady herself.

Kellan stood and walked to a side table. "Take it slow. Have something to eat first. You expelled a lot of magic before your panic attack took you out."

Felicity blinked as another spasm of pain rushed through her head. "Oh. Um—maybe you're right."

"I know I'm right." Kellan gave a half-hearted smile before he returned with a bowl in hand. "Eat. Maybe bathe. I'm surprised Meira hasn't bustled in and shooed us out yet."

"I asked her for some time." Avyanna smirked. "But she'll be ready when you are."

She took the offered bowl to find broth with rice and chunks of chicken. "Stay with me?" Felicity felt vulnerable saying the words aloud, her attention on her friend. To rely on someone. Hell—she would have never done so weeks ago. She didn't know if that made her weak, but she didn't care. Felicity knew that this allowed susceptibility was because of *him*. That he helped her see what she was so fearful of...having something to lose.

Tears welled but she willed them back. If she was alone—there was a good chance she'd break down. Kellan would ask too many questions. Would want to dote on her. Avyanna was the safer choice.

Avyanna nodded. "Of course." She looked at Kellan. "Will you ask Meira to bring my things here and the two of us will get ready together? If she is up for it, we can meet before dinner."

"It's important. I'll be there."

"I will." Kellan gave Avyanna a peck on the cheek and then shut the door gently behind himself.

Her friend stood and headed over to the bathing room. "Meira may be upset with me for getting this started, but you deserve a relaxing bath."

The sound of rushing water from the tap began before Avyanna returned. She paused, looking over Felicity. "Your brother was thankful for all the updates you sent while you were gone. I think it helped with his worry. As much as he knew you needed to go, I think he never wanted you to leave again."

"Well, I'm glad he overcame that." Felicity slid to the side of the bed, dropping her legs over to feel the rug under her toes. "Al—" She couldn't bring herself to say his name. "He has the start of the bond." Avyanna breathed a long sigh. Felicity couldn't look at her. "He kept it from me for as long as he could. Then this..."

"He loves you."

Felicity stared at the wall.

"And you love him."

Felicity shook her head. To say it out loud, even to hear it from another, felt wrong after the truth was revealed. Her secret...

"I had a feeling. Before you left, I wondered. It's obvious he was attracted to you for some time. At the beginning, I thought it was a similar infatuation he'd had with many others. It wasn't until..."

She trailed off, drawing Felicity's attention. "Go on."

"The celebration for Roald's birthday. The way he'd look at you. Knew where you were at any moment. I saw him searching for you and the relief when he saw you after the attack. I thought it strange he'd been relieved because you'd been with another man—Kellan—when he was meant to be courting you. It all makes sense now, but then it was confusing. Especially after the events in Koselig."

Felicity listened. Signs of his interest that she had never noticed. At least not until she began to realize that she might feel something for him.

Avyanna grabbed a robe and a few other items as she talked. "And Koselig—that had been another side of him altogether. I'd gone on outings with Alarian before since we were meant to court. His mother had scheduled a few for us. He'd never been as attentive as he'd been with you. Kind, yes. As much as the other ladies had bustled on at tea about him being a rake and that you weren't special, they were ignoring the truth."

"Like I did," Felicity whispered, still staring at her toes. "I guess for good reason. I can't love him. He killed..." The words were bitter on her tongue.

They didn't move or speak for a few moments. Felicity's robe was draped over Avyanna's arms, a tender expression in her tear-rimmed eyes. Those damn tears welled in her own. "I should be angry. But it just hurts."

Avyanna rushed to her side, wrapping Felicity in her arms. She crumbled against her friend, a wracking sob breaking free. None of this was familiar, but Felicity couldn't care. She needed this, needed a moment to break. Avyanna didn't speak. Didn't shush her or wipe her tears. She just held Felicity and cried with her.

The time that passed was too long. Felicity hadn't even been aware that Meira had entered—probably just in time to turn off the tap for the tub. She assisted Felicity from Avyanna's arms and gently removed Felicity's clothes, before she helped her into the warm bath, the calming scent of lavender mixed with something else filled the room—cedar. Rain-misted woods, a forest...him.

Meira scrubbed her body with a sponge and soap. There was a quiet hum of a song Felicity didn't recognize. When her bath was done, she no longer cried but everything was numb.

Avyanna held out the opened robe after Meira assisted Felicity in drying off. She wrapped the warm clothing over her shoulders. "Are you certain you're ready for this meeting? We can fill you in later. Kellan and your father will understand."

Her father. The mention of him brought Felicity back to the surface from the dark abyss she had been drowning in. "What does my father know?"

Avyanna shared a glance with Meira. "Kellan had to tell him of course. He doesn't know how far your relationship went with Alarian. He's...grieving for your mother all over again."

Felicity nodded. "I need to go. Do something."

Felicity donned her most comfortable clothing—uncaring about any advisors that may be present at the meeting. Avyanna had changed into a plain linen tunic and a pair of dress trousers—attire less formal than she would have usually worn. Probably, knowing the female, in solidarity. Meira opened the door, and Felicity almost hugged her for the kindness. There was no one better than her. Instead, she gave the handmaiden a sad smile. "I'm—"

Meira shook her head. "Don't you dare apologize."

"All right then. How are you doing?"

Meira reached out and took Felicity's hands in hers. They trembled slightly as the handmaiden looked Felicity straight in her eyes. "I know him. You do too. When you're ready, I'll be there for you."

Her heart crumbled a little. She squeezed her hands and whispered, "Thank you."

Kellan was waiting outside the door of the meeting hall when they arrived. "Are you sure?"

She was starting to get tired of that question. "Yes. Tine needs to be dealt with. We need to know about Avy's parents."

Kellan straightened. "It's more than that, Felicity. You need to read the letter from Thomas and tell us what you can to assist us in planning for the battle to come."

"Then let's get this over with." Felicity stepped through and Kellan moved in behind her. A figurative cloak that had once felt like a burden and now was exactly what she needed.

Chapter 41

Kellan

Felicity's shoulders drew back, her chin lifted. A mask in place that Kellan hadn't seen in a long time. She had donned the persona of the spy and assassin as easily as she had been a daughter the day before. Not separate identities anymore, but the multifaceted female she was meant to be. Part of him wanted to thank Alarian for that, knowing the male had been a guiding hand even if he also had broken his sister's heart. She didn't say it aloud. Didn't need to. He saw it.

He should be angry. Should want to tear the male apart. But the whole thing didn't sit right with him. The irony was poetic. He wanted Felicity to return her memories and confirm the truth—but asking her to do so now was insensitive. She would talk to him when she was ready.

Avyanna squeezed Kellan's hand as they took the seats to the right of his father. He smiled in greeting to King Bastien and choked back the emotion that wanted to pit in his stomach whenever he saw him. Fifty years. And so much loss. He'd taken the news of Alarian's admittance rather well considering. The king had demanded his arrest and then after Kellan informed him Alarian had turned himself in, he sat in silence as Kellan explained everything he knew about the male. That Alarian led a rebellion against his own parents. Had protected Felicity and Kellan in ways he hadn't known and sometimes still had trouble admitting. There was so much more he couldn't even speak of since Felicity had her own stories to tell. Few knew that she covered a broken heart with a steel gaze.

His father called the meeting to order, and Kellan glanced around the table. Only three others were present—Lord Chartow, Lord Dimitri, and Sloan. The only ones they trusted with the truth they were about to disclose.

The letter from Thomas sat on the table and Felicity stood behind the chair where it waited, still sealed.

Bastien stood and met her at the table. "I'm sorry about your friend. I'm here if you need anything."

She gave him a half smile. "Thank you, Father."

"For now, let's concentrate on what we need to get done tonight." He started back towards his chair and once he did, everyone else also took a seat. "Avyanna, you said it's been a few days since your parents have communicated with you?"

Avyanna shifted her attention to the king. He loved that she was there for Felicity, but she had every right to be concerned about her parents right now. He threaded his fingers through hers as she cleared her throat. "That's correct, Your Majesty. I'm trying not to be concerned, but their missives have been like clockwork until now. When they chose to do this, they said if anything happened to them, we shouldn't send in anyone to retrieve them."

Kellan scoffed. "I hope they know we wouldn't leave them if they were in danger."

Sloan glanced at the others. "Then what do you propose, Prince?" There was an edge to his tone. One that undoubtedly had to do with the current location of one of his closest friends.

"I'll go as a representative. Be the decoy while others locate Avyanna's parents. We can go in as though unaware of Marquette and Fiadh's presence."

Sloan snorted. "You think that will work? They aren't stupid." He rolled his eyes.

Felicity pinned him in a glare. "Then what do you propose?"

Sloan's jaw flexed. His entire countenance softened though as he looked to Avyanna. "This is going to sound hurtful, and I apologize, but this is war."

"You want to leave them there and concentrate on what's important." Avyanna lifted her chin, and Kellan could read her expression. Knew she was willing to concede for the good of the continent.

"Hell no," Kellan snapped, shoulders tensing. "Even if they weren't my fiancée's family, we wouldn't give up on anyone. They put themselves in harm's way on our behalf. If there is a chance to save them I—"

Avyanna gripped his arm. "Please. I understand."

His father shook his head. "This is not up for debate as far as I'm concerned. We take the advantage of this opportunity, do some reconnaissance and found out how deep Tine is in Marquette's pocket, and get your parents out of there in the process." He waited for someone to negate or agree.

Lord Dimitri cleared his throat. "I agree. Right now, we need the continent to know we aren't abandoning those loyal to the rightful rulers."

Others nodded, even Sloan, although he hesitated a moment.

Bastien turned to Kellan. "We will discuss the plan soon." He faced Felicity. "First, read the letter. Share what you can. How can we protect the continent and our magic?"

"Magic?" Lord Chartow cocked his head.

The others shared a glance. Felicity stared at the letter as Kellan took a deep breath. "The heartstones are being stolen and collected by Marquette."

Lord Chartow jumped to his feet, color leeching from his face. "And you're just telling us now?" He glanced at the others who unfortunately didn't look as clueless as they should have. "Or was it just I who was left in the dark?"

"We had to be certain who to trust." Felicity nodded towards Dimitri. "He knows only because we met with him in Aer and shared a secret that you know about."

Chartow slumped back into his chair, arms crossed. "I see. And why, do you assume, she wants the heartstones? It doesn't make sense to weaken the entire continent's magic. That takes time, as proven by Domhain's slow decline."

King Bastien nodded to Felicity. "We are hoping to uncover just what they want to do. Felicity..."

She breathed a long sigh and picked up the envelope. She stared at it for a moment, and Kellan saw the battle within her gaze. The crack in the façade. But before he could decipher what caused her to pause, she ripped open the letter and removed the parchment within.

Silence ate up the space. No sound but the occasional rustling of paper as she read. When she reached the last page, she folded the sheets and placed them back in the envelope again.

"Well, aren't you going to read them aloud?" Sloan asked.

Felicity shook her head. "I cannot. The information shared is directly from a text that the Fios only deemed myself and few others allowed to read. I can only share with you what is necessary for the safety of the realms."

"And?" Kellan couldn't read her expression.

She placed her hand on the envelope and met Kellan's gaze. "There is more than one veil and the heartstones are capable of opening each one with different spells and stones."

Avyanna gasped. "Multiple veils."

Felicity nodded.

Sloan shook his head. "What veil are they planning to open?"

Felicity kept her eyes on her father. "That's the problem. They have stones for different spells. Without more information, we can't be certain which veil."

"Can you share what those veils are?" their father whispered.

She shook her head. "No. But I can confirm she will undoubtedly do it on Samhain. And knowing that they will attempt this in Saol brings the options down to three."

"Three? But what three?" Dimitri rubbed his temples. "That was more than we thought possible just this morning. Certainly, you can give us a hint."

"I don't know how much I'm privy to discuss. Either way, we know we can't allow them to succeed."

If silence was a living thing, then its heartbeat echoed through the room.

A flicker, a sudden silhouette built of shadow and darkness appeared in the corner of the room. Kellan had the dagger he'd begun to wear in his hand, and Felicity had her own poised to throw.

Sloan positioned himself between the king and the imposter, his sword pointed at the disturbance. But with a shift of the light, he straightened. "It's you."

Shadows evaporated and a female with sharp piercing blue eyes, tan skin, and deep violet hair stood in place of the silhouette. Her brow rose at the blades at the ready and shot a snarky smile at Sloan. "The palace has deemed me loyal." She lifted her chin, giving a pointed glare at each of their weapons.

"You weren't invited." Bastien tilted his head. "I don't think we need to apologize for our reaction to your sudden interruption."

"Yes, that is true, Your Majesty. But if you're discussing the heartstones' ability to open veils, then you're going to want the knowledge I have."

Kellan stood with his dagger pointed towards the female. "Who are you?"

Sloan sheathed his weapon. "Ciana. A delegate of Scáth. She *assisted* with your father's retrieval." His pinched tone sounded like it was painful for him to say that out loud.

She wasn't the same delegate that had been sent prior. Who had left silently and had dismissed any chance of conversation.

He glanced at his father who was slowly taking in the female. "I don't remember you there."

"I was back up. Sloan didn't want to admit he needed my help, but you should be glad I was there otherwise his search would have taken much longer."

"Why are you here, Ciana?" Sloan grumbled.

Dimitri and Chartow shared a glance. Sloan didn't seem worried, but Kellan didn't lower his defenses.

Ciana crossed her arms and leaned against the wall. "We finally have decided you're worth our time and not another waste of space in this castle."

"I don't care for your insinuations," Bastien growled.

The female smiled. "Your mother didn't either. I wanted to ensure you were still her son. Not the male the traitor king spread rumors about and raised a coup against. Strength is necessary, especially if what you believe is true and Marquette wants to open a veil. We don't want that to happen."

"Who is we?" Lord Dimitri glanced at the papers atop the table with a furrowed brow.

Felicity shifted, her dagger flicked and disappeared. "The Shadows. Members of Scáth's guards, I assume?"

"Has the traitor spoken to you about our ways?"

Felicity took a defensive step forward then stopped herself. Sloan was on his feet and Kellan grabbed his friend to hold him back. His sister tilted her head and took the newcomer in. "No. But you just confirmed my assumptions."

Ciana grinned. "Maybe. Maybe not. And where is he now?"

"In prison." Bastien lifted his chin. "Now, do you have a reason for interrupting a private meeting?"

"You need to understand your enemy." Ciana nodded towards Felicity. "Go back to where it all began."

"We don't have time for this. The entire continent—even Scáth—is in danger."

"I don't know the information our council holds. But with the knowledge Princess Felicity has" —Ciana pointed at the envelope in front of Felicity— "and the story of the traitor queen and the witch, then you will have the answers you seek. This is information only the princess can retrieve." Ciana's brow quirked. "She needs to go to Scáth."

Kellan glanced at his sister, his father. "We have more vital matters with Samhain on the horizon." A handful of weeks remained, and they needed to prepare for the battle to come.

"Send her if you want to know the truth." She disappeared before any further question could be asked. All that remained were the remnants of shadows she once inhabited.

His father pointed to the door. "Send guards to find her."

Chartow went to alert the guard outside the door, but Sloan shook his head, rubbing his forehead. "There is no point. If she wanted to talk, she would have stayed. You're not going to find her, and she doesn't pose a threat." He looked like he needed a drink.

Kellan had to stifle a smile as he watched his friend. "I have a feeling you have a story you didn't tell us."

The Dorcha male shrugged. "In the end, your father is home. That's what matters."

Avyanna let out an exasperated sigh. "Well, we need more information about Marquette if we are to decipher what veil she plans to open. What else do you propose?"

Sloan cursed under his breath, and Kellan had a feeling the cause was the shadowy female rather than the situation they found themselves in.

King Bastien breathed a long sigh. "Well, this seems problematic on multiple levels. Do we even know what stones are still protected and safe?"

"Saol, Scáth, and Aer."

"Guaranteed?"

Felicity nodded "I trust them. Yes."

She had never been to Scáth. Which meant she was taking *his* word for it. There was more to unpack there, but he didn't want to push that now. Not as a shudder of frustration on behalf of his sister slid down his spine. He hadn't gone to talk to Alarian. None of them had.

"Is there any more information you can share with us?"

Felicity bit her bottom lip. "No, Father."

Damnit. Kellan ran a hand through his hair. He could see it—her mind reeling with ideas. The spy and assassin visible by the sharpness of her gaze. It was one of the tells he found over time but had been missing since the curse broke. She was coming back to herself, and he was glad to see that spark hadn't dimmed after Alarian's truth.

"Felicity." Kellan drew his sister's attention back to the present. "Before you start planning a trip to Scáth, we need to decide what to do about Tine." Her brow rose. The only indication that she was doing exactly what he guessed. "We're certain they have sided with Fiadh and Marquette. We can confirm to what extent while we are there."

"What? Walk through the front doors and pretend to say 'hello' and not expect to be killed on sight?" Lord Chartow rolled his eyes.

"Yes and no. We will expect to be killed on sight," Kellan offered. "Play the ruse that we're checking on the status of the realm since they have been lacking communication. Sidetrack them so to speak. There must be others who want to leave Tine if it's under Marquette's rule. We can offer them sanctuary. Cut off some of their resources while we find out what is happening there."

"We can't send you in alone. That is too much ground to cover on your own." Bastien thrummed his fingers against the table.

Avyanna nodded in agreement, but he saw the pain in her eyes. Kellan squeezed her hand.

"I'll go."

Felicity's voice rang in Kellan's ears.

"No. You've just got back." Kellan stood, cursing as he knocked his knee against the table. "This is a job I can do."

Felicity smirked. "This part was made for me."

"Except that Marquette and Fiadh know what you can do now."

Felicity's grin only widened. "Exactly."

Sloan chuckled. "You can't leave your greatest asset behind." He nodded to Kellan. "You should be with me giving the people guidance. If they see you there, they will be more likely to trust that this is their chance to escape. We just have to time it for night—when I and other dark wielders can create a large enough portal for them."

Felicity's eyes widened. "You can do that?"

It was Sloan's turn to smirk. "How do you think most of us escaped the night of Roald's birthday? Only a few remained to create a trail. One impossible for the guards to keep up with."

Kellan rubbed his neck. He hated that this plan made sense and their options were limited. No matter who they sent into that fortress, Marquette would already doubt them. "You're taking a few guards with you."

"And me." Lord Chartow straightened. "You'll need an advisor if you want them to think this is a political meeting."

"We need you here." Bastien shook his head. "It's too dangerous and you're not a soldier."

"You don't need me here." He nudged Lord Dimitri with his elbow. "You need him."

Avyanna shook her head. "It's too dangerous for all of you. To find my parents, assess the stability of Tine, assist those who can escape, and what? This plan puts important members of this court in harm's way. Concentrate on the bigger problem."

Kellan and his father shared a glance. Bastien cleared his throat. "This is a big problem. We need to know what plans are underway. And the people need to know that we haven't abandoned them—your parents included. The rest of us will begin preparations for the war to come. Felicity will go inside."

Fuck—he knew it was the right call. The expected call. It would be irresponsible to not consider the option with everything against them.

Lord Chartow ground his teeth. "And the dragon? What if it's there?"

Felicity shook her head. "That dragon is being used. We need to find out what they are using to control her. It's probably her nest."

Everyone turned to face his sister.

Kellan's brow furrowed. He was vaguely aware that his sister had an affinity towards animals, but this intel was unexpected. "Why do you think that?"

"I was face to face with that dragon. Its coloring signifies that she's from the mountains between Domhain and Saol. We had a little difficulty with them when we had to use the mountain pass—but only if we got too close to their nests. Otherwise, they ignored our presence. I have no doubt that they are holding her eggs hostage as collateral."

"And the other dragons are not helping because...?" Bastien's brow lifted.

Felicity shrugged. "Dragons are solitary animals. Gather in small groups at most, but when they nest, they are untrusting of even their own kind. Eggs are valuable. Dragons are hoarders. Whatever happened, the others have chosen to ignore for one reason or another."

"Why did you learn about dragons?" Avyanna's expression held more worry than curiosity.

She glanced at Kellan. "I had some time to read."

He chuckled at her vague response.

Their father ran a hand over his face. "We'll discuss dragons and Scáth after we know where we stand with Tine."

"And the other realms?" Felicity asked.

Sloan cleared his throat. "Dorcha will assist. It took some finagling from my father, but the abduction of our stone had the leadership angry enough to finally act. Especially as Advisor Heavin has abandoned his post. Seems that others were following him blindly and don't want to be considered traitors." He nodded towards Felicity. The advisor never arrived, and the tail lost him around the border of Domhain.

"Aer stands with you," Dimitri added.

Felicity nodded. "Saol will as well."

Kellan smiled. "Some good came from your travels. We received word from Lady Leana of Domhain—who is on her way—and a Lady Molyle of Visce who have stated their realms will side with us." Upon the news of her father's arrest, Lady Molyle had gone to Visce's council and spoke on their behalf. "Knowledge that you attended their ball was enough for Visce advisors to extend a hand."

"Domhain doesn't have much to offer." Bastien sighed. "They have their own issues to deal with to offer much assistance. Even Visce doesn't have many capable of fighting. We don't have soldiers—Dorcha and Éardrom are our greatest assets. But many of our warriors are in Tine."

"Then we have to hope we are able to call enough to our aid," Felicity said. "Until I can travel to Scáth, that is."

"Yes. We will take the next few days to concentrate on planning for Tine. There isn't room for any mistakes. General Sloan?"

Sloan blinked once. Twice. "I'm sorry—what?"

"It was a unanimous decision. You've been promoted."

Sloan stood, his eyes wide. "But I'm just—I was..."

"An ally for Talamh when many were not. An asset to the people. You deserve this." Bastien stood. "You're one of the reasons I'm here with my family again. And who knows" —he reached out a hand towards Sloan— "maybe one day we can call you family. Now do you accept the position? It comes with many responsibilities."

Kellan glanced at his sister who was studying the table as though it might share all its secrets.

Sloan swallowed. "Yes." He took Bastien's hand. "I mean, of course I accept the position. It's time to whip these guards of yours back into shape. Get this army under control."

The room chuckled, the tension easing. "Good." Bastien smiled. "I call this meeting to an end. Let's eat."

Sloan didn't rush out, waiting as the others filed towards the door. Kellan saw his gaze turn to Felicity more than once in the hubbub. He intersected the newly stated general with a shake of his head.

Avyanna gave him a small smile, staying close to Felicity as they exited. When the room was empty, he turned towards Sloan.

"Congratulations." It was best to start on solid ground.

Sloan's jaw worked as he nodded, rubbing his hand over his shaved head. "I don't want to marry your sister."

Kellan snorted. "Trust me, I think the feeling is mutual—if she was even paying attention to my father's comment. I think he noticed you glance toward her more than once and may have misconstrued your intentions."

"That wasn't why—"

Kellan laughed. "I know. Besides, I think you have something to tell me about Ciana?"

Sloan rolled his eyes and leaned over the table, resting his palms flat on the surface. "Has Felicity learned the truth yet?"

Kellan sighed. "She's grieving, and I don't think she's had a chance to return her memories yet."

"She must. I know Alarian didn't do it. I've known him for too long—" He began pacing, speed picking up with each word.

"When he was a youngling?" Kellan knew the answer.

Sloan paused. "No, but close enough."

"He was raised among the Shadows. His parents are vile—we don't know exactly what he was capable of then." Even saying the words out loud felt false on his tongue. This didn't sit right even if Alarian had always toed the line.

"You can't believe he did it."

"He admitted it," Kellan pointed out. "What else do you want?"

Sloan's shoulders slumped. "Before there is a trial, you have to make sure she takes those memories. Please? Promise me."

"She will. I won't even have to ask."

"You sound certain. I know how you feel about—"

Kellan cut him off with a shake of his head. "This is between the two of them. Felicity won't condemn him to death out of spite." And he did know that. Because his sister may have donned her mask for this meeting, but he could see the pain she hid in the moments her eyes flickered. The way her gaze had lingered on Ciana's shadows. She was going to bury herself in this mission—get lost in it for a moment. But she wouldn't stay there forever.

"So...Ciana?"

Sloan groaned, tossed open the door and flung a derogatory gesture over his shoulder as he stalked out. Kellan chuckled after him.

Chapter 42

Felicity

For the next five days they strategized, prepared, and assessed every angle. With so many unknowns, there were holes within every plan. Sloan sent out scouts in an attempt to gain some footing upon their arrival. They were as ready as they could be. Felicity had thrown herself into the mission, keeping her priorities and thoughts on Avyanna's parents. She had two goals. If they were in the fortress, get them out. And ascertain how much control Marquette had over the strongest soldiers and bladesmiths on the continent.

While she and Lord Chartow were within the fortress, Kellan, Sloan, and a small retinue would be getting as many of the citizens out of the realm. A way to weaken their enemies' resources as well as protect their Tine allies.

They'd arrived in Tine easily enough. Felicity took in the crimson rocky mountain that blocked the coastal breeze of the northwestern point of the continent. Townsfolk wore scarves to protect their faces from the occasional gale that pelted sand at their bodies. They passed hawkers and carts laden with produce brought in from other realms. Storefronts were inserted in small alcoves with wooden benches where they sold their wares. Doors had been built over entrances to the cave system that twisted through the mountain providing living compartments.

Felicity and the others had arrived at the meeting place—a small pub that was nearly empty in the late morning—to find two of the three scouts sat at a table, sipping bitter-scented coffee. The third had been sent into the fortress undercover—and had never reappeared. She and Chartow would be going in blind.

"There hasn't been any sign of a dragon in the past few days. I've heard no stirrings or whispers about Marquette or the witch." The scout with piercing blue eyes peered over at the barkeep who was cleaning a few glasses. One of the many who would be leaving via Sloan's portal today. "All I have is their bell toll schedule." He nudged it towards Felicity.

They had hypothesized that that it was doubtful Marquette would appear when she was close to getting what she truly desired. She wouldn't want to jeopardize her plan. But it was hard to be unconcerned about the amount of smoke coming from the forges. Or the blacksmiths who worked day and night within the village proper.

As they parted, Kellan gave her a nod instead of a hug before he and Sloan disappeared into the crowd. She was certain his worry was hidden by the scarf covering his face. Their small retinue, including Éardrom and Dorcha fae, left with the scouts, their group spreading out to prepare.

She and Chartow waited until the sun was nearing the center of the sky. After leaving some coins for the barkeep, they made their way to the fortress.

They reached the only checkpoint at the entrance gate of the fortress. The guard who met them gave a short bow. "I'll take you to our general, Your Highness."

Chartow raised his nose in the air, a small smirk on his face. She remained at the ready while they were led into a wide-open space where soldiers moved through their training regimen in the never-ending sun. Swords clashed. Arrows hit targets. Fire engulfed hay dummies. Others marched.

Felicity's stomach began to twist and turn. Even with all of their strategizing, every fiber of her body screamed to turn around and return to Éardrom immediately.

A bell tolled and the clang and magic stopped. What once had been organized turned into chaos of laughter and patting backs as the soldiers dispersed. That was their signal. They had one hour before their main exit filled again with training recruits.

Lord Chartow glanced at her again, giving a knowing smile. The only re-assurance she would get. Four of their own guards had escorted them into the fortress built within the caves of the red-stone mountain. They were surrounded by thick rock with no way out but the way they came in. According to the resources her father had on the fortress, there was a maze of tunnels built throughout the mountainside which no one truly mastered unless they had been trained to do so. Felicity memorized every turn, repeating the steps in her head as they walked. *Through the gated stone wall that enclosed the courtyard entrances to the caves. Down a long hall with only two obvious off-shoots, and then the third door on the left.* She counted six guards decked out in armor and strapped tight with weapons as they were led down the fire lit cave.

They were deposited in a room, the guard who brought them closing the door behind him. Felicity took in the long wooden table and the six chairs that surrounded it. Another door was at the back of the room next to tapestries that hung from the walls. It was simple. No other adornments.

Concern curled around her chest. She wouldn't be so worried if the advisor had listened to reason and stayed with the others. But Lord Chartow had assured her that he understood the risk and told her to worry about herself. Which only made her concerns grow.

The doors flew open, and a general Felicity remembered as a trusted ally to Roald and Marquette strode in with two guards who stopped at the door. "Your Highness, I apologize for the wait."

He didn't bow. Nor show any sign of deference as he walked around the table, barely glancing their way before stopping at the head chair of the long table. "Please take a seat."

"General McGrath, is this how your princess is welcomed?" Chartow glared.

Felicity spared him a quick glance, frowning at the venom in his words. The lord's gaze remained pinned on the general in front of them.

"We are quite busy and hadn't expected you." The general gave a pathetic bow that was more out of decorum than respect.

"Yes, you do seem busy. Is there a reason for it?" Felicity took the seat offered.

The general waved his hand, and the guard nearest to the door opened it to allow in servers carrying trays of food and drink and placed them at the table. No one reached for a plate as the general cleared his throat. "A surplus of metal was found in one of the mines. Some will be shipped to Aer, another load to Domhain, if I remember correctly. The rest was allocated for our smiths to start work on right away."

"I see." Felicity folded her hands on the table. "We're here to discuss the fact that, beyond Lady Avyanna Solfire, no other member of the realm has seen fit to arrive at court. Is there a reason for that?"

The general shrugged. "We have no need for politics. Seeing as you ensured the death of our recent advisor, I suppose you have the right to pick a new leader." His glare thinned on Felicity.

"She is the princess whose family was cursed by the previous monarchs, so I would expect you to be respectful." Chartow straightened at his warning. "Delegates are put forth by the realm before the council makes the final decision." He spoke to General McGrath like a disobedient child. "We need names so we can properly make a decision. If you're unable to help us, then point us in the direction of those who can. Tine is much a part of Talamh as all the other realms."

This wasn't going as planned. The air was heavy.

"It was." The sinister voice grated along Felicity's spine. The second door had opened on silent hinges, but the sound of her heeled boots was all too familiar—as familiar as that voice that faked unattainable perfection. "Now Tine's free to make their own decisions."

Chartow rushed to his feet. Felicity's magic spurred to the tips of her fingers, but she sat outwardly unmoved—ready. Lord Chartow was the first to speak. "You're under arrest for your crimes against the crown."

Marquette smiled at Felicity. It was similar to the one the queen had worn as she had watched Lady Chartow's blood slip from her body. Had watched her struggle for her last breath before Alarian had relieved her from her pain.

That familiar pang slid around her heart at the thought of him. Hell, she wanted to rip the female's head off for what she did to her son alone. Who and what she made him into.

Fiadh stepped in beside Marquette, her dark hair pulled back behind her shoulders in a loose braid. Pale skin reminiscent of a ghost—but all Felicity could think about was the power she held but couldn't control. That inconsistency had once saved them when Alarian had stood beside his uncle and Fiadh had mistaken the ex-prince's memories for the late advisor. The memory that saved her from his father's wrath that day...when he had stepped in on her behalf.

A sharp spasm had her nearly clutching her chest. *Not him, can't think about him now.*

Marquette brow rose. "There is little you can do. Tine has given us amnesty. You can either accept that or place us on your little council. No other way around it. Besides, it wasn't I who raised my hand against the crown." She batted her eyelashes. "It was my husband—and you've already made sure to punish him for his alleged crimes. Without a trial, I might add."

Felicity's grip tightened until her knuckles were white. It would be so easy—so easy to stand up, remove the dagger from her thigh, and channel her magic into the blade before slicing the female's neck.

"Amnesty?" Chartow glanced at General McGrath. "With him? He isn't the head of the realm."

"He was at the time. You left them without an advisor. Your prince and princess's insipid plan may have weakened our alliances, but they didn't destroy them all."

Marquette must have pieced together how she and Kellan had orchestrated the deaths of their allies. Of course she had. A sensation—like claws along the spine—curved against her skull. She cleared her mind, concentrated on the traitor and kept her attention off the witch. The anger. Use the anger...

Chartow growled, "You took more than you gave. Don't try to act innocent. My wife, my bonded, died because of you."

"A shame. Such is the pain of loss during the game of love and war. Much the same, isn't it? I feel this pain as well. Watched *her* slice my love in half." With these words, Marquette looked towards Felicity. "By the way, how is my son? Has he professed his undying love to you? Or did he leave you heartbroken after you gave up everything for him?"

See me. Felicity bit her tongue.

Felicity forced back a hiss as razor sharp claws tried to break through her defenses, a sharp pain to her head.

Fiadh's grin widened. "Or did the truth finally come out?" She snickered.

Marquette laughed, the sound echoing in the room. Felicity cleared her mind, angry with herself. *Use the anger. Don't let the anger use you.*

"When Fiadh mentioned he had been by your side, I wondered if he would be brave enough to confess." As her smile lengthened, Felicity's stomach soured. "I would have loved to be there when he told you that he killed your mother."

Felicity stood now, drawing her shoulders back as she did, letting her magic slip under her skin. "He's in prison." She glared at the former queen. "Where you will be soon enough."

The female tilted her head, assessing her. "You turned on him, did you? Threw him away because he followed orders. You're so much like me. Too bad you ended up being on the wrong side."

"I'm nothing like you." Words Felicity had wanted to say since the first time the bitch had uttered them. "This amnesty won't save you forever. You've left Tine once, you'll leave it again." She checked her defenses, kept Fiadh out. Felicity knew not to allude to what they knew about the traitor's plans. They might be aware that Felicity had attempted to protect the stones, but that didn't mean they knew why.

Chartow shuffled papers into a neat pile and picked them up. "This meeting is over. You've made your decision to not have a say on the council and harboring fugitives to the crown is treason. You're aware that this could be a call to war?"

The general laughed as he made his way around his desk to stand beside the traitor queen. "Why do you think we're making so many weapons?"

Chartow growled. Felicity was surprised that they were willingly speaking aloud their treachery. Then it hit her—they didn't think Felicity and Chartow would be walking out of here alive.

Felicity nodded to their guard. A signal. The guard nodded back. "We have no reason to continue this conversation." She hoped Sloan or Kellan had found Avyanna's parents. Sloan was to search the prison if they hadn't found them elsewhere.

She started for the door, Fiadh and Marquette watched as Chartow followed. It wasn't until they almost reached the doorway that Marquette laughed. "Leaving so soon?"

The second door behind Marquette and Fiadha sprung open, and Felicity's eyes widened as a couple clasped in iron were strewn on the floor at Fiadh's feet. The female looked up, her eyes puffy and bruised but distinctly Avyanna's. The male beside her groaned but barely moved.

"**D**id you think we wouldn't discover your little spies? A weak attempt for a princess raised among a guild of assassins." The sound of steel slipping from scabbards echoed off the stone walls. "And a scout who valued his life more than his integrity. That was before we killed him. You thought it would be that easy? That you would just walk out of here?"

Felicity's grin widened. "Of course not." Before any of the Tine guards could make a move, she called her magic to the clear pendant at her neck. Marquette and Fiadh hadn't seen this trick yet, the former busy calling the guards to attack.

But Chartow and their guards had been prepared, running before her light spread. One guard towards the prone bodies of Avyanna's parents while the others fought off the Tine soldiers. Chartow ran towards the wall, cowering. Thankfully he stayed along the perimeter and kept his eyes downcast. She didn't want him in harm's way and if he rushed to the door, he'd have met the guards now pouring in.

The Tine guards closest to them screamed as they were blinded by starlight, heat burning their skin. Others fought through the room while Felicity rushed towards Avyanna's parents to assist the guard, removed her dagger from her thigh and sliced the neck of the first Tine soldier who passed through her light's defenses.

There was a splatter of blood as the Éardrom guard who had run to help Avyanna's parents screamed out, a sword through his gut. Felicity didn't stop. Vengeance. Anger. She grasped onto familiar emotions. Honed it into the weapon she'd trained to be. Shadows moved through the guards, but Felicity dodged them, using her light to feign them back. She was getting close. Just a little—

Fiadh was faster. She thrust her hand out and Felicity felt a rush of pain slice through her skull. She gripped her head with one hand trying to ease the vise-like grip on her skull. "What the—"

Her light snapped out of existence.

"You're not the only one with secrets." Fiadh smiled. "Princess of Starlight. Your mind is already a mess. Pieces missing. So many questions." Her hand turned to a fist, and Felicity screamed as the pulsing ache turned into a pounding spasm. "No wonder it's hard to see who you are. The curse must have jumbled your thoughts before. But the missing things—"

"Shut up," Felicity yelled.

A scream wrecked the air, and the pain stopped. Felicity fell to the ground, gasping for breath, her head pulsing from the remnants of pain.

Fiadh faltered a step, a spear through her stomach. Marquette's shadows rushed back as she bent over her fallen friend.

Chartow formed in her clouded vision, rushing towards her. "Run."

Felicity reached the fae couple, grasped the female's hand and pulled. Avyanna's mother staggered to her feet. Chartow grabbed the male and forced him up. A loud groan from the male drew Marquette's attention, who screamed profanities as they ran down the hall. One of their guards took Avyanna's mother from Felicity's arms and she ushered them forward. With her allies running towards the door, Felicity sent bursts of heat behind towards their opponents.

She was barely cognizant as she kept their enemies at bay—her body working on muscle memory. She rolled out of the way of weapons, sent spirals of heated light towards oncoming guards, used glass to pivot attacks, dodged fireballs, and parried with her dagger in hand. Blood coated Felicity's hands and clothes. The stench of death, burnt skin, and fire was stifling.

Chartow used his free hand to cut off air flow and swirled magic around the room, causing upheaval as they fought their way out. The guard carrying Avyanna's mother fell with an arrow through his shoulder. Avyanna's mother broke away just in time before he was engulfed in flames. With a stumbling half run, she made her way toward the exit. Felicity sent a throwing knife into the throat of a soldier who tried to stop her.

Another Éardrom guard was about to open the double doors to the courtyard when a sword sliced through his gut. Their third guard tore through his comrade's killer with dark magic. He started to take up where his ally left off, Felicity and Chartow moving to catch up, when the doors were ripped open, and Felicity called her light to her pendant in preparation for another attack.

Kellan stood at the entrance with two guards at his back, fury in his gaze.

"Lights out," she called to him.

Kellan pulled Chartow who was still assisting Avyanna's father through the door. Then he sent a rushing wave of air down the hall, extinguishing the lights and blocking Marquette from using her shadows as he scooped Avyanna's mother into his arms. The guard urged Felicity forward, slicing his blade into an oncoming attacker.

They broke into the courtyard where Felicity's light would have little impact, even with the setting sun. But her light's heat—she could still use that. Nine Tine soldiers rushed towards them. Three had bows drawn, fire arrows nocked and aimed. Heart racing—she grasped the anger. Held it. Controlled it.

Protectiveness bubbled in her gut. She needed to get them out—get Kellan out. Talamh needed him. With a deep breath, she rushed after her brother.

A flamed arrow slipped by Felicity. A scream had her twisting to find Avyanna's father who had been hit in the thigh. He screamed in pain. Felicity turned and sent a slice of starlight through two more arrows before they reached their target, breaking them off from their trajectory as the pieces clattered to the ground, smoke lifting from the extinguished fire.

She ran towards Kellan who was in the middle of a double sword fight with two guards. With a call to her magic, she aimed the light towards the blade glinting from her wrist—the gloves she had been gifted by Lian and Dimitri.

It would take precision. A tactical move she had been practicing but hadn't perfected.

One of Kellan's blades crashed to the ground with a sickening clatter. He waved his hand to extinguish his burnt palm, red blisters visible from the distance. Then he pivoted, his sword meeting one blade while he dodged the second. One blade against two.

It was now or never.

With her palm up, Felicity pressed two fingers into the center of her glove, engaging the mechanism of the weapon. She released her magic and it caught the two blades as they flew. Powered by the heat of her starlight, one impaled the gut of the first Tine soldier while the other went through the front and out the back of the second soldier's shoulder. Kellan didn't wait, landing killing blows.

The high pitch sound of metal swiped through the air. Felicity dodging the sword just in time, twisting out of its path with her own blade in hand, ready to parry the next attack. Advisor Heavin glared at her.

Felicity's grin was feral. She had wanted this opportunity. "I warned you."

He swung his sword towards her again, and he landed a nick at her bicep before she could dodge it completely. He laughed as the wound swelled with blood. "For some reason, I don't believe you're a threat."

She assessed him. Smiled. Then ran right at him. He squealed as he dodged to the right—the direction she expected him to go. This time he was too slow. She grabbed hold of his wrist and the hilt of his sword. Then plunged her favorite dagger right into his gut, the squelch of blood and gasp from his lips a welcomed sound.

Heavin's eyes widened, a choking gurgle as he looked down between them. She dug the blade in deeper and twisted. "You should have." She called the light, concentrated it towards the metal and then sliced the dagger upwards, the heat of her magic making it easy to tear through muscle and bone.

A bell tolled.

Shit. Shit.

Yells sounded. They needed to get out of here.

She didn't wait to see Heavin's last breath but assessed her surroundings. Chartow pressed his hand against his bicep, blood seeping between his fingers.

Their remaining guard and Kellan were protecting Avyanna's parents as they neared the exit. Four soldiers and two bowmen remained above the gate.

She ran, grabbing Chartow as she passed him. "Hurry," she hissed.

Shadows cast from the walls curved at her back. Felicity turned in time to shine her light at them, breaking through the dark wisps as she made her way to Kellan's side.

Marquette appeared with her arms raised, her face red with rage. "Close the gates," she ordered.

The Tine guards rushed at them, other towards the mechanism to close the gates. The creak and groan of the metal gears as it closed was like a countdown to their doom.

Felicity looked at their remaining allies. Blood dripped from Chartow's injury, Avyanna's mother could barely stand on her own, and Avyanna's father hung between Kellan and their remaining guard. The door was right behind them. Kellan was here which meant that Sloan waited for them at the portal. Their escape.

Felicity's rage fueled her magic as she sent bolt after bolt of heated light at their enemy. They screamed as the starlight seared their skin. Whatever she could do to slow them down. With the last clank, the gate closed. No way out.

Marquette was joined by General McGrath. Shadows rose around the perimeter. The Tine soldiers' palms were engulfed in flames.

Surrounded. A useless, closed door at their back.

Shit...shit.

Felicity thought of Alarian—how helpful his magic would be then. She used her pendant to slice starlight through a shadow stretching towards Kellan. She whirled to cut off another but missed. The jagged shadow struck Chartow in the throat. With a gasp and gurgle of air and blood, he fell. Avyanna's mother screamed, trying to close the wound as the male choked. The remaining guard leaned down and pulled her away. Avyanna's father stumbled, his wife's name on his lips as he tried to pull himself from Kellan's grip.

Felicity dropped to Chartow's convulsing body. "I'm sorry." She pressed her hand around his throat to stanch the bleeding. Frightened eyes found hers. Chartow mouthed inaudible words, and Felicity felt that familiar prick of tears. "I'm sorry I couldn't save you. That I couldn't save her."

Chartow grabbed her arm. Squeezed. Held her stare as the fear drifted away and a small smile tilted his lips. Felicity tried to swallow past the emotions lodged in her throat. Then he stilled.

"Felicity."

Shadows writhed on the sandy ground. Reached for them at all angles. *No—shit, no.*

Without a second thought, Felicity stood. Took a step forward and called it all—forced her magic to her fingertips. "Close your eyes," she ordered her brother and allies.

She held the pendant in her palm, feeling the pain as her magic ripped through her and engulfed their enemies. She used the shields that hung against the fortress wall, the weapons and armor, everything around them to send shards of light. The shadows were forced away, writhing backwards from her bright starlight. She felt her body weaken from the expulsion of magic. Exhaustion and lightheadedness begged her to stop. The light sputtered. Her limbs were heavy, muscles ached.

Draining. She was going to drain. But first they needed to get through that gate.

So much screaming, the sound echoing in her ears. Kellan, yelling her name broke through the din. She whirled around to find Sloan in the center of a dark portal, beckoning them through. He took Avyanna's father from Kellan. "Hurry."

"You weren't meant to come," growled Kellan.

"Good thing I did." He passed Avyanna's father to awaiting arms—all they could see of the figure within the portal. "Heard the bell was off schedule."

Her weakening muscles slowed. Her magic shattered. As her arm fell, the pendant bounced off her chest, and the light snuffed out.

Marquette screamed orders. Felicity didn't look behind but heard the advancing soldiers as she ran to catch up. An arrow zipped past and disappeared into the portal.

Each one of her steps felt heavier than her last. Her head pulsed. Wind whipped around her as Kellan came to her side, grabbed hold of her and wrapped her arm over his shoulder while bracketing his arm around her waist. The battle around her was too close. The cavernous dark portal too far away.

Her legs folded, her body unable to hang on any longer. A scream sounding very much like Alarian wrecked through her brain as a different type of darkness took her.

Chapter 44

Felicity

Felicity's head ached. Scratch that—her entire body ached. She moaned, gripping her forehead as she woke—

She bolted upright with a gasp, her head spun and she pinched her eyes closed.

"You're all right," Avyanna said, the sound of liquid hitting porcelain coming from Felicity's left. "You're lucky. Kellan said you nearly drained to death."

Felicity leaned up on her elbows and peeked one eye open. Dawn light came through the paned balcony doors. Her warm quilt was wrapped around her. Back in the palace. She was home. A glass of water was placed in front of her. "Thank you." Her throat hurt, her voice scratchy. "Your parents?"

"Alive. My father has a lot of inner damage from Marquette's shadows, but I think after some rest I can finish healing him." Avyanna stalked to the door and uttered inaudible words before she returned.

"You should be with them," Felicity murmured, noting the dark circles under her friend's eyes. She gulped down the water, parched. It felt good on her sore throat.

"I was. Until about an hour ago. Kellan told me to go to bed and he'd sit with my parents for me. I couldn't sleep though." Avyanna crossed her arms, staring at her with an unreadable expression Felicity couldn't recall seeing on the female before.

"How long has it been?" She rubbed her temples, trying to relieve the tension.

"Three days."

Damn. That was longer than she'd hoped. The shortness in Avyanna's voice had her looking up at her friend. "Are you angry with me?"

"Worried." Avyanna sat back down. "So are your brother and father. Kellan said you pretty much gave everything to get them out without even considering yourself. Drained—and nearly to death I might add."

The images of the shadows as they sliced through Chartow's throat came unbidden. "Chartow didn't make it. We lost most of our guards. Those shadows—" She breathed a sigh. "I had to get Kellan out—"

Avyanna shook her head. "And you didn't think you were important? I don't like to be told that my friend and future sister-in-law is unconscious. That she almost died again."

"For Kellan. For your parents." Felicity was surprised at Avyanna's response. "I gave everything for them, as I know Kellan would do for me. Where's this coming from?"

Avyanna looked at her hard, tears collecting in her lashes. "Alarian was screaming."

"What?" Her mouth went dry.

"Guards rushed from the prison to find me." She wiped her eyes roughly. "They thought he needed a healer. This bond—he could feel your emotions. He screamed you were dying and was inconsolable. Why didn't you tell me?" She frowned, brow furrowed.

"I—"

But Avyanna wasn't done. "His pain—it tore him apart that he wasn't there to help. It tore me apart seeing him that way. To know that you were in danger, and there was nothing I could do about it." Avyanna met her gaze and held it. "He keeps saying he deserves it, Felicity. Don't you think you need to find out if that's true? If anything, to put him out of his misery."

Felicity's chest cracked open again. She broke the stare first and looked down at her hands. "I'll take care of it."

Avyanna snapped her mouth closed. "I'm sorry. That was so inconsiderate of me. I know this cannot be easy. That night was—" She shook her head.

Felicity stared at her hands.

The female twisted the ring on her finger. "I was terrified I was going to lose you. Not knowing...and with a war coming. I should have gone. I'm a healer. I could have helped and should have since they are my parents."

Avyanna shuddered, burying her face in her hands. Her sobs had Felicity leaning across and pulling her friend into her arms. Her body had moved on its own accord, as if this was common practice.

"You were needed here."

She hiccuped, looking up at Felicity. This time she really took in her friend. Her hair was in a messy bun upon her head, wisps hanging at odd angles. She wore no cosmetics and judging by the smudges of dirt and wrinkles, she had slept in the dress she currently wore—if she had slept at all. "I can't do that again. You aren't leaving me behind. Not if I can actually be of use. Maybe there would have been less loss."

Felicity gripped her tighter. "We never thought less of you, you must know that?"

Avyanna pulled away, wiping her eyes with the back of her hand. "I don't care. Next time, I'm coming along. Do I have your permission, Princess?"

She blinked in surprise, then laughed. "You never, ever, need my permission. What makes you think you did?"

"I—" Avyanna shrugged. "Well, technically speaking I do need the permission of the royal family."

"Not from me." Felicity shook her head. "And if Kellan has—"

"What?" The door opened, Kellan entering a step ahead of their father who carried a tray.

Felicity muttered under her breath about the fact that he didn't knock as Avyanna rushed to her feet. "My parents?"

"Resting. Your mother kicked me out and told me to check on you, and yet our room was empty." He shook his head. "Figured I'd find you here."

Avyanna glanced at Felicity then back to him. "I'm going to be a field medic. I'll meet with your current team tomorrow and find out what I need to know."

Kellan chuckled before her words registered. Silence expanded as his eyes widened at the seriousness in her expression. "Oh... well, if that's what you want to do, I support you all the way."

"Good." Avyanna's shoulders relaxed as she glanced at the ring on her finger. "I wouldn't want to have to throw this at you."

Kellan was across the room in a breath and wrapped his arms around his fiancée. "Don't threaten such hurtful things. Marquette and Roald may have silenced you—but you should know that's not me. Or us. Right?"

Avyanna smiled and nodded.

King Bastien chuckled. "Glad we got that taken care of—now, where is my girl?" He walked across the room, a tray with a bowl of soup and a roll in hand. Such a common gesture, yet it warmed Felicity's heart even as her thoughts drifted back to Alarian. Back to what he must have felt. The pain she caused him. She remembered what Marquette said. *So much like me.*

She told the traitorous queen she wasn't like her, but the first thing she did was let him be imprisoned. Then had sat too long on those memories. She'd ignored what she needed to do for long enough. He didn't deserve it, even if the truth would hurt.

"I want to hear every detail of what happened in that room." Her father's voice brought her back to the present. "With Chartow gone, you're our only source. The remaining guard was only able to give details for your escape."

Felicity sipped the broth, sighing at the warmth against her scratchy throat. Then, with a deep breath, she relived the entire events. The general's lazy disobedience. Marquette and Fiadh's appearance. The threats. Kellan took over the story once they reached the courtyard and she was thankful to take a break from talking.

Felicity saw Avyanna grip tighter to Kellan at certain parts of their story. While this happened, Felicity ate. "How many did you and Sloan get out?"

"A little less than two hundred. Many children were orphaned since Tine was one of the places Marquette and Roald hit for mine workers. We got as many of them out as we could, but it doesn't feel like nearly enough."

Felicity's stomach churned. "We didn't know?"

"Not the extent. It doesn't help that the realm has been hiding so much from us since the curse broke. They took advantage of our blind spots." Bastien sighed. "We have a lot of work to do."

When her last spoonful of soup was gone, the crusty bread consumed, she met her brother's gaze. "I need the memories and letter."

Kellan searched her face, then sighed at whatever he found there. "Are you sure now is the right time? The memories didn't treat you well last time."

Felicity cringed at the reminder. "I might have made a mistake then. Should have read the letter first."

He bit back a laugh—she could see it in the twitch of his mouth. "I'll bring them to you." He stood, squeezing Avyanna's shoulder as he left.

Her father cleared his throat. "Are you certain you're ready for this? I might not know enough, but I know the male is important to you. We're in no rush to move forward on his trial. And your mother—"

"Have you spoken with him?" Felicity couldn't help asking.

Bastien shook his head. "No. It—I have only listened to Kellan's recounts. He'd been a quiet youngling when I met him and his parents. Not the description of the male who your brother speaks of."

There was sadness in her father's eyes. Then she remembered that it wasn't just her and Kellan who had been lost—not just the two of them who had suffered. "It must have been hard all these years. Knowing, but unable to stop it. I was oblivious all this time, but you had known what was at stake."

She was beginning to understand more as to why the Countess had removed her memories. She became strong in the absence of trauma. Was able to deal with it now even if it occasionally landed her unconscious or unable to breathe.

"I can't face him." Felicity's father lowered his gaze. "If what he claims is true...I will rip him limb from limb." The growl in his voice held more anger than his stance. "I've lost my partners twice now. And while they each gave me you and Kellan, I'd be lying if I didn't admit I worry that I can't protect those I love."

Felicity flung the blankets aside and wrapped her father in her arms. He shuddered in her hold. She knew exactly what he felt, his words similar to her own emotions regarding the male in prison. But she didn't voice them.

Kellan returned and after putting the envelope aside, he silently placed a hand on each of their shoulders. It was Avyanna who broke the silence. "Sometimes we must realize that it's not in our control to save everyone, but it's in our control to love them as long as they are here." She met Felicity's gaze and held it. She nodded at her friend over her father's shoulder.

They retreated from each other, Kellan settling beside his fiancée, Felicity back in her bed. Her brother placed the packet beside her. "When do you plan to take them?"

"I haven't decided. But I have made another decision."

"About?" Bastien's brow rose.

"I'm leaving for Scáth. We need information about Marquette. Her history is the key to tell us which veil will be opened." It was a long shot, but she didn't have a choice. "There is a reason why they're observing us, and I think they are wondering what moves we'll make. I want to create a relationship with them, if possible."

Kellan scoffed. "Nope. Not a good idea. You're still healing and you need to rest."

"Do you have a good reason this time?" she asked, resisting rolling her eyes.

"I just said my reason. You're healing. It doesn't have to be you all the time."

Felicity couldn't resist now and rolled her eyes. "Actually, Ciana said that I was the one who had to go."

"That's beside the point. We don't—"

"She's going." King Bastien cut him off and settled deeper into his chair.

Felicity's brow rose as did her brother's.

"Father..." Kellan started.

"You're quick to protect her. I understand. But she's capable, and I don't think Scáth will harm her. We need to know if we can rely upon them. And sooner rather than later."

"Where were they when the coup was raised? They didn't protect us then, and they were meant to," Kellan ground out the words in bitter bites.

Bastien glanced between his two children. "They remained out of politics for a reason. My mother was their ally, but my father broke their trust and used their services in a backhanded way. They didn't have a reason to help us. Now they are interested. We need to be open to their offer. My mother always said that this was one alliance she regretted taking for granted. I won't make the same mistake."

"It's dangerous," Kellan grumbled. "They could be planning something."

King Bastien shook his head. "Were they present for the traitor king? Did they sit beside him and Marquette?"

Kellan's gaze lowered. "No."

"You can't make Scáth do anything they don't want to do. Felicity is correct—they are observing, wanting assurance we aren't corrupt or coming with vengeance in our hearts. The only way we can rule now is to protect our people and the continent." King Bastian met Felicity's gaze. "If they will listen to anyone, it's Felicity. They've made that clear."

"She just came back unconscious from the last mission. Are you sure this is a good idea? Especially when she's about to return her memories." Avyanna looked between them all, concern etched in her features.

Felicity looked at the packet by her bed. "I'm certain." Because no matter what was in those memories and letter, she knew she would need to leave. To put some separation between herself and this kingdom—between her and *him*.

Chapter 45

Felicity

*D*ear Alarian,

    It is hard to admit how much we all had a part in who Felicity is now and could have been if there hadn't been a coup. I meant it when I said that only the one who brought her here could return her memories. It was an agreement that you also do not remember making with me those fifty years ago.

You were so young, torn apart, and justifiably angry back then. I hate what these memories may do to you now, but we had an understanding. I hope you listened and didn't open this letter until the night before your return. And I hope that once you realize what is within these vials are not only Felicity's memories, but one of your own, that you're able to forgive yourself. I manipulated you in a way that night. Not that I wanted to, but it would set in course a future much more important for us all. For the realms. And while the guild never chooses sides, we are about protecting the place we call home.

We took your memories for specific reasons—and maybe one day we'll have an opportunity to explain them to you. For Felicity, we needed certain moments removed from her mind. In particular, that night. Otherwise it would be tainted by time. By thoughts. By experiences. Her life would have become something solely other than it is now. In the end, I know it will work out as it should. I've seen it. Trust in that above all else.

Sincerely,

The Countess

P.S. As a note, take them slowly. It allows the memories to settle as they should in proper order. I assume Felicity will have learned that lesson after the last time.

Felicity had said she would wait for her brother who was worried about her facing her memories alone. For her father who had wanted to be by her side. As she reached for the vial, there was a gentle knock at the door. Meira didn't wait for an answer, walking in with a plate of chocolate cake. "Thought you might need a little something sweet."

At the sight of the dessert, tears threatened but Felicity fought them back.

Meira paused, looking over Felicity as she sat poised at the edge of the bed, reaching for the packet.

"How do you do it?" Felicity straightened. "How do you know when I've woken, or moved?"

A corner of Meira's mouth quirked, and she settled the plate down on a table by the fireplace. "Magic."

"Well, I assumed." Felicity reached for her robe that had been left draped over a nearby chair. She made her way to the chair to eat. It might be a good idea to have food in her system first. "You don't have to tell me."

"I'm a Domhain Fae. Earth is my magic. The blankets you sleep in have been mended, cleaned, and sewn by me. There is a touch of my magic in them."

Felicity's eyes widened. "Meaning?"

"Meaning that I can tell when someone is near waking by the shift of the sheets." Meira didn't look at her during this explanation, hiding her blush. "But nothing more. It doesn't give me details of their private matters. Just when someone is getting in and then wakes in the morning. That's it."

"You knew I was up late and out of my bed when I first arrived here, didn't you?"

Meira sniffed. "Of course."

"And you didn't mention it to the traitor king or others? Didn't find it strange?"

"I found it curious. But I figured out you were a spy the night they believed someone broke into the castle, and I went straight to Alarian with that information." She winced at the words.

"Why?" Felicity glanced at the packet, and then at the chocolate cake. Now it was her turn to be unable to look at the handmaiden.

"Because I know he put you under my watch for a reason. I didn't trust the king or guards with such information. He told me never to speak a word of it. So, I didn't." Meira held a plate in front of Felicity's face. "Now eat up."

She didn't need to be told twice, even if her stomach twisted at the thought of her soon-to-be returned memories. Last time had not been an experience she particularly wanted to repeat. It seemed the Countess had known Felicity wouldn't be able to face her letter before running headfirst into the past. Meira hummed as she walked the room, making the bed and keeping herself busy. Once Felicity was done eating, she stared at the waiting envelope.

"Alarian is in prison for killing my mother." She hated the words, and the way they made her feel. She stood, walked across the room, retrieved the packet then looked towards Meira. "Do you believe him?"

Meira straightened. "I do."

Felicity blinked. "What?"

The handmaiden's shoulders slumped. "That boy has always carried a heavy burden. First it was his parents' expectations and their disappointment. Then the challenge of rising above them to do what he knew was best. So, knowing what I do about him, I believe he may have ended your mother's life—but I have no doubt that he's being harder on himself than anyone would be and that there is more to the situation than it seems."

Felicity removed her memories from the envelope. "There is only one way to find out."

"What's that?" Meira glanced at the vial.

"Memories. My memories from that night and many nights before. The truth." She looked at the female who had cared for her the last time she'd woken ill—who had cared for her many times, simply because the male had asked her to. "Will you stay with me?"

It felt right asking this of her. Wanting her close. Meira knew Alarian as no one else ever would. Had been beside him in Scáth as a child, as an advisor's son when he could never rise to the unrealistic expectations of his parents. Through all his good moments and his bad.

"Of course, milady." Meira took a seat. "I'm right here."

Felicity wiped her eyes, fighting back the tears weighing on her lashes. With a pop, she removed the stopper. This time, the contents smelled different—instead of grunge and death, the fragrance was a mix of spring rain, the lemon scents of Saol, roses, and sunlight that made her instantly think of her father. A heavy sigh. A quick breath, and Felicity took a small sip, sitting back into her chair as she did.

Immediately, her mind calmed, collected, drifted. Pieces settled, not jagged and unfettered like before. When it felt right, she took another small sip and the memories filled in blank spaces, some connecting pieces, others still open. She repeated the process four more times, counting breaths in between.

Then, as the last piece clicked into place, Felicity searched through memories of her family. She wanted to pause to recollect times too long forgotten, but knew now wasn't the time. Her head ached, but it wasn't as bad as it had been the last time she did this. Every experience she needed was finally in her mind and she had to get used to the amount of time her memories had been gone.

It was the last of the new memories, but she found it. Closed her eyes. Let her mind grasp hold as the past unfurled...

The grass tickled her legs as her mother ran with Felicity held tightly in her arms. She gripped around her mother's neck, pressing further into her body. She wanted to run, not to be a burden, but her mother wouldn't hear of it. Silenced her requests. "Hush, My Little Star."

Felicity whimpered, the echoing of hoofbeats grew louder behind them. Even off the beaten path, they were being followed. It had taken days. They thought they had outrun their hunters—but it seemed the predators would not let their prey escape. "Mama."

Her mother stumbled and Felicity flew from her arms. Her head hit a rock. Her body jarred on impact with the hard ground and grass.

Her mother crawled to her, pulling her into her arms. "Sorry, sweetie. Shhh..."

Felicity hadn't realized it, but she was crying, a sob building in her chest. Her mother pressed her close, soothing her. "Hush..." She searched around their surroundings, then she pointed. "Look, that tower. We can make it."

A horse whinnied, the clip clop of trotting hooves on the nearby dirt road. Felicity and her mother lowered in the grass. A male shouted, "Did you lose their trail?" The voice was crass, harsh.

Kaliana pressed Felicity closer, glancing at the tower before lowering herself further into the thick, long grass.

"No. They're close." This voice was more of a snarl. "What do you have, youngling?"

Felicity muffled a whimper into her mother's dress and pressed her eyes closed. The hunters were close. And the tower was so far. Grass tickled her exposed arms, and she wished to become one with it. That it would encompass her and her mother to protect them from the scary soldiers.

A voice answered, less jarring than the others. "Spread out."

The sound of riders dismounting horses filled the air.

Her mother glanced between the hunters and the tower. It looked nearly as scary with its iron gate and dark windows. Her mother leaned in and whispered, "Stay here."

Felicity gripped her mother tighter. "No."

The queen, her mother, was crying. Felicity knew that didn't mean anything good. Not since they had run. Not since they had no clue if Father, if Kellan, were safe. Not once had her mother cried—until now.

"You're going to run towards that tower as soon as you get a chance. Once they're distracted. Understood?" Her mother gripped Felicity's arms, searching her gaze. "Please, Little Star, you must."

"No, Mama, I'm too scared. I need you. Don't go."

Kaliana pressed her lips to her daughter's forehead, pulled her close, the taste of salty tears slid against Felicity's lips. It only made her cry harder. "Not without you," she whispered harshly.

Her mother held her face in her hands. "You're brave. You're wise—the most beautiful gift I could ever receive. And I need you to do this for me. To remember that, understood?"

She wanted to fight her mother, but the danger was closer now. She clawed to hold her tight. But her mother only kissed each hand as she removed them from her body. "Brave." She spoke the word as a command and with a wave of her hand, the roots extended, the grasses wrapped around her torso and arms, then muffled her mouth. Felicity could only silently cry as they wrapped her tightly, holding her in place. Her mother crawled on her hands and knees, disappearing into the grass. Felicity saw shifts of starlight and grass as she laid on her back staring at the sky. Even as she wiggled in an attempt to fight off her mother's magic, she knew to remain quiet.

"Here," a male called—and Kaliana screamed.

Felicity froze, no longer fighting the grass that held her in place.

One of the hunters passed Felicity, who remained unseen in his rush to the others. She breathed a sigh of relief.

"Where's that brat of yours?" the same male growled.

Someone spat, and Felicity heard the crack of bone, the scream of pain her mother couldn't bite back.

Her eyes watered as though she had been the one who had been hit.

"Where is she?" This time he yelled.

Felicity pinched her eyes shut, willing her mother's magic to let her go.

Another scream. Another crack. The magic loosened its hold. But instead of fighting them off completely, she gripped her hands over her ears and drew her legs close. She couldn't move—wasn't able to be brave. Not like her mother asked.

More screams, yelling, the breaking of bones, the squelch of blood—sounds that no child should ever have to hear. Yet she did. No matter how much she tried to tune them out. To disappear. To draw on some semblance of bravery to save her mother.

A sudden graze to her shoulder and Felicity flinched. A hand clamped over her mouth, and her eyes widened on a fiery red-headed youngling who stood over her, his attention pinned away to where she couldn't see. "I've got you," he whispered.

She bit his palm and he hissed. She tried to pull away and escape, but he pinned her to the ground, green eyes meeting hers. The hold over her mouth didn't falter. "Trust me. Please."

There was something in his gaze. Something she couldn't understand, but as if on its own accord, her body stiffened—she didn't fight him, didn't move.

He sighed. "Good. Now stay here. Once I can, we'll get you out of here. All right?"

She nodded against his hold.

He straightened, letting her go and made his way through the brush. She turned and crouched, remaining lower than the reeds of grass to watch. He circled the crowd. It wasn't until he was outside of the perimeter of the hunters that Felicity caught sight of her mother's body. A limp form hung between the two men, and Felicity had to bite back her sob. The scream built up in her throat.

"That's enough. She's not going to talk—not that she can now anyway." The red-headed youngling pointed at two of the soldiers. "She probably left the youngling behind somewhere. Trail back and search along the road and see if she crawled into the grass."

Felicity watched as the two hunters listened, and then the red-haired youngling turned his gaze on her mother. Hope rose within her. This youngling would save them—

"At least you will leave this world knowing you didn't give up your daughter." Shadows erupted from the male before streaming down the queen's throat. Her body slumped. The predators holding her dropped her like a sack of grain.

Felicity froze. She stared at the crumpled form. Willed her to get up. To attack. But neither happened. Her mother, the queen of the realms, didn't move. The mother that used to hold her, play with her, brush her hair...

But she still couldn't bring herself to react—to run towards that tower as she was instructed. Fists formed at her side. Gripped the grass underneath her. She wanted to tear them apart one by one to get to her mother's side.

The youngling gave orders she didn't hear. The last of the guards went searching in the opposite direction. The redhead leaned over and picked up her mother then she watched as he whispered words she couldn't understand. Then with a wisp of shadows, he disappeared. Hope clamped her heart. Was she alive? Had the youngling saved her? She still didn't move. Waited. He'd come back with her and then she and her mother would run.

It was sometime later that she sat there staring at the spot her mother's body had been. When that hand clamped once again over her mouth this time, she didn't meet his gaze but searched.

When he realized she wasn't going to scream, he moved in front of her. Tears glistened in green eyes. "I'm so sorry." He shook his head. "I wanted to save her. I swear." His tears were real.

Felicity stared at him. "Where is she?" This wasn't what she had hoped. He had taken her mother from her. Was meant to bring her to Felicity. The way he spoke—

A shudder moved through her entire body. Her mother was dead. And she was sitting in a field with the youngling that killed her.

"She was broken." He swallowed. "Suffering. I'm—" He shook his head. "There is no way you could forgive me. I know that. I shouldn't even say such words." He removed his cloak from his shoulders, wrapped it around her body. Blood spotted the fabric. Her mother's blood.

He glanced around and then picked her up before he straightened. He stumbled a little, catching his balance with her extra weight. "We have to hurry."

She stared at the splatters of blood. Fear locked her joints. Grief stole her voice. Everything was numb...but hurt at the same time.

Without a word, he walked her to the tower gate. The male glanced behind on multiple occasions to ensure they weren't followed. The gate was open slightly, and he hissed when he knocked it open further with his elbow—but iron never bothered her. She couldn't bring herself to care if he was harmed.

Felicity looked up, transfixed by their destination. The building itself was dark—foreboding. A lone spire that looked as though it had been plucked from a much larger structure then dropped here. Dark windows were barely visible amongst the lichen-touched stone. No adornments, etchings, or symbols. No lights or lanterns to welcome. As though it was abandoned.

Before the red-haired youngling could knock, the door opened. He stepped back, his grip tightening on Felicity. A figure appeared—not a guard as Felicity had expected, but a woman with raven black hair, a sharp nose, and features that resembled a beauty and a beast all at once. "What do you want?"

"She needs some place safe?" The youngling put Felicity down. Her feet wobbled, unsteady. "Please help her."

"My mother." The words scratched at her throat. "He—" Tears stung, but she couldn't bring herself to say the words.

The woman glanced briefly at Felicity. "The traitor king's son brings me his prize. Interesting?"

Felicity caught the phrase. "I'm not a prize," she snapped.

Felicity tilted her head. Took the woman in fully from this angle. She was tall and wore a pair of dark leather pants with a long coat. She was interesting and terrifying. Felicity wanted to cower—or run. But did neither.

"Ah, she has fire. You'll need that, youngling." The Countess shifted her attention back to the redhead. "What is it you seek?"

"How did you know who I was?" the youngling asked.

He killed her mother. Or saved her. His words were an apology, and he was helping her. Felicity's head was a conflict of emotions. She wanted so desperately to cry. To make it all stop. Now this woman was watching her. Observing. And she didn't know if she liked the way she looked at her.

"It doesn't matter. Now what do you expect me to do with a fae child?"

"Protect her." He shot a look over his shoulder. "I'll return when I can."

"No." The woman lifted her chin. "She can stay here. But to do so, you cannot return here until you're summoned, and there is something you must give up."

He looked down at Felicity. "Anything. But it must be quick—they'll be back, and I can't detour my party for long."

"Memories."

"What?" The youngling's eyes widened, and Felicity found herself staring up at him, confused. She should be fighting. Wanted to. Why didn't her body work?

The woman held out an empty vial. "It's simple. And they will be yours again, as will hers. But tonight, no one will remember what happened."

"What are you talking about?" He stepped back, pulling Felicity with him.

"You need her safe. We can offer that here. But to do so, you and your party will go to Scáth and settle along the outskirts of the forest within the brush. When the monster attacks, assist it with its hunt. Then my associate will arrive, retrieve your memories, and you'll return home to tell your father that you succeeded—take the queen's body as proof."

"How do you—"

"You don't have time." The woman held out a hand. "Hurry. They come now."

As if on cue, the sounds of grumbling echoed as the group started to congregate. He looked down at Felicity, before his gaze settled on the vial. "Agreed. But only if I'm allowed to return her memories to her. She has the right to face her mother's killer."

The woman's eyes shifted, and Felicity let out a small gasp as they whitened then came back into focus. A feline smile tilted her lips. "Agreed."

He took her hand in his, gave it a shake, then he stepped away. "I'll do as you ask." Shadows wrapped around him, and he disappeared.

The woman looked down at her. Felicity should probably scream now, but she stared right back. "Welcome to the Tower, Felicity."

Felicity found herself on the floor, weeping, a body holding her tight, gently petting her head. She clung to Meira as she sobbed into her robes. Clung to her as her past met her present—as she came together and fell apart. The fear, the anger, the shock, and confusion. For herself. For Alarian.

No wonder it had taken years for her to bury all emotion. To clamp them down tight—she had felt so much before. Felt it all. She gripped tighter to Meira and the handmaiden rocked her back and forth. Didn't shush her, or speak comfort, just hummed an unfamiliar song. Until she fell asleep.

Chapter 46

Felicity

Felicity wrote three letters the following day. One for Meira to show her gratitude for staying by her side while she fought off nightmares, and for staving off her family's many questions and concerns, giving her space that she desperately needed.

The second was a recount of the entire events from that evening fifty years ago. To say them aloud felt impossible—but through tears nearly dried, she wrote it all down. Gave her testimony on Alarian's nature then and now.

The third was to him. To the male in that cell for nearly eight days. Once written, she placed them in separate envelopes and wrote the names of their intended readers. She left Meira's on her bed, knowing the handmaiden would find it. After a final look in the mirror to be certain the cosmetics had hidden the bags under her eyes and her exhausted pallor, she headed towards her bedroom door. Felicity had skipped a meeting that morning for a quiet breakfast and a bath. It felt as though her tears had been wiped away with the soapy suds, a new purpose settled in the pit of her stomach and blossomed. She was ready.

She picked up the packet with the letter from the Countess' letter to Alarian when another page slipped out and fell to the floor. Her brow furrowed as she retrieved it and unfolded the parchment. It looked well used, folded and glanced over many times, creases worn.

A list in a familiar scrawl...

~~Dance~~ Whenever we get a chance because I get to have you close
~~Make you smile~~ The first one was like exploding starlight

~~Hear your laugh~~ The most infectious sound I've ever heard
~~Maybe have a little fun~~ Koselig—before the chaos, of course
~~See how committed you are to your mission~~ <u>Very</u>…maybe not?
~~Find out a secret about you~~ Soft spot for animals, strong, stubborn, guarded, loyal

I started this list before we went to Aer together. It didn't happen all at once but over time. I wanted to add to this list, but I've learned that I'm not meant to. There are no words to explain myself. No ways that can express how much I wish my past didn't affect our present. You must know that it was never my intention to hurt you. To be the cause of any pain. Maybe it was selfish of me to pass this to you, but I wanted you to know how I see you. How the world should see you. Remember that always.

- A

She refolded it and held it against her chest. He had mentioned a list that first night he'd observe her at the palace training hall. His reasoning for her to join him at the summer ball at Dimitri and Lian's manor. No tears came—only resolve as she slid the letter into the top of her dress, pressed against her heart.

Her body seemed to know where she was going as she found herself outside the door of her father's office. She knocked once and was beckoned with a gruff, "Come in."

King Bastien stood as she entered, rushing around his desk to pause in front of her.

She searched his face, noting changes she hadn't before. The wrinkles at the edge of his eyes. The scar at his throat. The peppered gray at his temples. She pinched her eyes closed as he opened his arms. And she fell into them, crying into his chest.

"I wanted to be there." There was no anger in his tone, only remorse.

Felicity tightened her arms around his frame. Tried to fight the tears, but she had no control of them. "You're here now. It needed to be Meira then."

He pulled away, holding her at arm's length, looking her over. "How do you feel?" He wiped her tear-stained cheek with his thumb.

"Better. I remember you, mother...everything." She swallowed. "I remember I used to feel deeply as a child."

"You did." He grinned. "Especially for animals."

"That stuck." She tried but failed to smile. "I think a part of me was exhausted from feeling. Was glad to have a reason not to anymore." Felicity shook her head. "I thought it was a weakness." She cringed at his knowing look. "All right, maybe I still do."

Her father chuckled and wrapped an arm around her shoulder as he ushered her towards a chair. After she took a seat, he sat across from her. "Emotions are not a weakness. If you don't mind me saying, your presence was always strong enough on its own but when you feel something—we all felt it. That's a power not many have. No one ever saw your feelings as a hindrance. And from what I've heard about you, no one would dare question that now."

"Well, Marquette and Fiadh would say differently. They don't fear me."

His brow quirked. "Judging by their reaction at Tine, I don't think that's entirely true. They want you out of the picture. That terrifies me—more than you can imagine—but also shows what you're capable of. Don't sell yourself short because you feel now."

One corner of her mouth lifted. "I'm going to try to remember that."

"Are you happy your memories are returned?" He tried to hide his concern, but Felicity noted he had the same divot between his brow as Kellan's tell.

"Yes." She made sure he heard the truth in her words. "Without a doubt."

His shoulders relaxed. "Good. I would have loved you either way, but I'm relieved you don't have to create all new memories. The ones we had, although ended in heartache, were beautiful." He winked and tapped his temple. She remembered that movement.

"You're a great father. I remember riding on your back through the forest." She looked out the window of his office towards the bluff. "We used to have picnics as a family overlooking the ocean."

Bastien's eyes glistened. "And your mother?"

Felicity's heart swelled. "She was perfect."

Bastien nodded, and Felicity could tell he was struggling to put words to his thoughts.

"She loved us all very much. I wish it ended differently." She swallowed, her attention on the corner of the garden. Ivy clung to the fence. Blossoms of white hydrangeas amidst the green. "That garden was her favorite place. To visit with friends. To sit for tea. For family dinners at dusk." A knot formed in her stomach. "My last birthday dinner was out there. Before the party, we had a private meal just the four of us."

"Yes."

"We sat on the ground among the roses and wildflowers."

Bastien reached across and took Felicity's hand into his. "You requested everyone's favorite dishes for dinner. We had beef stew for me, mashed potatoes for Kellan—"

"Roasted vegetables for mama," Felicity continued. "And chocolate cake for me." She almost choked on the words.

Bastien pinched his eyes closed, tears now falling down his face. "Even if I didn't know it would be our last meal all together, that was one of the best nights of my life."

"Mine too." Felicity met her father's gaze then. She tried not to think about the chocolate cake from only a few weeks before. A late-night visit to a kitchen.

Her father sighed and squeezed her hand. "You've come here to talk about more than the past, I can tell."

She held out the second envelope. "Yes, I have. This should have everything you need to know for his trial."

Her father hesitated before taking it. "Oh? Do you want to talk about it."

Felicity shook her head. "I've written down the entire account of that night with character references of what I know of who he is now. I hope it's enough to help with whatever decision is to be made." She fidgeted once the envelope was out of her hands. Her father could come to a very different conclusion to her memory than she did. "I'm asking for you to conduct the trial while I go to Scáth. I think it's best that I'm not here for it."

Bastien tilted his head. "We can wait."

She considered not answering him. Lying. "It needs to be done while I'm gone." Her shoulders drew back and met his gaze directly. "I love him, and I can't put those feelings aside." She waited for her father's reaction. Disappointment. But he sat quietly, listening. She swallowed and continued, "Therefore, I shouldn't be a part of the verdict. And that memory..." She shook her head. "I was honest in that letter. My accounts are fact and not based on my feelings. If I'm to stay here and watch his trial, I know I won't be able to separate the two. It's best I go."

Her father didn't seem as surprised as she thought he would be. He turned the envelope over in his hands. "How do you think he will feel about you not being here?"

It wasn't the question she had expected. She swallowed, looking down at her hands in her lap. "I hope he'll understand." She removed the second letter from her pocket. "This is for him. You can give it to him before or after the trial—your choice. If he's found guilty, I ask that you please wait until my return before any sentence is carried out."

King Bastien took the second letter. "You're putting me in a precarious situation. I don't want to disappoint you, Felicity."

"I know. That's why I must leave. But whatever is decided by the court, I'll accept." She stood, sitting no longer an option. It was time to pack. Prepare.

"When do you plan to leave?"

Her father didn't stand, his attention on both envelopes in his grasp. She reached for his shoulder, giving it a squeeze. "Tomorrow. It will take me two days to reach Scáth." Felicity had considered riding a horse over Reóta, but if Gaoth chose to join them, she'd let him. She knew the mates didn't like to be far from each other for long. Time was of the essence and the lynxes were much faster than any alternative mode of transportation. She knew how cruel separating the mates would be, so the choice would be theirs.

He nodded, finally looking up to meet her gaze. "I'm proud of you. I want to make sure you know that. Whatever is in this letter, whatever is to come—I know that you've survived much more than I can imagine."

Felicity didn't tell him that she hadn't survived. What she did in the guild wasn't even living. It was adapting and learning—it was going through motions in a direction she hadn't known to question. Because it hadn't been a choice then. Not really. Parts of her hadn't existed. But now, now she had infinite options in front of her—even with the title and her past. Alarian had helped her see that.

"Thank you." She bent to kiss the top of his head and left. Kellan was settled by the door with his back against the wall.

Felicity crossed her arms with a bemused expression. "Listening in?"

She didn't want to deal with a side comment or bicker about her choices. He nodded, pushing himself off the wall, and walked with her down the hall.

"What? Nothing to say?" She didn't know why she was asking for conflict, but his silence nagged at her.

He shook his head. Kellan turned down a corridor, and on instinct, she followed. "Where are we going?"

He chuckled. "Come. You're leaving for Scáth, so I think it's a good idea we touch on what we know about them."

He stopped outside a door that led to a room where they had spent hours together studying over books. She grinned, stepping inside when he held it open for her. "Thank you, *Ward*."

It might have hurt him to hear that title before, but he chuckled now. "Some things never change."

She glanced at him, grin widening at the recollection of memories from a childhood where he, being much older than she, had played games and indulged her in antics. Felicity touched his arm. "You know I love you?"

He stumbled, his gaze meeting hers, wide open and vulnerable. "Don't talk like that. Sounds like goodbye."

"I just realized I never told you that. Now seems like a good time."

Kellan pulled her tightly into a hug. "Do you need to talk?"

After a few moments relishing in his citrus scent—a comfort when she thought she had become an outcast to the guild that abandoned her. He'd always been right there. A reminder of what could be. She stepped out of his hold and gave him a smile she knew he'd be able to interpret. "No, let's prepare for Scáth. I thought there weren't many books on them?"

He returned her smile. "There isn't. But I need some time with my sister."

Without another question, they sat down at the table. Kellan used his magic to remove books from shelves, and they spent the next few hours, laughing about memories and pretending that hell didn't wait outside the palace walls.

Chapter 47

Felicity

S he glanced from the door to the key in her hand.

Second door on the left. I'll send food up soon. The innkeeper had muttered the words after a small dimple had appeared on his cheek at the sight of her. The city was its usual busyness and while she'd considered moving on to the next town to get a little closer to her destination—her original plan—as soon as she'd landed Reóta near Cnoc, she couldn't bring herself to continue on.

The familiarity called to her. Even if the memories ignited were not exactly a comfort knowing what she'd left behind. An understatement. What she had done was run. As fast as she could.

Today had been Alarian's trial. Another one…but this time she couldn't stay. A weakness. Her weakness and fear that her testimony wouldn't be enough. She'd failed in so many ways during these past few weeks.

Now his life was on the line, and she couldn't face it if the final verdict was his death. She'd come back to deal with it when her mission was over. They needed Scáth as an ally. After everything else hadn't gone as planned, this she could control.

Somehow. She would not fail.

Felicity entered the room and looked around. The blood Alarian had spilled was gone. The furniture was in the same place, and just like last time, she searched for peep holes, broken floorboards, or gaps at the windows or doors. As it had been before, everything was as it should be.

There was no need to unpack, so she took a seat in the rickety chair and removed her whetstone and blades. A familiar habit. One calming to do as her thoughts kept turning towards him. Was he still in prison? Free and walking the halls of the palace? Awaiting a final verdict with iron at his wrists?

Her eyes pinched shut—as if that alone was all that was necessary to stop her trailing thoughts. A knock at the door for her arriving meal interrupted her spiraling thoughts and after she had cleared off the tray, she placed it in the hall and turned to stare at the empty room.

Felicity returned to her chair and began the methodical rhythm of dragging the blade against the whetstone. Rain beat against the cobbled street outside. A steady thrum against the window, the scent of a forest permeated through the draft of the worn stone walls.

Footsteps, nearly silent in the hall, caught her attention. She paused her movements, listening. The sounds stopped. Or paused—the sound of metal against wood. Careful not to make any sound of her own, Felicity placed the whetstone down on the table beside her and got to her feet, palming the hilt of her dagger.

The twist of the knob was slow. Felicity debated using magic to wipe out the light in the room, but she had other ways to protect herself.

With her crimson pendant in hand, as soon as the door creaked open, it blazed to life—white hot light engulfed the room.

A hiss from her target—she walked through the starlight, grabbed them by the collar and flung their body against the wall by the door, her blade at their throat. "Business."

An order.

They dropped the arm that covered their eyes from her magic. "I have a letter."

Her magic dispelled as shadows inked from the male before her. Steady. Gently.

"It's nice to see you've started to use it as a weapon." Alarian grinned, carefully opening his eyes. "Now, are you going to keep this blade at my throat?"

How dare he try to sneak up on her. She considered making him leave—

Her eyes widened as the meaning of his presence sunk in. "You're here." Felicity loosened the pressure she had against him, but didn't move her dagger. "They let you go?"

"You seem surprised? It was your written testimony, a witness's account, that set me free from a crime I should be hung for." He didn't push her away, his shadows sliding along corners and the edges of the floor. Assessing for danger.

If it wasn't instilled within her own practices, she would take it as a slight, but they had been brought up the same way.

"You didn't deserve to be punished." She swallowed, holding his gaze. "You saved my mother from more pain and suffering. Saved a youngling from certain death." Those damn tears stung her eyes, but this time she didn't let them fall. "Now that I know who my mother was, I have no doubt she was thankful for your guiding hand."

In a split second, he twisted and easily had her pressed against the wall, her hand with the dagger pinned between his own grip and the door. A corner of his mouth lifted.

"Why?" She rolled her eyes, telling herself she hadn't missed the way he grinned. "I probably would have lowered my blade at some point."

"You have a hundred ways to get out of this, I'm sure."

"A hundred and one." And she leaned forward and kissed him.

Alarian sighed as their mouths parted for each other. Exploring. He pulled back just as abruptly, chest rising and falling as his hold loosened. Heat welled within, her body begged for touch.

He broke their stare first, and she could see the questions in his own expression. Ones she had asked herself over and over since she found the truth about herself. Those that had died at her own hand. She wanted to tell him they would get through it together...

But instead, she pushed into his space. "You shouldn't have come here. I'm glad you're free, but this is something I need to do alone." He had made it quite clear he never wanted to step foot in Scáth. "Go back to the castle. Once this is all taken care of, Marquette and Fiadh stopped—"

He snorted, letting go of her wrist but not opening space between them. "No, I'm done with the excuses." He held up a parchment she recognized immediately. The snapped seal caught the dimmed lantern light. "You wrote this and ran away—again, and had your father deliver this to me. Did you really think I wouldn't follow?"

"I didn't know what would happen in the trial." She swallowed. "I couldn't stay. If—"

"I told them they were making a mistake. Seemed your account from that night was enough. But my own guilt…"

"Is similar to my own." She reached out and brushed his cheek as a tear slid down his face. "You saved her."

He pinched his eyes closed.

Her brow furrowed. "How did you know I was here?"

"Gaoth sensed his mate. I'm glad he didn't leave as it made travel much faster. As we got closer, I could sense your emotions like a tether that led me straight here. As soon as we landed in Cnoc, I knew where you would be." He traced a finger down her arm. "You didn't exactly try to hide from me."

She glanced at the parchment that now hung at his side. "That letter said explicitly to stay in Éardrom."

Alarian rolled his eyes. "I'm not letting you run away anymore. Unless you have a good reason, we are finishing this now."

"You're my weakness. One I can't have right now. The realms need us both and it would be selfish to act on our feelings. We need space between us so our heads can be clear. Don't you realize I would give it all for you? I gave a heartstone to our enemy."

Instead of doing as she asked, he stepped closer until their chests nearly brushed. All she had to do was lean forward. But he didn't touch her, reach for her. He only stared with those emerald eyes that had drawn her in more times than she cared to admit. "Or, counterpoint, we're stronger together. As has been proven multiple times in the past few weeks."

"Alarian…"

"What is it, Starlight? Worried about your heart? Because you already have mine. It's yours. You're more than an addiction—an obsession. More than a want and a need. You're my beginning, my middle...my entire reason for existence. There is no end, no expiration for how I feel about you. Not even in death. If the veil opened tomorrow and Ankus entered our world, I'd be with you or waiting for you. So yes, it would be easier to walk away. But that's also why I'm going to stay."

She couldn't speak. Her heart raced as he leaned in to rest his forehead against hers, his hand gently slipping around hers to assist her dagger back into the sheath at her waist. "I don't need any declaration from you. It's not your thing, I'm aware of that. But I need...action. If you don't feel the same way then walk away. I read your letter. I'll know the truth as to why." He pinched his eyes closed for a breath. "And I'll wait until you're ready or leave Éardrom once this is all said and done if that's your choice." His hand brushed tears from her cheek she had failed to hold back. "Or give me a sign and—"

She didn't let him finish that sentence. With a gentle tug on his arm, she lifted slightly on her toes and kissed him.

A grin spread against her lips. She pulled back to find that damn smirk. Felicity rolled her eyes. "What's that smile for?"

"I had hoped these tears were because you were happy. I meant it when I said I wanted to be the reason for all of your good emotions."

"You couldn't already read them?" she grumbled, wiping the tears from her cheek.

"I told you I was working on blocking out your feelings. Especially during that conversation—didn't know if I could take another chance for you to push me away when you didn't really want to."

She winced. "I'm...terrified."

"Of me?" he whispered.

She shook her head, unsure she could put the proper words together. He'd been through so much for her. Because of her.

He cupped her jaw and on instinct she melted into his palm. "I need you to tell me why. Honestly. I can take it. Promise."

She met his gaze. "I've killed for no other reason than because I was ordered. I put my trust and loyalty in the hands—willingly—of people who didn't completely deserve it."

"And you're afraid to do so again?" His tone held no judgment.

"No." She shook her head. "I'm worried I'm not worth your trust and loyalty. And if that bond is offered...what if you come to regret our connection? If my past catches up to me?"

Alarian brushed a kiss to her forehead and pulled her against him, his arms wrapping around her. She rested her head against his chest. Could feel the rise and fall, hear the beat of his heart. He breathed in, held it, and then slowly dispelled it. Was this the end? Was he was preparing to walk away? She didn't blame him. He deserved for her to prove herself to him.

"When you said we could be friends, I thought that was all I ever would deserve. I'd failed you. Your family. When I received those memories from the Countess, I knew the truth. I would never have a chance and didn't dare hope or even consider another option. Even with the taste of the bond, the magic had to be wrong. There was no way that you could ever forgive me."

He pulled back with a small smile. "Your letter gave me back that hope. Made me realize that maybe the two of us felt the same way. Undeserving. And if I couldn't fathom you could ever care about me, then maybe you felt that too. We aren't perfect, but even Magic knows we are perfect for each other."

He'd wait, she realized, for as long as she wanted. Would resist if that's what she asked. There was no doubt about his feelings for her, and she didn't doubt her own for him. Only fear stood in their way, and she'd overcome that many times. Felicity stepped back from his hold, keeping her gaze locked on his as she reached for the top button of her leather vest.

She searched his expression and the knot in her heart eased.

"You must know though, there is one secret still between us. I can't speak of—"

She pressed a finger to lips, stopping him.

Alarian inhaled but didn't move as her fingers went to the second, then third, button. "Are you sure?"

"We've had many secrets between us, and we've worked it out before. I trust you."

He inhaled deeply as she stepped around him. She inched out of the vest, the slap of leather hitting the floor. His shadows rose around him, his gaze raked over her body, as she sauntered toward the center of the room. His concentration remained steady on the movements of her hands as she pulled the hem of her tunic from the waist of her pants. Heat began to pool and spread from her core. "I'm ready."

He snapped out of view, the shadows pulling him away before reappearing in front of her. He slid one hand in her hair and pulled her mouth to his, the other tugged her against his body. Her senses rose and skin flushed at the heat of his touch, her hands roaming in turn, tearing at his shirt before the two of them pulled apart long enough to remove each other's tunics.

The tail of the fox tattoo on his shoulder drew her attention and she followed the constellation of freckles across his chest, up his neck and back to his gaze that was doing the same as he smiled in appreciation of what he saw. Then they were back in each other's arms, his mouth trailing along her jaw as he loosened the stays of her bralette.

"You're certain?" He paused for just a moment.

Need clawed at her. "Don't you dare stop now."

He chuckled, his movements slowing just a tad as his fingers grazed along her side, over her waist. Her bralette fell, and she had little time to figure out how he got it off so quickly before he was hoisting her up, legs wrapping around his waist, his mouth on hers.

She kissed him hard, punishing, her mouth parting slightly as his tongue slipped in, tasting her as she did him. He carried her to the bed, laid her down carefully, his body hovering over hers. Felicity gripped his shoulders, refusing to let him stray too far away from her now. It wasn't just his words that made all of this feel right, but the sensation of his touch. The love she felt within his care and gaze. Alarian's hand trailed from her navel to her breast, a flick of her nipple, a knead of his hand—memorizing.

"Can you understand how this—how you could become an addiction?" He growled against her throat, the vibration causing her to arch against him. "How I could never have just one night with you. You feel and look incredible."

She dug her grip into his skin, her nails raking over him gently. "If I'm yours, you're mine. It goes both ways, Rian."

"That's all I ever need to hear, Starlight."

His mouth took hers again. Her hand reaching for the ties at his trousers. The groan he gave as she released him, brushed a hand against the smooth skin of his cock, was enough to cause every nerve ending to rush through her system and blaze to life.

She had never felt this way before. This was different. The need. The rush of magic at the tip of her breaking point.

His mouth trailed to her breasts and as he tasted her, he helped her shimmy from her pants. "Tonic?" she mumbled, uncertain she could form a complete sentence. The last thing they needed right now was a child.

"Yes. You?" he asked between grazes of tongue and teeth against her breast.

"Yes." She arched into his touch. "I've waited a long time for this. Please." She was actually begging.

He chuckled, the sound raspy and guttural. "You have no idea how long I've wanted this." Then he was over her again, and they caught each other's lips as he slowly slid between her legs, brushing against her entrance. "Not just this. But everything." He kissed her. "Every taste." His mouth at her throat, a small graze of his tongue against skin.

"Say it again." He shivered as he spoke.

"What?" She arched her body towards him in invitation. "Please?"

He kissed her throat, the curve of her neck to her shoulder, a small nip. "While I would love to make you beg, let's save that for another time. You know what I need to hear, Starlight."

She growled, and then with the agility trained into her, she rolled him over onto his back until she was the one on top looking down at him. "I'm yours. You're mine." Then she lowered herself onto him, and they groaned.

They fell into a rhythm as if they had been meant to do this forever. And as she came undone, wrapped up in limbs and kisses, she knew that there had never been another one for her.

Chapter 48
Alarian

How was it that he could make a mess of things so quickly? They spent most of the night entangled together. Then this morning, he'd been in such a haze of happiness he hadn't let himself consider where he was meant to go today.

Alarian stood beside Felicity and stared at the forest before him. Scáth. A home he had given up for his parents. And so much more. They'd arrived about two chimes of the clock before the sun would set, but the shadows within the forest weren't just the trees. It was pivotal they made it to the center before the beasts revealed themselves. They were nocturnal—which had been used for his benefit once.

Those same beasts that had torn apart the assailants of Queen Kaliana as he'd remained hidden within the shadows of the trees. He hadn't watched as they were slowly devoured, only bits and pieces remained when the Tower liaison had appeared the following morning. Held out a vial and performed a ritual to remove his memories. Pieces Alarian hadn't known were ever lost. Gone. A blip of his life that should have the female beside him requesting his head on a pike.

The liaison, Bishop, had told him what he was to do. To return to the palace with the story of Felicity and Kaliana's deaths. Report that the hunters hadn't listened to his warnings and camped on the outskirts of Scáth. New memories weaved into his story.

There was one secret left between him and Felicity. And while this was probably the worst time to attempt to fix what had been done, he needed it over with. For Felicity, he needed this final secret to end and to move on. It might tear them apart again, but he had more faith in their relationship now.

"You know you don't have to come." She glanced back at the cailleach, watching as they stood at the woods edge. "I know you haven't wanted to come here, but I've been invited. It's time I find out why and hope they will ally with us."

Kellan had informed him of Ciana's invitation. The Shadow wouldn't appear when he'd called her name the day he left, hoping for answers as he packed. After Kellan and King Bastien gave him their blessing to run after Felicity, the prince mentioned that the Dearmadta had made it clear Felicity was meant to come. It was their hope to gain an alliance the continent needed.

While they had flown, he'd considered backing out. Waiting for her to emerge and letting her do this alone. He wanted to tell her about the blood oath hidden by the ink of his tattoo, but it would only have been the cause of a slow death.

"No. I need to go." He sighed. "Just...remember that I had my reasons. I can't..." He let the words trail, hoping she'd understand. Her protectiveness he felt like a warm blanket over his shoulder. For this reason alone, he didn't tell her that he might not be able to follow her out.

A squeeze of his hand was all he received before she took a step and entered the forest. The smells, the sensations, the otherworldly essence of the realm wrapped around him as he followed. The shadows already coiled at their feet. There would be little time before the others noted their entrance—if they didn't know already.

Felicity led them, her steps silent even amongst the fallen leaves that signaled the upcoming change of season.

They were deep within the brush when they both stopped.

"Well, look who we have here."

Felicity whirled around, her hand at her hip along the hilt of the dagger but paused from drawing.

Alarian's movements were slow. Methodical. He faced the female, a smile ready. "Talia."

The fae leaned a shoulder into a tree, watching them. Her light brown hair was shaved to her scalp on one side, the other hung to her shoulder. Different from when he'd last seen her. "You weren't meant to return."

"I know. But the fate of our continent is more important."

She scoffed and cast a raised brow in Felicity's direction. "I see."

Felicity hadn't moved and he could tell she was assessing the situation. Ready to jump in if things went badly. Alarian squeezed Felicity's hand once and let it go. "She won't hurt us. Not the one to be worried about."

Talia laughed. "You sure about that? What's it been now…fifty years? Maybe feelings have changed." She shrugged, a smirk playing at the corner of her ruby lips. Alarian sensed them before they materialized. Four more Shadows surrounded them, weapons at the ready.

"Don't worry." Talia nodded at Felicity. "We don't pose a danger to *you*, Princess. Just to him. Unless he chooses to come peacefully."

Felicity stepped in front of him before he could respond. "If you think you can threaten him, then you better be prepared to fight. He's with me. As a representative of the crown. No harm can come to him or—"

He gripped her shoulder before she could continue. A warning. Reminder. They needed this alliance, and this was not the way to go about it. Felicity's jaw clenched but nodded as she glanced at the others. "What I mean is that we have more pressing matters. Whatever your grievances are with him can wait until later."

A small chuckle broke from the group. "That's the problem, Princess, they can't."

Felicity growled at the mocking tone of the nearest Shadow's voice. "Test me."

Talia pushed herself off the tree, straightening. "We have our own ways here." She glanced at Alarian with a brow rose in question. "Will you submit?"

He nodded.

She gave a small nod and one of the four stepped forward, a bag in hand. Hell—not again. It seemed he couldn't catch a break when it came to the iron manacles.

Felicity flinched. "No—he's not going to run. I'll vouch for him."

"Felicity—" He stopped himself from reaching for her.

"I understand that might not be your ways, but on my honor, if he leaves prior to any discussions with your leaders, I will take the blame."

Talia considered her, before she waved back the Shadow. "Fine. But I cannot guarantee I won't be ordered otherwise."

"Talia, you can't," one of the Shadows growled.

"She the one who needs us. Now, let's go."

Alarian squeezed Felicity's shoulder once more then moved in beside her. "Trust me?"

She glared at the others when one stepped a little too close. "Yes. But—"

He shook his head. "That's all you will need for the next few hours. Please. Their ways are their own. Follow my lead."

Felicity's fists clenched but after a few minutes, she nodded. "Fine."

A lie. But there was nothing he could say to her. Truthfully, he had no idea if everything would be all right in the end. He glanced surreptitiously at the female beside him. He didn't doubt Felicity would raze the entire realm before she'd let him be imprisoned.

They walked in circles, a common tactic used to confuse their guests. Or prisoners. One he was aware of, and by the annoyance that stole through the wall he attempted to hold in place, Felicity was too.

They broke through shrubs and the tree line to reach a clearing. Felicity came to an abrupt stop and her mouth fell open in awe as she took it all in. Alarian grinned at her reaction before a hollow pit formed in his stomach. He turned his attention to the place he had called home for a long time. Until he followed his parents' orders. The last time he'd tried to make them proud. And this, he thought, is what he lost.

Rope and wooded bridges connected one tree to the next. Buildings were structured around thick trunks at different levels with ropes or ladders leading to circular buildings. Overhangs hung over porches that protected walkways from the inevitable rain that gave the forest its greenery. Moss and lichen clung to rocky surfaces and tree trunks.

There was a graze of skin against his hand as Felicity leaned in. "This place smells like you. Your home."

Tears pierced the corner of his eyes. He gave her a thankful nod, lifting his chin as faeries of all castes looked down upon them—him. Watching. Waiting.

Louder, so Talia could hear this time, Felicity cleared her voice. "I don't know why you felt the need to take us the long way, but I'm impressed."

Talia's shoulders drew back, the only sign she was surprised Felicity had caught on. Years of training and she still had the same tell. Alarian stopped his chuckle.

"It's necessary."

"Since he used to live here, I assume you felt it was necessary for me. Next time, you can skip the tour." Felicity smirked. "Now, who do we need to speak to so we can get this mess figured out?"

Suddenly he was glad that he had left this place and went to his parents. It meant he had a chance to meet her.

Talia bit back a smile. "Well, the council was expecting you. Not him. So, I'll show you to a room and—"

"He's coming with me." Felicity crossed her arms.

Alarian opened his mouth to try to buffer the frustration he saw on Talia's compatriots. He recognized two of them now—fifty years ago they had been younglings beside him. Now he was Scáth's most wanted. Or unwanted. Well, second to his mother. Talia waved them off. "He can come with you. For now." She held out her hand. "Shall we."

Felicity stepped towards Alarian, understanding the offer.

Talia sighed. "I've allowed him to remain uncuffed, but he is prohibited to shadow travel."

One of the Shadows stepped forward and held out a hand to Alarian, although begrudgingly. He wasn't going to complain. Not if the alternative was another moment with those manacles on his wrists.

They arrived by shadow to a third story porch outside of a bungalow. The male gripping Alarian's arm, rather tightly, released him with a sneer and a nod to Talia before he disappeared into the shadows he still held close.

She nodded towards the door. "Wait here."

Felicity glanced over the edge of the railing to take in the bridges and houses that zigzagged between trees and around the forest clearing. "This is the highest place you have. It wouldn't stop him. When are you going to realize he's not going to run?"

"I'm trusting you." Talia rolled her eyes. "This is so the others are more likely to leave you alone. Listen, Princess, a little understanding might go both ways. I assume you don't know why he's banned?"

"How could she?" Alarian grumbled. "I wouldn't be here otherwise, would I?"

"Why did you come back, Alarian? She could have come alone." Talia shook her head. "We had an understanding."

"How is Clarice?" His brow rose.

Talia swallowed. "She's doing well. Don't change the subject."

"Time to deal with the past. Need a clean slate." He was forbidden to speak as it was.

Talia glanced at Felicity. "You know how he is like, don't you?" A grin. "The gossip said about him?"

"You've left the comforts of your realm long enough to find out?" Felicity growled. A challenge in the bite of her tone.

"She's rather snippety. Not your usual type, Rian?"

He stepped in between Talia and Felicity, her emotions brewing like a storm cloud. "I'd be careful of what you say. Not only is she a princess, a spy, and an assassin, but she's also—"

"His." Felicity stepped up beside him. "As he is mine."

Talia glanced between the two of them and grinned. "Good. You're going to need that resolve for what's to come." Her expression softened. "You finally found one worth sticking around for. Happy for you."

Felicity ignored the comment. "You should know Ciana sent me. I need information on Marquette. This is for the entire continent and you're wasting our time with frivolous issues that are fifty years in the past."

Talia shrugged. "Not my call." Then the shadows whisked her away.

Felicity didn't relax even though they were now alone. "Who is she?"

He considered how to answer. All the ways that the words could bite him in the ass since he couldn't explain. At least, not easily. "Do you remember how I asked you to trust me?"

She nodded.

"There are some things I can't...say." He sighed. "Many questions I won't be able to answer. At least not yet, or maybe not ever." Instinctively he brushed a hand over his shoulder, to where the scar burned in reminder and warning.

Felicity watched the movement, her brow furrowed. "Remove your tunic."

He smirked. "Don't think this is the time, Starlight."

"Don't patronize me." Her lips pursed.

Alarian leaned forward, and with a look alone, asked for a kiss. She rolled her eyes, crossed her arms and stared hard.

"Fine, fine." He undid the buttons and shrugged out of the sleeves. Before he could even finish, she was behind him, her fingers tracing over the tattoo on his back. Images, sensations of the night before, caused him to still. He tried to concentrate on their surroundings instead of her touch. The two cots on either side of the room. The chair and small table against the third wall. The hardening of certain body parts...

Her movement stopped at the raised skin along one of the thick lines of the fox's tail. She leaned in, her breath warming his skin.

Damnit.

"Really?" She moved around and looked down at his waistline. "Now?"

He shrugged. "I still have to get used to you being close to me. It does something to every single cell in my body."

Her jaw feathered and he watched her fight back a smile before she turned her attention back to his shoulder. "A blood oath?"

He didn't react. Couldn't.

"And you can't speak of it?"

Again, he remained still.

"Then I can only assume you broke an agreement you had with Scáth when you returned to your parents." She watched him carefully. "Can you tell me who Talia is? A friend or what?"

"I wish..." Hell, he didn't want to lie to her. Even if he couldn't explain.

Felicity went wholly still. For a moment he wondered if she even breathed. "Is she your wife?"

He swallowed. Unable to speak.

She stepped into his space, holding his gaze. "I trust you." She kissed him, and he enveloped her in his arms. Held her close.

"Touching as this may be..."

Alarian sighed, recognizing that voice. "It's been a while, Hayden." He didn't let Felicity go as he met the new arrival's gaze over her shoulder. "As obnoxious as always."

Hayden grinned. "Of course, otherwise, I wouldn't have interrupted."

"You didn't interrupt," Alarian growled, his hackles rising.

"Down boy." The male grinned. "The Díomhair is ready to see you."

Well...at least that would quicken the process. The Secret Keeper would not leave anything to chance.

"We're waiting for the Council." Felicity stepped aside, glaring at the male. "Who are you?"

"Trouble." Hayden winked. "And the council will see you soon. He has a date with the witch first."

Felicity opened her mouth, and Alarian could tell it was going to be a biting remark when he squeezed her hand. "Don't worry. It will be fine."

"You sure about this?"

"Yes, stay here. I'll be back soon. Right?" He glared at the male at his side. One he'd once called a friend.

The male chuckled. "Of course. Piece of cake."

Felicity worried at her bottom lip. Alarian kissed the back of her hand. "I'll explain when I can." If he could. "I have to do this if I'm to face the council. Best alternative, actually. Maybe it's a good sign." A lie—one she could read in his expression. The bond hadn't been offered yet. He itched for it to be soon.

Her glare thinned. *Trust me*. He wanted to say again but instead he flung his tunic back over his head.

Felicity shifted to face Hayden. "If he's not back before midnight, I'll hold you personally accountable."

Hayden's grin widened. "I'd like to see that actually." He held out his hand toward Alarian. "Shall we?"

Hell, he wanted to use his own magic. With his hand in Hayden's, the shadows wrapped around them and an instant later, they landed outside of a quiet building. A few Shadows stood nearby, glaring at him, but most had begun to head to the meeting hall for the evening meal.

"You know she could tell you lied, right?"

Alarian nodded, not wanting to give this male any insight into his relationship.

"Talia says she's protective of you. And you over her."

"And?"

Hayden pulled aside the rug hanging over the entryway to one of the smallest buildings built amongst the trees. "Does she know what you're about to face? Who the Díomhair is?"

Alarian rolled his shoulders back. "No."

"You kept our secrets? Even from the princess?"

With a deep sigh and a lift to his chin, he stepped into the room. "Yes."

The Díomhair stood in the center of their nearly empty room. A chair in the center. Ready. Waiting. "Take a seat." They were human. A witch. Wrinkles crinkled at the corner of their mouth, skin as thin as paper. Except for thinner hair and a few extra wrinkles around their eyes, they looked the same as they had the last time Alarian had been here.

There was no moment of welcome. Not a second of formalities. "Always straight to the point."

"I remember that you used to like that about me." They pointed to the chair with annoyance written in their expression for having to ask twice.

Alarian took the place offered for him, resting his clammy hands on his thighs.

"Remember to relax." They sat across from the chair, staring with unseeing eyes.

"You mustn't take. I need it all," Alarian muttered. His memories were his, and he'd never bargain for them again.

The Díomhair smiled as they stalked towards him. "Never take, only borrow. They are yours." Then they placed both hands on top of Alarian's skull and immediately his eyes fluttered closed.

The screaming that followed, he didn't recognize as his own.

Chapter 49

Felicity

She'd paced well into the night. Talia delivered food but had no news of Alarian's whereabouts. It made her want to tear apart the realm for him, but she kept her word. Remained in the space that was beginning to feel like a cell. Kept the promise to trust him despite knowing that he lied about it being all right. Whoever the Díomhair was, she had seen the rigidness of his shoulders. The smile he forced.

Felicity looked out the window, the moon visible through the trees. They were near the top of one of the highest branches of the forest, the building just hidden from view of any who would fly over. Midnight was nearing, the full moon inching towards the center of the sky.

The light shifted, the flame moving on an unseen wind when shadows appeared in the corner. Felicity touched the hilt of her dagger. Ready. Careful.

Hayden stepped from the shadows with Alarian slumped against him. Felicity rushed to his side and took his arm. "What happened?"

"Díomhair," Hayden answered with a wince as he assisted Felicity in dragging Alarian toward the bed. "He'll be all right after some food and rest. It's mentally exhausting."

Once Alarian was on the bed, a groan enough of a sound of life that she didn't remove her dagger as she turned on the male standing beside her. "What did this Díomhair do to him? Tell me."

Hayden grimaced, a tentative step back towards his waiting magic. "It's not exactly my place to say."

Her magic flared to life, and she directed it through his shadows. "No escape. Not that easily. Tell me—"

The male's eyes widened in surprise "Impressive. Didn't know you could do that."

She hadn't been certain, but figured it was worth a try. "Answers."

Hayden sighed. "The Díomhair is a witch. They can go through your mind—find out the answers they seek. All they have to do is ask the right questions." He glanced at Alarian then back to her. "It's not an ideal experience. But you knew he was lying so..."

"I also told you that I would hold you responsible." Her light edged to a point and settled right below his groin. "I want specifics."

Alarian had been through enough. Dealt with enough.

A raspy chuckle sounded from the male on the bed. "You know, Starlight, I kind of like this overprotective side of you. What does that say about me?"

Her light dimmed as she whirled around to face him. "It says that you shouldn't lie to me. Or I might hurt you." With her sidetracked by Alarian, Hayden disappeared with a snap of shadows.

She kept her attention on her Cridhe, even when a plate of food arrived on the bedside table. "Hayden must be terrified of you."

Felicity's glare thinned. "What happened? Tell me."

He pushed up to a sitting position, and she moved on instinct to assist him. Once he was comfortable, she held the plate just out of reach with an arched brow.

Alarian gave that half smile that turned into a grimace. "You know when you have a real bad headache? Light hurts. Sound hurts."

She nodded, putting the plate in his waiting hands.

He took a bite of bread, chewed, swallowed, then he continued, "Well, this is like that. While it feels like your skull has fingers digging through it, they ask questions into your mind and the answers come. If you fight it, the process is worse. Your muscles and limbs lock up. It's near impossible to protect the answers, but it can be done depending on the ability level of the one searching.

But the Díomhair is ancient and has the experience of time to get what they want."

They reminded her of someone else. "Did you know Fiadh could do something similar?"

Alarian startled. "What?"

She explained what happened in Tine. "I couldn't tell what she was looking for. But it felt like my nerves were on fire and I had no control over my body."

"Knowing her, it was just to torture you. Cause pain. Her magic is volatile."

Felicity sat down at the foot of the bed. "I was glad my memories weren't all intact yet."

Alarian swallowed another bite. "The Díomhair wanted to know if I'd shared information and the secrets of the realm. I wish I could say more, but I'm sworn to secrecy. Tomorrow I'll be taken before the council."

"Another trial? Really?"

"No." He shook his head. "They aren't exactly trials when the Díomhair is involved. They will speak for or against. Others will state their claims. Then a sentence will be stated and carried out."

"Would they lie?"

Alarian shook his head. "I've known them my entire life. It wasn't the first time I've faced the Díomhair."

She sat and considered. Wondered at all the threads connected by that oath scarred into his back. Felicity brushed a finger over the scar on her palm.

"I hope, by the end of this, that the oath between us is all that remains," he whispered.

Felicity's chest ached at the words. She hadn't even considered it. "I still owe you a dance."

"And you will—until the end of our lives. I'm not ever letting that mark leave your body—unless, of course, you ask it of me." He put the plate aside and shifted back into a lying position in the bed. "Now, my head is killing me, and I can't think anymore. Can I hold you?"

Weak. He had made her so weak. But she couldn't resist the offer. She never would again. She lied down beside him, his arm pulling her flush to his chest, the other arm sliding under her pillow. "Good night, Starlight."

"Good night." She breathed out a slow breath. Pulled his hand to her lips and kissed the scar at his palm.

"I love you," he mumbled, the words barely indiscernible.

Before she could return the sentiment, his breathing evened out, the soft whisper of it brushing her ear.

***

Talia arrived as soon as the sun had settled above the horizon, slowly making its way into the sky, the trees hiding most of the light. "Are you ready?"

Alarian sat up beside Felicity, his head in his hands. While he'd eaten and rested, he complained quietly that his head still ached. Felicity glanced at him, and then back at the female. "First, I have some questions." She had time to consider, think it through.

Talia's brow rose. "Oh?"

"Yes. Who is it that he is blood-oath bound too?"

Talia swallowed. "How? He can't—"

"Speak of it? I figured it out on my own." Not a complete lie. "Is it you or can you not speak of it either?"

"Why would you think it would be me?" Not an answer.

Felicity stood, ignoring how stiff Alarian had gone next to her. "Because you two were intended for marriage. Isn't that what this all about?"

Talia smirked, glanced from Alarian back to her. "How did you come to these conclusions?"

Felicity crossed her arms. "Everyone here has looked at him as a pariah. Not you. When you chose not to put the manacles on him, I wondered if it was out of guilt that you felt for his current predicament. As for the engagement, the others follow you. Must mean you're up in hierarchy. You two are around the same age, if my assumptions are correct. Alarian is a powerful male." She ignored the fact that he preened at her compliment. "So the two of you would make an advantageous match for Scáth. Am I on the right track?"

"Interesting. You're not what I expected. Even if there were whispers of a spy princess." Talia shrugged. "Maybe. It could be a part of it."

"And is it you who he has the oath with?"

She crossed her arms. "Yes."

"Let him out of it."

"What?" Talia's brow furrowed.

"Do you want him to have a chance to plead his case?"

Talia's mouth thinned. "Of course."

"Then give him that chance. With the oath the two of you have, he won't be able to openly speak for himself."

Alarian chuckled under his breath, his head lifting slightly to peer at them. "It doesn't work that way."

Talia ground her teeth. "The agreement we have is so he *can't* speak to the council."

"Talia—shut it," Alarian growled, standing unsteadily. "Let's get this over with."

"Whatever it's about, I doubt he deserves to carry all the blame."

Alarian stared at her. Swallowed. "Starlight?"

She met his gaze, hardening her expression. "I'm not leaving without you. You've taken on the burden enough. This time you're not doing it alone."

He leaned forward and pressed a kiss to her forehead. "My fate isn't the priority." He held Felicity's gaze. "I mean it. You need to concentrate on why you're here. It's not because of me—it's because you need allies. Because you need information about my mother. We need to know her plan. Remember that, Starlight. I came because I couldn't have anything else between us. Understood?"

Felicity glared. "I can handle it all at the same time."

He smiled. "Never doubted you, but don't let me be what holds you back. You and I both know stopping my mother and protecting the people of Talamh should come first."

There was no reason to argue with him. Not with the pain she could see he was trying to hide. She looked at Talia and took the female's hand to shadow transport. "Let's go."

They arrived outside of the largest circular structure from what she could see of their tree house community. Many stood along the railing outside, silently watching. Talia ignored everyone and entered the meeting hall, Felicity a step behind with Alarian coming in last. There wasn't an empty seat on the elevated benches that wrapped around the space filled with spectators. In the center, near the thick tree trunk the hall was built around, were three chairs. And upon them sat one male, a female, and a woman. Talia took them to stand in front of these individuals and gave a small bow. "Council, I bring to you Felicity, Princess of Talamh, and Alarian."

"The traitor," someone whispered. Another chuckled.

Felicity bristled inwardly. This was all a waste of time. Why couldn't they understand?

The female in the center tilted her head, watching Felicity carefully. With long brown hair that reached her waist, a petite frame, round tan face, and piercing deep gray eyes, wrinkles at her mouth that showed she smiled. "We invited you here, Princess, but not him. Is there a reason you chose him as your traveling companion and guard."

"I didn't choose for him to accompany me." Best not to lie after all. "Yet, he came despite what it would mean for him personally." A united front. And she wouldn't start their alliance with untruths. "He's mine, and I won't be leaving here without him."

Whispers and gasps broke out from the group. Talia leaned against the wall beside another female and Hayden. The female in the center glared at the male beside Felicity. The other two began to try to calm the increasingly agitated crowd. The female clapped twice, silence spreading through the room at her reaction. "I see. We will deal with him later. Plead your case. Why are you here?"

"I was invited by Ciana. She sent me to speak on behalf of my family to ask for your assistance in stopping Marquette and, in the process, Tine from destroying the magic of our realms."

A tilt of her lips was all the female gave as a sign that she even heard Felicity. "And what makes you think that was why Ciana sent you here?"

"Everness, it's pivotal you help." Alarian straightened. "My mother—" He winced. "Marquette and Fiadh are planning to open the veil. They—"

"Silence," Everness, the female in the center, hissed. "You'll not speak until it's your turn. Your words mean nothing unless we deem otherwise, traitor."

He bowed his head, glaring at the ground. Every muscle in Felicity's body begged to react. But he was right—one hurdle at a time. She would get what she wanted to prove just how wrong they were about him.

"Ciana interrupted our private meeting. She told me that if I wanted information regarding Marquette's motives, then I needed to come here to get it. That information can help us know her goals and how she plans to achieve them."

"And you brought him as a bargaining tool?" The male beside Everness grimaced. He seemed to ink the shadows as though they were permanently a part of him.

"I explained his presence. If you can't accept it, then that's your problem. But he's not the reason for this request—you once stood beside my grandparents. We need you to stand with us again."

"Yes, we did." The voice came from the other side of the tree trunk. They appeared with uneasy steps, a cane in hand, hunched over. A chair was immediately pulled beside the council as they sat down, their joints almost creaking with each movement. Wrinkles covered every inch of exposed skin and gray hair curled out from under a dark thick cloak. "Until a king used us for selfish gains."

"We aren't that king," Felicity countered.

The male snorted. "Same family. We don't make the same mistakes twice. We already did that with him." He pinned Alarian with a glare. "We may have been cursed like all of Talamh, but we didn't forget what *she* did. We tried to do what we could to fix those mistakes. That ended badly for us too."

She swiftly grazed her hand against the sheath of her dagger. Everness tracked the movement, but Felicity didn't care. It was a reminder. *Don't let the anger use you.* "If you keep bringing up Alarian's supposed crimes, then we will deal with that issue now. Otherwise, let's stay on task, shall we?"

Everness' mouth twitched in a half smile that immediately disappeared. "She's right, Gibbons. The traitor should not be the reason for our decision." Her gaze hardened on Felicity. "Why should we stand beside your family?"

"What do you think will happen if you stay here and ignore what's happening outside of Scáth?" Felicity glanced around at the people. "When the other realms' magic is depleted? When stories and monsters are no longer reason enough for others to not cross your border? I've been to Visce. Seen the creatures there. If they lose what they have, where do you think they will go next?"

The murmurs began again. Worried words shared among the others. The newcomer glanced at the council at their side. "She speaks words of truth. Even without seeing her thoughts, it would be detrimental not to assist if we want to keep our way of life."

This must be the Díomhair. It was hard to believe that such a witch could cause Alarian so much discomfort when they could barely walk themselves.

The council members shared a look, and Felicity's brow rose. She wondered if they were having a private conversation that no one else could hear.

Everness rolled back her shoulders. "Ciana spoke highly of you in her letter. We don't want that witch and the traitorous queen to open the veil. Our stone is safe, but we won't tell you where. That is a secret no one is privy too. Not even a princess."

Could it be that easy? Or was the fight soon to come? "Understood. As long as you continue to do everything within your power to protect it, I'm comfortable with your decision. We do have a spell you can add to it if necessary."

"We shall consider, but you will have to show us how to do it ourselves." The woman to Evenness' right, who had remained silent until now, folded her hands in her lap. "We will ally with you to stop Marquette. Once the dangers are neutralized, we will reassess any continued relationship with your family. Is that acceptable?"

"It is." Felicity bit back a smile. "And greatly appreciated. Thank you."

"When do you need us ready?"

"We plan to arrive to in Saol two days prior to Samhain." It wasn't much time. Only twenty days to finish preparations. "But that isn't the only reason I came. I need whatever information you can give me about Marquette. Your insight may be pivotal to our fate."

More whispers and talking from the audience followed by another clap from Everness to silence them.

The male council member nodded. "Whatever Ciana promised was out of turn. But you're welcome to ask our elders." He raised his chin. "In the meantime, Talia will return with you and four of her most trusted compatriots. Prepare her, fill her in, and she will communicate with us what you need."

"Thank you."

Everness nodded and waved a hand at Talia. "Have your four chosen make preparations to leave."

With nothing more than a glance from Talia, four fae stood and headed towards the door. With their exit, four others from outside entered and took the empty chairs.

"You didn't seem surprised about Tine," Felicity added.

The Díomhair grinned. "We are the Shadows, Princess. We know everything."

"You didn't know that Alarian was with me."

The others bristled, a nerve hit. Gauntlet thrown, and a chance to switch to a new topic.

Everness' grin turned savage, as if she knew what Felicity had meant to do. "We would have soon enough." Her attention drifted to Alarian now. "Thank you for your time, Princess. Hayden will see you out—"

"No." Felicity straightened, her shoulders drawing back as her light fluttering to life. "I'll stay."

"These are matters of *our* realm."

"He is a representative of the Light Palace. As the princess, I see things differently."

Alarian had lifted his head, a glance out the corner of his eye in her direction.

Talia leaned against one of the wooden pillars. "Let her stay, Mama."

Mama? Interesting.

"If you stay, then you'll have to swear never to share any of our ways with anyone. Do you understand?"

Felicity removed her dagger, a few withdrawing their own weapons at the sight of the blade and held its hilt towards the Council. "I'll make a blood oath now."

Alarian shifted beside her, but she ignored the movement.

Everness grinned dangerously, her face brightening. "Not yet, Princess. Your blood comes later if you're deemed fit."

Alarian growled, a warning. "Over my dead—"

"Silence, boy. You don't want to finish that sentence," Everness ordered. She turned her attention to Felicity. "If you stay, then you can only speak if asked. Understood?"

Felicity grinned. "Of course."

Alarian reached for her hand. Gave it a squeeze before Felicity let go and stepped back, remaining close. Ready.

Chapter 50
Alarian

Alarian stared straight at Everness. The female had never warmed to Alarian. Not when she'd been alive to witness his mother's betrayal. Tried to wipe them all out. Been there when they had to pick up the pieces. The others had accepted him over time. Took him in and hadn't held his family against him. Everness remained wary—even when she'd ordered her daughter to marry him. Saw him for the power he contained and nothing more.

The last bit of control she thought she needed—wanted—to ensure he was loyal.

Talia had moved closer, either armor at his back or a weapon poised for attack. One could never be too certain after fifty years apart. She hadn't forced those manacles on his wrists, but it didn't mean that she had accepted his return. He'd broken their spoken agreement after all.

Everness tapped a toe against the floor. "Well, what is it you have to say for yourself?" She eyed Felicity as if daring her to interject. It was already a great show of trust from the council that she had even been allowed to stay.

But that look was a warning. One word, one wrong move, and that allowance would be revoked.

"Ask them." He nodded towards the Díomhair. "They asked the questions. Got the answers you seek. I have the headache to prove it."

Gibbons grumbled under his breath and glanced to the woman down the line. Coralie—the woman wasn't a witch, but her cunning ability and sharp mind had earned her place. If his intel was correct, she was the newest member

417

of the council, starting nearly three years prior. Which could either hurt or help him.

Coralie's hands fidgeted in her lap. "You left. Abandoned us and your duty. For the traitors that not only hurt our own, but the entire continent with their misdeeds."

"I did." Again, Alarian glanced at the Díomhair.

"No." The Díomhair cleared their throat. "That's not the truth."

Everyone went silent as they stood again. "He did leave, but it was out of hope that the family he wanted would finally be his. Not to abandon us."

"He was betrothed," Everness snapped. "To my daughter. He was in line to sit upon this council. To complete his training and lead. Instead, he betrayed our trust."

He glanced at Felicity but if she was upset or frustrated by this confirmation of her suspicions, he couldn't tell. They would speak about it later, but he still wouldn't peek into her emotions without her consent.

"No, he went to their side and allowed the pieces to fall into place that caused the break of the curse."

A few inhaled sharply. Alarian eyes widened. "What do you mean?"

The Díomhair sighed. "If you hadn't gone back, she'd be dead." They pointed at Felicity. "She wouldn't have been raised among spies to become who she is today. Rebels wouldn't have collected under one banner but would have been spread out upon this continent with no rhyme or reason. Inside knowledge wouldn't have been shared. And she wouldn't have been hired to be the downfall to a traitorous king. The knowledge of the heartstones wouldn't have been uncovered nearly as quickly and more chaos would have wreaked havoc upon the continent. You're the piece Magic has played on the game board that connects this all together."

Everyone started talking at once. Alarian pinched his eyes closed against the sound, his head pounding and temples aching. A hand brushed against his. Warm. Comforting. He grasped hold of Felicity, grounding him in the moment and he concentrated on that sensation alone.

A clap had his body shuddering. Silence spread through the room at Everness' call to order. He peeked through hooded eyes, the light increasing the pain in his head. Hell, he had hoped it would be over by now.

The council female's eyes held the real truth to her emotions. A touch of pain. "You left my daughter. I take it as a personal affront. After everything we'd done for you, you hurt—"

She bit back the last words with a shake of her head.

"No, Mother." Talia moved in beside him. "That's not completely true."

Alarian inhaled, his heart pounding in his chest...

"Alarian and I had an agreement." She held up her forearm to show a small scar. "He left for two reasons." She winced when her mother's sharp eyes turned on her. "A blood oath."

Fuck—she was going all in.

Felicity's grip tightened on him.

"I didn't want to marry him. He and I weren't meant to be bound in that way. When his family sent word, we took the opportunity, knowing that he could never return. But to cover my tracks, he offered an oath prohibiting him from speaking of our agreement with anyone. That he would bear the pain of this decision for me. And being selfish, I accepted."

An icy chill centralized at the scar on his back.

Everness whirled to the Díomhair. "Lies—it must be."

They shook their head. "It is not. They both have scars to prove it. I couldn't see what he protected, as even my search only showed a wall around a part of him. That is why we are here now, because I wasn't certain what that wall was."

"Our agreement." Talia glanced at Alarian. "And one that I no longer hold you to."

At her proclamation that coolness suddenly eased—gone. A lightness settled in his shoulder. The blood oath complete. "Thank you," he whispered.

The Díomhair stood and walked across the space, stopping in front of Alarian. "May I?"

He balked, his head still aching from the last time they had pierced into his thoughts. Every part of him wanted to tell her no.

Felicity was on edge beside him. Even with his attempt to block out her emotions, he could feel her desire to remove every threat in his way. Instead, he gave her a small smile, squeezed her hand. "It will be all right."

He nodded at the Díomhair.

They raised a hand, pressed it against his temple. Immediately, Alarian called forth the memory, giving it unbidden to the spectral fingers that prodded his thoughts, tearing away at his past. Anything to make it as short and painless as possible.

He hissed against the affront, fighting back the desire and need to scream out. Tried not to concentrate on Felicity and cause other memories to come to the surface even as her grip tightened.

Then, it all stopped. He breathed a sigh, gasped for a breath.

When the Díomhair stepped back, Alarian fell to his knees. Felicity stepped between them, her hands tight fists, cursing profanities at them until Talia pulled her back.

"I'm all right," he gasped out. "Felicity—"

Talia must have let her go because she pulled him into her arms. He let himself slump against her, using her to keep himself upright.

Felicity didn't try to raise him up but stayed there. Even as the council members stood before him. It was Gibbons who spoke. "You're free to leave. We will not extract a punishment with this new information. But you're not meant to hold a space on our council. Understood?"

He nodded, all he could muster before the pounding in his head took over and he let consciousness go.

***

He woke curled up in a bed that wasn't his.

Felicity, noting the movement, was by his side with food and a concoction he didn't recognize. "For the headache. Talia brought it."

He pinched his eyes closed for a moment before mustering the energy to sit up. "What happened?"

"You were freed from the oath and were dismissed by the court. Then you passed out."

He drank from the cup first and almost spit out the bitter contents. "That's disgusting."

"She said it should work quickly. Drink up."

He did as she ordered while Felicity walked around the room, adjusting the curtains over the window and moving their packs from one corner to another. "I'm all right," he muttered between bites. "You don't need to worry."

"You said that before you passed out. So excuse me for not believing you." She stopped at the end of the bed and glared. "And then I had to give Talia an earful for not bringing you this medicine earlier."

"Probably wasn't allowed to." He took a sip of the water.

"That's what she said." Felicity began to pace again.

As vile as it was, the medicine began to work, the ache in his head dulling as he ate more and more. He watched as Felicity's nervous energy had her packing and then unpacking only to re-pack their bags again.

"Starlight?" He moved to the side of the bed.

She paused, her glare thinning on him.

"Come here." He reached a hand for her.

She stared at it and pierced him with a look. "I was worried."

Alarian leaned over and grabbed her wrist, tugging gently until she finally sighed and stepped closer. Not close enough. He pulled until she was straddling his lap, then wrapped his arms around her, holding her close. "I have wanted to tell you everything for so long."

"That's not it. I understand why you didn't tell me this. You couldn't or I'm assuming pain and death is all you had to look forward to."

He nodded, resting his forehead against hers. She felt so good in his arms, and he realized again how much he never wanted to let her go.

"I'm angry that you felt the need to lie to me when everything wasn't going to be all right. You can't do that. We can't do that. War is coming. A battle we might not survive."

He hated the finality in her words but didn't interrupt, reveling in the feel of her in his arms. On his lap.

She brushed his hair back from his forehead and placed a kiss on the bare skin. "We can't hide the truth from each other anymore. Especially since you can read my emotions."

He grinned at her, then rested his forehead against hers. "Can you tell what emotions I'm feeling now?"

Felicity rolled her eyes. "Already you're—"

"Come with me. There is a place I want to show you." He was going to take advantage of his newfound freedom within the realm. Wanted to show her places he had only visited in dreams since he'd left. The shadows already started to slink towards them at his call.

"You passed out just a little while ago and have a headache. This is where your mind goes?"

A chuckle. "You'll find that I'll be thinking of you in many ways. A wide imagination some might say." Some being him. "And my headache feels better."

His shadows curled around her, and she arched into him at the caress. The question they possessed. "Do we have an agreement, Alarian?"

He kissed her, breathing in her scent of star drenched wildflowers as he did. "Yes. I won't lie to you about what's to come. And how I feel about it."

"Good."

"By the way." He nipped her neck. "I feel really good about where we're going right now."

"You'll wait."

The shadows dropped, and both of them turned to find the Secret Keeper standing in the doorway with their cane in hand. "We need to talk."

Felicity removed herself from his hold and pulled a chair out for the old witch to sit. "I'm not certain how I feel about you," Felicity warned them.

"I can understand your hesitancy." They took the seat with ease, even if they couldn't see. "But I have information you want."

Felicity and Alarian shared a glance. "Marquette?"

They nodded. "Yes. But in this sharing of secrets, I'm breaking an agreement held for over seventy years. The weight of this secret has been heavy on my shoulders for too long, but if it will save the continent, then you deserve to know."

Felicity took a seat, rapt attention on the witch. "We need whatever information we can get."

Alarian's jaw clenched momentarily. His headache wasn't completely gone. "Will you need to use your magic?"

The Díomhair shook their head. "No. Just your ears to listen. So shut your mouth so I can talk."

Felicity chuckled, and Alarian rolled his eyes as the witch sat back in their chair. "The youngling known as Marquette was a timid thing. Most thought her shy, while others found her stuck up. The truth was she was neither. She was biding her time. You see, Marquette thought she deserved everything she wanted. Before her twentieth year, I'd caught her stealing parchments meant only for our scholars. She promised she'd never do that again. I had thought she meant that she'd never steal. Later, I learned that she meant she'd never get caught again."

Alarian's brow bunched. There were a few stories he had of his mother growing up. This was not one of them.

"When she was nearing her forty-seventh year, she was sent on a mission. Powerful many would say, but in truth, she didn't know the full extent of her powers yet. Certainly not how to yield them. All she had been meant to do though was find the governor of a nearby town in Visce and discuss the grazing grounds for our animals. Instead, she returned with meat and produce. The

Shadows sent to uncover what happened had thrown up at how the people were torn apart from the inside out. According to Marquette, they had attacked her.

"That was when Visce chose to attack us. She survived. Her family and countless others had not. But she blamed us for her loss. Said we hadn't wanted to protect her. It was then that I was first asked to read her secrets. She'd nearly escaped, but I was able to collect."

This is what they needed. What Felicity needed. Not the accounts of a female who considered herself a victim, but of one that had been pushed against a wall. Where his mother had found herself after running from Roald's death.

The Díomhair leaned forward on her cane and stared blankly in their direction. "The witch."

"What?" Felicity tilted her head. "Fiadh?"

They gripped the chair tightly. "Yes. The witch was whom she had found in that town. A young woman hiding amongst monsters, as she considered the faeries of the village she lived in. Fiadh told her stories of heartstones and power she'd never considered. A heartstone that she hoped to steal from the people. Visce's attack was meant to be a diversion, but since they were not under Marquette's control, her family had been among the first lost. As a result, she hid and couldn't retrieve that stone."

They breathed a long sigh. "Due to her actions, we handed Marquette over to Visce for punishment as they deemed fit. In the end, I believe it is what brought her closer to the witch. Two minds alike with greed at the center of their souls."

"What was it that she wanted though? It couldn't have just been the stone?" Alarian asked.

"It was more. Power was not the only thing she wanted—but control over life and death. A whole new possibility."

Felicity inhaled, her eyes widening. Alarian swallowed, glancing between the two of them. "But only Ankus and Saol..."

He trailed off, air stuck in his throat. He looked to Felicity for confirmation of his suspicions. She had told him she would share the letter from Thomas when they returned. Until then, he was kept in the dark. He opened the bond, could feel her fear, shock. With her nod, he expelled a breath. "Shit."

The Díomhair tapped her cane once, then creaked to a standing position. "You have the information you need, I believe. There is no need to ask the others. I must leave before the broken oath takes over."

"What does that mean?" Felicity stood to assist them to the door, their movements slower than before.

They gave a halfhearted grin. "I've held that information for a long time. Many secrets in fact. But that is one of the most dangerous. For the continent, I gave it up, and I don't regret it."

"You're not going to die, are you?"

Alarian heard the concern in her voice.

A little chuckle broke from their lips. "Not yet, but soon. I have a little time to get my affair in order before that happens. Secrets, to me, are like years of a life. By giving them away, I give my life away. And now I am nearing the end of my time."

"So, the secrets you told about me?" Alarian whispered. "Were they killing you?"

She nodded. "I didn't have to say more than if you were innocent or not. But you deserved more. Your story, or what could be told of it, shared. I don't have any regrets. It is time for me to leave this plane. But I ask that you protect my resting place from the likes of Marquette and Fiadh."

While Felicity continued to assist her out, Alarian gripped the back of the now empty chair, settling himself. The truth was out. His mother, the witch, his father—they were going to open the veil to hell itself.

Chapter 51

Felicity

Felicity had assisted the Díomhair to a fae outside their door waiting to escort them back to their room. When she returned, she found Alarian still gripping the back of a chair. Just moments before he was going to take her away. If they had left, the truth wouldn't have been uncovered. The truth of what Marquette had done and what she and Fiadh planned to do.

"How do you feel?"

Alarian shifted, his knuckles white. "I remember hearing stories of my father's kindness when he was young. My aunt had told me that my mother had changed him. That the bond they shared changed them. I never knew how they became bonded, and now with my knowledge of how it comes to pass, I wonder what trouble their relationship went through that was against all odds."

Felicity straddled the chair in front of him and looked up into his face. "To assume that Magic is good or bad, sentient in such a way, is an assumption one shouldn't make. For reasons unknown, it thought they had found each other through hard and difficult times and chose love anyway. That was enough."

"But it changed him. He allowed her to turn him into something vile."

She swallowed and his gaze snapped to her. "I wouldn't do that to you. You know that, right?"

"If anything—" She almost wanted to bite back the words but resisted. "I fear that I'll do that to you."

He leaned in and kissed her. "We never would. Remember—I call you out for your shit and you do the same for me."

"I promise to always call you out when you mess up."

He grinned. "We are great apart, but we are better together."

She rolled her eyes. "You're getting mushy on me."

He gave a small chuckle, then leaned back and stared at the floor. "The veil to Ankus? Is that really what she and Fiadh are planning to do?"

Felicity stood, resting a knee on the chair, and took his face in her hands. "Yes. I think it is. She needs four of five stones. They have three for certain." She rested her forehead against his and closed her eyes. "Saol and Domhain. She needs only one of them—and with Domhain's lost..."

"Saol's stone is in danger."

Felicity nodded.

"I'll send a letter to warn the Countess."

Felicity opened her eyes. "She probably already knows. But it doesn't hurt."

Alarian breathed a slow sigh. "True. You know, I had thought we could just enjoy each other. Hide away for just a moment longer from the real world and all its problems."

Felicity's mouth quirked. He was right—they had a lot to deal with and needed to return home as soon as possible. "It's nearly dark."

When he didn't move or respond, she continued, "Even if we traveled all night, we would be exhausted."

"Meaning?" He stepped closer, the damn chair between them still.

"Which means we could technically leave early in the morning and be more helpful if we have a good night's rest tonight."

"I think you should be aware that rest wasn't my plan for you tonight, Starlight."

"Good." She kissed him as the shadows wrapped around her, adjusting herself around the chair to be closer to him.

The sensation of floating was fleeting and just as quickly, her feet met the ground.

Alarian never loosened his hold on her. Felicity pressed further into him, reveling in his heat, his scent. When the shadows began to disperse, she pulled from their kiss long enough to take in their new surroundings and let out a whispered breath of awe.

Trees overlapped a beautiful lagoon. A small waterfall trickled from rocky terrain, the little river flowing from it lapping against stone and earth. Vines of leaves hung above, sliding from one tree to the next. Openings in the canopy above let in a little moonlight. Moss covered stones and little toadstools popped up along fallen logs and the river's edge. Frogs and crickets sang in the distance.

"It's beautiful here."

Alarian leaned in, pressing his lips to her forehead. "I've dreamed of taking you here. Never thought it would be a reality."

She bit her lip, that ever-present realization of all the truths she laid at his feet just a few hours before.

He must have picked up on her thoughts. "What is it you want, Felicity? I know you still think I'm a liability right now."

She remembered his words. Even after the night in Cnoc, she knew he'd step aside for now. To pick this up later. As if that was a choice anymore. "You're my weakness," she whispered the words between them. "That scares me more than I can fathom."

Felicity looked into his eyes. His mouth quirked, but only for a moment. "You're my everything." There was a finality in his words. "I know—"

She leaned in, interrupting him with a kiss. Reveled in the way his hand gripped her waist, his other arm curved around her back, holding her close. There was a lingering taste of sadness, as if he was preparing for goodbye. Even after she claimed him in front of a council of his people. He deserved for her to say it.

There was no way this would be the last kiss. That she could resist the sensation of his emotions. She needed years, a lifetime more of them. "Alarian, I'm yours," she breathed against his mouth.

A small growl, and then the kiss was all consuming. His hand sliding up her neck and tangling in her hair. She panted, breaking away from him, then traced a finger along his jaw, forcing him to meet her gaze. "I'm not going to walk away from you anymore." He needed, deserved, the reassurances he had offered her. "You're more than worthy."

He shuddered at the words. She drew his head against her chest. She could sense his doubt. It made her want to find Marquette and tear her apart. To kill Roald all over again for this male who had been shattered by his parents. "I need you, not because you make me better, but because you've seen me long before I even saw myself." He straightened and she reached up to brush the tears from his cheek. "There is no beginning and end to us—just a continuous loop." She met his gaze. Held it. "I love you." She hadn't said it aloud to him. It felt wrong not to speak the words when he could sense it.

His lips were on her in a heartbeat. He pulled her up, her legs instinctually wrapping around his waist. He carried her, his grip firm but gentle. She had no clue where they were going, but when it came to him, it didn't matter. Together. That was all it was now.

Felicity giggled as he lowered her to the ground, an unfamiliar sound, un-bidden as the bed of grass tickled her body. He chuckled, the feel of his body reverberating against hers, the feel of him. She laid down, his arms bracing him above her. "I love you too."

"How's your head feeling?" She brushed a finger along his brow, his dark red hair shining in the limited light.

"Great." It was mostly the truth, she could tell. "I'd honestly forgotten about it as soon as I got you here."

She smiled at him, her finger tracing over his lip. That smile of his quirking at the corner of his mouth. Damn that smile, the way his gaze warmed her to her core. "Alarian, please don't take your time."

He recaptured her mouth with his, already roaming, touching—taking her in as she did the same. Firm muscle, soft skin. This was different than the Cnoc inn. That had been filled with a need. This—it was exploratory, teasing. His hands dipped to her trousers, releasing the stays. She was at his ties, releasing his shirt then traced a finger along the hemline of his trousers. His hand inched up her tunic, grazing her stomach, and she shuddered as they brushed along the base of her brassiere.

Alarian's lips trailed along her neck, then skimmed the top of her breast. She sighed against his touch, heat growing between them as their movements became hurried. Anticipation growing.

He pulled her tunic over her head, hooded eyes roaming over her body. She reached up and slid the straps of her undergarments down and he inhaled as she tossed her brassiere aside. He glanced over her appreciatively, then met her gaze. "I can feel your emotions right now—and there is no need to be doubtful. You're beautiful."

She smiled. "You're cheating."

"I didn't think about it before, but this may have its advantages." He leaned in and her body arched into him. "It does help to know exactly what it is your feeling." A nip to the curve of her neck had a shudder of need rush down her spine. "Almost like a window into what you like." A graze of his tongue against her breast, a brush of his teeth around her nipple and she gasped. "What turns you on."

"Rian," she whimpered the word.

He chuckled between a trail of kisses to the waist of her trousers. "I've dreamed of making you feel this way. Thought it would never be reality." He looked up at her as he sucked her nipple between his teeth. "Reality is already so much better." Then his head dipped between her legs, a gentle kiss that had her gripping the grass to stop herself from begging for more.

His tongue slid against her, a groan she didn't recognize broke from her lips. As he worked her, Felicity's hand dug into his hair, felt his firm shoulders, her body begging for release as she hung on tight.

Just when she was about to break under him, to scream in ecstasy, he stopped, looking up at her. "So close, Starlight."

"You damn asshole."

Fire lit in his eyes then, and he pulled off his pants in a swift movement she barely caught, he dipped between her again, his cock grazing against her.

Felicity reached down, her fingers wrapping around him, stalling him from his attempts of control. As she tightened her grip, sliding her hand up on down his shaft, he shivered. "Fuck, Felicity."

She kissed his neck, wrapping her legs around his, pulling him closer. "Yes?" The innocence in her voice held a teasing lilt.

"You know exactly what you're doing."

"I do." She kissed his collar bone, her other hand trailing down his chest. He shuddered above her as she stroked him again. "I'm going to learn every touch that makes you come undone."

She angled his cock between her legs, sliding it against her slick opening. He didn't hold back but plunged within her. As he filled her, he groaned out her name.

Their movements quickened, panting between kisses as their heated bodies were cooled by the mist in the air. They came undone together, both of them riding the wave of desire, Felicity's body shuddered under his touch. Magic—not hers, not his—curled around her. Slid through her blood and along her muscle. Beckoned. Offered. And she knew what it was as Alarian's breathed into her, holding her tightly against him. They met each other's gaze. He brushed a thumb against her jaw. "Always, Starlight?"

"With you."

And she relaxed into his touch. Magic's offer. And a snap rang through her body beginning at her heart. A strong sense of love, acceptance, appreciation, overcame her. And she knew those emotions weren't only hers. Knew that he was now as much a part of her as she was of him.

The bond. He looked down on her, their gaze met, and he grinned. She smiled. His eyes shined as she rested her palm against his cheek. "I love you."

Alarian squeezed his eyes shut for a moment. "I love you too."

They dressed then he curled her into his side and Felicity's eyes fluttered closed for a moment, a sense of bliss and peace washing over her. The grass, the flowers...everything seemed so much brighter. More alive. With him beside her, they could keep it that way. Would keep it that way.

He must have known where her thoughts, or emotions, had drifted too. "I wish we didn't have to return tomorrow."

"Are you going to your aunt's house after this is all done?" The words were out, the last of her concerns a whisper on the breeze.

Alarian kissed the top of her head. "Only if you are. It's you, Starlight. Always you."

"What is?" She didn't know why a part of her needed to hear the words. Maybe it was the fear that she wasn't worthy of him.

"Where I'm meant to be."

She smiled. "If we make it through this—I want to go back. To Domhain. To help them."

Alarian kissed her temple. "My princess. My starlight." He nuzzled her. "I knew I'd never have to ask."

When they had finally deigned to get up and dressed, a rustling caused them both to reach for their weapons.

"Beasts?" she asked, knowing *things* hid in these shadows.

Alarian shook his head. "It's not late enough yet."

"How do they not enter the village?"

He winked at her. "Secrets." Then lowered his own dagger as Talia and Hayden emerged from the trees.

Hayden glanced at the ground where they had laid moments before then back to them. "At least we came after the show."

"Jump off a ledge, Hayden," Alarian ground out.

"Can't." He nodded towards Felicity. "We have some business with her first."

Alarian shifted in front of Felicity, his shoulders bunched. Felicity couldn't hide her smirk.

Talia laughed. "Don't worry, Rian." She smiled. "It's only Dearmadta business."

Felicity's breath caught in her chest. "What?"

Shadows cleared and others stepped from the edges.

Talia grinned. "Ready to take your rights?"

Felicity glanced from Alarian to Talia. Something she couldn't quite decipher snapped into place. Her shoulders drew back as she slid her blade into the sheath at her hip. "Yes."

Alarian moved to follow, but Talia placed a hand against his chest, stopping him. "You can't come. Sorry, friend."

"But—"

Felicity moved in beside the others and grinned at her bonded. The male she would always claim as her own. "Sorry, Rian—as you said—*secrets*."

And she knew that these were secrets they were allowed to keep and wouldn't separate them from each other. The excitement of having this for herself, the pride in his gaze—Felicity knew this was the correct choice to make. For herself.

The traveling party arrived on the outskirts of the castle, a mile on foot from the entrance. Felicity walked with purpose, Reóta remaining at an easygoing stride beside her. Success. In the end, she'd done exactly what she'd planned and although Alarian was certain she hadn't realized the ramifications of her actions, he was thankful all the same. She was one of the Master Spies now. Had been given the offer and took it. Since then, it seemed like the last fragments of her identity had snapped into place.

Scáth no longer despised him—even if it was only tolerance, he could accept that. It had been too long since he'd breathed in the air, felt the humidity, been surrounded by the earth and trees...he'd missed his home.

Talia cleared her voice. "Did you get word to your family, Princess?"

Felicity shook her head. "No, we decided Alarian's magic was best preserved for emergencies since it was weakened."

Alarian winced at the words. "Not weak. Just needed a break. The Díomhair took a lot out of me." His headache had mostly dissipated but even though the herbs had briefly helped, he wasn't healed completely. It would be another day or two before it would be gone for good.

"Sure," Hayden grumbled. "The Díomhair took a lot out of you."

Felicity smirked and he winked at her. His bonded. Damn, that sounded good.

Talia groaned. "Don't start being cute."

They reached the gates, Éardrom guards rushing to attention and offered to escort them in. Felicity waved them off. The Shadows that joined them sent out a wisp of their magic around them and the guards straightened, their eyes sharp on the new members of their party. It would already create a stir and with the upcoming call to arms, it would be helpful for all to see that they had allies within their midst.

They entered through the side door that Alarian had become accustomed to returning and exiting through. The staff started whispering immediately, darting furtive glances as their group walked along the halls towards the throne room.

The guards, seeing them coming, quickly opened the double doors. He watched as Felicity drew back her shoulders and raised her chin. As if this was rehearsed, Alarian took a step behind, Talia beside him, with her four associates bringing up the rear.

Everyone turned, their gazes taking in the procession. King Bastien smiled with a gleam of pride in his eyes. He was the first to rise, making his way down the steps to drag Felicity into a hug.

Alarian clasped his hands at his back, taking on the role of dutiful soldier who had assisted his princess in her return. It was a moment of clarity though when Prince Kellan looked over Felicity's shoulder and actually smiled at him. There had been a change in the male over the past few weeks when it came to their relationship. A change Alarian still wasn't certain he deserved.

Prince Kellan led his sister up the stairs, and King Bastien stood when all three members of the royal family stood side by side. "Friends from Scáth have arrived. I apologize for this unexpected distraction but if you would all be so kind, I will meet with you regarding any concerns tomorrow. If you've been waiting, please step in the hall for a moment, and I'll be certain the staff sends you on your way with a meal."

It wasn't until the last of them had left and the council members stood from their chairs, that Alarian saw that Lord Dimitri was present. They clasped hands while the others talked with the newly arrived Scáth members. "How is everything?"

Dimitri glanced at the others, then back to him. "Lian—I haven't heard from him and I'm worried."

Alarian's jaw clenched. "The stone?" he whispered.

The male shook his head. "I need to go home to be sure. There is so much left to do here now that Chartow is no longer with us."

Alarian had been told about the incident in Tine. They may not have seen eye to eye, but Chartow's death was still a blow.

Dimitri glanced towards the large windows overlooking the garden. "If anything happened to him..."

"We'll find out. I should have stopped and checked in."

Dimitri shook his head. "Don't take this burden, Alarian. You and I both know the dangers were there either way. Lian was aware too. He's still alive. I'd be able to tell otherwise."

King Bastien cleared his throat, drawing them out of their private conversation. "Let's allow our allies a moment reprieve. They can settle into their quarters with a meal in their stomachs. We can reconvene in the meeting hall at the fifth toll of the bell."

Everyone started to head towards the door, Alarian walking alongside Dimitri. "Does the king know?"

Dimitri nodded. "I told only him."

Alarian's name was called, and he glanced over his shoulder at Felicity standing with her brother and father, a tentative smile on her face. His stomach dropped. Were they doing this now?

Dimitri chuckled. "Seems like you have a family affair to deal with."

"What do you mean?"

He rolled his eyes. "I was at your trial, my friend." He patted his shoulder. "Don't worry. I'll receive an update from Lian soon, I'm sure. It's likely I'm over-analyzing his silence. If I don't hear from him tomorrow, I'll head home." Then he waved over his shoulder as he left Alarian behind.

Alarian tried to not think the worst of Lian's current situation as he turned to face the others and met them halfway.

King Bastien spoke first. "Well, I think we all want to know—is there an impending marriage?"

A snort from Felicity and Alarian's eyes widened in her direction. "Marriage—Your Majesty, I assure you that I would ask you first for—"

Bastien chuckled, clasping him on the shoulder. "It was a joke."

"Oh." He swallowed, trying to recover his composure.

"I'm glad to know you would do the proper thing."

He wasn't accustomed to humor, the firm but gentle grip on his shoulder, the smile from a male that held so much power. As if he could read his mind, Prince Kellan nudged him with a grin. This was a side that he was still working to accept. Even when King Bastien and Prince Kellan gave him the news of his freedom, he had expected them to re-clap on the manacles and take him straight to the gallows. Instead, not only had they freed him, but suggested that he should follow Felicity. Despite what her letter said.

Felicity sighed. "This is edging towards heartfelt... let's move onto the more important matters."

Prince Kellan guffawed. "Like when you two finally—"

"Nope." Felicity cut him off. "Let's go."

The two siblings continued to bicker as they walked towards the door. Alarian looked towards the king. "I promise to do my best by her."

King Bastien's jaw clenched. "I know you will. Long after I'm gone."

"Let's not have that be anytime soon, Your Majesty. We still need you here." Alarian clasped his hands behind his back again, uncertain what else to do with them. With himself.

The king took a deep breath. "They are more ready to lead than I was at either of their ages. Especially together. They've collected an army, allies. I'm proud of who they became despite it all."

Alarian nodded. "Despite my parents."

"Despite anything. This isn't your fault. The male before me isn't calculated and cold but one who stands united and strong. And as much as she allows it, my daughter will need you by her side. That letter told us more of your character than any of those rebels could. More than your parents will ever know. I didn't think it would be easy for me to forgive you. Until I read that letter, I wanted to blame you for everything. But I couldn't—even if she didn't love you."

Emotions bubbled up inside Alarian at the words. The truth in his tone. "Thank you."

"Come. We have an important meeting to prepare for. A war to win." He clasped Alarian's shoulder once more before heading towards the door.

"Let me know what you need of me."

King Bastien chuckled. "Oh, we have plans for you."

***

Everyone—an advisor from each realm—had arrived and settled around the table in the meeting hall. He was surprised to see his aunt who gave him a regal nod and a knowing smile as he took a seat across from her. "It's good to see you again."

He smiled. "I'm glad you're here."

"Me too," she mouthed.

Unlike when Alarian had been forced to attend his father's meetings with a large throne-like chair at the head of the table, King Bastien had ensured all the chairs were the same, the table in an oblong shape so that no one side was considered the head. A table of presumable equals—and Alarian had been asked to sit at it by the king as a representative of the people. Not one realm, seeing as he'd spent so much time and had connections throughout the continent, but it seemed his efforts with the rebels had shown his willingness to serve no matter someone's stature or means.

It was an honor he wouldn't let go to waste.

Sloan stood, his hands resting on the table. "My contacts within Tine have informed me that the ex-queen and their armies are preparing to move. Within the next few days, if they haven't already. They will take different forms of travel—some by sea, others by land, and some by darkness or shadow."

"The dragon?" Felicity stared at the map in front of her.

Alarian couldn't help the small tilt to his lips. Of course her concern would be for the beast.

Sloan shook his head. "No concrete information on why the dragon is assisting them just yet. It's difficult to uncover since the creatures are enigmatic as it is."

Prince Kellan stood pointing at the map, along the crags of the hills. "With the cailleach and horses, we will have means for both an aerial and land attack. The dragon will make easy pickings of our air forces, let alone any within the distance of her fire or talons. If Felicity's correct in her assumptions that she's being used, we need to free her from Marquette's clutches as soon as possible. If we can get a few to travel ahead, assess our situation and search the mountain caves, we might find what the dragon desperately wants back."

"Unless she's a Tine dragon and then what we want may be on the other side of the continent," Lady Grandeur added.

"It's from the mountains along Saol and Domhain. Of that I'm certain." Felicity glanced at the advisors. "Tine's dragons are usually covered in clay and dust—red in color. Saol dragons try to meld into the terrain to remain hidden. This one was green and tinged gray."

Alarian added, "I'm also under the belief that Tine's dragons usually wouldn't care what was taken from them. They would kill without question or a second thought if they felt threatened, even if it meant the loss of their young. They don't play well with others."

Felicity bit her lip in consideration. Her emotions simmered under the surface, but he blocked them out as best he could. She was still grasping how to do the same with him but was catching on much faster than he had, able to sometimes block him out on her own. He respected her privacy and understood her reasoning.

"And was your trip to Scáth helpful?"

Alarian glanced at Talia. During their trip, they hadn't confided with her what the Díomhair had shared with them. Both Felicity and Alarian decided it was information best not divulged on the road. "Yes."

The silence was deafening. Stagnant. Waiting. Felicity stood and leaned over, resting her palms on the table. Her chin lifted, glancing at each of the advisors in turn, before settling on her father. "Marquette plans to open the veil to Ankus." She swallowed. "To hell."

No one spoke. Moved. The entire world went still. Except Alarian knew that for many outside those doors, life continued. Oblivious of the truth just spoken aloud.

"Are you sure?" Prince Kellan whispered.

She nodded, as did Alarian.

Avyanna stared in horror at the center of the table. "The oath. That's what it meant. They are bound to them even in death."

Avyanna removed drawings from her pocket and placed the papers down on the table to flatten them out. "Every one of the imprisoned, dead or alive, was forced to take an oath. No one can remember the words properly. They are convoluted and changed in each survivor's account."

Everyone stood and took in the crude drawing of a barren and withered tree. The dead roots. The flourishing branches.

"What are the similarities in the oaths?" King Bastien asked.

Prince Kellan ran a hand through his hair. "Unending fealty to Marquette and Roald."

Felicity reached for the drawing, and Avyanna held it out.

Felicity gasped. "I didn't even consider. They have what they need for an army of undead."

Sloan slammed a fist into the table. "We can't let this happen."

"Obviously." Dimitri rolled his eyes. "The question is how do we stop it with only days between now and Samhain."

"We have to be there. Ready." King Bastien's shoulders were slumped, bags under his eyes hinting at the exhaustion he hadn't yet succumbed to.

Before they could discuss further, there was a knock at the door and the king beckoned them in. A guard held it open. "Your Majesty, there is someone here to see you. They said it was urgent and have vital information."

The door widened further and a female walked in, her body clad in brown and black clothing. Her face was nearly fully covered, revealing two teardrop shaped eyes. When she was in front of the king, she bowed, before lowering a mask from the lower half of her face. "Marquette and Fiadh have made their move."

King Bastien glanced at the others. "For those who aren't aware, this is Ciana of Scáth. She's been collecting intel for us."

So, this was the infamous Ciana. Talia had only shrugged when Alarian had asked about her, unwilling to give more information.

She glared at Alarian out of the corner of her eye, then turned as Prince Kellan stood.

Prince Kellan glanced at the map ahead of them. "We know—"

"No." She shook her head. "They are riding the dragon separate from their army. They recently left Aer."

Alarian's gaze immediately shifted to Dimitri. The male was stiff in his chair.

The king glanced around the room, purposely diverting his gaze from the Aer advisor. There were no words of comfort. Nothing that anyone could say as Dimitri clutched his chest. Not when only a select few were privy to what Lian protected. "We don't have time to wait anymore. It's crucial we start our move towards Saol. Spread the word to your realms. I expect them to be ready within ten days to move. Extra supplies shall follow with us.

King Bastien glanced at Sloan. "Send ahead your fastest messengers and a small guard for protection. We need to clear the towns of Saol as much as possible."

"Consider it done, Your Majesty."

"And what of Éardrom's royal family?" The new advisor from Dorcha tilted their head in contemplation. Felicity had told Alarian of Heavin's demise. He was glad she was able to keep her promise. "Will you be following?"

"Yes." They all answered at the same time and everyone chuckled.

Prince Kellan gestured to his fiancée, Avyanna rising to her feet. He cleared his throat, before taking her hand. "Tomorrow, we would like to invite you all to a small ceremony. Before the fight, we want to wed. We'll keep it quick."

Felicity's well of emotions opened to him. The others stood and began to congratulate the couple, and Alarian watched as his Cridhe pulled Prince Kellan into a tight hug before turning to Avyanna. Happy. If only he could guarantee she could feel this way forever.

King Bastien clapped, calling the attention towards him and the room quieted. "Tomorrow evening it is. I'm happy for you both."

"This should be a large celebration." Aunt Leana smiled. "Are you certain you don't want to wait?"

Avyanna was the one to answer. "No, my parents are here. We are all together. That can't be guaranteed soon. When this is all over, we shall celebrate with the entire continent." A difficult decision since most of her friends and family were in Tine. Only a few had returned, most still remaining within the realm. "We want to be officially married before all of this."

Alarian's gaze turned toward Felicity, longing settled in his chest. Someday. He knew, without a doubt, that she was his forever. No matter how long forever would be. For him, everything began and ended with her. No matter what this battle would be, as long as Felicity survived, he knew he could handle it all.

Chapter 53

Kellan

Kellan met Felicity's eyes for a brief moment over Avyanna's shoulders. The smile and contentment on her face settling him before he turned his attention back to his bride. Sometimes he needed those reminders that she was still here. And now his sister was standing beside his almost-wife as he was getting married. It felt surreal.

Avyanna squeezed his hand and he smiled at her, an ache in his chest at the overpowering sensation of love. This was what he'd worked so hard for. What he had dreamed but never dared hoped would happen.

His father spoke clearly of the vows between them, overseeing the ceremony. As the final vows were spoken, Sloan handed him the bracelet he'd had made for Avyanna—fire opals imported years ago from Tine and had been within the palace vaults. He'd had the gems set with diamonds from his mother's marriage bracelet. He placed it around Avyanna's wrist, and with the heat of her magic, she welded the clasps closed.

"It's beautiful," she whispered.

"I'm glad you like it."

Felicity held out a steel band to Avyanna who took it and welded it closed around his wrist.

"Just as these pieces signify a never-ending circle, may their lives be filled with never-ending love. And now you may close these vows with a kiss."

He tugged her close and Avyanna laughed, her head tilting back slightly to show off the smooth column of her throat. One of the first places he would start tonight—when they were alone. Kellan kissed her, unable to wait a moment longer.

She rested her hand against his chest, kissing him back.

Everyone cheered, the sound comforting even if it was just a handful of guests in attendance. They had sent out food to the nearby townspeople in the hope they could find some solace and time with their families before they were to leave the following day. For war. No matter if they were fighting alongside them or not, many would lose loved ones in the days to come.

The thought forced him out of the moment. He pulled back gently, resting his forehead against hers, eyes closed, concentrating on the feel of her hands on him. Applause broke through his dark thoughts. Thankfully. He wanted to remember this moment.

They made their way to the garden where the staff had set up a small feast and tables. A quartet played lively music from their place on a small platform.

They danced. They ate. Guests made toasts. Everyone kept the mood light and cheery. No one brought up what the following day would bring.

The sun was inching towards the horizon, the last of the food shared amongst the guests and staff. Guards and soldiers were invited to join in when the mood had shifted. Couples wanted to be with one another. Family close together.

Bastien gripped his son's shoulder and smiled. "I'm happy for you. The two of you complement each other very well."

"Thank you."

"Nothing to thank me for. It's the two of you that found each other amidst a curse."

He watched as Avyanna giggled, a champagne glass in hand, at something Alarian had said. "Is it wrong that I want to tell her that she shouldn't come tomorrow? Her training in field medicine just started a few days ago. What if—"

"There are always going to be what ifs, son. Avyanna is smart and resilient. She won't be alone, and the other medics would have told her she couldn't come if they didn't think she could handle it."

"But in every fiber of my being, I want to protect her."

Bastien snorted. "And why do you think she wants to come? It's not just because she has purpose out there—it's for you."

Avyanna glanced his way and her smile widened, her face glowing. He winked and watched as Felicity drew his wife's attention back to their conversation with Alarian.

"How are you taking it that she came back *with* him?"

His father gave a small smirk, gaze pinned on the couple. "He's growing on me. The talk we had with him helped."

"But for Felicity?"

"He's a good male. I know Felicity won't let him get away with anything."

"Even if…" He didn't want to say the words. "Can you forgive him?"

"You heard Felicity's account." Bastien peered at Kellan from the corner of his eye. "There is nothing to forgive. From his own mouth, those that killed my wife were torn apart by beasts. He watched to make sure." Bastien shook his head. "It would be easier to blame him, but I can't. He'll do good by her. I have no doubt he loves her."

"Why?"

Bastien grinned. "Because they're bonded, Kellan."

His eyes widened. The bond…it was something he had heard of but never understood. When Felicity had asked about it, he couldn't imagine speaking to his sister about love. In his eyes, she was meant to be a youngling forever. "How do you know? Did he tell you that?"

"He didn't have to." Bastien nodded in their direction. "I remember that feeling."

"You and—"

"Your mother." Mist settled in his lashes as Bastien faced his son. "It was an honor and a blessing. The time I spent with her could never be replaced. I loved two fae in my life—but she was the one who I defied all the odds for and would do so again. Kaliana always understood and that is what made her my second love. Because she never tried to be a replacement but cared for us the best way she could."

Kellan had never known his mother. She'd died giving birth to him. It was hard to grieve someone you never met. His thoughts of her, the stories his father had told him before Kaliana came into their lives, had only settled a longing within him for something he couldn't have. Or so he thought, until his stepmother lovingly filled that role with no expectations.

"Is that something Avy and I can have?" Kellan asked in awe.

"The bond is not something to hunt for. I don't fully understand it."

"There is no one else for me." Kellan shook his head. "It's always been her."

"Then you already have it, son. And remember those words and these feelings and you will always have it."

They stood in silence for a little bit longer. Kellan watched as Sloan talked with some of the newly arrived Shadows. Ciana had made an appearance but now was nowhere to be seen. Alarian's aunt danced with Lord Denizen and a few others.

"Thank you, Father."

"For what?"

Kellan gripped his father's shoulder and pulled him into a hug. "For always being an example."

"I'm not perfect," Bastien grumbled.

Kellan chuckled. "Never said you were. But you tried to show us how to be the best we can be."

"I'm glad I'm able to see the male and female you two have become."

Kellan grinned, pulling out of his father's hold. "I'm just happy your back."

Bastien sniffed, wiped his eyes.

Felicity and the others came over. Avyanna rested her head against Kellan's shoulder while Felicity wrapped her arms around their father's waist.

Silence spread as the clock chimed the hour.

The music came to a stop.

Kellan looked at his friends. His family. Sloan met his gaze and nodded. Alarian's attention on the clock upon the wall as it came to the stop at the tenth bell.

The guests whispered congratulations. Some gave hugs to others. Then they all left for the privacy of their own rooms. To prepare. To contemplate. Hold loved ones close.

For tomorrow.

Avyanna pressed a kiss to his cheek. And he reminded himself of his promise. Tonight. For them, he was going to present tonight.

# Chapter 54

Felicity

The moon was lowering over the horizon. She and Alarian were still tangled together, her head resting against his chest. His breathing had turned heavy a while ago, but she couldn't sleep. Her eyes were pinned open as her mind reeled with all the possibilities of what tomorrow meant. What could happen over the course of the upcoming days. The planning, strategizing. The fact that they couldn't control the possible deaths of hundreds if not thousands.

"Talk to me, Starlight." The words were a whisper, and Felicity instinctually tightened her hold.

He brushed hair from her cheek, then traced a finger along her jaw to lift her chin up to meet his gaze. "Tell me."

"Just thinking. A lot." There was everything and nothing.

He kissed her forehead, then his gaze searched hers. She'd been working on blocking his emotions. It felt private. But right now, she searched his. The warmth of his love and comfort caressed her skin.

"I have a question..." Alarian trailed off, deep in thought.

After a breath, two, she said, "You can't start and then not ask." She rolled her eyes, and rested a palm on his chest, her chin on top of her hand. "Well?"

"So impatient." He flicked her nose. "I worry this is too soon to ask."

"Tomorrow isn't promised. Remember."

The light in his green eyes dimmed a little at the reminder. "Would you ever consider marriage?"

She blinked in surprise.

He rushed ahead. "I was just thinking, you know, because of Kellan and Avy's wedding today. If that was something you ever wanted. In the future. When you are ready. There's no—"

She pressed a finger to his mouth, stopping him. "I didn't fawn over wedding dresses." His lips pursed together. "I didn't think about proposals or plan my perfect wedding."

Felicity lowered her finger and replaced it with her lips, kissed him. "With you, though, yes, I want to marry."

Alarian's shoulders loosened and relief etched his features. "I thought I would frighten you."

"A little." She winced at the admittance. But it had been brief. The connotation of the word, not the act itself. With him. "Just because I won't lie to you."

"Thank you. For your honesty. I don't mean to pressure you in any way."

"Alarian?"

His brow rose. She smiled at the inquisitiveness in his expression.

"If we make it through all of this—"

"It's not if, Felicity. Either we both make it, or I follow you into death. There is no other option for me."

"You could live."

"Not without you. You could go on—for your kingdom, your family and people. I don't mean to sound dramatic, but for me there is only you."

Felicity considered his words. "I can't live without you either, Rian."

He chuckled. "Yes, you could. And I'd want you to, but I don't think that was what you were going to say."

She rolled her eyes, recognizing the change of topic. Her fingers fidgeted against his chest. "Fine, then. If we make it through all of this, I want to marry you. Understood?"

Alarian gasped, covering his mouth in fake shock. "Felicity, did you just propose?"

She groaned, rolling off him and onto her back. "You're ridiculous."

The resounding laughter told her just how much he cared.

"Goodnight, asshole."

He turned, bracketing his arms on either side of her head, hovering his body over her. "I'd marry you now. Tomorrow. Anytime."

"I'm not offering anymore," she mumbled.

He chuckled, kissing the tip of her nose. "Then I'll ask. The day after all this is done. You've been warned."

She was a little annoyed at the smirk that played on his lips. She knew it was in response to the love that he could sense had spread at his words. She really needed to learn how to block him out for moments like these. That was until his amusement turned to adoration—a warmth like a blanket spreading through her chest.

He returned to his place at her side and rested an arm over her stomach. "I love you, Starlight. Always."

She sighed into his touch. The contentment that slid through their bond. "Always."

Chapter 55

After days of preparation and long meetings with their allies, the royal family left for Saol with an army at their backs.

Alarian and Felicity often rode the cailleach ahead, scouting what was to come and finding places to rest for the night. Evenings were spent strategizing before Felicity and Alarian curled up in their tent, holding each other close. Each step, each flap of wings, was like a countdown to the battle to come.

They passed signs of a traveling army. Areas scorched with campfires. Homes along the outskirts of the realms were torn apart and the remaining inhabitants claimed they hadn't antagonized the Tine fae but they wreaked havoc along the way. Along the routes, birds didn't sing, insects didn't chime or buzz. It was as though the wildlife knew what was to come and hid because of it. This only caused more to join their cause, falling into line with whatever weapons they had, while others gave food and supplies.

Dimitri had left directly after the wedding and although Alarian had offered to go with him, the male went alone. On their fourth day of travel, Dimitri caught up with them at the border of Aer and Domhain with upsetting news. Lian was nowhere to be found, and the stone was missing.

Alarian frowned at the news. Felicity's heart cracked open. "We should have hidden it elsewhere."

"He won't give up the information on how to access the stone." Dimitri swallowed. "Not even if it would cost him his life. I may never see him again, but I know he is currently alive. I can still feel him. Even if it's just a touch—I know he's there. Whatever is to come, we should know soon enough where he is."

She wanted to ask him what he could sense. With the upcoming war and the bond between her and Alarian, she needed to know. But it would be insensitive to do so. Instead, she reminded herself to continue practicing blocking his emotions. Alarian did the same. While it was a benefit, they also knew it could be a distraction.

Dimitri patted his horse's neck, and she saw the heaviness in his shoulders. The male was putting on a brave front, but she could only imagine he was breaking inside. Felicity could feel the fear in Alarian.

His brow furrowed, and as his friend walked away, he turned to Felicity. "Do you think they followed us?"

She tilted her head. "What do you mean?"

"That, somehow, they trailed us without us being aware? They arrived in Visce, now Lian is missing after we had visited them."

Felicity's eyes widened. "We didn't search anywhere else in Aer. Would they have assumed we had found the stone?"

"It's a stone that's not required to open the veil to Ankus..." He had read Thomas' letter the night they had returned to the palace.

She blinked and considered. "But could be an attempt to divert our attention."

Alarian's body went rigid. "If they followed us from Dorcha or if Heavin had someone trailing us, it would have been difficult to know. But in Saol—"

Felicity froze, her heart bottoming out with her stomach. *Shit*. "The life heartstone."

He nodded.

Without another word, she mounted Reóta and nudged her upward. "I need to tell my father."

The flight back to her father took less than an hour. They relayed the information in clipped sentences, only insinuating the danger. With a squeeze of Felicity's shoulder, Bastien urged his daughter to the sky. "Go ahead. Find out what you can. We will make camp at the border to Saol. Return with your intel when you can."

They flew quickly for the next two days, only having to divert once when they caught sight of a straggling group of Tine soldiers. To remain unseen, they landed in a small orchard and continued on foot. If she was correct, once they broke through the tree line, they should have a view of the Tower.

And when they did, she stopped, nearly stumbling at the sight before her.

Without a word, she jumped onto the cailleach's back, Alarian doing the same. And they took off towards the Tower. "We need to be careful. They could still be here."

Felicity barely heard the warning, glancing around her as they headed towards the remains of what had been her home for years. Rocks and stone walls were broken, scattered and singed. Very little of the actual structure remained standing. Smoke billowed from certain locations, burnt bodies laid in macabre positions among the remains. She rested a hand against the lynx's neck. "Careful girl. Find a safe place to land."

The cailleach's chest rumbled as if understanding. Something she had noted during their travels. Felicity filed that thought away for later as she leaned in close as they began their descent.

And she took it all in.

Gone.

Everything was gone.

No sign of life or what used to be of the guild of assassins and spies.

As they landed, Felicity jumped off in a fluid movement.

"Felicity?"

Her name sounded foreign. Unfamiliar.

"Let's look for signs of the Countess. We must find out if she was abducted and if the heartstone is still safe."

She swallowed. "Abducted?" Her eyes widened. "Shit, she's taking them."

Alarian stepped in front of her, forcing her attention on him. "What?"

"The book." Her body shuddered. How had she not considered this sooner? "Thomas said the spell alluded to needing blood and soul of the realm. I thought it meant to heartstones. What if it needs an actual sacrifice? That's why she took Lian."

Alarian held her gaze. Didn't move. Didn't even seem to breathe.

He turned and stared at the remains of the Tower. "It's the Countess—the leader of the Tower. We know she saw this coming. She wields magic and knowledge we can only fathom. Let's not jump to conclusions just yet."

It was sound judgement, but she remained frozen, unmoving. This had been her home. For years. Yes, they had taken her memories. They hadn't loved her as a normal family should or could. But suddenly, with the vision before her, Felicity didn't care. If they had taken the Countess, it meant she wasn't immortal as she appeared. Wasn't untouchable. Her heart raced. Her stomach twisted and she almost fell to her knees. Throat constricting, her breathing turned raspy.

The Tower had always seemed like a fortress. A pinnacle that didn't change. Didn't shift with the times. But now—

Alarian caught her as she stumbled, holding her at arm's length to meet her gaze. She blinked as he came into focus, his grip on her shoulders grounding her to the present. "Marquette will pay."

"Yes." She swallowed her emotions. His emotions too. Blocked them all out. "Let's see how much we have to collect." He turned and her body followed on instinct, pulled out of anxiety's attempt to take over.

They reached the wreckage, nearly choking on the stench of death and soot. Instinct led Felicity towards the center of the remains. With little thought, she began to pull aside stone, digging through rock and debris.

Her senses spread out, searching for any familiar scent—the Countess' perfume of honeysuckle, Harrison's aftershave. Harrison. If anything happened to him...

Her knuckles and nails were bloody from tearing at the hard compacted debris. For any sights. Familiar fabric or bits of furniture. Sounds.

"She's not here."

Felicity turned, almost falling over a rock as she did.

Bishop hobbled, dirt smudging his skin—burns and jagged scratches grazed his entire body, revealed through ripped clothing that hung like scraps from his frame. "The Countess." He cleared his throat, then spat. "They took her."

Alarian stumbled across the rumble. "And Harrison?"

Felicity crumbled to her knees, a sob stuck in her throat. She hadn't wanted to voice her fear. But the male she loved knew she had looked for him too. Knew that the man who had been a pivotal presence during her time at the Tower was still important.

"She foresaw. Not soon enough for us all to escape, but many of us got out. The first she sent away was Harrison. Said it was important that he left." Bishop caught her eye.

"Good." Alarian nodded. "That's good."

Felicity ran a hand over her face. Pulled herself together just enough. "Do you know where they took her?"

"Not exactly. We were attacked by a dragon. Hell had broken loose already when the army, arrived but I'm almost certain she was taken west, towards the mountains. That's the last I saw of them while I was trying to get the others out."

Felicity rose to her feet. "Where are the others?"

"Hidden. Safe." Bishop shuddered when she took a step towards him.

Felicity stilled, glancing at Alarian. He hadn't moved. The liaison still had a wall erected towards her. She was here to help. Bishop glanced at Alarian, then back towards her with a sharpness in his gaze. "You fear us?"

Bishop's chuckle was almost a whisper. "Not exactly. I more fear what's to come. What your presence signifies."

"What does that mean? We can help by moving everyone to safety and they can receive medical care. Our camp isn't too far."

He nodded. "Yes, that's true. But it also means a battle is at our doorstep."

"You had to know it was coming."

"We usually stay out of politics. Or so I thought—until you showed up." Bishop grimaced.

Felicity and Alarian shared a look. The Countess seemed to have her hands in everything.

"Should we look for any other survivors?" Alarian glanced around the destruction.

Bishop shook his head. "We found who we could save." He turned, a limp in his step as he cleared a path in the remains. "I'll lead the way."

Felicity moved in step with him and Bishop bristled.

"What is it?" she snapped, no longer feeling obligated to ignore his reactions. Not after so many years of silence. Alarian stayed at her shoulder as they walked, a solid wall of support. "Why have you never liked me?" Years of snide remarks, dark gazes—she never understood why. Even with her memories returned, she couldn't pinpoint a certain incident to make her believe she deserved his scorn.

Bishop turned to face her, his shoulders drawing back. "My sisters were always the smart, conniving, manipulative ones. Not me. It was easier to ignore that which I couldn't control. To pretend it wasn't there."

"So, you couldn't control me therefore you ignored me?" That seemed far from the truth. Then the rest of his words registered. "Wait—sisters?"

He laughed, the jarring sound causing a shiver to run down Felicity's spine. Once he stopped, he glanced over her. "The best spy on the continent and you still didn't want to see. I should have known how much alike we really were. That you, just like me, ignore what we don't want to understand. Where do you think she got a potion for memories from if her ability was seeing the future, not the past?"

Felicity blinked, trying to understand what he was insinuating. He snickered, glancing at Alarian who had moved in closer to her side.

Bishop shook his head, disappointment in his gaze. "The Countess is one of my sisters. My other sister—I assume you know—is long gone. In truth, we lost her when our parents were murdered. She gave her life for a false belief. Or maybe because our eldest sibling was all-knowing, and she was tired of it. Either way, I could never get a straight answer from the Countess. She only shares what she deems important. But I'm a witch."

"A witch?" Alarian growled. "That was your spell? I thought you were just the messenger. Not the one to take her memories." He stepped between the two of them, his body rigid. "Who held our memories."

Felicity didn't know what it said about her that heat pooled in her core instead of anger at Alarian's protectiveness.

Bishop sighed. "My ability is spellwork. And one of those was the memory spell. And no—I never stole. You both gave them willingly. You know that."

Felicity wanted to reach for Alarian but stopped herself.

Alarian had Bishop's collar twisted in his grip before the liaison's words registered.

Bishop sputtered, holding Alarian's grip. The male stepped in closer, his grip tightening. "Fuck you. The shit you caused. The hell you put her through. Us through. Who else suffered at your hand?"

Felicity took a step forward, tentative and slow. A tail had spread in whipping shadows, Alarian's magic shifting off him. Resting her hand on his arm, her own anger cooled at seeing his. "Let him go."

His emerald gaze turned to her, his grip loosening enough for Bishop to take a gasp of air. Alarian didn't let go.

"This is not the way. Not now." She bit her lip, then sighed. "Many of my memories were taken by my choice. This is not all his fault. And the Countess said there was a reason for her choices. We have to trust that." She had to trust that.

"After all this time, you still want to believe her?"

Felicity pinched her eyes closed. Considered all the transgressions and proof against the Countess. But it all came down to one thing. "It brought you to me. Ended the curse. I don't agree with her tactics, but they've worked so far. There must be a reason for it all and even why she's missing now."

Alarian let go, stepping back from the man. Bishop gripped his knees, catching his breath in ragged inhales. "She" —he gurgled— "always has something" —he let a slow breath out, then looked at them— "up her sleeve."

They waited, watching the liaison finally straightened. "Every step was meant to lead up to breaking the curse and..." He trailed off, his mouth pursed tight.

"What?" Alarian growled. "What else aren't you telling us?"

Bishop swallowed, taking a step away before resting his attention on Felicity. "You asked why I kept my distance from you. It's because I didn't agree with the secrecy, but more so, I didn't want to get close to someone destined to die."

Chapter 56

Felicity

Nature went silent. The world stilled. His words echoed in her mind. It wasn't until Alarian buckled beside her, falling to his knees that she finally comprehended what he said. "What?"

There was a bob of Bishop's throat. A deep inhale. "My sister didn't believe in premonitions. Prophecies. That's why she never told others about her ability. People would expect her to warn them. Foresee the future. She believed to her core that it was wrong to share the future—but there was one image she entrusted to me. I think she wanted someone to share the burden with."

Bishop pinched his eyes closed for a moment. "I know she cared for you like a daughter. Please don't think ill of her for this. Of me either. There are many things to despise me for, but not this." When Felicity couldn't make such promises, he continued, "She told me that when the battle came, you would sacrifice yourself to save the continent."

Alarian's shadows had expanded and cocooned the three of them. But they were beginning to feel suffocating, entangling around their limbs. Felicity hadn't even been aware of it but before she could reach for him, he roared.

The raw sound forced her to cover her ears. Bishop cowered, attempting to block out the bellow.

"Alarian!" she called.

Shadows shot upwards into the sky, snuffing out the light in a rush of darkness and mist. Then they twisted, charging downwards. Bishop wrapped himself into a ball at Felicity's feet. She stared at her Cridhe. Tried to reach him with the last of her emotions—anything that could break through. "Rian," she whispered.

His gaze fell on her. And with a snap, the shadows broke, light blinded them and Alarian fell to the ground unconscious. Drained.

She dropped to his side, checking his breathing, turning him over to rest her head against Alarian's chest to feel his heartbeat. With a shake, she could tell he was out cold. "Damnit."

"What happened?" Bishop hadn't moved from his curled-up position, only his ears now uncovered.

"He drained himself." A tear slid from her eye, but she brushed it away. She rested Alarian's head in her lap. "How?" She bit her lip, stared at Alarian's pained expression. As if he felt everything, even unconscious. "How does it end?"

Bishop swallowed, sitting up. He glanced around and stared at the male in her arms. Probably looking for signs that he was going to lose it again. When he deemed it safe, he answered, "She didn't give specifics. I don't think she wanted to give life to the words."

A nod was all Felicity could muster. "He'll need food and water when he comes to. Grab my pack for me so I can reach my rations and then I'll call on the cailleach so we can be on our way to the others."

Bishop fumbled to his feet and grabbed her bag. "I'll go to the others and have them begin to pack. We will meet you at the tree line."

"Might be for the best. You won't want to be here when he wakes."

Bishop took it as the warning she meant it to be, even if she knew Alarian wouldn't be able to draw on his magic once he came to.

When Bishop was out of sight, Felicity turned her attention to Alarian, running a hand through his soft hair as she battled the emotions caused by Bishop's words. A sacrifice. Throughout her short life, she knew that her end could come in many ways. A mistake on her part. A moment of luck from one of her targets. Even that day so many years ago, in a field she could see from her current vantage point, when she had chosen to believe a red-haired youngling.

It was strange, but she wasn't frightened. Maybe she should have been. Or at the very least, upset with the Countess and the hand she was dealt. But all she felt was peace. Understanding. As if a part of her had always known.

Felicity pressed a kiss to Alarian's forehead. His brow furrowed. And slowly he blinked open his eyes. Alarian groaned as he came to. "I can't remember the last time I drained like that," he muttered, pressing a hand to his forehead before he pinched his eyes closed again.

"We all have our moments." She continued to run her hand through his hair. "I won't tell if you don't want me to."

There was no chuckle. Not even a pretend smile at her pathetic attempt at lighthearted jokes. "It doesn't mean anything," she whispered.

Alarian didn't look at her but stared out in the distance. She wondered if he had the same thoughts she did. Of what had happened in that field fifty years ago. If her mother's blood still soaked the soil.

"You won't sacrifice yourself, Felicity."

"I won't." She turned her hand until their fingers were entwined. "Never. But if what she spoke does come to pass, I need you to know two things."

He shook his head, but her gaze requested his silence. Alarian let go of her hand, pulling her close to his body. "What do you need me to know?"

"That I'm thankful for any time spent with you." He shuddered around her. "And that I started to fall in love with you when we danced in Koselig."

He stared at her, searching her face. But he didn't say a word. She kissed his forehead. "You need to rest." She reached across for her pack, attempting not to jostle him as she removed rations and water. "Bishop's having them pack up their camp in the meantime."

"I want to say something witty. Come up with a comment to make you smile." He didn't move, obviously not caring that he was currently weighing her down. "But nothing comes to mind. You're my everything, Starlight. I can't lose you."

"Tomorrow, the next day, we aren't promised any of it. The realms might need me to be more than a princess and a spy to keep them safe. If that's the case, I'll gladly give my life. As I know you would. Don't diminish this. Please. There is no turning back."

"But—"

She shook her head. "You can't tell anyone, Alarian. Promise me. There is a reason that the Countess didn't tell me about this. Just like she kept so many other secrets."

He breathed in a long sigh, then patted the spot beside him, and she curled up into his arms. "I love you, Felicity."

A teardrop fell against her forehead as he nuzzled her, and she gripped his arms tighter as they laid in silence and concentrated on feeling him breathing. The contraction in her chest as she felt as his heart ache—the sensation of love pouring through the bond. The anger pulsating at the edge of his desire to control that which no one has a say in. A future.

Neither of them spoke. The only sound was the occasional breeze through the grass. The chirps of a bird. They held tight to the last bit promised to them. Until she had to force him to eat. To move. To live.

Chapter 57

Felicity

Felicity could see that Alarian was still exhausted when they returned to camp a few hours later. His head bobbed as they rode, his eyes heavy. The trailing assassin and spies were forlorn and while some had battle-ready gazes, others looked lost. Had she looked like them when she'd been told she couldn't return to the Tower? Now there was nothing to go back to.

Kellan and Avyanna rushed to them as soon as they were in view of their camp. The latter wrapped her tightly into a hug, mumbling worried admonishments into her ear that she couldn't or didn't want to understand.

Avyanna squeezed Felicity's arm. "Who are all of these people? What happened?"

The guild members were huddled together, Bishop breaking through the crowd to stand before them. "Where should we set ourselves up?"

Felicity swallowed and Kellan only gave her a small glance before leading the liaison away. She gave her brother an appreciative nod before turning to Avyanna. "The Tower has been destroyed. These are the survivors."

Before Felicity even had to ask, Avyanna jumped to action. "I'll grab my supplies." She whirled around then stopped short. "Is Alarian alright?

"He used too much magic." A safe answer, keeping what they learned from Bishop to herself. It was bad enough that Alarian had overheard.

The female sighed. "I'll leave him to you then." She called over two others to assist her. Felicity smiled at the authority in her sister-in-law's voice and how she had also found herself in these past months. Change. Opportunity. That was why they were here.

A familiar figure appeared, a healer's bag in hand. Felicity smiled at Fiona Molyle. "You're here."

Lady Molyle lifted her chin. "Water Fae heal. It's one way I can help after..."

"We don't blame you for what happened," Felicity whispered. Felicity led Gaoth towards Alarian's tent, the male in question slumped over the neck of the beast. She took the moment to assess the female who walked beside her.

"I know. Otherwise, I would be hiding at home. But I had to do something when the call for aid came."

"We appreciate your support." She squeezed Fiona's shoulder then pulled Gaoth to a stop outside the familiar tent. She nudged Alarian awake gently. "Come. We need to get you inside."

He nodded, sliding down from the lynx's back into her arms, her legs braced for impact.

She assisted him to the cot placed against the side of the tent. With a grunt, she laid him down.

"Do you need anything?" Fiona asked gently from the entrance.

"I've got him. There are others that need you more."

Fiona nodded and before she walked away, Felicity grabbed her into a hug. "I'm glad you're here."

The female blushed as Felicity stepped back. "Thank you, Princess Felicity." She walked away, and Felicity couldn't resist the warmth that grew in her chest.

Alarian groaned, bringing her back to reality. As Felicity turned to leave to collect more food and water, Alarian gripped her wrist. "Stay."

"This is the worst I've ever seen you. I need to get you more—"

"No." He tugged gently. "Please."

"Rian."

He smiled at the nickname. "All I need is you. I've had enough food, and no amount of water will make me feel better." Alarian let go and moved sideways to create space on the cot. "Just you, Starlight."

Felicity nodded and sat down beside him. "You know, if something happens to me—"

"I won't let it."

She gave him a half-hearted smile. "First off, get a dog. They make wonderful companions. Second—"

"Again..." His mouth a hard line and his brow furrowed. "Nothing is going to happen to you. I won't allow it. We will get a dog—together."

She brushed a strand of hair from his eyes. "War, Rian." A gentle tug had her curling into his side, his arm pulled her against him. "We aren't guaranteed a lifetime."

He kissed the top of her head. She closed her eyes as he nuzzled her hair. She breathed in his misty pine scent.

He whispered in her ear. "It's you. You're the future I'm fighting for. The reason I'll survive, and you will too. If either of us is to be a sacrifice, it will be me."

"Rian—" She'd never let that happen. He had to know that.

He shook his head. "You have a kingdom that looks to you. A brother who relies on you. A father who is proud of you. So much to live for."

She twisted in his hold until she was facing him. "We both do."

He tried to smile but failed miserably. "We know that's not true."

Every one of her emotions were heightened. All the little words she didn't say. The words she couldn't and wouldn't voice mixed with the feelings she could sense wafted off him.

"I love you," he whispered, his head resting against her forehead.

"I love you too." She kissed him. Then they held each other close and wished they could stay there forever.

She bit her lip, duty battling with the need to stay. There was a sense of concern, melancholy, not weakness as much as exhaustion in the emotions she felt that belonged solely to him.

Alarian kissed the top of her head. "I can tell, you know?"

"Tell what?"

"When Bishop told us—you felt a sense of peace before you blocked it all out. Was that because I was draining or...?"

Felicity sighed, uncertain how to explain herself. "I wondered if I could figure out how to stop you from sensing my emotions. I had hoped doing it then would help you not to go too far. But I suppose it didn't surprise me."

He rested his chin on her shoulder. "I don't believe in prophecies either. Never have. So, I have only one request for you. Until your dying breath, please fight. Don't give in just because it's foreseen."

She brushed her fingers along his jaw. "How well do you know me, Alarian?"

A chuckle, a graze of his lips against her forehead. "My Starlight. Stubborn. A fighter."

"A weapon," she uttered.

He stilled, meeting her gaze. "We've discussed this. You get to decide what you are. That is still the case. One does not sacrifice a weapon. One uses it. You wield the weapon. Not the other way around. Because you have a choice."

She closed her eyes, considering his words. "I'll never give up." She opened her eyes again, meeting his penetrating gaze. "Don't lose faith in me."

Worry. That's what rushed from him now. And she couldn't try to cheer him up, because she knew that if it came to it, she'd give her all to stop Marquette.

***

Alarian was in a deep sleep when Felicity unfurled from his hold and headed towards the center of camp. While they had been gone, more tents had been erected as allies from Dorcha, Visce, and other realms arrived. Some semblances of comfort created—as much as one could find in the middle of awaiting a battle. Fires had already begun to burn, and troops met around them. Felicity had never been in a war, but even with the uncertainty of what tomorrow would bring, she saw conviction with the carefree chatter. They didn't know a veil could be opened, but they did know they must stop a threat to their continent and that was enough.

She moved aside the flap to the large meeting tent to find her brother, father, Sloan, Shale—who had arrived from Dorcha, Lord Denizen, Dimitri, Aunt

Leana, Talia, and even Bishop were congregated around a crude drawing of the mountain pass overlooking the alleged location of the veil.

All attention turned towards her as she entered, and she didn't miss a beat. "We diverted around a straggling army, but we saw what their numbers could do. The dragon is going to be a problem." She couldn't say it again—that the place she'd known as home for so long had been decimated. That the woman who had raised her and protected a heartstone was taken.

"Marquette has at least three of the ritual's necessary stones. Possibly four." She had to hope that Harrison had escaped with the stone. The reason he was sent. And maybe a gift for Felicity as well that he remained out of the fray. But if she was wrong, Marquette already had the fire, dark, and light stone. With Domhain's stone lost, they needed Saol's heartstone to fulfill the ritual.

"Marquette may be collecting them for sport, unless she has other plans. The information on the actual ritual to open the veil wasn't found." Not a lie, just withholding some of the truth. She had to keep the information vague. A promise to the magic of the Fios.

"Which doesn't help us." Avyanna entered and settled in beside her. "How is Alarian?"

"Resting." She bit her lip. "The others?"

"Most will live. A few are still being cared for and two lost limbs. They are lucky to be alive." Avyanna gave her a tentative smile, then nodded to Bishop. "My understanding is the uninjured have spoken to you about assisting in our cause."

Everyone turned towards Bishop, who stood a little straighter at the attention. "We have not been trained for war. Our styles are much different than what will take place on that field tomorrow. That being said, they are free to make the decision that's best for them. The younger trainees will not be a part of this though. They see glory and envision something that isn't promised."

"And what is that?" Sloan asked.

"Revenge," the liaison grumbled.

King Bastien cleared his throat. "There is a lot of speculation about what is meant to happen. All we are promised tomorrow is that there will be a battle that could tear our continent apart. Chaos will reign. And if Marquette and Fiadh succeed, they will have too much power and will tear our kingdom apart. But more so, it would shift the magic our continent needs. We cannot let that happen."

He pointed to a location on the map. Two mountain peaks that jutted in opposite directions and a small pass that led to the ocean. "This is where we believe she will attempt to open the veil. Within these mountains there is a system of caves that lead to different outcrops. This one" —he pointed to a ridge overlooking the point— "is the perfect location to overlook the opening of the veil and may be where the ritual takes place."

Kellan's jaw flexed. "And with a dragon and magic they are able to cut us off from that pass quite easily."

"Can we find a way to blow it up and destroy their troops in the process?" Sloan crossed his arms over his chest with a critical look at the location the king pointed to.

Talia shook her head. "According to my Shadow, the caves are heavily guarded. He wasn't able to give us many details. We almost lost him in the process of uncovering that information. The chance of getting anyone in there with enough magic or explosives to not only destroy the caves and cause a rockslide, would be nearly impossible. We would have had to be prepared prior to their arrival."

"And we didn't plan that well," Kellan grumbled under his breath. "We should have."

Their father rested a hand on his son's shoulder. "We needed to be certain. We only had speculation and little concrete proof as to what was to come."

The sun was dipping into the horizon as they discussed strategies and debated options.

"The dragon will be difficult. We need to free her from Marquette's clutches," Felicity pointed out. "With the dragon out of the way, that will open us up for more aerial attacks and take out a pivotal obstacle."

She felt him before he spoke. "Felicity should handle the dragon," Alarian said as he settled in beside her. "She knows enough about them to ascertain the location of her nest and dispatch whoever is causing trouble."

A chuckle curled around the room. "True," said Kellan. "I don't think anyone else can traverse through those caves as easily as you could to find the dragon's nest."

Felicity glanced between her brother and Alarian. "Trying to keep me out of the battle?"

"Never." Alarian shook his head. "I'll even come with you."

"We need your magic on the field, Rian," Sloan pointed out. "You have the ability of short-and-long-range attacks. Besides, the rebels present will want to know you're here."

"Not rebels anymore." Bastien's shoulders drew back. "They are the people of Talamh." He nodded towards Alarian. "He won't be needed there. With Scáth as allies, I'd prefer Alarian with my daughter. The two of them will watch each other's backs. Kellan—your wind should assist our archers."

Sloan and Ciana were given the job of leading a group of soldiers and finding Marquette and Fiadh. They would enter through another entrance closer to the opening their enemies were expecting to use for the ritual.

Their planning continued until stars littered the sky. Food and drink had been delivered to them. Other advisors were brought in to discuss plans or provide input when necessary. The king took a seat, resting his head against his chair. "We have planned for all that we can foresee. There are only two days until Samhain. Hopefully we can bring this all to an end before then."

Felicity analyzed the map, confusion marring her brow. "I feel like we're missing something."

"There are always unknowns. It's war." Sloan sighed. "I wish we had more, but Tine also doesn't know what we have planned. We have to concentrate on that and pivot where needed."

"They have the army of Tine behind them. Some of the best strategists in the entire kingdom. We definitely need to be prepared for the unseen." Sloan's voice held a hint of uncertainty even within his firm resolve. "For the people, we cannot fail."

"That's why now we all need rest." With that, Bastien dismissed them. It was decided that they would attack at dusk the following day. When the enemy wouldn't expect them—as long as Marquette didn't make a move sooner. It would also allow Felicity and Alarian a chance to sneak into the cave system undetected before nightfall while they were sidetracked by battle. Besides the outcrops, the scouts uncovered on entrance not heavily guarded that they would use. Yes, Tine had an army almost entirely of fire-wielders, but they had light and Aer's inventors had come up with their own ways to assist.

Felicity and Alarian walked back towards his tent. Alarian's fingers brushed hers. An invitation. Not that they had ever spent a night in a separate tent since the beginning of this trek.

They went inside and Felicity came up short when she found her pack on the cot. "Did they know?" Usually one or the other had to go get their things from their respective tents.

He chuckled, pulling her in close to his body, brushing the hair from her neck to kiss her throat. "It's the night before war begins. What do you expect?"

"I figured you needed rest." She pressed her hands to his chest, gently pushing him until his legs touched the cot. "Tomorrow is a big day."

Alarian leaned in, resting his forehead against hers. "Do you remember what I asked of you that night after the brothel?"

Her brow furrowed. "When?"

"After we returned to the castle. I asked—"

"That I would not allow myself to ever be used again," she finished for him, the memory coming unbidden. "Yes, I remember."

He closed his eyes for a moment. "When I made that request, I had just felt your first emotions. The beginning of the bond. It took everything in me to leave you that night. All I wanted was to make you see what I felt. But I couldn't. Not yet—not when you didn't know me or who I was. I meant it though—I never wanted you to be used. To be a pawn in some larger game."

She swallowed. Felt that familiar pang. *A weapon to be used.*

"No." He shook his head. His tone demanding. Without speaking he must have ascertained where her thoughts had gone. "You're not a pawn."

Felicity met his gaze. Held it. Allowed all her insecurities to be felt through their bond. He inhaled, blinking in surprise.

"The Díomhair basically said it. You were the one who was necessary." She made sure he felt the love too. "If it hadn't been for you, then all of this wouldn't have come to pass. It's because of you that we're free now. It's because of your actions, choices, and your goodness that we are alive. Maybe all this time I was just the piece that needed to remain on the board for this reason alone."

Alarian's expression softened. And she brought down that final piece of the wall she'd been learning to erect against his emotions. And adoration, love, pride...feelings she hadn't expected came through that bond.

He kissed her brow. Breathed her in. "Ah, Starlight, that's not it. I was the tool used to ensure this all came to pass. Because it all centered around you. You were the key."

"Agree to disagree," she breathed, closing her eyes, reveling in his touch as his thumb brushed her jaw.

"I think we will have to. Or maybe agree that in this, we were both important. Played a part we hadn't known we were meant to be. No matter what, I have no doubt that it still led me to be right here, by your side."

She opened her eyes to meet his gaze. "That we can agree on." Her chest ached, not only from his words, but the concern, fear, and love that tied them together. Instead of speaking, she pressed her lips to his, pulled him in close. Tight against her body. Words would fail her now. She had to show him everything she felt.

And she did. With each caress. Each kiss. The way she pulled him closer and whispered his name.

She groaned as he nipped her neck.

He sighed as he captured her mouth.

She peppered his body with kisses. Touched every divot of muscle and inch of skin.

Completely undone. For him.

And when he entered her, their breaths synced, their hearts raced, and she opened that bond between them wide. Felt every emotion mix with her own. Love, lust, possessiveness, and protectiveness that mirrored her own. He growled at the sensation, and she couldn't help the small chuckle that escaped. Their movements were slow. Each one instinctual. Important. Matched perfectly together. Memorized. Each sensation and touch tattooed in her memory.

They were curled up in the bed afterwards, holding each other tightly as if it would keep tomorrow from coming to pass. She stared at his face, his eyes closed, but she knew he wasn't asleep yet.

"I promised you then." He blinked his eyes opened and she continued, "I didn't blame you for leaving, but as you disappeared, I promised you—and myself—that I wouldn't be used again." Her finger brushed his cheek. "You made me see myself when I didn't want to. And find myself when I thought there was nothing to find. Before you, I was empty. With you, I'm...complete."

A tear slid down his cheek, a small crack appeared on his lips, that signature grin that she loved so much. He kissed her once more. "I don't deserve you."

She scoffed. "Oh, you do. I'm trouble and that's exactly what you deserve."

He laughed, pulling her in tighter. "Forever, Starlight."

Chapter 58

Alarian

The following day, a few chimes before dusk, Felicity and Alarian had taken the cailleachs to the edge of the groves nearest the mountain, hidden from view. The few Tine folk they had found within the citrus trees were easily dispatched. Now they waited. Watching for the signal.

He reached across the small distance between them and took her hand. "Be careful. All right?"

She chuckled. "I always am."

"This is an angry dragon we're talking about. Whatever has her upset, especially if it's her nest of eggs, she's going to be dangerous if she thinks we're a threat." He sighed. "Don't try to make friends."

Felicity had an idea, and they had found out that they could now converse when he was in his fox form. She tried again to communicate with Reóta who had looked as though she'd rather hunt than talk back. She'd attempted to talk with a few horses, and although one had actually listened to her words, it didn't respond back to her, so neither were certain it was part of their bond's magic or not. He just hoped she wouldn't attempt to negotiate with a dragon.

"You think I'd try to make friends with an angry dragon?" Her gaze thinned to slits and he chuckled to himself at the fact that she had missed out on Domhain's bloodline and the ability to shift. She'd be formidable.

"Starlight, you'd make friends with the most vicious of creatures, I don't have a doubt. But in this case, I need you at the end." He brushed his thumb over her hand.

She glanced down at her hands, then back up to meet his gaze. "I'm not going to rush into a decision that will put me at risk based on Bishop's words. Understood?"

He'd been trying not to bring it up since their talk last night. Alarian pulled her close, pressing a kiss to her cheek, then buried his face in her neck. "You make me worthwhile."

Felicity chuckled. "I think we both know that you were important before I came along."

They leaned in for a kiss when the first swell and clangs sounded. Bright beams of fire filled the air, smoke following in their wakes. The signals that they had seen at the Inventors Fair what felt like a lifetime ago. Screams and yells followed. The two of them broke apart, turning to see smoke rise in the distance. The battle had begun.

When a streak of light broke through the sky, this firecracker flinging colors in a star-like pattern, they mounted the cailleach. Alarian gritted his teeth, a final check of his weapons then faced her. "Lead the way."

***

They remained low to the ground, riding the beasts around trees and over bushes until the copse ended at the base of a sheer mountainside.

They picked this location because there would be limited access for anyone without aerial assistance. They flew close to the sheer walls and blended in amidst the gray stone. Their bodies pressed closer to the lynxes, careful not to be seen by anyone who may divert their attention, but the battle was doing what it is meant to do by keeping everyone engaged.

Above them was the cave entrance. Even if the side of this mountain seemed near impossible to scale, it was doubtful that Tine hadn't posted someone at the opening of the caves.

The cailleach landed silently on a thin shelf underneath the outcrop of rocks that opened to the caverns. Felicity and Alarian looked at each other, silently trying to decide what to do next to ensure that they weren't seen. Stealth was key.

Alarian grabbed hold of a piece of shale and tossed it over the edge. The rock clattered on the floor of the cave opening. They waited in silence, listening to whether or not anyone came to investigate. There was a slither—a growl and sniff as whatever was above smelled the stone. A great maw peered over the opening and Alarian's eyes widened. Shit.

Fomorians.

Neither of them moved. The darkness would be an ally to the beasts and not to them. The Fomorian stepped away from the edge with another snort of disgust. This wasn't what they expected to come up against. And they should have been. The promise of battle and bloodshed must have been enough for them to side with the traitors. No wonder they had been spreading through Domhain—they were heading to the mountains.

Felicity and Alarian regarded each other. This was their best entrance. The other options would leave them too visible. If the Fomorians were within the cave, they would need Felicity's magic to get past them. With the darkness and the nocturnal practices of the faerie beasts, the only other option would be to wait for morning and hope they slept. Not a guarantee with the battle waging and tensions high.

Felicity reached into the curve of her armored tunic and removed a clear crystal pendant from its hiding place. They'd practiced using other conduits—a reflective surface that could handle the heat was what was necessary and although the gem was helpful, her blade would work just as well. A distraction—they needed to force the creatures out of their way, one way or another.

Felicity glanced down at the cailleach, and Alarian breathed a sigh. An unnecessary agreement and understanding already between them. He leaned closer to Gaoth. "We need your help," he whispered.

The cat gave a guttural growl. If that was in agreement or not, Alarian didn't know, but he dismounted, settling his feet on small, jagged stone and gripping tight. Felicity did the same, whispering words he couldn't discern to Reóta. The cats flew off into the air, then turned sending a roar to draw the attention of the stone faeries.

An arc of an arrow, the growl of the Fomorians. The creatures were at the edge of the rock outcrop roaring at the two flying beasts. Felicity and Alarian climbed up on either side of the opening and as they reached the edge, they remained out of sight behind the three Fomorians.

With silent steps, they made their way deeper into the darkness. If the creatures were here, others would undoubtedly be interspersed throughout the cave. They could only hope that many of them were drawn out to the battle on the field below.

At the first fork, Felicity stilled, pressing her body against the cave wall. His eyes watered from the stench of piss and death. The Fomorians must have been stationed here for a while.

Alarian glanced at her then down the openings. They needed his animal senses right now.

He passed over his pack and couldn't resist a wink as he stripped. He was completely aware how her cheeks flushed—even in the dim light she emitted with her magic, it was obvious that she was taking in his body. "Not the time."

"I bet I could change your mind if I wanted to." She bit her lip.

As he shifted, he chuckled. His fox form was always a little rough around the edges. He had control—though it had taken a lot of practice—over all of his limbs. His magic inked from his tail, but he called back the shadows. At least his gray fur would allow him to meld into the stone.

"Follow me," he said into her mind.

"Have I mentioned how cute you are this way. I just want to cuddle—"

He stifled a growl.

She chuckled through the bond. *"What, your surprised? Your fur is so soft. How often do you groom yourself?"*

"Are you saying you wish me to be soft with you?" He ignored the comment about grooming. As if he preened in front of a mirror...

"Let's make it through this and you can have a lifetime to find out."

Just hearing those thoughts gave him hope.

Alarian headed down the hall to the right with slow and careful steps, letting his fox instincts take over. A pause, his nose lifting to the air. The smell was worse now with the heightened senses, but he worked to separate the scent of piss, sweat, faeries, humans and…

There it was. Something other. He'd never smelled a dragon before. It was a mix of soot, sulfur, and beast.

A roll of a pebble had him jumping, turning to find Felicity a step behind, surprised at the sound she'd made.

"Do I have to ask you to be quiet?"

"It's not exactly easy when it's so dark. I don't have your eyesight. Warn me if you can."

They had agreed to keep her light dimmed for now, just enough so she didn't run into a wall. Otherwise, they would be a beacon to anyone. When they came to a corner, Alarian turned back towards the direction they'd been traveling, considering. This didn't feel right. Something had him wanting to turn and run in the opposite direction. But that could be the fox's instincts, not what he knew he needed to do. A few more steps…

Then he paused. Low whispered voices. The clank of chains. The smell of blood. *"Lights out."*

She did what he said.

He peered around the corner and paused. Lord Lian sat chained with blood streaking his brow, his eyes puffy, and face bruised. Two humans were bound with three faeries, their backs to them. What was this?

"Fae and humans," he whispered into her mind. *"Prisoners. Lian is with them."* Alarian stepped back and when he was certain no one else was present but Felicity, he began the shift. She handed him clothes as he formed, and he rushed to put them on.

"The ritual," she whispered. She handed him his pack after he dressed.

He strapped on his weapons and then tightened the straps of his bag. "We need to get them out of here."

She nodded in agreement. They curved around the corner, sticking to the shadows Alarian created to keep them hidden.

A silence greeted them, the lords shushing each other. Felicity stopped first, holding her hand out to signal Alarian to stop. Footsteps sounded from down the hall. *Shit.*

"Who do they want?"

Two Tine soldiers entered, armed to their teeth and holding familiar crimson bags. The ones that protected the fae from the iron chains. Alarian rose the shadows around them to keep them hidden without being obvious.

"All of them." The guard leaned over the two humans first. "Let's start with these two and we'll come back for the others."

Felicity started to rise, ready to attack, but he gripped her arm. When she glared over her shoulder, he shook his head. *Patience.* No matter how tempting it was, an attack would draw more attention, and they should free the ones they could and then go for the others.

And if Lian was here…then the enemy had another stone. He'd tried to ignore that. But the frustration that they had failed only made it harder to stomach the truth. Marquette could very well get what she wanted. The idea of it made him sick to his stomach but he pushed it back. Because they could be a step ahead now. And hopefully keep Felicity far away from any scenario that could lead to her sacrifice. Maybe he should send her off to find the dragon and deal with this himself.

The two guards walked out, dragging the two humans with them. They balked, fought, but the soldiers didn't falter. Once they were gone, Alarian dropped the shadows and rushed to Lian's side. "Hi friend."

Lian's eyes widened, and he silenced a cough. "No, Alarian. Get out of here."

Felicity was already working on another fae's bindings. Alarian ignored the male. "We're getting you out of here."

The feel of cold steel pressed against the back of his neck and Alarian stilled. "Hello, Son."

Marquette's voice held a twinge of pride. Not towards him. Alarian knew she'd never have that emotion for him. When he turned around, still crouched on his knees, the blade traced his throat. Felicity was fighting against two guards, her mouth covered. One guard grabbed hold and ripped the crystal from her neck.

"Let her go." Alarian glanced back at his mother. "Now."

"I don't think you're in the position to be giving orders. In fact, you're in the one place you always deserved to be. At my feet and at my mercy." She pressed the blade deeper and nicked his throat.

Marquette tilted her head to the side. "I had hoped the two of you would arrive. It's like you expected what I would need and offered yourselves up."

Felicity continued to struggle, a growl breaking from her gagged mouth. Alarian held his mother's gaze. He couldn't let her know how much the female at his side meant to him. She was already the princess who'd retrieved a stolen crown and the one to kill Roald—Marquette didn't need another reason to kill her.

"What are you talking about?" Alarian growled.

"The sacrifice of course."

At her words, Alarian froze. It took skill beyond measure not to look towards Felicity. Not to offer himself up in her place.

Marquette's grin widened. "Blood, soul, and stone. Magic of the earth, given to break a bond. Well, you're going to help break that veil right open for me."

His gaze narrowed.

"You knew." She smiled. "I can give you credit for that. But you still couldn't stop me."

She gestured to a human guard and two others came over, quickly locking iron manacles to both their wrists. The two guards grabbed hold of Alarian on each side. The human stepped back, slipping the key down his shirt.

Fuck, fuck, fuck. "Do you realize how insane this is?" He needed to keep his head, remember his plan. The one he had made while he was meant to be sleeping. As he had held Felicity and knew there was no way he would allow her to be used again. Even if it was fate. A prophecy. She would survive this, and he would give his own life to ensure that happened.

Marquette tilted her head. Stared at him. "You're a smart boy. Just not smart enough." She stepped back and then turned to the guards. "Get them all to the cavern. We have a ritual to begin."

They took a step, and then Marquette stopped, turning to the largest male Alarian had ever seen. "Silence them." She flicked her chin towards Alarian and Felicity. The last thing Alarian saw was the hilt of a sword—felt pain—then darkness.

Chapter 59

Felicity

They had made too many mistakes. Been a step behind even when they had thought they were catching up. There hadn't been enough time, or enough information to stop Marquette. Not when she had years of preparation.

These were the thoughts racing through Felicity's minds when she woke with a terrible headache, the side of her face against the cold stone. She hadn't moved yet. Hadn't signaled to anyone nearby that she was lucid.

The ritual—blood, soul, and stone. They had walked right into a trap. Hadn't considered the Fomorians as allies. All they ever had was hope and even now that was dwindling.

She couldn't see Alarian. Had no idea where he was, only the sensation that he was there, alive—and waking up. The knock to the head had done enough to keep them both unconscious until dawn, the light coming in from a nearby outcrop that overlooked the valley below. The view she faced when she peeled one eye open.

Samhain.

She heard the battle in the distance but all she could see was blue sky, and in the distance, clouds were coming in...

"Is the fire ready?" Fiadh's voice was cold. Distant.

There was a gruff exchange of words, but Felicity couldn't understand a single one of them. Not until Fiadh spoke again. "Good. It's time. Prepare the offerings."

Offerings. That's what they had been debased too. Rough hands grabbed her shoulders, and her head lolled, pounded, as the guard dragged her body towards the base of a large pyre. Others were unceremoniously dropped alongside her, but with her mouth gagged, she couldn't do more than meet their frightened gazes.

Felicity could not recognize any of them from the quick glances—

A flash of red hair. She tried to sit upright to get a better view, but the guard pressed her back. Fuck him. When she got out of here, he'd pay. Which she would—Marquette didn't know that Felicity wasn't affected by the iron manacles. But she could tell that the metal was draining the strength from the other fae.

To Felicity's left was the lit pyre that warmed the cave wall at her back. To the right, the mouth of the cave opened to that cloud-spotted sky. She took in those who were forced beside her noting she was amongst the group of fae and human offerings for the spell to open the veil.

And then the pieces of a plan started to come together...

Now she just needed to wait for the bitch to arrive and get the female to talk. Felicity smiled to herself. If she had learned anything about the traitorous queen, it was that she loved a good story—as long as it was about herself.

Felicity didn't have to wait long.

Hurried stepped and quick whispers made Felicity believe that they were on a timeline, and judging by the congregating clouds, it was when darkness spread over the land. Felicity had hoped to be wrong, but if she was right...

Marquette entered, cutting Felicity's thoughts short. The female glanced over the eight beings at her feet, a smile stretching wider as Fiadh joined her. Marquette's gaze pinned to Felicity for a brief moment, then continued on. The witch held a wooden bowl, but Felicity couldn't see the contents within. She didn't move, allowing the twisting in her head to ease. To collect herself. She needed to remove this damned gag from her mouth and get the woman talking.

"What is this?" Alarian growled from farther down the line.

Fiadh sliced a look his way, but Marquette held out a hand stalling her. "The future. You're going to be a part of it."

"This, what you've planned, isn't a future."

Silently, Felicity thanked him for fulfilling her unspoken request, using it as a distraction while she worked at her bindings. He knew his mother, as well.

Marquette straightened. "You don't even know what you're talking about. You just think you do. Followed the breadcrumbs I laid out for you all this time." She scoffed. "I knew you were against us, and you may have tricked us with your lazy attitude to lead a rebellion—who knew you had it in you—but it doesn't matter now."

Anger came unbidden. A deep desire to tear her head from her neck. Felicity realized her emotions were mixing with Alarian's, the bond heightening every feeling.

Fiadh caught Felicity's gaze. "She's awake."

"Oh, I know." The turn of Marquette's neck was almost serpentine as she regarded Felicity. "She wouldn't miss any chance to spy."

Felicity's magic pulsed through her skin and bones. Up her arms and through her chest. Alive.

"Remove her gag. I want the princess to be a part of her continent's undoing. I want to hear her scream for her people."

A guard grabbed her and did as ordered. Felicity didn't fight. Yet.

Lian struggled against his chains. "You can't be serious. Why would you want to open the veil to the human realm? It doesn't make sense."

Fiadh was the first to laugh this time, but the traitorous queen joined in as if there had been a joke within the lord's question.

Felicity straightened. "It's not the human realm she wants to open a veil to." Lian wouldn't know. Most of those bound by her side probably had no inclination what their lives were to be used for. "She wants to open the veil to the Ninth Realm."

Silence expanded, only the crackling of fire remained. Every head had turned in wide-eyed shock towards the ex-queen. That is what she and Alarian needed. The finality that this was her plans for the stones.

"You still think too small." Marquette's smile expanded. "But it's a start. I should thank you for assisting my husband in preparing our new troops. I didn't expect you to be the cause of his death—the one to send him—but in truth, it's poetic now. Because, as I sacrifice your life, you'll be creating a path for his return. And then further desolation of so much more."

Alarian roared, the walls shaking from his rage. The others reacted, Lian shifting to his knees.

Felicity continued working at the manacles. "You can't—" She caught Marquette's meaning. Fiadh grinned. Wider. A dangerous emotion written in her expression. "You plan to open both realms."

Marquette sighed. "We all have lost, haven't we? It took my innocence and for a young girl, it took so much more." Marquette looked at Fiadh and took her hand. "Her people have mostly abandoned this continent. We can take it all back."

The witch's smile was all teeth, nodding. "We deserve all of it."

"And to tear down the world that failed us. Failed my husband. My parents. The magic of this realm. Talamh must pay." Marquette reached into the bowl in Fiadh's hand. "These stones are the way and if the veils weren't meant to be open, then we wouldn't have been given a key."

Felicity's gaze narrowed on the heartstone Marquette levitated into the air. The one necessary in place of Saol's stone.

Alarian was the first to breathe a loud growl. "Where did you find Domhain's stone?"

The female glanced at her friend. "Stories hold truths, Alarian. I've told you that since you were a little boy."

"You weren't there when I was a little boy. That must be some other child you took the time to raise because you never told me shit. Meira taught me those things." Alarian fought hard, but Felicity could feel the iron deplete his energy with his hope. His anger was getting the better of him, and in their current predicament, he'd need both.

"And who do you think gave those books to Meira?" She tilted her head. "I'd hoped it would guide you to our way of thinking. It seems your time in Scáth only poisoned you against us instead of making you stronger."

Through the bond, she sent calming energy, hoping he read her signal. Wait. Patience. They would stop this.

There was a swoop of air, a gust of wind that rushed over them, stoking the flames, and they all looked towards the opening to catch sight of the passing dragon. A ball of fire erupted from its mouth before she flew from view. The screams and yells, the sounds of metal banging and orders given were distant. The battle was waking strong, but Felicity had no idea what side was winning. Her family, the people, relied on her. The dragon needed to be freed. At least the sunlight had stopped the Fomorians. But that wouldn't last long if those storm clouds continued their way.

"Bring him." Marquette pointed to one of the faeries. She dropped the heartstone into the bowl.

A female Tine guard grabbed the wing-bound pixie who struggled as he was thrown to the ground at Marquette's feet. Felicity and Alarian fought against their bindings. Another guard punched Felicity in the face, the back of her head meeting stone. Alarian tried to stand, yelling profanities but was forced back. The others joined in, but between the manacles, the ringing in Felicity's ears, and the might of the guards, it wasn't enough. No matter how much she wanted to stop what she knew was to come.

But only her anguished cry was heard as the pixie's throat was sliced open, Fiadh holding the bowl under as the pixie's blood sprayed over the stones. Only her screams as the pixie's body was thrown over the edge of the opening. Alarian roared with her. Their pain emanated through the bond.

As the Tine guard was about to step back, Fiadh grabbed hold of her. "Thank you for volunteering."

The silence that followed was deafening. The other Tine soldiers froze in place as Marquette repeated the sacrifice with their comrade. The female's blood soaked the witch's hands and the bowl of stones before her body was tossed over the edge with the other.

Marquette cackled as she made her way towards the bowl that Fiadh held. She sliced her palm and squeezed her hand over it. "A part of the sacrifice. But you will be the soul necessary," she mocked Alarian. "This I can give for the family stolen from me. For the loved ones torn from my life by hate. I will have them back."

"Hate you caused," Alarian roared.

Felicity shook with rage. Called forth that anger. Held onto it hard. Allowed the training that she had mercilessly fallen into for years take over.

Marquette glared at him. "More whispered lies by those you call allies." She spat on the ground. "Now, who is next?" Her brow rose as she took in those cowering before her and a guard stepped forward.

Felicity took the chance to make her move. The guard forced her to her feet, and she head-butted him in the nose, timed perfectly with the dislocation of her thumb. He slapped her across the face. With the grind of her teeth from the pain, she silently slid her hand free, adjusting herself to snap the finger back in place as he threw her to the ground. She held the iron manacle in place, ignoring the pain in her hand that rushed up her spine from the impact of stone.

Marquette laughed, the sound of rumbling chuckles from the guards—of Alarian's fighting attempt to break free at her treatment—to silence. "Enough. You know when you've lost. You're smarter than this."

"Don't—" Alarian's shadows had expanded around them, his face bright red with rage, but they were cut short quickly by the iron. He fell back, unable to fight off the seeping power of the metal. "Don't touch her. Ever."

"Don't worry, Son. You'll be with her soon enough. For eternity, if you prefer. Chained side by side in hell. Now she must have a front row seat for what's to come. Because she won't be here to witness the veil to the human world opening. That comes later." Felicity was dragged closer and settled in front of them. Marquette didn't move forward though and neither did Fiadh.

Felicity willed her magic to the pain in her hand, hoping the warmth of her light would remain hidden while reducing the swelling. She would need it soon enough. And she could only hope it was enough. That she was enough. Alarian would hate for her it. He'd never understand why she made this choice, but she knew now what the Countess had meant. What she would need to do.

As if the thought of the witch was enough, the Countess was dragged between them. Felicity's eyes widened in disbelief. Bloodied and beaten yet the woman still held a stoicism in her posture. On instinct, Felicity tried to stand, to move towards her while still feigning bound arms, but the guards flung her back to the ground.

"Leave her be!"

"Aw, I assumed correctly." Fiadh smiled and Felicity's hatred grew. "I recognized her in your memories. A witch beyond her years. Just as I am. She survived by the power of the life heartstone."

The Countess laughed bitterly, blood seeping from a wound at her forehead and her cheek bruised. "The stone grants its abilities to those who protect the Magic. You stole your survival for selfish deeds. You're going to meet your end."

The truth dawned on her the same time it did Alarian. "You're the daughter from the story? The one about the girl who tried to save her mother."

"Tried?" Fiadh's grin turned savage. "Succeeded. I saved her. For years we lived in peace. Until others tried to take the stone. Claim it as their own."

"It was never yours," Lian growled. "The stones are the heart of the Magic granted to those who care for the continent. Not for you to use for your bidding. To use them for your selfish gain will only result in—"

"Shut up," Marquette snapped, sending a wave of shadows at the lord. Her magic slid down his throat and he sputtered, gasping for air.

"But soon I'll have her back. *We* will have our families back." Fiadh placed a hand on the Countess' arm, and Marquette retreated her shadows. Lian fell forward on his face, breathing heavily.

The Countess caught Felicity's gaze. Held it. "It protects us all." Her eyes slid down to Felicity's throat, then up again. A small nod. A signal. Another thing Felicity was right about was now confirmed.

Marquette grabbed the witch by the hair, forcing her gaze to break from Felicity's. "Well, it can't protect you now."

"You don't have Saol's heartstone." The Countess grinned. "My death will only be the blood—not the power you seek."

"True. But there are alternative options, and you are of Saol and a soul must be given."

"No," Felicity screamed as Marquette sliced a blade across the witch's throat.

Chapter 60

Felicity

There are moments in Felicity's life that stood out once her memories were returned. One came to her now as the Countess slumped to the cavern's floor. Her head bounced on the stone.

She was young. Kellan had sat down beside her in the garden, sprawling out on the blanket they had all just picnicked upon. He nodded at a growing between two stones. "The weeds are starting to grow."

Kaleana smiled, her face bright from the sun. "Not a weed, but a wish."

"What?" Felicity leaned in. "It doesn't look like a wish, Mama."

"Sometimes the most unassuming things can be so much more than expected. Pick it and think of something you desperately want, or dream of...then blow on it. The wish and dream will go into the sky to be remembered or will find the one you're thinking of."

Then just as quickly it snapped to another memory.

The Countess walked beside her. A breeze picked up, and puffs of dandelion snagged in Felicity's hair. She tugged a piece out and the Countess reached out, stopping her. "Don't do that."

"Why?"

"Because those are someone's dreams and wishes they sent to you."

One piece of dandelion was clutched between two fingers, and she stared at it. "I think I've heard that before."

The Countess' expression softened. "I imagine you have."

The image of the Countess' convulsing body brought Felicity back to the present. But she couldn't move.

She had wanted desperately to blame the Countess for so much of what had happened. For the decisions made on Felicity's behalf. It wasn't until that moment that Felicity knew how much the woman had done to protect her. For a chance to stop what was happening now. To be someone beyond a weapon for a guild of spies and assassins. More than a princess with a crown on her head.

She was neither. And she was both. Felicity was exactly what the continent needed.

As hot tears slid down Felicity's cheek, the Countess' blood collected over the stones as she slowly suffocated. She tried not to scream at herself for not moving. For not interfering. She hadn't been ready then. Hadn't called her magic soon enough. But she was ready now. Had collected it properly. Prepared so she wouldn't drain.

Marquette muttered words that Felicity barely understood. The few phrases that stuck out were familiar—the spell. A flash of lightning struck through the sky and hit the ground, causing screams from the battle below. Thunder followed, the outcrop of stone that overlooked the valley below shook. Felicity looked toward the black clouds that shrouded the sky in darkness. The dragon roared as it darted another flash of lightning.

The traitorous ex-queen glared at Felicity with malice and spite. "Now, one last thing we need to take care of." She pointed to Lian and he was dragged forward in front of her. "Tell me, how to open this." Marquette removed the spelled stone, still in the form of a quill, from her pocket.

"Never," Lian growled.

Damnit—she almost had Aer's heartstone.

Felicity noted the hesitancy of the guards. They glanced at each other as if the loss of their fellow soldier had sunk in and they were beginning to question what they were doing here. She glanced at Alarian, but his attention was solely on his friend. Felicity concentrated on the bowl in Fiadh's hand.

"It was the only object on you when you ran. We know what's inside. So, give in" —she nodded to Fiadh— "or she can force it from you."

Fiadh stepped forward, the bowl in one hand as she held out her other. Lian screamed. Felicity knew that pain. Knew she was searching his mind for what she wanted. What Felicity had to be sure wasn't given up.

Felicity stood. Her body moved on its own accord. Did exactly what it needed to do. No one paid her any attention, focused on the scene at Marquette's feet.

She saw red. For the woman who had raised her. Been a mother to her. Told her stories. Grounded her in moments that led to this decision. For her Cridhe—the male she loved and hoped would understand.

The manacles clattered to the floor behind her, and she tore away the chain of the red crystal pendant still at her neck, hidden under her tunic. The one taken from her when they had been caught was a decoy and had done its part. She tossed the pendant to Alarian. "You know what you need to do."

The necklace fell at his feet as magic blazed to life at her fingertips. She glowed white hot, Alarian warning the other captives to get down, to close their eyes. Lian bellowed as Fiadh twisted her fingers, the whites of her eyes showing as she searched his mind.

But the witch wouldn't find what she wanted. For her people. Her family. Talamh. Felicity would be a memory—a sacrifice. Just as the Countess foresaw. It hit her then she had never known the witch's true name. But power came with such knowledge. She'd learned that when she broke the curse binding her brother.

The guards were too shocked to move, unprepared, they screamed as the starlight seared and blinded. She kept it above waist height, to protect those who cowered. The world was moving in slow motion, like trudging through sap.

Marquette screamed as Felicity appeared in front of her and backhanded the female, sending her body sprawling. Then Felicity grabbed Fiadh and held tight to the witch, the bowl of heartstones still in her grasp.

Lian gasped, warning Felicity too late as Fiadh's vision came back into focus, pulled out from his mind. Her gaze pinned on Felicity. She grinned, twisted her fingers. Pain ran through her entire being—the sensation of fingers pinching nerves as they looked. Searched. Wanted.

With a strength she didn't know she was capable, Felicity ignored the pain as she dragged the witch to the edge of the stone cavern.

"Don't you dare."

She could hear the sound of manacles, the crash of chains as he fought, but she couldn't bring herself to look at him. Not even as Alarian repeated his orders. Yelled her name.

"It's not meant to be this way. Not you," he pleaded.

Fiadh fought her grip, unaware of their destination, concentrating solely on her power even though Felicity's own burned the witch's skin. Her mind was connected now. Felicity could feel her searching. A gust of wind whirled around the cavern's edge. The battle raged below. The dragon flew overhead, fighting off lynxes and dodging arrows...and with the witch still holding her body and mind, Felicity jumped.

The last sound she registered was Alarian's scream before the wind echoed in her ears.

The witch's mouth was open in a silent scream as she fought Felicity's scalding hold. The bowl was clutched between their bodies. The stones and blood still inside, staining Fiadh's front crimson.

Felicity didn't let go until the witch finally opened her eyes, meeting Felicity's gaze. She smiled. "For them." The Countess. Her mother. All of those who had suffered.

Then she flung the woman away from her. The witch hit a rock, the sound of her neck breaking, but Felicity didn't look. She closed her eyes, blocked that bond that made her feel so much. And waited for oblivion to claim her.

Chapter 61
Kellan

The fucking dragon.

Aside from his sister's wish to free the beast, he didn't take the dragon down because even as she attacked, she seemed to purposely be practicing bad aim. Their line of fifty archers were left untouched, the land around them scorched and their skin heated from the flames but unharmed.

That didn't mean she wasn't vicious or a problem for the others. When the cailleach attacked, the dragon acted in defense. And even though Kellan tried to call them back, feathers, embers, and carnage dropped around them, and he could see that the dragon's patience was dwindling. She wasn't going to hold back much longer.

The dragon was the least of their worries. Even though Dorcha and Visce had publicly aligned with them, a few armies had broken away from their realms and allied with Tine. Once night fell, they would be dealing with more than the current battle—but surprise attacks by the Dorcha fae was inevitable once the sun set.

The roars and movements from the caves were proof enough that the Fomorians waited in the wings. An unexpected addition. And there wasn't much to hold them back. Not with the rising smoke from the dragon and Fire Fae blocking the light from view and creating a sepia haze over the valley. Clouds had appeared as if from nowhere and spread quickly by an indiscernible wind.

At the crack of lightning, Kellan hailed the archers, each of them sending an onslaught of arrows. With his wind, he diverted the arrows' trajectory towards their enemy. Screams, the clang of metal, the ting of arrowhead banging against armor.

A horse came to an abrupt stop beside him. "We need to advance," his father called. "If we don't move soon, we will lose any ground we've gained before nightfall. We must force them back."

It was time to enter the fray. Kellan gave his father a half-hearted salute and repeated the order. The archers dropped their long bows and began their run, removing swords, daggers, or crossbows.

As he ran with his troops, he saw a group of Dorcha soldiers sending their cailleachs towards the dragon. *Shit.* He diverted his attention, running towards them. Obviously, fear was interfering because they were explicitly told not to attack unless the dragon attacked first. It might not stop all of them, but if he could control a few, maybe it would spread. "Stop," he shouted.

But it was too late. Fire engulfed the cats and their riders.

Kellan dodged the falling remains and remnants of flame that fell. Another onslaught was preparing, but he screamed again, attempting and failing to get their attention.

This time the dragon ignored those coming for her and swooped down, grabbing hold of four Aer soldiers within her claws—and squeezed.

Felicity needed to hurry or there would be no choice but to kill the beast. They had hoped with the freedom of her nest, she would seek revenge on those who had imprisoned her. Become an ally. That hope was disappearing.

Smoke cleared to reveal that the clouds now covered the sun. Kellan removed his sword just before a Tine fae lunged for him. He made quick work, cutting the male at the heels and sending him sprawling to the ground. He ran just in case the male was able to heal himself. There were too many now.

Dorcha and Scáth fae slipped in and out of view. Fire Fae fought against Visce and Aer. Bastien's light expanded, enough to keep most of the Fomorians back.

Lightning blasted through the sky and hit the ground. The earth trembled, thunder bellowing. Enemies and allies screamed as they ran. Others still fought as though the sky hadn't been ripped in half one thousand paces away.

Blood splattered as he cut and sawed through his enemies—warm and sticky on his skin. Others came to his aid, some falling to blades as others were caught up in their own fights. Kellan didn't stop moving, worried that if he did, he'd be cut down. Especially with the way the Dark Fae moved, appearing unexpectedly behind or to the side of him. He had to keep them on his toes.

There was a scream, and Kellan whirled around as someone pointed towards the mountain, hoping to see the dragon assisting them or gone from the skies, but instead what he saw was much worse: a body fell through the sky.

Reóta was suddenly in the air. Kellan moved, as if he could urge the cailleach faster. The lynx darted others, another flash of lightning, trying to reach for the falling figure. A roar of pain echoed through the canyon from above. And Kellan moved on instinct. Ran as the falling body broke into two, a second figure crashing into the stone, the first still falling.

A scream from another cailleach, and Kellan whirled around as Reóta's path was intercepted by arrows, the dragon catching the lynx in her sight and lunging towards her.

Kellan yelled, but a slice to his arm had him whirling around to parry another attack. He fought a Dorcha female, but forced her back, slicing his blade through her chest before running again, searching the skies. But Reóta disappeared, the dragon banking right from the mountain and swooping to the ground.

And he ran with fear stuck in his throat.

If the cailleach had failed—if that was his sister's body falling to the ground...

He couldn't let himself think that way.

Growls rumbled from the opening above. Wisps of shadows battled slips of darkness. As magic collided and a pulse of lightning shocked the air. He turned on his heels and froze—nearly fell to his knees. The dragon slipped from his mind. As did everything else as a giant rip started high in the sky tore the world in two as it spread towards earth. A darkness visible within the seams.

Another scream as a man fell to the ground, clutching his forearm. More echoed as allies and enemies tore at armor or clothing. Kellan rushed to the first and knelt beside him, trying to pin the man to the ground. He fought, tearing into his own skin with his nails. "Stop it. Now." Kellan pinned the man down, trying to get past an invisible foe.

"What is it?" He finally pinned the man's arms, his heavy frame holding him against the ground. "Tell me."

"The mark," the man cried out. "It burns. It wants—" His gaze thinned on the Kellan. "They're calling me."

Shit. The oath. "She's calling you."

The man pinched his eyes closed. "No." He shook his head violently. "He is."

Then he went still under Kellan. Stared up at him. "Run, Your Highness."

Kellan glanced around at the others who had just been writhing on the ground around him. They stared. Some with vengeance in their eyes. Others with regrettable sorrow. Kellan swallowed. And the man underneath him whispered his next words, "We can't stop it."

Then he threw Kellan off of him.

Chapter 62
Alarian

Numb. That was what Alarian felt. Not a sense of the fierce female who had just taken his heart over the edge. He couldn't feel her. His Cridhe.

He stared at where she had been. Stumbled. Swallowed, his throat sore and scratchy like thorns.

A movement behind him. A groan. The guards were either blind or incapacitated. Alarian pulled himself out of the grief that begged him to crumble. That was for later.

His shoulders drew back, a mask he'd seen his Cridhe wear many times slid over his features.

He bent over and grabbed hold of the pendant before he rushed to the closest guard and searched, grabbing the bag of keys. The iron keys bit at his palms as he freed himself then tossing the keys to the nearest human. "Hurry. Help each other."

The woman didn't wait, shaky fingers twisting the key into the lock. Alarian shouldered another guard towards the edge and the male screamed as he fell. He slid the necklace around his neck and stuffed it under his shirt. It was hers. He'd never let it go.

His mother was on the ground, screaming. Crying. Her hands covered her face as she rocked back and forth on her knees.

Lian reached him first, a limp in his step and anger in his eyes. He blinked as the crying stopped and felt his mother's shadows before he saw them.

His friend spared a quick glance before Alarian nudged him towards the opening. "Go. Take the others. Sloan is somewhere in these caves. Find him."

Lian nodded, turned and ran with the others.

Alarian shook his arms, relieving the strain in his muscles. Called his magic.

His heart was in two pieces. Resolve was the only thing that kept him together.

He turned slowly. He wanted to grieve. To rage. But right now, Felicity would want him to end this.

Marquette sliced a look up at her son, her face blotchy but the shadows already culminating around her. "Your bitch killed her."

He wouldn't think of that right now. "You've done this to yourself."

Her smile lengthened. He could sense the shadows she created behind him. Ready to attack. Growing. She had always been stronger than he was. Not for lack of trying on his part. But maybe there was something to say about the fact that when you crave power, you crave strength. He'd never craved power. That had been a disappointment to her.

Marquette got to her feet. "I still have won. Their sacrifice will be enough. The veil to Ankus is opening." He didn't allow himself to look out over the valley below. "And it might take time for Fiadh to regenerate, but after your death, you and your princess will only know torture and pain. We'll ensure it. Then we'll open the other veil to the human world and wreak havoc on the entire continent." The look on her face was maniacal. "Stand aside and accept your fate. Take the place you always were born to be—at my feet, begging for mercy."

The hairs on the back of his neck rose with the shadows. "I may not have been able to stop you before. I might have been a step behind. But there is one thing you weren't prepared for."

"And what is that, you useless welp?"

"That I'd be here to tear you down."

With his words, her shadows attacked, but Alarian rolled out of the way as his own magic pierced her through the back—her own magic impaling through her front, her control lost as his magic had mixed with hers. She'd grown too cocky. Too sure of herself. Believing she was still ahead of him.

She gagged, misty gray blood slipping from between her lips. She wiped it away with her hand, staring at her palm for a moment before turning to him. Then her shadows disappeared in a snap. Alarian's chin rose, softening the edges of his own shadows as they lowered her body to the ground. "Goodbye, Mother."

He stood there for a moment. Unable to move. Watching the last rise of her chest. The life leaving her eyes. They needed to close that veil immediately if they were meant to succeed. Otherwise, if what his mother said was true, Fiadh and Marquette would be at Roald's side in no time.

He stumbled, his balance faltering. Felicity. He gripped his head, steadying himself against the stone. His limbs pulled him down, begging him to curl up in despair.

A scream echoed from beyond the cavern, and he turned in time to see a dark tear in the sky. The screaming grew and spread. Both sides terrified. Shit—Éardrom, Saol, Scáth, and Domhain. Blood and soul. He'd failed. In the end, it hadn't been enough. And he may have been the one to finish the spell by taking his mother's life.

No—she would have killed him instead and then there would be no way to stop it.

The two remaining guards were still moaning on the ground. A roar brought Alarian out of his grief, the dragon flying away from the rip. Just a moment. That was all he needed. A little longer to put a stop to this. The dragon would need to wait. Then he could grieve. Could break.

The tear lengthened, nearing the ground from the plume of dark clouds with a jagged spark as sharp as lightning. The earth rumbled at the impact.

Ankus—the realm of the dead. What the hell had his mother done?

With a sharp whistle, Gaoth appeared. Alarian mounted and the two shot downwards towards the battle waging. The Tine soldiers seemed just as frozen in fear and wonder as their side. Alarian scanned the crowd.

He searched for her. A body. A presence. Her emotions. Anything. But he found and felt nothing. His entire being ached at the loss. Temptation clawed at him to turn back to the outcrop and search closer among the stone and rock for what remained of the female he loved, but first things first—warning her family of what was to come.

Prince Kellan waved at him from below and Alarian veered Gaoth towards him. As he came in for the landing, Prince Kellan yelled, "Where? Where is she?"

Alarian already saw it. Fear. So much fear in his eyes. He already knew the answer. "Prince Kellan." It was the only thing he could say. He wouldn't be able to speak it otherwise.

"Where. Is. My. Sister?" Tears mixed with sweat and blood. He grabbed hold of Alarian's tunic. "Please—"

Alarian hated this. That he had to be the one here now. It was a weird sense of déjà vu. He hadn't been able to protect her mother. And now he failed to protect his heart.

"I don't know." Not a lie, but not the truth either.

Prince Kellan's jaw twitched. He inhaled before he wiped his face, smearing blood, dirt, and sweat against his cheek. "We will find her. Or she will find us." That same sense of resolve that Alarian felt passed over Prince Kellan's expression. Then he turned and ran, shouting over his shoulder. "We need to find my father and to close this damn veil."

Alarian wanted to fall to his knees. Didn't want to move. But she'd hate him if he did, so he followed. He noted the battle around him. Watched for an attack. Then his brow furrowed as he caught up with the prince. "Why are some walking towards the veil?" A large mass collected, some with jerky movements, as though forced by a puppeteer.

"The oath. They are forming their army."

Chapter 63

Kellan

Alarian had caught up to him and as they ran, he shouted over the din. "Did you stop Marquette?"

"She's dead," Alarian huffed beside him.

He'd seen it in his eyes. The truth. Felicity was gone—but he had to hold it together for a little longer. They both had to.

Alarian lengthened his stride. "So is Fiadh. It sounds like it will take time for their bodies to regenerate before they can join Roald's army of the dead. Then once they have control here, they plan to open the veil to the human realm too."

What the actual... "Shit. We can't let that happen." Even with the news that the veil would lead to Ankus, he couldn't fathom or even attempt to wrap his mind around what that meant.

The battle waged around them, swords clanged as he dodged around the fight. Some had stopped, shocked. The rip in the sky was about to touch down to the earth. They needed to hurry. Needed to find a way to stop it.

"Do you know how?" Kellan hoped he had the answers from his studies and the time he'd spent researching the veil. "How do we close it?"

Alarian grumbled under his breath, his shadows wrapping around them to keep them out of the fray. It made it harder for Kellan to see where they were going...but anything to dodge a fight they didn't need.

"No." The whistle of steel whizzed past Kellan's ear, a knife lodged in a Tine male poised to strike him through the shadows. The male fell to the ground with a grunt.

"Shit—thanks."

Light blasted in front of them, and Kellan knew where to go. The shadows wavered within the presence of the magic. The King of Éardrom. Of Talamh. Fomorians peeled back with shrieks, cowering closer to the mountain's edge to hide from the magical sunlight that glittered like a barrier from the rest of the battle.

They passed Ciana and Sloan, fighting back-to-back, protecting the king. Alarian sent a slice of shadows through their foes and stepped into Sloan's face. "Where were you?"

Kellan pulled Alarian back. Shocked at his outburst at his friend.

"Lian found us. We were—" He swallowed glanced at Kellan. "We had just found where the prisoners had been kept. He filled us in, so we left our soldiers with him to get everyone out and came down here to help. We were too late."

Alarian wavered on his feet. Kellan recognized what that look was. Defeat. He'd felt it before. But he wouldn't abandon Alarian now. "We can still stop this. There must be a way."

Alarian pinched his eyes closed, and Kellan ignored the sight of tears on his cheek. Couldn't think of his sister now. The fate that Alarian couldn't speak.

Alarian nodded, and the two of them turned and rushed to Bastien's side. Alarian slid his shadows under the sunlight barrier and into the crevices of the closest Fomorians. Whatever the male was feeling, he took out on their foes, the Fomorians closest exploded in dust and stone.

Kellan sent a wall of air at their enemies, helping to hold them back as Alarian breathed heavily beside him. "Father—what the hell do we do?"

Bastien roared as he sent another rush of sunlight, burning hot and bright, pressed the remaining Fomorians farther back. "Where is she?" He pinned Alarian with a glare. "The dragon is still under their control—where is my daughter?"

Kellan blinked, then glanced at Alarian. The king's expression fell, darkness seeped into his eyes. "I can't—not now..." Pain etched his features, but there was a hardness around his mouth.

Kellan shook his head. If Alarian spoke the words aloud, he knew they would all crumble.

"Not now," Alarian growled. "She'd never forgive us. We can't fail."

Kellan's heart cracked. "This can't be how it ends—"

"It's not." Bastien straightened and he peered over his shoulder. "She's not—" Even he couldn't finish the sentence. "What happened up there? What was the ritual?" The question directed at Alarian.

He explained what he could. Blood-soaked stone sacrifice. Bodies thrown over the edge. Kellan shuddered at the mention of the Countess' death. How Felicity must have felt then. He wanted to ask what happened to her. But grief would come later. When they had time for it. Alarian was right—she'd want them to end this.

Bastien breathed. "To open it, death and souls were needed."

"So, to close it?" Alarian faced the veil just as the earth shook, the mountain quaking. His brows were drawn together. "I think..."

"What?" Kellan glanced at the tear. It was dark blue, shining—like lightning hung stagnant in the air. Except it was widening and instead of a cloud-filled sky, darkness like the pitch black of death hung in its wake.

As the seam hit the ground, a shock reverberated like an echo, causing each of them to falter, grabbing hold of each other to catch their balance. The fighting paused as the world stopped shaking, stilled. The veil split. Figures appeared at the base, hundreds of them.

"Fuck," Kellan breathed. He wheeled to face Alarian. "Do you have a plan or not?"

Alarian reached under his tunic. He yanked and Felicity's pendant hung from the end of a chain. "Life. Felicity said I'd know what to do." He met their gazes. "If I'm correct, this a piece of Saol's heartstone. We noticed it was broken. This matches it exactly, and she has worn it all this time." His grip tightened for a moment. "The opposite of what was needed to open the veil, is needed to close it."

He was about to ask why Felicity didn't have her necklace when Bastien cut off his magic and grabbed hold of Alarian and Kellan. "Take us away."

Alarian didn't hesitate. As Bastien's sunlight snapped from existence, the Fomorians moved, and Kellan was suddenly weightless, shadows encapsulated and blocked everything from view.

The ground met his feet, and he stumbled. His father stepped away, Alarian's shadows dispersing and stared at the opening that was much wider and closer now.

And from the veil's depths, an army of the undead marched. From this distance, it looked like they were led by the witch—the Countess' sister—by her side was a grotesque beast. One that Kellan could recognize anywhere. He glanced at Alarian. Any trace of fear was wiped from the male's face. He was poised, his head held high as he locked eyes with his father—Roald.

The battle around them had stopped, everyone turning their attention to the amassing undead. Tine's soldiers were in shock, staring. The Fomorians didn't move. Even they knew what stood before them was unworldly. Unjust. The only ones who remained moving were the branded. Their cries of anguish as they fought to get away from what awaited them. The dragon landed upon the side of the mountain, her great serpentine body plastered against the stone.

The reinforcements of deceased screamed, the sound sharp and painful like those within the throes of death. Fae, humans, and the like covered their ears—cowering to protect themselves from the awful screech.

When it cut off, the undead stopped and stared at their quarry.

The scent of death and blood that had clung to the field evaporated. The grass under their feet began to die, spreading from that opening.

Bastien glanced at Alarian. Kellan looked between the two males. Alarian nodded, a calmness stretched over him. Bastien turned to his son, his fierce gaze searching his face. "You've made me so proud. The male you've become. The female you've chosen to be by your side. I'm so glad I was able to witness it."

Kellan blinked, brow furrowing. "What?"

Bastien unsheathed the sword from his back. Alarian stepped in front of him. "No, it's meant to be me. I have nothing—"

The king, Kellan's father, laughed. "No, boy—it's not. Life is light. A living soul is needed. Now, find her. Tell her I love her and that I wish there had been more time."

"You're meant to—"

The words rushed around Kellan. "No." They started to make sense in his muddled brain. The screams of those running away from the onslaught. The rush of fear. He reached for his father. "No."

Alarian glanced at him, and King Bastien ripped the pendant from Alarian's hand and ran as he swung his sword in an arc. Unlike the masses of people running away, he ran towards that great maw. Towards the army of death that cut down anyone who dare stray in their path no matter their lineage.

Kellan started forward, instinct telling him to stop him. Stop his father from whatever absurd thoughts that must have plagued his mind. "No!"

Alarian grabbed him, shadows erupted around Kellan's legs, holding them to the ground. "Let go," he screamed at the male. "Let go of me!"

Kellan fought. Yelled for his father to stop. To turn around. Cried out when his sword met Roald's muscular shoulder.

Alarian wrapped his arms tighter around him as Kellan continued to thrash—scratch, kick, hit—whatever he could to get out of the male's hold. To get to his father. "Let me—"

"I can't," Alarian growled. "She'd hate me if something happened to you too."

"I'll hate you if you don't let me go," Kellan snarled.

"I can live with that," Alarian snapped. "But Avyanna's grief? That I can't live with."

Kellan stopped, heart racing and chest heaving. Avyanna's bright hair, her dark skin. Her smile and laughter. He choked on a sob.

A nearby scream pulled him back. A woman cried as she was forced towards the army. "I don't want to go," she yelled.

"Help them." Kellan met Alarian's eyes. His brother in arms. "We need to help them."

Alarian peered around them. "All right. But I'm trusting you." He let him go. And they ran, following in his father's wake.

A roar sounded above. The dragon disappeared within the ravine. Their forces saw the chance, took it. Turned on the Tine who had been running in fear. Pushed the Fomorians further into the mountains as light burst brighter from Bastien.

He saw more than heard as his father's blazing sword met Roald's talons. Alarian sent a wall of shadows ahead of three branded, forcing them together and attempting to hold them back. Kellan did the same with his wind, creating a small tornado around others. They grabbed hold of comrades, dragging them towards the magic-made corrals. Some pleaded. Others cried with hope.

And Kellan glanced at his father who was in the midst of a battle for their continent. Bastien had the upper hand, but barely. Kellan met Alarian's gaze.

"I've got them. Go." Alarian's eyes pierced. A warning. *But you can't follow.*

Kellan ran, calling his magic to the tips of his fingers. He pulled the wind from the corral, Alarian's magic taking its place to protect their people.

And he used it all. Sent a giant gust of wind that came in from both sides of the spreading undead army. He roared as he asked for more. Pulled more. It met in the middle with a crash, right behind Roald—leaving him to deal with Bastien alone. And he pushed. Asked the wind from the mountains. The breeze from the coast, the gales of the plains. Called them all to his aid.

Bastien and Roald fought as the veil arched upwards. His father pushed him back, took the upper hand. Kellan couldn't look anymore as the glaring light forced him to close his eyes. But he kept up that wall of wind and air. Pushed them back through the veil with all of his might.

Nothing registered. Not even when the world shook again. When he opened his eyes to see a bright light snap with the veil—his father's light. The clouds that had hung in the sky almost seemed to quake as they lightened to a misty white instead of the heavy gray.

He was on his knees, barely realized when Alarian slid in at his side and wrapped his arms around him.

Alarian kept speaking in his ear, unintelligible to his muddled brain. Then the veil was gone. The army of undead had disappeared. Alarian let go. Stepped back. And Kellan ran. He was only somewhat aware of Alarian following. That the battle around him had nearly stopped, most of Tine's forces surrendering. Those who had been forced by the oath cried and hugged each other—free, while their enemies were taken into custody. But he barely paid any attention to them.

When he reached the center of the scorched earth, a crack in the ground where the veil had pierced, Kellan fell to his knees. Stared at the place where he'd last seen his father.

Alarian gasped for breath beside him. "I'm so sorry."

Tears already drenched his face. He stifled a sob, his hands spreading over the barren, burnt ground. "Why? Why did he do this?"

"I tried to be the one—"

Kellan looked up at him, his own eyes wide. "I'm not asking why you let him. I'm definitely not asking you to be the one to take his place. I'm asking why he took it upon himself. You stopped me. You understood." He wiped his face, grimacing as he felt dirt smudge against his cheeks.

Alarian cleared his throat and dropped to the ground beside him. "Life. The opposite of death and souls was life. Your father crossed through that barrier alive with a shard of Saol's heartstone. The light—I think that was his final goodbye to you."

He nodded, trying to put the thoughts together that felt too far out of reach. "I just got him back," he said weakly.

Alarian wrapped an arm around his shoulder. "I know."

Kellan's body felt so heavy. He leaned into the male at his side for a brief moment. "Thank you, Brother."

He ignored the way Alarian stiffened. "You stuck by me. I—I appreciate it." Tears he hadn't allowed finally slipped down his face. He was so tired. Felicity—his father.

Alarian sighed and got to his feet, pulling Kellan with him. Exhaustion clung to every portion of his body. He turned to find that their armies had started to clear the injured from the battle. Others searched for fallen comrades. Tasks he should be doing now. He desperately wanted to check on his wife. "Let's go find her."

The male beside him shuddered. "Prince Kellan—"

Kellan shook his head. "Enough of this *prince* stuff. And you don't need to say it, because I'm with my father on this."

"No—you don't understand. There was a prophecy. She didn't tell any of you. Honestly, if I hadn't been there, I don't think she would have told me either."

Kellan's jaw clenched and unclenched. His gaze thinning. "Go on."

"Bishop told her that the Countess foresaw that she would sacrifice herself. For us. For Talamh." His voice was so low, but Kellan could see the grief he attempted to fight back. How much pain he was in.

"Can you sense her?"

Alarian shook his head. "She learned how to block me out. But I've never felt such...silence." He was crying too. When he stumbled, Kellan reached out to grab hold.

"I won't accept it. Not until I see her body."

Alarian nodded, straightening but just barely. "I'll try."

Kellan saw something catch the light. He trudged through the mud and muck, the smell of burnt earth lifted by his movements. Alarian walked beside him and stared down at the sword at his feet. "He must have thrown it over here."

It pointed towards the mountains, the ravine. King Bastien's crown sat a little further ahead. Kellen bent over to retrieve the sword and the crown. He stared at them. Listened. Then looked up to the sky. "Alarian, the dragon? Where is it?"

"The dragon is taken care of." Bishop's voice caused them both to turn.

The liaison held his arm close—it hung at an odd angle against his chest. Alarian was in the man's face before he could take another step. "How could you tell her?"

Kellan stood a step away from them, understanding Alarian needed to confront the man. He'd be next...

Bishop shrugged. "The Countess told me years ago. She said when it was time, I would be allowed to tell her. But she wasn't to be raised as a lamb for slaughter. Felicity was raised to be prepared."

"What the hell are you talking about?" Alarian stepped back, holding his chest again.

Bishop glanced at Alarian's hand. "She needed you—a protector."

"What? That's the last thing—"

"If she knew any sooner, would she have ever allowed you in?"

Alarian blinked.

Kellan was beside him in a heartbeat, sword raised. "What does that mean? Explain now."

Bishop grinned. "My sister was wise. Smart. Even if I hate to admit it. I've been where you've stood so many times. Doubted her. But by waiting, Felicity allowed herself to fall in love. Was able to find reasons to keep living."

"She had her brother. Her father—"

"Yes, but it's been proven they would go on if she was gone. But you—"

Alarian's hand went slack, he stumbled and fell to his knees, his hands clutching his chest. He looked up and met Kellan's gaze. "She's alive. I feel her."

Bishop grinned. "She needed to have someone to live for. And if I had never told her, she wouldn't have planned for the inevitable. Would have just given her life when the time was right."

Kellan glanced from Alarian to the mountain. "The dragon, Alarian. It's gone."

Before another word could be uttered, the male was on his feet and running.

Bishop watched him go. "I wish my sister could have seen this."

Kellan could only have assumed he meant the Countess. The witch who had orchestrated much of what had come to pass. He glanced back at the spot the veil had once been. "She knows. They both do."

The sun pierced through the clouds then. Kellan leaned back for a moment, enjoying the sensation of the heat against his skin. He looked at the man beside him, the quieting of chaos. "Come, let's meet with Tine to figure out the logistics to their surrender."

"Going to put that on?" Bishop pointed at the crown in Kellan's hand.

It was a small circlet. Simple. A marker for the male who had once worn it so well. No jewels or intricate adornments. "No."

Kellan made his way towards where the veil had closed. He struck his father's sword into the ground, kissed the spot that would have covered his father's brow and hooked the crown on the hilt. Then he walked away from his father's resting place and towards the female who loved him.

Chapter 64

Felicity

Moments before...

The impact when Reóta caught her in midair forced the air from Felicity's lungs. She grasped tight to the cat's tuff of fur to settle herself before she was able to peer over the jagged rocks below and found Fiadh's ruined body.

For a moment, she considered going back to Alarian to assure him she was alright. To explain what the pendant was. A piece of the life heartstone. The Countess had confirmed her suspicions with that nod. It must have been why she had allowed them to see Saol's heartstone in the first place. She hoped Alarian would know what to do with it.

Before she could, the dragon appeared and a ball of fire pelted her way. Reóta dived towards the ground, Felicity's stomach in her throat as she pressed her body closer to the cat. The cailleach veered a sharp right, then left, twisting around stone and boulders to lose the angry beast that had caught them in her sights.

With a deft agility Felicity couldn't help but be in awe, Reóta curved into a crevice, hiding from view and melding into the terrain. Felicity didn't breathe, not wanting to be the cause of catching the dragon's attention. The serpent flew overhead, its shadow passing by.

Minutes passed.

As she raised her head, she sensed it. Felicity's gaze slid up to the sky as the veil opened.

Fuck.

With a quick brush of her hand along the cailleach's nape, the cat burst upward. Again, her heart pulled her towards Alarian. To return to him. But when the dragon sent another ball of fire at the armies below, she held onto her resolve. The dragon needed to be a priority. Needed to be freed from the enemy's clutches.

She leaned into Reóta. "I hope you found the nest."

As if that was enough of a request, the lynx moved into the side of the mountain, turning into a blur against the stone. Perfect camouflage.

Felicity checked her surroundings. Above them was an outcrop of jutted stone. A cave entrance maybe. It was large enough for the dragon, so there was a chance...

Before she could make a move, the opening in the sky impacted the earth and the entire mountainside shook. Rocks tumbled and Reóta lurched, taking Felicity with her but debris hit her, tearing her from the lynx's back. She fought for purchase, grabbing hold of stone, the rock biting into her hand as the world stopped quaking. With effort, a growl, her feet found footholds in rock divots. She pressed herself against the mountain to catch her breath. Reóta let out a small purr, peering over her shoulder at Felicity.

"I'm all right," she breathed. One reach and step at a time. Felicity pulled herself upward, making her way to the outcrop of stone. She needed to end this. When she was at the edge, she peered over to see if the coast was clear. Listened. Sensed.

Nothing.

She pulled herself upright, remaining low as she climbed onto the flat stone. The cave was deep but already Felicity could see the jutted sprigs of branches and the fluttering of dead leaves. The nest was built across the entire expanse of the back end of the cave. And there, at the only open visible was the general of Tine and a handful of soldiers.

And he was smiling at her. "Aw, you thought you were sneaky." Swords were released from scabbards.

Felicity sighed, straightening.

No chance for the element of surprise on this one.

General McGrath grimaced. "Disappointing. To think you are meant to be some fierce spy and I've already caught you."

She laughed and shrugged. "Caught me?"

He smiled. "Of course. If you move against me, then these eggs will suffer."

Fire erupted within the palms of several of the guards, illuminating two eggs in the center of a nest. Felicity's jaw tightened—but she knew something the general did not. Which could work to her advantage as long as they didn't turn those blades on the eggs.

The plan settled into her chest, her brow furrowed as she transformed into the part she was meant to play. "No. You can't."

The general's grin extended. "Yes, I can."

"But then you'd lose your hold on the dragon."

A snort. "You think that matters. We already won. Look behind you. The veil is opening. Either way, you should surrender. I'll make it quick for you instead of Marquette's plan to draw out your death—if you ask nicely."

She shuddered not daring a glance behind her. "You're not giving me much of a choice."

"That's because you don't have any."

Felicity walked forward, almost to the edge of the nest when the fire erupted, the flames now licking the ceiling of the cave.

"One more step and the eggs will be destroyed."

"You wouldn't cook defenseless eggs, would you?" She kept the sincerity in her voice. The fear. Fought back the smile trying to force itself to the surface.

General McGrath held out his palm, a ball of fire forming. Growing. Waiting.

Without giving him a moment to consider, Felicity rolled out of the way. Flames gushed towards the eggs. A roar echoed from outside of the cave and a ball of fire flew over Felicity's head, the heat grazing her hair. She grabbed hold of her blade, called her magic and with a tuck and roll, she hopped to her feet and sent an arc of starlight straight at her enemy.

The soldiers screamed. The nest was ablaze, and Felicity took the chance and sliced her magic-laced blade through the first two guards. The conduit pulsed, searing starlight spreading, moving through bone and muscle with ease.

Another fireball shot by, dodged barely but its flame grazed her shoulder. She hissed, patting the area to put out any flames and rushed towards the general who had another ball of fire forming.

With little thought, she sliced the blade straight into his abdomen. His wide eyes met hers as his magic sputtered.

A ball of fire hit her chest, sending her suddenly rocketing backwards into the nest amongst the flames.

She jumped out, screaming in pain as she rolled to smother the fire. Her clothes had protected most of her body, but her arms were burnt, one side of her neck sizzling. Nausea churned from the pain and scent of her own burning flesh, but she held back the bile.

The general laughed but then he stumbled. The pride vanished as he glanced down at the sword in his gut. He fell to his knees, orange bright blood seeping down his front. "You can't save them." His breathing turned ragged. "The eggs are destroyed. The dragon will go on a rampage. The veil is open. Even in death, I still won."

Felicity glanced at the eggs, the fire smoldering, then back to him. "You helped the eggs. They need to be kept warm. Fire is how most dragon's hatch over long period of times."

The general's eyes widened. "No."

The world shuddered again, and Felicity grabbed for a charred branch to keep herself upright, nearly knocked off her feet. The pain of the burn forced her to let go quickly.

When the floor stopped moving, she took a step and pulled the blade from his stomach. Felicity grabbed the general by his shoulder, forced him around to the opening of the cave. "And I think the veil is closing."

He yelled out before blood spluttered from his mouth, a cough stealing his voice.

"Don't worry," she whispered. "I'll make it quick for you. Just as you would have done for me." The dagger slid easily from her thigh, and she stabbed it in his neck, the tip protruding through his throat.

He choked, his airway torn open. His body slumped to the ground and Felicity stepped back as blood pooled at her feet.

She stared at his limp form for a few moments before heading towards the opening. She stepped back as the dragon appeared, and Felicity felt the heat growing in its chest. Her already burnt edges coming to life with a new sense of pain. She would need a healer before infection could settle in.

The dragon regarded her with narrowed slits and tilted reptilian head. The beast glanced at the nest behind her. The fallen guards. The blood soaking into stone, then back to Felicity.

She stepped aside, not wanting to seem a threat and to give her access to her eggs.

The dragon's entire countenance relaxed and with a coo that only could come from a mother, the dragon walked into the cave, holding her wings tight to her side to fit into the space without brushing Felicity.

She sighed, glancing over her shoulder. "Be careful with them."

Before Felicity could reach the edge, the dragon's nose nudged Felicity's arm and a cool mist covered her burned skin. Relief was instant.

The dragon settled back. Regarded her.

She didn't dare reach out, no matter how tempting, to pet her nose. This had been enough of a gift. "Thank you."

Reóta appeared on the edge, her tufted ears in the direction of the dragon, watching warily. She turned her to Felicity. *I hope you still prefer me to that beast.*

She heard the words in her mind and couldn't help but smile. She scratched the cailleach behind the ears. "I'd always choose to fly with you. Although it would have been appreciated if you'd shown signs you were listening to me sooner. I had to put a lot of faith in you."

A purr echoes in her head. *Well, now you know.*

Felicity chuckled as she mounted and exhaustion took hold. She didn't know what awaited her below. Whether a battle was still waging or not. But there was only one way to find out. As they took to the skies, she opened the bond between her and Alarian. Felt him there. And sighed at the relief and love she felt.

It was as though the world had gone still. The only movement was the slow progression of the clouds across the sky. Soldiers leading Marquette's allies by knife point. The veil had been closed. Felicity breathed a long shuddering sigh when she found Kellan walking back towards their camp, an arm around another fae, assisting them to the healers. Felicity urged Reóta to land.

"Kellan!"

He turned as she dismounted, his eyes widening at the sight of her. He assisted the man to the ground with incomprehensible words then ran, grabbing hold of her and pulling her in for a tight hug.

"Shit, Felicity. I was so scared." He gave her one final squeeze, then held her at arm's length, really taking her in. He immediately dropped his hands from her. "Oh hell, sorry. That must have hurt. What happened? Let me take you to Avy."

"Barely felt it." The dragon's breath had helped, but now shock was taking over. She knew that. "I'm fine. Where's Father? Rian?"

Kellan glanced away, towards where the veil had once torn the air. Her throat tightened. Eyes stung. There, barely visible, was the outline of a sword and crown stuck into the ground. "Kellan?"

"Father—"

Felicity wouldn't make him say it. It was written all over his face. She flung her arms around him, ignoring the pain. He buried his head into her neck. "I tried—"

She shook her head. "No, don't. Don't try to take the blame." And then she cried with him, sobbing for the loss of the father who had just been returned to them. For what they wouldn't get to have. More memories. More time.

Kellan nodded against her. They stood there for a moment. Their skin drenched from each other's tears. Her own sliding through the cracks of his armor at his shoulder.

"Damnit." Kellan pulled back. "Alarian. You need to find him. He went searching for you."

She wiped her eyes. "Where is he?"

Kellan shook his head. "I don't know"

Felicity gave her brother one final hug, even if her skin tightened and seared at the movement.

"Maybe you should head to Avy and the healers? I can find him and send him to you."

She shook her head. "No. I can find him." With the help of their bond. Felicity squeezed her brother's arm and he winced, his pinkish blood against her palm. "You're hurt?"

"Who isn't?" He chuckled. "Go, hurry."

"I love you."

He gave a half smile. "I love you too. When this is done, I'll take you to where father left us so you can say a proper goodbye."

She stifled another sob as she mounted Reóta. "Thank you." Before Kellan could try to talk her into going to Avyanna again, they took off into the air. She flew over the battlefield first, then leaned into Reóta's ear. "Take us to Gaoth."

The lynx growled in satisfaction. *If you insist.*

A speck appeared in the distance. Hope fluttered in her chest, and she maneuvered the lynx in the direction of the cailleach taking form. She couldn't see if Gaoth had a rider. Not yet.

When a shot of red hair glimmered in the sunlight, hope expanded, filling her chest. Gaoth was lowering to the ground now, over the rocks at the base of the mountain. Alarian was looking for her. For her body. She urged Reóta faster.

They landed a few feet ahead of the lynx and she felt it as soon as Alarian caught sight of her. Felt his gaze holding onto her form as she dismounted.

A gentle brush of a breeze as Gaoth landed and before she could see through the tears that now slid down her cheeks, she was in Alarian's arms. He sobbed as he held her, inhaling big gulps of air as he buried his face into her hair. She did the same, inhaling his intoxicating scent and finding comfort. Misty forest. Even the pungent blood and sweat. It was everything. He pulled back enough to press his lips to hers. Then he leaned back, looking in her face. "I love you."

"Don't ever do that to me again," Alarian growled. Then a small lift of his lips, and he brushed a finger along her jaw.

That's when he saw the burnt skin and pulled back. "Shit, did I hurt you?"

She shook her head. "The dragon cooled it for now." With a step back, she flinched slightly. "How bad does it look? Do I still look like a princess?"

"Looks like a badass way to mark this mission, Starlight."

Felicity couldn't help it, she laughed.

Alarian pulled her close again and she rested her head against his chest. "We're all right."

He breathed a sigh. "Felicity..."

She could hear it. Regret. Sadness.

"I know," she whispered against him. "He's gone."

His grip tightened around her, and she felt the dampness of tears on her temple. They were his.

She nodded as fresh tears came unbidden. "I saw Kellan. I couldn't..." She breathed a sigh. "How?"

As they stood close, he told her of everything she had missed. How her father had known he had to reverse the spell. His guilt for holding Kellan back on Bastien's behalf. That he'd told him to share a message with her. That there had not been an ounce of hesitation when he'd gone against Roald. "I'm so, so sorry. I should have stopped him. I should have—but then Kellan would have gone, and I couldn't save them both for you."

Felicity pulled back and kissed each of his cheeks in turn. Kissed away the tears streaming down his face. "You did what my father wanted." She swallowed, looked in the direction where that sword stood sentry. "He has been preparing us since his return. I just wish I had been there"

Alarian rested his forehead against hers. "He knew you were exactly where you were meant to be. I thought—shit, you scared the hell out of me."

She swallowed. "I'm sorry. I'd hoped it wouldn't come to it, but I thought by taking out Fiadh and the stones it would end it all. Give you the chance to save the others but also, if necessary, find a way to use the pendant."

"How?"

She explained how, before they had parted at the beginning of the caves, she'd asked Reóta to search for another entrance to the nest in case the one they entered wasn't correct. How the Countess had laid hints about the true origin of her pendant. The fact she shouldn't have healed faster than other fae since it wasn't a part of her magic but always had. "She gave me the shard to protect me."

"I guess we can't hate the Countess. And you did stop Fiadh, Starlight." He chuckled. "Otherwise, two veils would have opened. Who knows what would have happened then. What would have been required... Marquette is dead."

He told her what happened after she'd jumped with Fiadh. The finality in his voice, not an ounce of grief for his mother. "It's over," he breathed. "Truly."

She kissed him. "I love you."

His face crumbled. "I should have known you had a plan. But when I saw you go over that edge. When I couldn't feel you anymore—"

She gasped, cutting him off. "What? You couldn't feel the bond."

He shook his head.

Felicity's shoulders fell. She brushed his cheek and then tilted his chin to meet her gaze. "I'm so sorry. That was not my intention when I blocked it. I didn't know it was two-sided. I just knew I couldn't be distracted. What with falling through air and having the catch a flying cat."

He pulled her into his chest and whispered into her ear. "I can forgive you. If you promise never to do that again."

She chuckled between her tears. "I don't know—you might want to block me sometimes. I feel a lot."

Alarian kissed her temple. "I want to feel it all. Always."

They held each other for a little longer. She worked to control the wave of emotions that slid between them until their breathing was evened out.

Felicity stepped back. "Come. We should go back to camp. See the others."

The two of them flew. The armies below were finding their injured. At the far edge of the once battle, Felicity caught sight of Avyanna amidst a group of tents and supplies. Kellan was there, ordering people about as they collected those able to help.

Everyone worked alongside each other, even some members of Tine built tents and brought in the injured. As Felicity and Alarian landed, she felt hesitancy in his emotions. The fear that he'd be turned away. His guilt a sharp pinprick to her skull.

She gripped his hand as they moved through the crowd. "They are here for Talamh. Many are alive because of you."

"Many died today."

"But that's not your burden to carry. As a continent, we will take care of each other."

His guilt lessened, but only slightly, as he threaded his fingers with hers.

Kellan rushed to them. "Avyanna is ready for you, Felicity." He led them through the crowd, Avyanna catching sight of them and hurrying to meet them.

Her eyes widened as she took in Felicity. "Oh no, sweetie."

"There are others much more important—"

"Shut it." Avyanna nearly pulled her to the nearest seat. "Is this dragon fire?"

Felicity shook her head and explained.

Avyanna bit her lip. "This won't be easy. Some of the scars will remain. The dragon may have helped with the pain but—"

"It's fine." Felicity glanced at Alarian whose expression held love and reassurance.

Avyanna turned to Kellan. "Well, I'll need..." She paused, caught short. "Where is your father?"

Felicity reached for her friend's hand. Squeezed it. Avyanna inhaled, understanding lighting her eyes as she swallowed and nodded.

Once she got to work, the skill of a healer in her touch and movements, Felicity stared at the two males who sat at her side. Her brother. Her Cridhe. The female who worked relentlessly, one she was lucky to call friend and sister.

Felicity's mind wandered to a time when she would have considered this a weakness. This crying, friendship, and relying on each other would have meant she couldn't handle it all.

Alarian stepped by her side and took her hand. Sloan passed by, giving his condolences, before assisting another injured fae to a nearby tent. Lady Molyle arrived with a tray of supplies. She chatted away about what she brought, Avyanna nodding along.

Felicity sighed. Smiled at Kellan who was rolling his eyes. Felt Alarian's fingers thread with hers.

With them. Even with the pain of the loss of a male she was just beginning to know again—she knew they'd get through it. Together.

Epilogue

One Year Later

To receive a bonus epilogue, scan the below code to find out what Felicity, Alarian, Kellan & Avyanna are up to one year later.

prousebooks.com

Acknowledgements

This is a story beyond lore, curses, kisses, and smut. It's a story about being who you are, despite what box the world wants to put you in. Defining your story for you and surrounding yourself with people who are going to lift you up and be there for you through the ups and downs.

And those are the people I want to recognize today.

To my writing community. The ones that understood when I said the characters spoke to me and I couldn't ignore them. That got it when I said I couldn't just 'let them kiss'. In particular, because names have to be mentioned here, to Ashley Wilson (I wouldn't have made it without all the sprints and check-ins), C.C. Tyler (thank you for being one of the first readers of ANO), The Secret Writers Guild, Jen Thrill, my fellow Query Wenches, the Butt Kickers (Tania and Samara- the OG CPs), and Writing With The Soul!

Megan Amato—editor extraordinaire—who needs her own paragraph but deserves a whole page. You took on this venture and edited each sentence with a fine tooth comb and I know it wasn't always easy. You loved their story and helped make it what it is now. Thank you is only a phrase.

Then there are the readers. The ones who messaged me on social media. The awesome supporters on the Street Team. Those who left reviews. Reached out with affirmations and positivity. You don't know how much your words kept me going when there were times I didn't think this book would make it. If I would make it through writing it correctly.

My parents and in-laws—thank you for checking in with me while I've been writing this book. For dealing with my shy responses, uncertain replies, and blushing silence. There is a deal in the beginning of this book that applies to you and I'm asking again that you remember it from here on out! Love ya, guys!

My friends—the ones who cheered me on when I finally was brave enough to talk about my craft. Who didn't judge, but supported (to name some super stars: Alissa, Lori, Lizzie, and Nicole!). Who showed up! I'm glad I had a chance to choose you, but you also chose me back.

Finally, my husband and kids. The greatest gift that God could have ever given me. Thank you for your patience while I disappeared at times for hours. When I freaked out about my self-imposed deadlines. And loved me through it all. Someday, kids, when you don't live under my roof, you can read these words. That way I don't have to know about it. Either way—Love you all the most.